PRAISE FOR \

*"Historical crime doesn't ge\
world, characters that leap off the page, all wrapped up in a\
delicious whodunnit. Just fabulous."*

– Jonathon Whitelaw, author of *The Bingo Hall Detectives*

*"I adored this fantastic first book in the new series by Victoria\
Dowd. I raced through* Death in the Aviary *in a matter of\
days and was gripped all the way to the fiendishly-clever\
reveal. Dowd's characters leap off the page, and her humourous\
touch makes* Death in the Aviary *not just a superbly-clever\
puzzle but also a thoroughly entertaining read. With this\
brilliant innovation on the 'locked room mystery', Dowd firmly\
establishes herself as the modern queen of 'golden age' detective\
fiction. I cannot wait to read the next instalment of Charlotte\
Blood's adventures."*

– Phillipa East, author of\
Dagger short-listed *Little White Lies*

*"Utterly brilliant. Victoria Dowd proves yet again that she's\
in the top tier of mystery fiction writers, with wit, a fabulous\
puzzle, and the odd frisson of spookiness."*

– Tom Mead, author of *Death of the Conjuror*

*"Victoria Dowd's brilliant evocation of 'Golden Age' crime\
with her 'locked lift' mystery wonderfully captures the spirit of\
the age without ever reading as pastiche. Certainly, I detected\
echoes of the 'queens' of the genre, especially the aristo vibe of\
a certain Miss Sayers (although also the 'whimsy' of a certain\
Mr Waugh) but* Death in the Aviary *remains very much Ms*

Dowd's book, not simply a celebration but a compelling and ingenious reimagining very much on her own terms. A very bright beginning for Miss Blood!"

    – Tom Benjamin, author of the *Daniel Leicester* series

"Charlotte Blood is a wonderful new heroine set to take the world of detection by storm. Feisty, intelligent, and deeply sensitive, she jumps off the page in a beautifully written, terrifyingly atmospheric gothic page turner, that keeps you guessing to the very last line. Family feuds, hidden secrets, windswept moors and talking ravens, an irresistible combination!"

    – Sam Blake, author of *Three Little Birds*

"A beautifully-crafted ode to the Golden Age of detective fiction. There's much here for fans of the classic genre: a forbidding stately pile set on windswept moors; imperious aristos; viciously-loyal servants; a sinister occultist; and even a 'locked lift' mystery. Hugely entertaining! I look forward to the plucky Charlotte Blood's next exciting adventure!"

    – Phil Lecomber, author of the *Piccadilly Noir* series

"A richly characterised detective story with a haunting atmosphere and a terrific puzzle at its heart. Delicious!"

    – Daniel Sellers, author of *Murder in the Gallowgate*

"An atmospheric, gothic deep-dive into the Golden Age of crime fiction, Death in the Aviary *is a thrilling start to the Charlotte Blood series. Dysfunctional families, lies, betrayals, ravens galore and a 'locked lift' crime scene make this a brilliant puzzle of a story that keeps you guessing to the end. Perfectly executed!"*

    – Eleni Kyriacou, author of the 'Between the Covers'
    book club pick, *The Unspeakable Acts of Zina Pavlou*

Victoria Dowd

DEATH IN THE AVIARY

THE CHARLOTTE BLOOD CHRONICLES
BOOK ONE

DATURA

DATURA BOOKS
An imprint of Watkins Media Ltd

Unit 11, Shepperton House
89-93 Shepperton Road
London N1 3DF
UK

daturabooks.com
A little birdie told me…

A Datura Books paperback original, 2025

Copyright © Victoria Dowd 2025

Edited by Ella Chappell, Saxon Bullock and Alice Abrams
Cover by Alice Claire Coleman
Set in Meridien

All rights reserved. Victoria Dowd asserts the moral right to be identified as the author of this work. A catalogue record for this book is available from the British Library.

This novel is entirely a work of fiction. Names, characters, places, and incidents are the products of the author's imagination or are used fictitiously. Any resemblance to actual events, locales, organizations or persons, living or dead, is entirely coincidental.

Sales of this book without a front cover may be unauthorized. If this book is coverless, it may have been reported to the publisher as "unsold and destroyed" and neither the author nor the publisher may have received payment for it.

Datura Books and the Datura Books icon are registered trademarks of Watkins Media Ltd.

ISBN 978 1 91552 353 2
Ebook ISBN 978 1 91552 354 9

Printed and bound in the United Kingdom by CPI Group (UK) Ltd, Croydon CR0 4YY

The manufacturer's authorised representative in the EU for product safety is eucomply OÜ - Pärnu mnt 139b-14, 11317 Tallinn, Estonia, hello@eucompliancepartner.com; www.eucompliancepartner.com

9 8 7 6 5 4 3 2 1

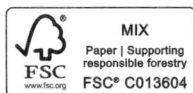

To K, D, J & S

"They considered the great house as in some degree their own; their pride was bound up in it, and their life was complete within the square of its walls."

V. Sackville-West, *The Edwardians*

"Quoth the Raven 'Nevermore'."

The Raven by Edgar Allan Poe

VICTIMS, SUSPECTS & INNOCENTS

Charlotte Blood	Journalist at *The Comet*. Gossip columnist who writes under the pen name Nosferatu
Mrs C	Her landlady and author of the "Burnt Rose" series of books
J H Fulman	Editor-in-chief at *The Comet*
Charles Ravenswick	Murdered heir to the Ravenswick fortune
Rachel Ravenswick	His widow
Edward Ravenswick	Younger brother to Charles and now the heir
Elizabeth Ravenswick	Wife of Edward Ravenswick
Celeste Ravenswick	Young daughter of Edward and Elizabeth Ravenswick
Mary Ravenswick	Youngest sibling of Charles and Edward Ravenswick
Lord Melhuish Ravenswick	Press magnate. Owner of *The Sunday Review*. Head of the Ravenswick family. Incapacitated and left bedridden by a series of strokes
Lady Violet Ravenswick	His wife
George Jeffers	The gardener
Patrick Bartram	The raven master

Heskins	The butler
Mrs Thornycroft	The housekeeper
Nicodemus Bligh	A spiritualist
Philip Pembroke	A solicitor
Nanny Austin	The family's nanny
Nurse Sidmouth	The nurse who attends to Lord Ravenswick

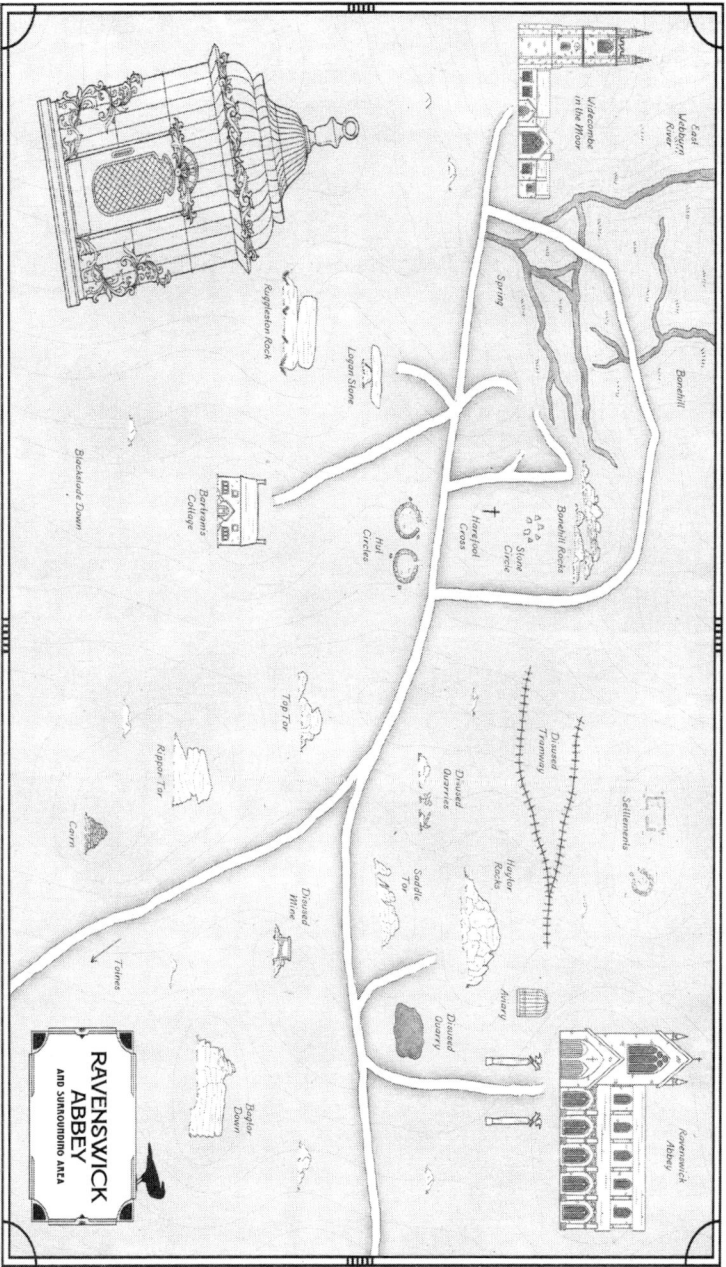

RAVENSWICK
ABBEY
AND SURROUNDING AREA

East
Webburn
River

Widecombe
in the Moor

Spring

Blackhill

Rugglestone Rock

Logan Stone

Blackslade Down

Barham's
Coltage

Hut
Circles

Stone Circle

Blackhill Rocks

Hareford
Cross

Top Tor

Rippon Tor

Carn

Disused
Tramway

Settlements

Disused
Quarries

Hayler
Rocks

Saddle
Tor

Disused
Mine

Totnes

Disused Quarry

Aviary

Ravenswick
Abbey

Bagtor Down

1

"Miss Blood, you can go in now." The voice was flat, disinterested. The sound of chattering typewriters drowned out any answer.

The tall young woman walked with overkeen steps, her dark, bobbed hair bounced in time at the edges of her face with metronome perfection. Everything about Charlotte Blood was synchronised.

The secretary gave her one knowing look and then dismissed her like all the other people she had cast off through that frosted door. Charlotte let her eyes travel along each painted letter in turn as she walked past. *Mr J II Fulman*, the dull gold announced. *Editor in chief at* The Comet. She took a deep breath and her mind pulled up a quick image of a replete fat man sitting back in a large chair – a full man. It was not too far from the truth.

The room smelt like the warm remains of a meal, a yeasty, salt aftertaste on the lazy air. He was a sweaty man, even then, in the grip of a brisk winter. There was always a fan going in his office, just recirculating his heavy breath and everything he said. He said a lot.

This man was made of words. He produced them on vast conveyor belts and breathed them out constantly like the great chimney on top of a factory. He sat behind the desk, spreading himself out along one whole side of it, a grey-skinned growth emerging from the wood. He was all layers – a mound of face, a roll of jowl drifting down to a bulging neck, then the turn of his chest slipping over the top of the enormous dome of his belly. He leaned back to accommodate it all. He was broad and undulating in the off-green shirt, his own land mass with rolling pastures and hills.

"Blood." He said it like he could taste it.

"Sir." She remained standing with her long arms held back and her chin pointed upwards, parade-ground ready. She squeezed her hands together so tight the knuckles stretched white.

He glanced up at her, already disappointed. There was a moment of assessment. Then he spoke as if he was delivering an unwelcome diagnosis, an unpleasant detail that had to be dealt with swiftly, surgically. "I need you to go to Dartmoor."

"Dartmoor?" She frowned.

"It's a moor. In Devon."

She didn't flicker.

"*Hound of the Baskervilles*? Sherlock Holmes?" he offered slowly. "Never mind. Someone will point the way."

"I am aware of its location, sir."

He stared at her before looking back to his desk, littered with random papers as if he'd just thrown them up in the air and let them land in a tickertape parade. He picked up one file. It curled at the edges and had enough different stains and fingerprints to imply this had passed through a lot of hands. He skimmed it a little way across the desk. "I want you to go to Ravenswick Abbey. You're going undercover."

Her face visibly lit. "In disguise?"

He drew his fleshy eyelids closer together until all that was left of his eyes were two black slits with furious eyebrows pushing them down. "I don't want any of your hooey," he growled. "Charles Ravenswick was shot and killed almost a year ago on New Year's Eve. No one's been fingered for it yet."

"I *know*. I remember." She sounded scandalised. "So utterly awful."

Fulman let his large head fall to the side and gave a doubtful look.

His strained breath whistled down his nose. This was a man for whom breathing didn't seem to come naturally. "Listen, Blood, get down there and find out what's going on."

"He was shot."

"Yes, but by who? That's what I want you to discover." Fulman tapped his pen repeatedly.

"Were the police called?"

"Yes, the police were called, Blood! A man was killed In a lift. No one could have got in or out. Lights went. It was someone in that lift but no one knows who did it."

"Aha! A locked-lift mystery." She laughed a little before adding, "Or perhaps… if the crime is impossible to *solve*…" She saw his unmoving face and cut it short.

Fulman paused and his thick, stony jaw fell to reveal the dark, wet inside of his mouth. He took another laboured breath.

"Charles Ravenswick was the eldest son of Lord Ravenswick, who also happens to be the millionaire owner of *The Sunday Review*. They're not touching it, of course. It could be the story of the year! *And*, what's more, some strange things have started coming out of Ravenswick Abbey."

"Sounds just too *odd*."

"Blood, this is not one of your ridiculous escapades! If you can't take this seriously…"

"I can! I can!" She felt the floor beneath the thin sole of her shoe. She knew how silly and frivolous she appeared to men like this. It was useful sometimes, but she could be serious alright, if it was going to pay. "See!" She gave him a studious look, fixing him with those forget-me-not eyes.

He looked bewildered for a moment, his face wrinkled with irritated confusion. "Blood, manuscripts and rare volumes have started appearing on the market from Ravenswick Abbey's library, and there's a whisper that they are harbouring something very special indeed there. Nobody knew about most of these books. They thought they were either lost or *mythical*, or some such nonsense, but now they're appearing with a distinct regularity. Lots of spiritual, ancient pseudo-religious texts… that kind of rubbish and drivel. You'll know all about it. Anyway, there's a man."

"A man?"

"Yes, a man. Nicodemus Bligh." He pronounced the name as if he was introducing a notorious devil. "A mystic or shaman, something like that. He started out as Lady Ravenswick's *spiritual guide*, but he's been digging through the library, says he's made these discoveries and there's something mind-blowing to come. I want you to go and find out what's going on at Ravenswick Abbey, who shot Charles Ravenswick and what they've got in that library that's so special. So, you're going undercover –"

She took a thoughtful breath and looked pensive. "A librarian or ancient spiritual text expert…"

"– as an ornithologist."

"Right."

He searched for a sign of recognition. "A bird watcher, Blood. Our parent group has a small publication – *The Ornithologist's Weekly, Monthly,* whatever. You are going to be one of its journalists. No one reads it except sad old men with too much time on their hands."

"Is it good?"

He closed his eyes slowly. "*Blood.*" He ground out the word through clenched jaws.

"I'm just forming a picture. What kind of tone am I aiming for? Academic journal or intrigued amateur? Am I specialising in exotic birds of paradise or common garden sparrows?"

"Ravens." He nodded at the folder. "The family are very proud of their ravens and keep them in some sort of fabulous aviary. They wouldn't usually let press anywhere near the place. They know the game too well. But they've agreed to let a bird expert in to interview the raven master. They love the bloody birds. It's the one little crack in their wall and we're in."

"I don't know anything about birds. I'm not a bird *expert.*"

"You just need to look like one."

"What does one look like?"

He paused, analysing her. "I don't know, Blood. But these are your kind of people."

"My kind of people?"

"Toffs."

Her mouth tightened.

He raised one of those thick eyebrows, taunting her. "*Nosferatu* would definitely want to sniff around that mansion, wouldn't she?" His mouth spread into a vulgar smile.

She stiffened. "I suppose she might."

"Surely you don't want to spend the rest of your life trawling nightclubs and bars, sucking up gossip about rich people?"

She felt herself flush. Not many people outside this room knew the true identity of Nosferatu, *The Comet*'s salacious gossip columnist, but if they did, they certainly wouldn't let Charlotte party with them anymore. Or maybe they would. There were definitely more than a few of her "friends" who read the column with delighted horror, desperate to find out if their nightly antics had been included.

Charlotte consoled herself with the idea that she was just feeding on the appetite for scandal. Readers were desperate to know how the elusive upper classes spent their money, lavishing their exotic affections on one another in the riot of London parties and myriad country-house *weekends,* as they'd become known. And she was perfectly placed in their set to drain them of their secrets and lay the scandal bare for the public to feast on the next morning. Sometimes she even caught the scent of her victim's enjoyment the next day when they read her column, not knowing the author was right in front of them. But Charlotte had no wish to go on with this grubby game forever. It barely paid the rent, for a start. She needed more, and here it was – death in a dirty folder. She could not waste this chance.

Fulman wiped a flabby hand down his greasy face.

"This is serious, Blood. A man is dead, and they're not getting any closer to finding his killer. *Rasputin*'s taken over at the Abbey and they're selling rare books like penny dreadfuls. I want you to get in there and find out what's going on."

She opened her mouth to speak but he held up his finger. Charlotte's lips remained parted, waiting for the word to arrive. His eyes sharpened into the look of a man who could see the headlines being typed out in front of him. "This could be the scoop of the decade. This is real news, not inane back-page gossip. I wouldn't usually let someone as flimsy as you –"

"*Flimsy*? I covered *the* midnight treasure hunt round London!"

There wasn't even a trace of acknowledgement on Fulman.

"Chips Caruthers and Boy Jespers? Climbing Anteros?"

"Eros, surely?"

"Actually, Anteros." She gave a coy smile. "Sir."

His frustration was growing. "Look, you're not the kind of girl I'd usually want within a country mile of a big story but you can get close to these sorts of monied people. You know them. Know their cut. This is a big opportunity for you, Blood, to prove yourself. Make a name for yourself. A real name, not some sharp-toothed joke." He picked up a copy of a paper and, with a stubby finger, pointed to the Nosferatu column. "Time to break out of *'who got slaughtered at the Embassy then raced a Rolls round London before making a splash at a pool party in Trafalgar Square'*!"

"Fruity Montague, and it was really the Kit-Cat but they threatened to sue."

Fulman glared at her over the top of the paper, the

finger still hovering mid-air. His face gathered in the middle, creating fresh folds. He nodded to the folder. "It's all in there. Everything you need to know and a train ticket. They're sending a driver for you at the other end."

She leaned forward and inspected the folder before picking it up cautiously. "Sir, I..."

He threw down the newspaper. "Blood, do you want to make an impression here or not? This is a big story."

"Thank you."

"I'm not looking for thank-yous! I'm looking for answers. I'm looking for the scoop. The *scoop*, Blood! Do you understand? No one wants to hear about the Crash and misery anymore. It's Christmas time. They want a good old-fashioned murder mystery. Ask Mrs Christie." He pointed at the front page of the rival newspaper showing the novelist in a cloche hat looking wistful. Below it was a picture of her latest offering, with a glamorous couple and a strange, malevolent shadow on its cover.

"*Partners in Crime*, sir. Like us."

He looked appalled. "Get out and get me a story, Blood. I want the scoop. You hear me? The *scoop*."

"Yes, sir. You can count on it. The scoop."

Before he could speak, she turned to go with a deliberate enthusiasm in her step that she hoped he noticed.

"Oh, and Blood?"

She paused at the door. "Yes, sir?"

"They're all still there, the people from the lift."

"Yes, sir." She looked confused.

"Well, that means there's a murderer there, Blood."

"I thought that was the idea, sir. After all –" she smiled "– it takes two to have a murder. One to die and one to –"

Fulman made a frustrated noise of defeat. "Just don't

end up dead." He flicked his hand dismissively. "It's messy for the paper."

"Understood, sir."

"Now, get out."

The platform at Paddington Station was dank and marbled grey by rain, the dirty fog as thick as damp wool in her chest. Charlotte Blood pulled her tweed coat up higher round her face. It smelt mildewed from Mrs C's house. She and Archie had moved into the flat at 44 Mecklenburgh Square just after they were married. Almost nine years of that air, and now everything Charlotte owned was thoroughly impregnated with the smell of boiled veg and damp. Mrs C only ever felt the need to point out that she "ran a clean house" when she wanted to insinuate that Charlotte's job or way of life were somehow seamy and morally depraved.

"What kind of girl wants to spend her time grubbing around in other people's business, anyway?" she'd say. Charlotte didn't tell her, the kind who wants excitement and a life outside the bland existence that was always snapping at her heels, threatening to drag her back. The kind who'd sooner stay a widow than be married off to the highest bidder.

Anyway, she'd had worse disapproval for her choices from supposedly *better* people than Mrs C and that hadn't deterred her, so far. Even when her own family cut her off without a penny *"for her own good"*, Charlotte remained firm. Maybe they *were* right to stop the money. After all, no rich, little "*It* girl" living off Daddy's money was ever going to make waves with a man like Fulman. But she had to make this job work. It was her chance to earn real money and make a real name. It was almost seven years since Archie's lungs had dissolved and finances were starting to look as bleak as this wet December day. Work on her column at *The Comet* barely paid rent money. Although, Mrs C never mentioned all the missed months.

Charlotte huddled deeper into her coat. She was tired of wearing thin clothes on cold days and passing them off as the new diaphanous fashion. Things were going to be different now, she could sense it. Charlotte boarded her carriage quickly with a new, determined clip to her heels, her head full of opportunity and thoughts flicking randomly through Fulman's instructions.

There was a harsh, mineral edge to the winter air today and it burned deep into her bones. The usual London fog was thick with an odious smell to it, sinking the day into a perpetual gloom.

She watched a train full of people pull alongside, coming in from the country, their dubious eyes peering through the grey lens of the windows as if they were seeing some new, alien world.

Her train dragged out heavily through its own smoke, white rapids misted over the station, leaving the sharp smell of acrid coal trailing behind. The beat of metal grew faster beneath her feet, cold rattling through her body in the cloudy-windowed little carriage.

Charlotte stumbled from side to side as she swung the small, battered suitcase onto the luggage rack. The carriage was empty, and she settled quickly into the worn seat. First-class travel was a distant, fond memory. But she reminded herself again, that *this* was "for her own good." Not any of that life she'd left behind.

From her worn leather satchel, Charlotte pulled out the folder Fulman had given her. Some of those large, greasy finger marks were there, as if he was pointing up at her from out of the thick card cover.

Inside were press clippings with dramatic announcements.

Lord's son shot in mystery lift incident!

There was a grainy picture of a house that had easily embraced mourning. The vast stone façade of Ravenswick Abbey was already swathed in ivy, and curtains were partially drawn in spite of the morbid light. There was a distinct melancholy to it.

A circular picture of the dead man had been inserted at the side of the article. Charles Ravenswick looked rich in a way that took it for granted. She knew that self-satisfied, languid look all too well.

Charlotte glanced down at the tracks darned into her old stockings. She remembered cultivating that look of bored wealth. She'd been very good at it. One of the best of the season for a while. But seasons fade.

There weren't too many details in that first article. Lots of intrigue and suggestion, even some sensationalist stories about ghosts at the Abbey. A monk, Thomas Cowper, was said to haunt the great hall, leaving behind the sulphurous smell of unguents and potions that were used on him as he lay dying of the Black Death. Another was the tale of one monk who suffered death by immurement – walled up with a table, chair, book and candle. His skeleton had been found during some modern-day renovations undertaken a few years ago by the family. The piece continued with the inevitable, *legend has it*... At this point, the writer of the article seemed to lean in and whisper to the reader wide-eyed. It was a technique Charlotte had used many times to manufacture that scandalous effect. The article continued in a similar vein. Apparently, when death was imminent in the house, the spirit was said to unleash a terrible caterwauling and screaming from behind the stone, its noise circling the walls of the Abbey. There were reports from various parlour maids, presumably paid a few bob and desperate for attention, that on the night of Charles Ravenswick's death, just such a frightening sound had been heard to echo all around the house before that fatal gunshot.

Of course, what was missing from these early reports were hard facts. There wasn't much more beyond, Charles Ravenswick had been shot in a lift and died instantly. It had happened on New Year's Eve 1928 and so it was the first story *The Comet* had run to mark the arrival of 1929. Shameless was a word the paper was very comfortable with. A small amount of detail followed about the deceased, but not much beyond what Charlotte already knew. He was the son of the press magnate, Lord Melhuish Ravenswick, who had been bedridden for the last few years, and Lady Violet Ravenswick, a dour woman who seldom ventured beyond the confines of the family home. They'd printed a severe photograph of her with a turpentine look that could strip someone back to the bone.

The article went on to say Charles left a wife, Rachel. There was the obligatory stern family photograph, tragically posed and lifeless. His widow was admittedly attractive in a cold, austere way.

Charlotte paused on that one black word. Widow. It always came with its own sadness. Eyes fell a little when people murmured its name, voices softened with a touch of embarrassment, concerned that some of her ill luck might rub off. None of them could understand why a young, attractive woman like Charlotte would insist on clinging to her widow's weeds.

She turned the page and there was a similar stiff photograph of the younger brother, now heir to the fortune, pictured with his family. Edward Ravenswick stared directly into the camera with decisive eyes. His wife, Elizabeth, had an altogether frigid look about her. The daughter, Celeste, aged nine, already looked rebelliously stubborn in a Peter Pan-collared dress that obviously wasn't her choice.

The last picture was of a young woman, surly and plain with a fitting name, Mary. She was prim in brogues and what Charlotte considered to be a very ill-judged dress. The girl's hair was unstyled and clearly a source of aggravation with its wild, unruly nature. It sat on her head in mocking opposition to the rest of her.

Charlotte looked out of the murky train window and watched the condensation slowly rolling down the glass. The world had already changed. Scraps of countryside flew past the window. Flat, bleak fields were hardened with frost. Black, winter-stripped trees stood like abandoned pitchforks. It was a leaden sky, exhausted by cold, the low sun no more than a pale oyster in that grey mottled shell.

A raw scene. She shuddered to imagine the unheated room waiting at the other end for her. She'd stayed in enough country houses to know that however wealthy they were or pretended to be, however many innovations they had, the grate would be as icy as the coal in the scuttle the next day. Her own childhood home had been no different, waking into those cold, graphite mornings.

She let her focus slip away on the long reel of the landscape outside.

The carriage rocked and tilted, shaking out fresh memories like loose change. Bladesworth was forever lingering in the back closet of her thoughts. The sound of those angry waves never stopped finding its way in.

It was always there, that great, white palace on the Devon coast, standing on the cliffs looking down on a brutal sea, a crumbling pile bought by her father in an effort to elevate his status to match his money. Even though the guts of the old beast were ripped out, remodelled and decorated to the highest modern standard, in the depths of a storm-lashed winter there was no escaping that cold. The nights were the worst. The fire in her room made up at ten o'clock would burn down overnight. By first light, with the ragged sea wind battering at the window, her breath would stiffen on the air, her face burn with cold.

Charlotte shuddered to think how she was willingly stepping back into the bleak icy mornings of a country house where her privacy was never her own. It was a world she'd vowed never to return to. Mrs C's might be small and cluttered, but it was warm, the hum of London outside, and Charlotte's days belonged to herself. It was luxury far beyond any she'd had in the splendour of Bladesworth.

But futures changed fast these days. Only this morning she'd been a backroom gossip columnist. Now, she was on her way to being a serious journalist. On her way to another future, back into a past she'd left behind. And what was already very clear was how broken the world was at Ravenswick Abbey.

Charlotte's eyes fell back to the folder. There were yet more press reports, with information leaking out as if it was a carefully regulated stream of curated secrets. Lord Ravenswick was gravely ill and had been for some time, having suffered a series of increasingly debilitating strokes. He'd summoned his family and others to see him at his bedside on New Year's Eve last year, and they'd all apparently used the large old lift that had been installed for His Lordship when he could still move around.

An arrow labelled the astrology tower at the furthest end of the long façade of Ravenswick Abbey that had always been the haunt of the old Lord and, clearly, there'd been no surrendering that, in spite of his illness. It was somehow easier to build a giant mechanical contraption to transport him, rather than contemplate moving His Lordship's rooms.

Unattributed sources said that on the fateful night, the lift just stopped when the power to it failed, as it did regularly, and the lights went out. There was a shot, and when the lights came back on, Charles Ravenswick had collapsed, dead, and a gun was on the floor in the middle of the lift. There were no exits or entrances other than the main gate to the lift, which had remained closed throughout and was in any event facing a solid brick wall at the moment the lift stopped.

It had to be one of them!

the report announced sensationally, and then went on to list all those present in the lift at the time.

One black word hung above them all in bold type:
WHODUNNIT?

3

It was a strange menagerie of people in that lift on the night of the murder. A gardener, a raven master and even a spiritualist had gathered together with the family. The newspaper report listed them in turn, each now cast as a suspect simply by virtue of their presence.

WAS IT...

Rachel Ravenswick, his wife?

Edward Ravenswick, the brother?

Elizabeth Ravenswick, his sister-in-law?

Mary Ravenswick, the younger sister?

George Jeffers, the gardener?

Patrick Bartram, the raven master?

Heskins, the butler?

Or Nicodemus Bligh, a spiritualist?

Charlotte's frown deepened. It struck her as odd that in such a household, a kind she was all too familiar with, a number of members of staff had also been in the lift with the family heading up to see His Lordship on New Year's Eve.

And she wasn't the only person to find the various occupants of that elevator unusual. Speculation had been rife at the time as to why this selection of people were all together in the lift at that particular moment on New Year's Eve.

Last year, she remembered the clubs and bars of London had been alight with the gossip about it. Some said it was a sort of last hurrah party for the ailing Lord, but the guest list certainly didn't seem to bear that out.

There was also mention of the fact that the family solicitor had been summoned earlier in the week. The two incidents could have been unrelated, but it instantly cast a more serious, grave tone over that assembly. No one invites a lawyer for fun, especially not someone like Phillip Pembroke. Charlotte was very aware of the infamous fixer, renowned for dealing with the scandals of the upper classes. It was said that his head was so full of the secrets of the important and influential that if its contents were ever opened up and put on display, the whole structure of society would be rocked. Fulman would definitely have liked to have had a rummage around in there. But there was a reason Pembroke was one of the wealthiest lawyers in England. Secrets and indiscretions were literally worth a fortune. His silence, golden.

Something had clearly needed his attention at Ravenswick Abbey. The whisper of wills was in the air, which always cast an unhealthy suspicion over any country house. An indiscreet maid had reported there'd been arguments in the house for weeks prior to the shooting and the family was haemorrhaging money. Another member of staff confirmed they'd heard there had been a change to the will.

As she made her way down the list, Charlotte's attention lingered on that last name, Nicodemus Bligh – a spiritualist. There were plenty of those around these days, ask any widow. There was a whole army of people ready to bring back your lost soldier, consumptive wife or fevered child. So many people had suddenly discovered *the sight,* and they only increased with the unemployment rates. It seemed there was a whole host of dead people wandering around nowadays just waiting to be seen by those who had the gift.

She turned the page and a glowering picture of this modern-day, self-professed shaman stared back at her. They'd clearly printed the most menacing picture they could find of him, although he looked like the sort of man who might have quite a few to choose from.

The press had lapped it up, from his flamboyant costume to his slick of beetle-black hair and carefully groomed beard. Those wide, penetrating eyes were as white as zinc. There'd been the inevitable Rasputin comparisons, particularly when information was leaked that Lady Ravenswick was completely in this man's thrall. A bearded Mephistopheles, one headline announced. An unnamed, recent guest even hinted that Nicodemus Bligh might in some way be linked to the School of Night, an atheist group of clandestine intellectuals, poets and playwrights. Charlotte had heard of it in the clubs but mostly it was dismissed as a group of pretentious effetes who styled themselves as dilettantes and imagined they were some modern Hellfire Club. There was a rash of these supposedly risqué, underground societies recently. Dressing up, chanting and using their own little secret codes. All "just too dull", according to Fruity Metcalfe. "Embarrassing," Lady Feathers had told her. "The only sin they were guilty of was the worst one – being boring!" Noel had announced and written a song to prove it. Even Nosferatu found it too tedious to mention in their column.

But as Charlotte studied the picture of Nicodemus Bligh, those vibrant, intentional eyes looking out of the paper did seem to have something captivating about them. Something spectral. The sockets were unnaturally deep, and the eyeballs looked screwed down into his skull. It was an impenetrable face. He was definitely someone Charlotte was not looking forward to deceiving.

She leafed through the pages, landing on a drawing of the lift in question. It was a large structure, easily big enough to hold all nine of the occupants. With its ornate bars and scrolling metalwork, it had the look of a vast bird cage. It was the main way up to Lord Ravenswick's rooms in the astrology tower, which he never left now as a result of his illness.

The article said the lift had been known to stop on many occasions when the electricity supply to it was frequently interrupted. Although hidden in a remote part of Dartmoor, Ravenswick Abbey had been fitted with many new and some eccentric modern embellishments – the hydroelectric turbine was one of them. It provided electricity for the mansion, but the article said the supply had, in recent years, become more intermittent. Charlotte had been to many a long weekend in a remote country house that had to resort to candles and fires. In fact, even in spite of its isolated setting, it sounded as though Ravenswick Abbey was more modern than most, with its own power supply, as unreliable as that may be.

She closed the folder and looked out the window. Another new world lay out there. The snapshots of different places blurring past the windows was disjointed but was weaving together to form a journey back to the kind of hidden, country world she knew too well. She'd grown up amongst it but grown away. Bladesworth had always been stranded in the past, a time capsule of a place, broken off from the world.

She had such a definite future mapped out for her back then, as predictable as all the rest of the past's solid golden promises. But the war had blown great, unhealing holes through all that. The scars were still deep the last time she had seen Bladesworth House.

The world slipped by beyond the train window. The sea, brown and rippled by wind. A sandy shoreline, empty and perfectly corrugated by waves. Through the dusk, rags of mist were already hanging low across the water. Occasional abandoned wrecks were half visible. Their masts leaned too far, and the blackened skeletons of their hulls lay sideways on the shore. There was an exposed bleakness to it all that unsettled her. She buried her face into the collar of her coat and another wave of Mrs C's house filled her nose. Even that was somehow comforting now. Charlotte was travelling back to an ageing world. Her stomach coiled tighter. She pulled the folder into her chest.

She just had to remember, this was a chance. A chance to make a name, Fulman had said. The question was, what kind of a name would it be this time?

4

Totnes Station was deserted, with the kind of unwelcoming air that drives people to scurry along damp platforms with their heads bent low. Muted lights cast a grimy scene, the winter sky already black and thick with stars. This was not a place to linger. Charlotte bent a little to shield her face from the cold flurry of wind that came in waves. The last few winter leaves felt slippery beneath her feet. Her shoes leached in the freezing water from a large puddle, the leather already stained around the soles.

She didn't know whether to wait here on the lonely bench or head out of the station. Fulman had said a car would pick her up. Maybe someone was waiting for her outside. Was this really what was *"for her own good"*, standing on an abandoned train platform in the bullying wind, water seeping through the holes in her shoes and the cold smell of damp rising up from her clothes?

"Blood?"

There were times when she didn't thank Archie for everything.

"Miss Blood?" The voice was tired and cracked from too much rough tobacco in the trenches. Charlotte knew that sound well.

The face matched it. He was wearing a hat that he

didn't take off and a sullen expression that suggested this was somehow outside his usual duties. He didn't offer to take her bag. Lines were always drawn early by men like this. Boundaries that should never be crossed. It was obvious he'd firmly marked her down as staff.

The resentment was clear when he opened the door to the old green Rolls Royce for her. It was a begrudging gesture, presumably born from force of habit. She gave him a weak expression of gratitude. He looked away disapprovingly.

There'd been some grave breach in the order of things, but Charlotte was very used to ignoring such perceived violations. Her mother always thought there'd been at least ten before luncheon.

Inside, the car seemed to expand beyond its own dimensions, a great room opening out. The deep buttoned seats and heavily polished wood, stately and sedate. It had an air of undeniable authority, that old club smell born from generations of privilege. The chauffeur got behind the wheel and made no effort to speak. She was glad of it.

Charlotte watched the lights of the small town fade away into countryside and fields. Stone walls and deep hedges rose up in a thick corridor either side of the car. For all the great expanse of land, this was as claustrophobic as any London street. An enclosed world. Ahead, the air was grey with mist, charged with more rain.

The journey shifted again at some imperceptible point. As they headed out onto Dartmoor, there were only sparse dots of light from houses and farms, the hedges falling away to reveal a hardened land. Against the iron moonlight, outlines of gnarled stone tors rose from the earth as if they'd forced their way up like teeth. It was a harsh world, and more than ever she felt everything about her would be inadequate for this. A thin coat and worn shoes wouldn't be any match for a land that seemed like it was ready to consume her.

A drizzle of fine rain began to blur the windows, gathering at the edges in beaded trails. The headlamps formed two white search lights in the mist. She nestled herself back into the soft, black leather seat. It had been a long time since she'd felt this kind of luxury. It used to be an everyday thing. That phrase, "for her own good", circled above her again, watching, waiting for her first fall.

At Bladesworth, she'd been driven everywhere by a chauffeur, and at very specific times. Shopping trips or tea, she'd always be accompanied by someone, her mother, a footman or someone to carry her purchases. She was never alone.

Charlotte felt the damp, moorland fog seeping through to her skin. The beam of the headlamps picked out skeletons of tortured trees dotting the barren landscape, offering up no shelter for the occasional sheep or bedraggled pony. With each mile, the thought festered – what kind of a family would choose to live in such a desolate place? The answer she was trying so hard to ignore, was of course, one like her own – one keen to preserve their isolation from the world.

So many old families had gone to the wall. The Ravenswicks clung on. But city men like her father swooped on these remote, old estates, snapping them up for sums they could afford ten times over, keen to dull the shine of their new money. One thing her childhood home of Bladesworth never lost though, was that sense of separation, of being cut off from the outside world.

She stared into the darkness ahead. It was the kind of vast night that only existed outside cities, overwhelming, as if it might go on forever.

When they arrived at Ravenswick Abbey, the car slowly passed through the two stone pillars at the end of the drive, each set with a large carved raven. The great birds crouched with their wings bunched in tight to their bodies, ready to take flight. But thick ivy had crawled up over them and roped them down. Their potent, stone gaze seemed fixed on her, with eyes vaguely tragic.

Ahead, the disembodied lights of the house floated in the darkness as if it had somehow come untethered and drifted in its own space. The house watched their approach.

As they travelled down the long drive, the outline of the Abbey became clearer. Cut from the black sky, the building seemed to create its own light. The grainy photographs she'd seen in the press cuttings had not even begun to hint at the colossal weight of this great house and its grounds. It had clearly been designed to rival the vast landscape and perhaps even the sky. Built by a god, or at least someone who thought he was, this had originally been the home of monks, but there was nothing humble about it now. It had burst out of its cilice with bloated opulence. Every new addition had been constructed to make mortals feel small before it. Any ghostly monks that did wander these vast corridors would be bewildered by its new size.

All the holy men had long since been replaced by this Father of the press. But the papers would have people think otherwise, of course, with their salacious stories of people frightened to death by the lingering spectres of those long dead monks. They'd focused heavily on the possibility that it could be some supernatural entity that had killed Charles Ravenswick. Charlotte could never quite understand people's willingness to think ghosts had committed a murder when the culprit always turned out to be a living person. But people were willing to believe it if the papers told them it was true. The press was a powerful beast.

Lord Ravenswick might have been silenced by illness, but his paper, *The Sunday Review*, still had a certain refined reputation. This story would not only elevate *The Comet;* Fulman was clearly aiming to bring down a giant.

The chauffeur begrudgingly opened the door and Charlotte gave him as much acknowledgement as he had afforded her. She had been more polite when she could afford it.

The fine rain had lifted but the air was still damp and cold. She started to walk towards the door but finally the man found a use for his mouth.

"You'll need to go round the side." There was the hint of a smile on the end of his statement. "Trade and staff." He slammed the car door in confirmation.

She wanted to question why he'd brought her to the main entrance then. But she knew why.

The engine started and gravel crunched as the car passed her with the slow, satisfying sound of money rolling by.

Charlotte was alone with that empty winter moon watching her, a single abandoned eye rising over the silhouette of the house. She leaned back and looked into the dark.

The sky was broader here, the darkness already

threaded with stars. There'd been hardly any room for daylight at all. Charlotte sighed out, watching the cold, white tendril of her breath misting her view. For a moment, she thought she caught a small movement at an upstairs window and squinted into the darkness.

What faces lived behind those windows? What shadows? There was no one here to ask. Even if someone had been watching her arrival, the vast, ornate door remained closed. Perhaps they were looking out now. Or perhaps it was just those spirits of holy men, trapped behind the walls of this strange, disorientating new world.

Charlotte took a steadying deep breath as if she was about to dive into cold water. She'd imagined this would all be achingly familiar, but she was wrong. She was re-entering this world in a very different way.

When Charlotte finally found the correct door, it was opened before she could knock.

"Now then, what's this the cat's dragged in?" A pinch-faced woman whose features had prematurely aged her stood in the doorway, with her hands on her thin hips, jutting out a provocative little chin.

"I'm Miss Blood, the ornithologist." Charlotte had practised this countless times on the train and it still sounded unusual, even to her.

The woman's eyes narrowed into a guarded look. Perhaps it was the combination of the surname with the *ologist* part that had a vaguely worrying sound to it.

"If you say so." The woman had a naturally snide edge to her voice and she gave it extra emphasis now.

"I'm here to see the birds. The ravens," Charlotte clarified to make it sound more plausible.

The woman bent the sides of her mouth down in a

contemptuous little arc. "Right. You'd better come with me." There was no acknowledgement of whether or not she had been expected.

Charlotte was taken through myriad corridors with smooth floors and rough walls. They weren't well-lit but that was probably a kindness. It was a grim place down here, a warren of tunnels burrowing under the house.

When he came back from the war, Archie used to talk about never wanting to be in holes in the ground again. That wasn't a place for men, he'd say. That was for animals. A trench had collapsed near him and killed a lot of men. He could hear them but couldn't get to them. He said he could still hear them when he returned, when he choked out his own words through blood and spit. Some of the men who had survived had come back to these tunnels in houses like this.

Charlotte carried on down the narrow corridor, following after the surly woman. There was one small room to the left with bench seats and a dresser but no people. A kitchen was to the right, with some bitter-faced women washing and cleaning. They had a raw, scrubbed look to their skin that gave them a pulpy appearance.

"Food's done for the night," one called out in a curt voice.

Charlotte didn't answer. She hadn't eaten since the single slice of toast and one small, boiled egg she'd had that morning. She was glad though that Mrs C had brought it up and stayed to see her eat it. Food was easier to forget now it was just her. It was simply a function of living rather than an event to linger over.

Her head pounded and she realised she hadn't had anything to drink since then either. She couldn't remember if the lukewarm, brown liquid Mrs C had offered her before her journey had been tea or coffee. Mrs C's drinks all tasted vaguely similar. Some were hot, some were cold. Sadly, none were ever just right.

But Mrs C had been adamant Charlotte could not go without drinking whatever it was that had been sat on the side for a while with a thin film shining on the top. Charlotte would have been thankful for a cup of that brew now though. But this was not Mrs C's anymore. It was already very clear this was somewhere much more serious than that. Much more cautious.

The woman who'd led her down the dim corridor gave Charlotte another spiked look before rapping hard on a door and leaving with a simple, "Wait there."

Whoever was inside that room took their time before finally saying, "Come."

Charlotte entered the room and was immediately looked up and down by a solemn housekeeper who wore the expression of a woman born with a headache. "Ah, the *journalist woman*, I presume." Charlotte couldn't tell which part of this the housekeeper disliked more. She said both words with equal disapproval. Some jobs just weren't for women. Some women weren't for women.

"I am. I'll need –"

"You may call me Mrs Thornycroft. Your room is ready if you follow me." She spoke efficiently as she walked past her. Charlotte followed dutifully out of the room.

"It's vital that you adhere to the routine of the house whilst you are staying here, Miss Blood," the housekeeper continued without glancing back at Charlotte. "The scullery maids rise at five thirty but they will be busy with the range. Do not disturb them. The junior housemaids will be cleaning the grates so under no circumstances must they be distracted from their work. I'd suggest you remain in your room until we breakfast at six thirty downstairs. Mr Bartram will be at the aviary from seven. He's aware you are arriving. Meadows will take you over after breakfast."

The regimented schedule was delivered with military precision, leaving no room for Charlotte's opinion or thoughts. Although similar to Bladesworth's routine, she was increasingly aware this was going to be an experience from a whole new side of the fence that she hadn't anticipated.

When they arrived at the room, Mrs Thornycroft opened the door but didn't look for any acknowledgement.

"What a charming..." But when Charlotte turned to speak to her, the dark figure of the woman was already halfway down the corridor. She had gone so silently Charlotte had not even heard her move.

Charlotte was alone at the door to a small room that would have been more appropriately described as a cell. It was not hard to imagine those devout men who had once drifted through these rooms. There was a very monastic, stark feel to it, an imposed silence that seemed to resonate and implied any behaviour was being watched and judged.

Her shoes felt dirty and damp on the clean wooden floor. Each step seemed to release a new note from the creaking boards. The pure whiteness of it all had a brutality to it, an efficient cleanliness as if worn away by constant, hard scrubbing. The bed's painted metal tubes were surgical. She imagined all the hands tasked with scouring away any sign of her time here the minute she had left.

Even the air was stark and unforgiving. A dead cold. The only sound, a small clock ticking loudly, each second lingering too long as it echoed into the next one. Even time felt wrong here.

She put her small, battered suitcase on the bed and felt slightly ashamed of it. There was very little inside – a nightdress and underwear, the remaining few smart clothes she had, some soap and one pair of spare stockings. She draped the black, beaded cocktail dress over the chair back in the hope of hanging out the creases. But her stay was looking very different to the one she'd imagined when she packed that. Charlotte had never got out of the habit of travelling with an evening gown, even if they were beginning to look a little worn. Mrs C had some talent with a needle and thread, and had been called in to rescue more than one gown that had seen too many parties. Some were beyond repair now, but the Lanvin dress had survived so far.

Charlotte remembered a time when a long weekend – or "Saturday to Monday", as her mother always insisted on calling it – used to revolve around her wardrobe. Her mother, unlike her father, was from an ancient family. Another attempt by Sir Richard to buy himself some pedigree. And she insisted on adhering to the old ways. The day would be partitioned in accordance with the need to change her outfit. Charlotte loved those frequent periods when everyone was dressing and redressing. The promise of a new phase of the party, the little gap to be alone and find some privacy.

Although Charlotte was by herself here at Ravenswick, there was nothing private about it. Even the room made her feel like an interloper. She didn't belong here, in this part of the house. That much was clear from the reception she'd already had downstairs. But when she looked into the sorry suitcase, it was obvious she had drifted very far from the world above stairs.

Charlotte undressed, self-consciously. There was no one else here, yet it didn't feel like that. She felt observed. She was surrounded by other souls that she couldn't see, all manner of servants for every describable job. She was very well acquainted with the requirement for *every* need to be met in such a house but she'd not had much experience of life this side of the bell and she'd certainly never slept in the servants' quarters before. The lack of a lock was the most obvious and disconcerting removal of her privacy. But there were so many little invasions that left an all-pervading air of close scrutiny.

Charlotte didn't linger but slipped quickly between the stiff sheets. They were rough and well used. She didn't care to think just how many other bodies they'd covered.

The folder had slipped out from the open flap of her satchel on the floor and the edge of one of the papers peeked out. The face of the bearded spiritualist was staring up at her. He watched her intently, his eyes following her every move. She gingerly poked her foot out, made slightly braver by Archie's socks, and she quickly flipped the bag shut before whipping her foot back under the covers as fast as a child afraid of whatever might be under the bed.

She barely slept that night, half waking and imagining figures in the room, robed figures drifting across the moonlight with heads bent and hands clasped in prayer. Charlotte was very glad for the comfort of Archie's socks that night.

5

Before dawn, Charlotte lay awake nursing her doubts, listening to the murmur of the wind and the movement of the house. A dense silence seemed to magnify every sound, a thick darkness wrapped around everything, smothering it. She had sunk into that unreal time when dreams and truth mingle until they become indistinguishable. Each time she tried to put her thoughts in order, they drifted out there onto the moor. Finally, she gave up on sleep and flicked on the light.

She saw it straight away, there in front of her.

A chair had been placed right beside the bed, facing her. It hadn't been there before. Surely she would have seen that. She tried to remember her first view of the room. The rough, wooden-slatted chair had been in the corner, hadn't it? She pushed herself up further in the bed, her face drawing into confusion. The air was cold and the lingering scent of something medicinal, almost cleansing, clung to it. There was a familiar, herbal astringency about it. It was the smell of the apothecary. An indescribable incense of treatments, medicines and trickery.

The door to her room was still closed. She would have known if that had been opened. Charlotte looked closer at the chair, with its wicker seat. It would have made a

43

sound if anyone had sat on it. The room was as empty as it had been when she arrived. But she could not escape the overwhelming feeling that someone else was in the room with her.

There were knots as heavy as stones in her head. She was tired, her eyes fried by the sudden white spark of light from the bedside lamp. She must have missed the chair when she arrived. That was the only explanation. Exhaustion, that was all.

Charlotte rubbed a brisk hand across her forehead, trying to sharpen up her thoughts, but they spun like bobbins, rattling around. Nothing would settle.

She reached beside the bed for her satchel and held its comfortable, tired leather close to her. It felt warm. It had been Archie's, and the tracks of his initials were still there ingrained in the surface. She remembered the first morning he left for work after they were married, how he'd shown her that he'd had her initial added. Charlotte ran her finger along the groove of the letters now, *AB + C*.

She opened it and glanced down at the folder. What was very clear, even from those first few pages she'd read, was that the Ravenswicks were shrewd, hidden people. She'd have her work cut out deceiving them, let alone wheedling out any information.

Something faltered in her, a wave of doubt. What if they spotted her? Unmasked her? She felt so unprepared. There'd been no time. She'd not even had much of a chance to consider what an ornithologist would look like. She knew there should be binoculars and she'd managed to borrow a pair from Graham Snellworth, who spent most evenings in the gardens of Mecklenburgh Square. From her window Charlotte had often seen those glass eyes glinting in the light behind the bushes, she told him. He'd flinched and a pattern of mottled red had spread up his face. She was going on a bird-watching weekend, she'd explained, so wondered if it might be possible to borrow his binoculars as he wouldn't have any use for them while she was away. He'd flushed so hard she'd thought his face might combust. He'd handed them over complete with the well-thumbed leather case.

There'd been no real time to ready herself so the only other addition to her new persona was a copy of *The Bird Watchers' Book: A Compendium for Amateurs, Teachers and Students with more than 300 questions and answers* by Nathaniel Hardacre Dillworth. Mrs C had rooted it out for her. Her landlady's real enthusiasm though had been to make sure Charlotte "embraced the character of an ornithologist".

Mrs C had just got back from the Bloomsbury Super Cinema when she found Charlotte packing. The old landlady had only walked ten minutes from Theobalds Road but the way she was sucking for breath and coughing, it sounded like she'd walked the length of London. The fog had been bad recently, hanging in the winter cold, filling everyone's lungs with its thick vapour. Mrs C still had enough puff left though to tell Charlotte all about the film. Her dramatic landlady loved the cinema almost as much as she loved her books.

"Oh, you should have seen that Ivor Novello! Frightening he was. I'd have shown him the door, alright."

She'd been to see a rerun of *The Lodger – A Story of the London Fog* which Mrs C thought was particularly relevant as it involved a landlady suspicious that her lodger might well be a killer.

"That's comforting, Mrs C," Charlotte commented.

Mrs C frowned as she watched Charlotte continuing her packing. "What's all this then? You leaving me?" There was a note of genuine concern in her voice.

Charlotte explained her new ornithological role which prompted the multi-talented landlady to practice a few bird calls on Charlotte. They didn't sound like any birds Charlotte had ever heard before. Mrs C explained she'd added her own interpretation for artistic purposes.

The bird book had been on one of the many bookcases that lined the hall and staircase, floor to ceiling, at number forty-four. There was never any need for fresh wallpaper or paint. Mrs C just added another row of books, most of them old detective novels.

"You can read this on the train. You'll have plenty of time," she said, shoving the bird book into Charlotte's satchel. "Let's see..." She searched around the shelves before finally pulling out a dog-eared copy of *Bradshaw's Railway Guide*. It was Archie's old one, the last he'd bought. 1922. There were no more journeys after that year.

Mrs C looked at the ticket on the bed, then back to the book. "Thought so. Paddington..." She ran her finger down the page. "4.15."

"4.50?"

"No, 15. 4.*15*. Gets in at 9.28 tonight. You'll have plenty of time for bird research on the train then! You just stay safe now."

Charlotte sat in the cold bed at Ravenswick and let her mind meander down that narrow hallway at Mrs C's again with its dark, peacock coloured floor tiles. Cluttered and warm, an untidy array of books lining the walls. She imagined herself sitting in her usual spot on the stairs.

The eye of her imagination ran along the shelves. *The Mysterious Affair at Styles, The Hound of the Baskervilles, The Secret of Father Brown, The Thirty-Nine Steps, Clouds of Witness, The Billiard Room Mystery, The Crime at Black Dudley, The Man in the Queue, The Roman Hat Mystery.* Too many to remember. Charlotte had spent many comfortable hours sitting there buried in those pages, waiting for Archie to come home from work or return from one of his trips away. Mrs C would always bring her another cup of the extraordinary brown liquid that tasted somewhere between tea and coffee but always had the lingering smell of whiskey trailing along with it.

Of course, nestled away amongst all these treasures were the books written by Mrs C herself. Charlotte's very own landlady was none other than a self-professed crime writer. The first day she and Archie moved in, Charlotte remembered meeting Mrs C – this unbelievable woman in a cloud of floating velvet and cigarette smoke, offering a shot of the warm stuff at nine o'clock in a morning. Mrs C was never without her whiskey. She even brushed her teeth with it, then soaked her jewellery in the bottom of the glass. "Comes up nice and shiny. Strip the dirt off anything that would," she'd say. There'd often be an old ring looking out at Charlotte when Mrs C tipped up the glass to drink. There were so many more uses for scotch than Charlotte had ever imagined.

She remembered the exaggerated conspiracy in this theatrical woman's eyes when she announced that she was not just Mrs C, brewer of the worst vegetables and tea in London, she was also Ella Crossity, novelist extraordinaire. Her introduction had more the spirit of the circus ringmaster than a member of a literary salon. She'd whispered a confession that it was really a pseudonym and searched both their faces for a glimmer of recognition but could see it was necessary to go on to explain that she was the author of the *classic* – her word – "Burnt Rose" books featuring an undercover female detective who worked in a mortuary. Why anyone would want to read about a woman whose employment involved spending all day in a morgue with dead bodies was beyond Charlotte but, it turned out, her landlady had quite a few avid readers. Mrs C had explained that her books appealed to an older, more genteel audience who still had a lingering Victorian love of all things mourning and morbid, coupled with a salacious need to read about incredibly violent murders.

Charlotte had even managed to read a couple – *Rose and the Cadaver*, and *The Autopsy of a Rose*. They were eye-wateringly gruesome in their detail and raised the very worrying question of why her landlady would know so much about internal human anatomy.

But as Charlotte sat there in that sparse room at Ravenswick Abbey, it warmed her to think of Mrs C in her flat, scribbling away about bloody slaughter, a mug of whiskey to hand.

Charlotte took out Mrs C's bird book. It smelt of London, her flat, and, for a moment, she was there on the top step of the stairs, next to that lukewarm cup of tea.

The book wasn't particularly in depth, and the section on ravens was relatively brief but, as a journalist, Charlotte was well acquainted with the concept of a little knowledge going a very long way.

She absently flicked through the pages.

They didn't look like the sort of birds people would keep as pets, but then Lord Ravenswick wasn't just "people". The book said these birds were one of the two largest corvids. The picture showed a powerful, solid creature with a rich blue-black sheen. Its glass-bead eyes reflected the world, seeing everything. The slight tilt of the head was inquisitive, with a sharp intelligence. They'd apparently lived alongside humans for thousands of years and were hugely successful because they could eat everything, live off anything from carrion to small animals. They would snatch baby birds from nests or feast on remains. Nothing was untouchable.

Yet, the book went on to say these violent, ruthless birds would mate for life and aggressively defend both their territory and their family. If a member of the pair was lost or died, its mate would reproduce its partner's calls to encourage its return.

Charlotte leaned back against the pillow.

She had made no noise when Archie finally slipped away from her. She was silent for days. It had been a quiet, unassuming death, just as he'd lived. Her grief mirrored it. The house and everything around her had grown still as if it was all falling away into the air. Mrs C had brought food that Charlotte didn't touch and whiskey that she did. It was almost peaceful. The lull before the storm. Before the rest of the flock came hunting their carrion.

The family all wanted to be there then. Not before, to hear his struggled breathing and ruckling chest deflate with pain every time. No, her only companion had been Mrs C, who helped her to discreetly empty the bowls of rusty blood and vomit. She remembered Archie's words

on the day they married. "I'll always keep you safe."
Always had only been two years, one month and four
days, and ultimately there had been no way she could
keep him safe from the inevitable. In the end, he wore
the regretful look of a man who was deeply aware he'd
given her reason to doubt him.

After his death, the mourners came in a long cortege
of extravagant grief. They wanted their mourning.
They wanted their crow-black clothes and outpourings.
Charlotte had given him her silence, her devotion, in spite
of anything else. And she wore his socks. They reminded
her how comfortable and easy it felt to walk with him by
her side. They reminded her she was no longer a wife.
She was someone new – a widow – a whole different,
darker creature.

And now she was an ornithologist with a very distinct
interest in these clever, merciless birds who had a taste
for survival. Charlotte's eyes settled on the last words the
book had to say about these fearsome birds. A collective
group of them, it explained, was known as either an
unkindness or a conspiracy of ravens.

6

The morning bristled with cold. Small crystals had formed on the window and her breath chased her round the room as she hurried to get ready. It was still dark outside, but Mrs Thornycroft had been quite firm about timings last night and Charlotte couldn't risk missing food again. Her stomach was sharp with hunger and griped. Through the thin walls, she could hear the muffled sound of other people readying themselves, dressing in their meticulous uniforms that were worth more than anything else in these rooms. The sound of so many busy lives around her was an immediate reminder that she was in a house full of strangers.

At Bladesworth, when it was too wintry in her bedroom to contemplate making the morning breakfast gong by nine, she'd sometimes be tempted to hide in bed too long. But that was always a mistake. There would inevitably be an invasion of strangers and staff with no room for privacy in a vast house that needed tending. The housemaid, scouring the grate; the watermen hauling enormous cans of water dangling from wooden yokes over their shoulders; coalmen, whose skin had soaked up so much black dust they had a mineral look about them. It was never wise to linger in your room in the morning, no matter how cold it was.

Charlotte dressed quickly, spurred on by the spartan air. She chose a fresh crepe de chine blouse with a long, blue bow, but pulled on the same drop-waisted tweed skirt she'd travelled down in and rolled on yesterday's stockings, taking care around Mrs C's darning. When she was ready, Charlotte fastened the suitcase and pushed it far under the bed. She slipped the folder, bird book and binoculars in her satchel, and smoothed down the bedspread, taking care to leave everything exactly how she'd found it. It seemed important to make as little impact as possible. If she was going to survive here, she'd need to blend into the house seamlessly. Charlotte considered herself splendid at blending in. Even Tipsy Ketteridge had said so, and she was famously good at mixing in any social circle.

Before she left, Charlotte paused and then took a moment to move the chair back to where she thought it should be, next to the window in the corner. She nodded in agreement to herself. "That's where it should be."

As she turned away from the corner, she paused, her eyes drifting to the window beside her. She looked out into the dark world and let her breath pool and fade on the cold glass, watching the grey circle contract and disappear. It was a lonely view. But then, she'd grown around her loneliness. Seven years living alone creates a solitude that becomes difficult to break. It was becoming harder to remember another way of life. Charlotte's social life was an enforced necessity these days for the column, but the door into her flat still closed every night. And there was always silence waiting for her. London had a loneliness like no other. The slow torment of being so close to others living lives rushing by, ignorant of all those silent watchers.

Sometimes Charlotte still sat on the bottom step with Mrs C's books. She wasn't waiting for Archie to come home anymore but it still felt like she was waiting for something.

That first month after Archie's death, the only constant was Mrs C, needlessly wafting in and out of the hallway in black kaftans, lace and fake pearls. It was an anchor in the dark river of grief, breaking the spell of all that time trapped in her own thoughts, holding up every memory to the light, preserving its details, unravelling moments, the things she didn't understand, the doubts, and reworking them into something else.

Familiarity was slow to return, but there was always a lukewarm cup of tea on the side when Charlotte came in from a club, a slice of toast outside the door to her flat the next morning and the occasional signed copy of a new Burnt Rose book. It created a sort of home, or at least somewhere to live without being entirely alone.

Charlotte leaned on the rickety chair back and it moaned in disapproval. Something felt sharp on her palm and she lifted her hand.

There in rough letters was etched a single word: "*No!*" A very unassuming looking word, but with enough power behind it that someone had been driven to cut it deep into this wood, scratching at it repeatedly like graffiti carved into a school desk. Charlotte touched it again and wondered what this small rebellion might have been provoked by. These servants' walls must have known many grievances, some greater than others. Some requiring retribution, others, like this minor act of vandalism, to vent some perceived frustration.

Charlotte left the word on its own in the room and ventured out into the deserted corridor.

Downstairs in the servants' hall, there was a more hurried air than last night. People busied themselves around the breakfast table, not sparing a glance for the new stranger in their midst but avoiding her in such an obvious manner that they were clearly aware of her presence. They seemed quite used to efficiently dealing with intrusion.

The warm smell of food and bodies was almost homely.

But there was no welcome at the Ravenswick breakfast table. There were the occasional side glances and dismissive, closed looks from the servants. It wasn't that Charlotte was a stranger, presumably they were used to visitors' staff dining with them. But this woman who sat in their nest was a cuckoo from a different world entirely.

A wraith-like man entered and everyone immediately stood to attention. He saw Charlotte instantly but said nothing. In his immaculate black suit, he stood like a pastor in front of his flock, his arms spread wide, his collar too tight.

"There is only one announcement this morning." He had a reedy voice that went straight through Charlotte's tired head. "We have a *journalist* in our midst."

He might as well have said leper. Their eyes were quick to land on her. It was a strange reaction given their employer's profession. Perhaps that was why. It had nurtured their suspicion.

"Miss Blood is here to speak to Bartram about the ravens. There will be no necessity to speak to her about *anything* else."

They all eyed her warily. The sense of being an outsider, overwhelming now.

"I am Heskins, the head butler. Do you have everything you need?"

It took a moment for her to process that she was being spoken to directly.

"Miss Blood?"

"Oh, yes, thank you. Some tea would be nice." She smiled ingratiatingly and then wished she hadn't.

"You may serve yourself, Miss Blood. You will be taken over to Bartram shortly and any further requirements during your stay may be directed towards Mrs Thornycroft." He sat down in a firm statement that didn't require a response.

Charlotte wanted nothing more than to walk out, head held high, but her stomach said otherwise. Instead, she reached for the large tea pot that one of the maids had put down in the centre of the table.

It was an uncomfortable start to the morning but she was determined to stay. She ate eggs and toast quickly. There'd been a time when she embraced that feeling of hunger, keen for the latest flat-look dress to hang just right. But an empty belly wasn't something to ignore these days and she was more than ready to put aside politeness when faced with a full plate. When she'd finished, she paused to enjoy the feel of the hot cup of tea in her hands for once. But this wasn't a place for lingering and the atmosphere was growing colder by the second. The message was very clear, they'd feed her, but her company was another matter entirely.

A small bell rang and a coloured disc moved in one of the apertures on the electric indicator board displaying the names of all the rooms in the house in a small, glass-fronted case.

"Miss Mary's up early," one of the maids remarked with a sour look.

Charlotte's eyes ran along the line of names, some familiar from the file. There was Miss Mary's window, which had turned red, and next to that was Mr & Mrs Edward. There were various other named rooms such as the billiard room, drawing room, dining room, library and smoking room. But it was one name on the board that Charlotte's eyes settled on – Mr & Mrs Charles. There'd been no attempt to change this in almost a year. Perhaps they were waiting to be told what to do. No decision had been made. It had just been left. This name loitered like an unanswered question. There'd been no closing of this death. Charlotte felt that spur again. Too many men had died without reason, without answers.

Heskins nodded over to a young boy who came and hovered by Charlotte.

"Meadows, I believe it is time for Miss Blood to visit the ravens," Heskins commanded.

Charlotte raised an eyebrow and carefully placed the almost full cup down before pushing back her chair. Without ceremony or acknowledgement, she stood. No one else did.

"Well, this has been just wonderful!" She gave them all a tight smile which nobody returned. She smoothed down her shiny bob of hair and flicked her head. "You must remind me to do this again sometime. Maybe tomorrow." Charlotte turned and walked with decisive steps, the only sound, the little heels of her pumps clipping on the stone.

When she got outside into the corridor and paused, she had a sense that the room behind her sighed with relief. Then she heard the sharp murmur of their judgemental voices start up.

The boy looked at her expectantly. He was a thin needle

of a lad, with a nervous, agitated edge to him. He didn't speak, but simply lowered his head and blushed before leading her through the stone-paved corridor, still cold with the early morning.

Outside, the air had an earthy, damp smell. And across the lawn, the first skeins of a weak, saffron-coloured light streaked the underside of the clouds. The boy intentionally walked a few paces ahead, the orb of his lantern muted by the mist. He didn't turn or speak and had an anxious, quick way of walking that suggested he didn't usually get entrusted with guests. But then, she wasn't meant to be a *guest*. At least, no one had treated her like one so far. Yet, like the rest of the staff, this boy certainly didn't consider her one of them either.

Admittedly, the less attention they paid to her the better, but she could see already that she was caught in a no-man's-land. She hadn't foreseen this problem but there was no real reason why the family should have accommodated her, a backroom journalist, in rooms alongside themselves. It had just never occurred to Charlotte that she'd ever be put in the staff rooms at such a house. The problem was already glaring out at her – how on earth was she going to dig any deeper into the family if she didn't have access to them? She wasn't here for birds or servant breakfasts but she had been housed as far away from the family as possible. They were, after all, newspaper people, and presumably any form of press was treated with distrust, even ornithologists. They knew exactly what they were dealing with, particularly after the frenzy in the papers surrounding the death last year. But if she couldn't get near the family and the servants wouldn't speak to her, what was she supposed to do?

Fulman presumably had no idea about the intricacies of the unbreachable boundaries at play in an old country house. But Charlotte knew them all too well and her position seemed insurmountable. There was already the creeping feeling that she was very much being kept at arm's length, not just by the staff, but by the Ravenswicks as well.

With the rumoured state of Lord Ravenswick and the death of the heir, they had good reason to be reclusive, but that didn't make her job any easier.

Charlotte glanced back at the house with its turrets and towers all added to the ancient, simple monastery by successive generations. There was nothing simple about this place now.

She caught the glimmer of movement in an upstairs room and immediately sensed eyes on her from behind those dark windows. They didn't trust her here. Clouds of suspicion hung over this house. It seemed strange that she'd been invited at all. What was already very clear was that someone had let her into their world but not everyone wanted her here.

7

The walk over to the aviary was much further than she'd imagined it would be. The silent boy just scurried on ahead across the lawn, offering no explanation.

The day was still, in those dark, dawn hours outside. Coal hours, Archie used to call them, when the air was stiff with cold in his thin lungs, the brisk salt and charcoal smell of winter raw on his chest. She'd hear every ruckled breath, so abrasive that she struggled not to openly wince. He'd light a fag, "just to loosen things", he'd say, before heading off to work. Each moment another second gone.

She looked out across the unchanged landscape of Ravenswick Abbey, the great canopy of ancient trees in a land that seemed untouchable, the vast mansion standing amongst it all. As a child, she'd run across those lawns at Bladesworth, down to the cliff's edge staring out to sea, thinking all the world was wide and full of wonder. The daughter of gods in her castle high above it all. The muscular waves would swirl and howl up over the rocks below, so aggrieved they couldn't reach up and smash down those ivory towers.

The white memory of it all was crystallised in her mind now. A glittering expanse of water lying out there, new worlds awaiting her discovery. She'd watch lithe seals tumble in waves, green waters fringed with seaweed, her hair always sticky with the saltwater air. Those memories were filled with the sweet grass smell of never-ending summers, staring into an unimaginably vast sky full of possibilities. All her days were ahead of her then.

But time had stalled here at Ravenswick Abbey, so formal, grand and fading into timeless obscurity, suspended in a past they'd all left behind somewhere in the trenches.

It was an empty picture now. All the faces at the party had been blown away on a bitter wind. They'd been sealed off from the outside world that burned. Separate.

It stood alone. These vast lawns spreading out towards the bleak moors, a house imposed on an ancient landscape.

Only a curve of light traced over the horizon. Charlotte's exposed skin stippled in the damp morning air. Back then at Bladesworth she'd have been at garden parties on lawns like this, all exquisite gowns and soft music. Men in white suits and hats. Now, she wore yesterday's skirt with a coat that was still too thin, stockings splashed with mud and a cloche from Marshall and Snelgrove that had seen far too many days. Mrs C had trimmed the frayed velvet on that hat so many times now it was almost bald in parts.

They walked further out across the lawn, leaving shadowy footprints in the dew. It was the first time she noticed a great lake, hidden from the drive by a small dip in the land. Mirror-still, the water was dead, its black surface only occasionally interrupted by weeds and high plants. As she and the boy drew closer, the abandoned air became more obvious. There was a fathomless, unkempt nature about it. Everywhere, a gentle fall into neglect.

The stone sculpture of a woman stood in the lake's centre, clawing her way up to the sky whilst being dragged back by a sea creature's coils. At some point it must have been a fountain. The smears of algae running down her head and over her shoulders told of water tracks long since run dry. She was lost, abandoned forever in the moment of her capture.

"It's very beautiful," Charlotte called to the scurrying boy.

He paused and turned a little towards her, deciding whether to speak. "Stopped working when the 'lectric went again few months 'go. Mister Jeffers deals with all that now no one else working in the hydro. He ain't got round to fixing it yet."

"Oh, I see." She smiled encouragingly. "So where is the..."

But the boy had started walking again.

8

Charlotte could hear the birds before she could see them. The witch-cry calls of the ravens echoed over the high trees and down across the lawns towards the house, as if they were calling out to it, or at least, to someone in it.

The boy led her through a clipped arch in the high yew hedge, and there standing before them was a peculiar, incongruous sight. The aviary was a magnificently delicate construction of green-bronze metal, filigreed and painted with gold. Charlotte paused to look in awe at this strange, misplaced confection. As frivolous as a French queen's intricate gown, it sat bell-like in the clearing. The severe looking, black feathered creatures that ambled around in front of their home seemed untroubled by how jarring they looked next to this ornate creation.

The birds were much larger than she had imagined, sinister with their long, shadowy, plague doctor beaks. Their feathers shimmered, iridescent in the rising morning light. Their eyes had a polished sharpness. A clever little light was in them all. One paused and angled its head to the side as if leaning an ear in, keen not to miss a word.

"I'll leave you here." The boy scuttled away before she could protest. It had the look of a fearful exit, his lantern swinging in the lingering white mist before disappearing.

She was alone with the ravens. One cocked its head and started to analyse her. Another swayed towards her, dipping and bowing as it hobbled from one leg to the other, a learned figure, caped, holding its hands clenched behind its back, approaching in solemn, grave judgement. The bird's hunched, dark-spine walk had a strange, undulating rhythm, rocking from one thick-clawed, leathery foot to the other. Glassy, coffin-black feathers rippled over the old, ominous shape. Charlotte instinctively stepped back.

"They won't hurt you, Miss Blood." The voice was as guttural and rough as the sounds the birds made. It had an ancient sound to it that seemed more at home with the moors and crags than this decorous bird house.

The man was standing at the wire-scrolled door to the aviary, looking like a weary sea captain incongruously stranded in a gilded picture frame. His face was hardened but the eyes still soft. He wiped his hands on some cloth and walked towards her. "Patrick Bartram, raven master here. Thanks for coming down, Miss Blood." It was the first truly welcoming voice she'd heard.

Her eyes widened and she looked down at his extended hand. For a moment, nothing seemed natural about this simple act of politeness. An awkward air passed through the space between them.

"Hello." She grabbed his hand a little too hard and began shaking it up and down. "I'm Charlotte, please, call me Charlotte."

"I quite like Blood." He paused and looked suddenly mortified. "I mean..."

"It's fine. It happens a lot." She smiled and continued to shake his hand.

"Do you think we can stop now?"

"Stop?"

"The shaking?"

She looked down. "Oh yes, sorry. I'm *delighted* to have this opportunity to meet you." It was a little too eager.

He cleared his throat and frowned, drawing his other thick hand down the grey peppered beard and slowly stepping back from the handshake. "So, you want to see the ravens I hear."

"That's right!" She was aware it sounded too enthusiastic again but assumed he might appreciate her being keen about his birds, so added, "Our readers are *fascinated* to know more about these birds."

He looked at her doubtfully.

"They're so marvellous, don't you think? Particularly their behaviour patterns and how they... fly." Her smile began to wilt.

"These don't." He nodded towards the large, black shapes meandering across the lawn.

"Oh, I see. I just assumed with them having wings... It just goes to show there's always more to learn about these intriguing birds."

He pulled back his head and looked puzzled. "They do usually but their wings are clipped so they can't."

"That's *awful*. Who would do such a thing?"

"Me."

There was a pause filled only by the throaty, rattling noises from the birds.

"Which publication did you say you came from?"

She grimaced. "*Ornithologists' Weekly*. I haven't been there very long."

"You surprise me."

"I am here to *learn* about the ravens, Mr Bartram. To expand our readers' knowledge of these birds." She paused and steadied her voice. "So, I take it you've worked with birds for a long time then?"

He nodded. "Been here twenty years, apart from when I was –" his face darkened in that painful way she'd seen too often from men who had fought "– over there."

She nodded once.

"Twenty years. You must have an extraordinary bond with these wonderful creatures, living *here* amongst them for so long –"

He looked bemused. "I have a home elsewhere."

She attempted a laugh. "Yes, I realised that. I didn't think for a moment you lived *here* in a… bird cage."

He shoved his hands into his grey tweed trouser pockets and took a long, patient breath. "Shall we go and take a closer look at the birds?"

"Yes, yes, the birds, sorry. I was forgetting about them. I suppose that must happen as well occasionally."

"Not really, no."

This hadn't gone quite as smoothly as Fulman might have liked. The only talent Charlotte was demonstrating so far was one for making everyone she met wary of her. She had to start making some allies or else she'd never find a way into anyone's confidence. But it seemed so insurmountable. She was facing closed ranks.

Even the ravens were starting to grow suspicious now. Their thick beaks turned slowly towards her in concert. Their shrewd eyes grew inquisitive. The one nearest to her crooked open its mouth and let out a raucous cry. Charlotte drew in a sharp breath and flinched.

"Honestly, you're in no danger." Everything in Bartram's voice had a questioning undertone to it now. He took out a small stubby knife from a leather sheath and absently started to run it round under his fingernails, making a dull, repetitive clicking noise.

A liminal light was breaking through. Amber was just starting to muddle the dark sky but her coat still felt too thin, a sour reminder that Charlotte definitely wasn't a smart, respected journalist or even an ornithologist for that matter. She had binoculars though, she remembered that much. She pulled them out of her bag and put them ostentatiously round her neck.

He glanced down and frowned. "You should get a good enough view of them from here."

One of the birds roamed around their feet.

"Shot in the dark."

"I'm sorry?" She let the binoculars fall onto her chest and looked at Bartram in confusion.

"It's the bird," he said.

"Shot in the dark," the bird obligingly responded.

Charlotte's face gathered in disbelief. "It spoke. Did you hear that?"

"Yes."

He paused, a perplexed look caught on his face, and added slowly, "She's a mimic. Repeats things she's heard when actually she has no idea what she's talking about." He continued to look at her deliberately. "What was it you said you did again, Miss Blood?"

She rapidly turned her attention back to the birds and pulled herself up a little taller. "I see. I suppose you could call it Ravenspeak?"

"No. No one has called it that before."

"Well, I think our readers might appreciate the new terminology. Ravenspeak has a good ring to it."

He eyed her sceptically.

"Now Mr Bartram, perhaps we could go into a little more detail about the ravens." Charlotte took out a pad and pen, turning the top page efficiently. Written clearly on the top of the pad in large letters was a note she'd idly made after speaking to Fulman. *Who killed Charles Ravenswick?* She pulled it in to her chest quickly and looked at Bartram, who appeared to still be focused on the birds.

She carefully folded the page around on the pad. "So, Mr Bartram. What was it that first drew you to the ravens?"

He turned to her with new, astute eyes. When he spoke, he used a low, quiet voice that could barely contain his mounting irritation. "They are very intelligent creatures." He waited until she looked up from her writing.

"Right," she said, adopting a look of intense interest. "What in particular leads you to believe that? What traits do they exhibit?"

He leaned in close and Charlotte could feel his breath on her cheek. She drew back a little.

"Because," he began, "when Charles Ravenswick died they all gathered round and stood in silence on this lawn as they do when one of their own passes. Mobbing, it's called. An act of devotion – *loyalty*. These birds *mourned* him, but they were the only ones who did." He nodded towards her pen. "Now, you write that down, Miss Blood. That's what you came for."

She attempted to look aghast. "I'm sure I don't know what you mean. I am here to conduct a thorough, in-depth analysis into the practice of keeping ravens. Our readers are keen to know more. And, speaking for myself, I am a great admirer of these extraordinary birds. *That's* why I came."

He studied her for a moment. "I'm a great admirer of whiskey, Miss Blood, but they don't ask me to go and interview distillers."

She sniffed the air. The familiar flavour of Mrs C honed in. He clearly was partial to whiskey.

His voice sank to barely above a whisper. "Listen to me, Miss Blood. These people are powerful. If you don't think they'll spot who you are, that they won't sniff you out as press, then you're a bigger fool than you already look. It's their world, the press. They know it. They'll know *you*."

She stiffened. "Of course I'm press. I work for *Ornithologists' Weekly.*"

"It's monthly. They don't have enough to fill it every week."

She felt sure Fulman had said weekly. She looked down at the intrigued bird who was standing between them waiting for her to speak. "As I said, I'm new on the publication."

Charlotte set her face at a decisive angle and smoothed her hand over her hair.

She looked down into the melancholy eyes of the raven that seemed to be just as unsure of her as Bartram was. The bird looked back at Charlotte as if it was the one that was making a study of her.

It seemed to her that there was something vaguely maudlin about this creature. Perhaps she was only imagining that now she knew of its flightless life. But she couldn't shake the idea that there was some dim air of tragedy to the bird, a mournful edge to those incisive eyes.

"They seem somehow... sad."

He looked disarmed. "No, not at all, Miss. They can actually be quite playful. Like children." He paused before adding. "Like all sorts of games. Take a closer look." He nodded towards the creature.

She paused before crouching tentatively in front of the bird. It stood almost as tall as her when she was squatting down. Up close, there was a petrol-coloured sheen to its sleek feathers, its horned beak thick with traces of grey at the top. For the first time, she saw that its eyes were not entirely black but ringed with a deep hazel, tortoiseshell frame. The bird studied her. She could see herself reflected on the surface of its green-black eyes. There was a cold, unmerciful gleam there.

"That's Circe," Bartram said, a new gentleness edging into his voice.

The bird shifted in acknowledgement and its feathers flowed in a fluid movement up and down, like fingers running through a sequined dress.

"She's beautiful," Charlotte said quietly.

The bird seemed to hear her words and dipped its head in gratitude. There was a cunning note to this one. A certain aloof nature. As it moved, she could hear the rustle of its wings against its body as though they were fine ruched silk.

Bartram crouched next to Charlotte. "I've got some biscuits if you'd like to feed her." He reached into his pocket.

"Yes, I'd like that very much." Charlotte didn't take her eyes off the bird, part from fascination, part wariness.

"I just need to go and soak them in blood," he added softly. "I'll be back in a minute.

***

Although there was still an undercurrent of caution between Charlotte and Bartram, they both relaxed a little more into the next hour with the birds. The raven master introduced each one like an old friend or relative. It felt like a privilege he bestowed on her.

Along with Circe, there was the bird's partner, Nostradamus. Then there was Morgana and Merlin. The latter was injured recently by a fox, Bartram told her, but he'd nursed the bird through. Medea and Paracelsus were the youngest. Bartram spoke about the creatures as if they were his equals, not just birds. Charlotte couldn't help but be intrigued by this glimpse into their strange, rare world. Yet, there was a dark fascination to this man who deprived the birds he respected so implicitly of the one thing they were meant to do – fly. But there was somehow a mutual regard from these captives towards him too. He was much more than a gaoler or even a keeper. Master seemed like a very appropriate title for him.

The book had said they were called a conspiracy of ravens. And Bartram was clearly part of that. He was part of their society. It was a very beguiling cooperation that was being revealed and Charlotte could not help but let herself be intrigued.

"They're interesting names. Did you choose them?"

"No." He left it there.

Charlotte couldn't lose this growing opportunity. She tried again to impress.

"And they mate for life, don't they?"

He gave a wry smile. "You have been reading up then, have you?"

"For my new job."

"Not likely," the bird creaked.

They paused.

Bartram cleared his voice. "Like I said, the birds don't understand," he said. "They just mimic. And yes, in answer to your question, they do mate for life usually. But this one here, Paracelsus, he visited Morgana a few times when her partner was injured." He looked over at one bird in particular. "Thinks I don't know what he's been up to." Bartram turned to face Charlotte. "I know most things that go on around here."

They both stood up without looking away.

"They quarrel a lot," he continued, "the birds, that is. But you need to remember that these creatures possess a lot of devotion to their families, and they do not welcome outsiders."

She took a breath. "I see."

"Look, Miss, old Lord Ravenswick, he loves the ravens. Has a real passion for them. It's the only way he'd ever let someone like you come anywhere near here, I'm sure."

She folded her arms. "Someone like me?"

"I mean press. Nothing else. He's in the game, or he was. He might be ill now, but he knows every move. They all do. They know people come digging around here looking for a story – *the* story! You're not the first. Don't be the last. Just be careful, Miss Blood."

She looked at him with rising concern. "You make it sound like the others didn't survive. What happened? Are they buried under the aviary?" She smiled but he didn't return the gesture.

"Shot in the dark," one of the birds offered again.

Bartram looked off into the grey daylight and sniffed as if testing the air.

"Day's getting on. You should be setting off now. Do you want me to take you back over or do you think you can manage to find your way? It's a pretty big house. You can't miss it."

She was a little taken aback. This was an abrupt ending and had the distinct tone of a dismissal. "I'm sure I'll manage, thank you very much." She attempted to mirror this new cold attitude and readjusted her hat with a firm, decided manner.

Charlotte had been a past master at the art of curt detachment, and she certainly wasn't about to be dismissed.

She paused, reminding herself that she wasn't on a country weekend now and this man wasn't *staff* to her. She was on his side of the fence now. Or at least partially. And she'd made a connection here, albeit a tenuous one. She couldn't afford to lose this. She dropped the haughty attitude.

Charlotte brushed down her coat absently, trying to appear natural. "Thank you for showing me your birds. I may need to return as I will require a little more for the article."

He let out a dismissive laugh. "Right you are. I'll be here if you need me. You know where to find me."

She thrust out her hand to him. "Thank you for your time, Mr Bartram."

He looked down and paused before shaking her hand. "You're very welcome." He didn't let go immediately. The hint of a smile spread across his lips. "And just one last thing."

"Yes?"

"Next time you need to choose an undercover

pseudonym you could try choosing something a little less conspicuous than Blood."

She pulled her hand away. "I can assure you, Mr Bartram, that is my name. Blood. For better or worse."

9

Charlotte followed the same route back towards the house. The trees were bare, but a smell of fresh dew softened the sparse landscape. The bitter tang of the fires being lit at the house brought wood smoke on the air. Another frill of grey smoke lifted from one of its chimneys.

The sky was sickly with rain, a dour mist settling in. It was not a crisp December morning but a dull afterthought of the year. The dead remains of another year. There'd been no real Christmas this year. Mrs C had left her a card on the hall bookcase and a gift of another Burnt Rose book – signed, she pointed out. They'd had a lunch of sorts together but the main focus seemed to be on getting to the whiskey at the end. She'd covered Mrs C with a blanket and left her to sleep it off in the chair. Charlotte spent the rest of the evening alone in her room.

There'd been no Christmases now for seven years.

She wondered if they'd celebrated here at Ravenswick Abbey. There weren't any decorations in evidence.

A thin drizzle had begun. The rain seemed to follow her around here. She was deflated already. The first morning of her inquiries and she'd gathered nothing more than warnings from Bartram. She hadn't achieved anything and was no closer to finding out about the lift or even meeting most of its occupants on that fateful night.

It was still early but the day already had a halfway-over feel to it. Lying was harder work than Charlotte thought it would be, even though she had been a journalist for a while now. As Nosferatu, dresses, parties and the latest gossip didn't really require this level of subterfuge. She just had to be what people expected her to be – carefree and always ready for a good time. The truth was, she had more cares than she ever wanted.

She paused by the lake she'd passed before, its surface mirroring the dark grey marl of clouds. Daylight was steadily crossing the moors but there was a jaded quality to it.

Charlotte looked towards the house being dressed for yet another day without an answer as to who killed her heir. They lived in such a frigid, broken world of rules and boundaries that denied one simple truth. Someone in that house had murdered a man.

It must be constantly disturbing to be so powerless. Every time Charlotte felt too cold, or her stomach complained, or the flat looked tired and small, she forced herself to remember the glittering cage she had escaped. But she'd be lying to herself if she didn't admit that it was starting to wear her down. This was too much like visiting the past wearing someone else's shoes.

Her chin fell onto her chest and she closed her eyes. It had been nine years since she left Bladesworth, but it was a lifetime ago. She was tired to her core. Tired of trying to find another way. Tired of missing Archie, of all those unanswered questions. She just felt weak. It was a loose, boneless feeling as if nothing was solid anymore.

A bright flicker caught Charlotte's eye over on the opposite side of the water. The light moved again for a moment. It was something reflecting – glass or metal perhaps. It flickered out for a moment. But when it reappeared, it was closer. She needed to get back to the house.

Smoke was lacing up from more chimney pots, the lights coming on in some of the upstairs windows. She rearranged her hat, turning up the edge over a particularly worn, almost threadbare patch, and passed the strap of her satchel over her head with renewed purpose. She set off, but as she did, she saw that drifting light move again, matching her movements.

She walked hurriedly now through the gathering mist, more aware of the rustling leaves growing louder behind her. She paused again and looked over her shoulder. The noise stopped when she did and there was a cold silence. Charlotte scanned the grey air but even the lake had disappeared beneath the blanket of fog now. Ahead, the outline of the house was blurred, its lights floating in the blank air.

A quick snap cut the silence.

The breath stuck in her throat. A dark shape drifted through the bushes. Someone was there.

She frowned. "Hello?" Her voice was weak as if she didn't want an answer. There was none. "Is someone out there?"

A quick flurry of movement was the only response. It seemed to be moving in her direction. Charlotte's eyes darted around but could pick nothing out. A shape began to emerge. A figure. It was moving fast, directly towards her.

Charlotte didn't call out again. The only impulse

she had was to turn and walk briskly away. She shot a look behind her again and the dark figure was quickly slipping through the mist. It was much closer than before. Running now. Faster.

She broke into a jog, then a run, her heart gathering pace. Her breath clouding the air.

Over towards the right, under the faint pattern of a great tree's branches, Charlotte caught sight of a small, partially disguised structure. If she could make it there fast enough through the mist, she might lose them.

She darted off with a renewed speed towards the small, round shape. As she drew nearer, she could see the stone pillars, thick with moss and marbled with white-green lichen. An old folly.

Charlotte ducked in quickly, careful not to make a sound on the stone. She searched the dead air but the figure seemed to have fallen back.

It was small inside with barely enough room for the weathered old bench. Quickly, she crouched down behind it, her heart pounding, her wide eyes searching the view through the entrance. There was nothing but empty mist now. The figure had disappeared. Perhaps she'd lost them. Why would they chase her? Why didn't they answer her?

She leaned into the seat, resting her forehead on the cold, damp wood. Her face filled with the mildewed scent. The stale air mingled with the faint decay of leaves and stagnant lake water.

A disarming silence settled over the small, round room. The wind picked through the leaves piled at the edges and round the bench.

She put her palms onto the small slats of the bench to steady herself.

Her fingers instantly made out something, a disruption in the grain. It grew clearer as she traced around the edges. Letters. A word. Carved into the wood.

She pulled her hand back.

The small word looked up from the seat.

Power

Charlotte's finger traced around the letters. It had been cut deep, each letter picked out with something sharp, a knife or something finer, digging out the wood as it peeled off in tiny wet splinters. It was fresh, the wound new and unblemished by any of the dark dirt settled in the grooves of the rest of the bench.

She whispered the word and heard her voice echo back.

Instinctively, she looked quickly to the door. It was there, only a few feet away, standing in the mist. A dark, still figure. Waiting.

Charlotte froze, her fingers poised on the word.

The outline moved. Slight and fast. Charlotte's imagination was racing. If they came in, she would...

But the figure simply walked back into the mist.

Charlotte waited, listening to her breath, looking out at the dead scene. It was as if nothing had been there at all.

A flurry of startled birds rose up from the trees opposite and her heart clenched tight.

Their raucous, angry voices called out and turned up into the sky.

The black shapes were gone in an instant, disappearing beneath the mist along with the figure. But Charlotte could still picture those eyes out there somewhere in the gloom.

She looked back at the bench and the small word staring back at her.

Power.

***

Charlotte couldn't say how long she waited there behind
that bench, looking at those gouged-out letters, a coppery
taste of fear in her mouth, her chest gripped tight, but
when she finally emerged and scurried back to the house,
she was completely unaware of the small, round eyes
watching her from the woods.

10

Charlotte was thankful when she returned to the house to find the kitchens were a busy hive, the air rich with the hot smell of cooking and hard work. No one acknowledged her at all. She might as well have been a ghost travelling round the corridors. No one saw her until she passed Mrs Thornycroft's door at the end. It instantly opened as if the woman might have a spy hole she'd been looking through.

"Miss Blood."

Charlotte faltered.

"Lady Ravenswick wants to see you in her drawing room in ten minutes."

The breath stuck in Charlotte's throat. Surely Bartram couldn't have got word to the house that quickly about his doubts over this so-called ornithologist.

Mrs Thornycroft looked her up and down. "You'll have enough time to smarten up and then Mr Heskins will take you over to Her Ladyship. I do not have time. There's a new seamstress to instruct and a parlourmaid to reprimand." Mrs Thornycroft's face was merciless. Charlotte pitied the poor girl who was about to encounter that.

The housekeeper closed the door before there was time to say anything else. Charlotte walked hurriedly back to her room. There seemed to be no space down here for any extra words or sentiment. Politeness was just a rigid adherence to protocol performed with a cold detachment. Every requirement was observed immaculately and correctly, but there was nothing spontaneous or genuine. Nothing unnecessary. It was all stripped back, military style efficiency that left no room for emotion or sentiment. It meant there was no time for complacency or, crucially, to think. Everything was automatic and swift, which made it unquestionable.

The machine worked impeccably. It was exactly the same above stairs too. There was no need for thought, just routine. It was mind numbing. Charlotte remembered as she grew older those long, dreary days at Bladesworth spreading out week upon week with nothing to do but wonder when the next engagement would be, the next meal, the next outfit change, all in the brutal pursuit of a husband for her. It was almost as if it was designed to blunt the mind to such an extent that it became impossible to question anything. A mechanical world that ran like clockwork and, on the surface, it still did at Ravenswick. But someone had removed an integral part quite purposefully. The heir. Evidently someone did question the machine, and that someone must still be here, living behind one of those names on the indicator board, perhaps waiting for their moment to disrupt the system again. Was that the intention?

But remove the head and another one just sprang up. Did that leave Edward Ravenswick, the new heir, in a vulnerable position, or had he been the one who had done the removing? At least now Charlotte had the chance to finally meet some of the other pieces on the board. She needed to look the part, if she could remember what that was.

Back in her room, it was clear someone had been in and gone through her things. The contents of the suitcase were moved around and the coverlet on the bed had been left with an impression where someone had sat as they'd riffled through her belongings. It was very clear that privacy was not a luxury afforded to people this side of the house either.

Charlotte brushed her hair and quickly changed into the drop-waisted tweed dress that had been altered many times. It was worth it though. Charlotte had bought it in Liberties almost a decade ago, when money didn't matter quite as much. She held it close and ran her hands over the fabric just as she remembered Archie had.

It was good quality and hadn't worn, unlike some of the clothes she flippantly bought without thinking they'd still need to be serviceable in a different life. Right up to the end, Archie had been earning well at the Foreign Office and was promoted even though it must have been obvious that he'd never make it to retirement. Perhaps that was the idea, to shuffle him through the ranks quickly. He didn't really talk about it. But it wasn't quick enough to provide a very substantial pension. There were none of her own savings left now either.

Escape money, she'd always called it before she was married, and had been saving for years, creaming a little off any dress allowance or socialising money she was given for outings or shopping trips. Purse strings were always immaculately controlled at Bladesworth to maintain a constant state of dependence. Who could bolt on the money for two good cocktails and a hat?

But she didn't need to bolt. So few men returned from the war, that it was de rigueur to invite officers to pad out the numbers. A room full of husband-hungry debs was an uncomfortable look even if it was the truth. Her parents had been forced to extend the guest list like everyone else to afford the parties, luncheons and shoots a more palatable veneer. But what the old guard and, most especially, her mother and father didn't foresee was that the officers were easier to fall for than the stale remains of society.

Colonel Blood's name alone had caught Charlotte's attention at Lady Trethwick's shooting weekend. But he also had the intelligent look of suffering the smart men brought back from France. An alert, anxious melancholy all dressed up in a damaged hero's uniform was very compelling to a young girl who'd been offered nothing but old men or whey-faced boys hunched under the weight of their families and titles.

Colonel Blood, or Archie as he insisted, was utterly riveting. He talked about books and plays, artists he knew and poets. He even drew her the rough sketch of a bumblebee – the first of many. It was a new world.

Charlotte stood in the stark servant's bedroom now, holding the dress tight. She breathed in the smell of that night in Bloomsbury when he'd carried her into their small, Bohemian life. As they lay as close as two pages in a book, he whispered again that he'd always keep her safe. There was a simplicity to the way he spoke, to the way he moved and looked at her. Those were the naïve, early days before Charlotte discovered there was very little else that was simple about her husband.

But she'd escaped far from the stultifying air of Bladesworth and, in those moments, she was free.

Now, standing here, isolated and alone in the cold of Ravenswick, she was stranded back in that foreign field once again.

She powdered her face, slowly put on her lipstick, and climbed into the dress like she was stepping back into that world. A little smile curled across her mouth as if Archie had just held her face the way he always did. "My clever Charlotte," he'd say. He believed that. Now all she had to do was prove it.

***

Mr Heskins walked at a steady, funereal pace through the servants' hall. Various members of staff nodded to him and he pursed his lips in response. It was a careful labyrinth of loyalties and order, adhered to instinctively.

Charlotte, following behind, was left unacknowledged, in the same way that some embarrassing item he had been called upon to remove might be studiously ignored as he dragged it along.

Finally, they reached the green baize door that led out into another world – the world she remembered being part of. She avoided the word "belonged."

It had been a two-stage process of escape – her marriage, then her job, but as Heskins led them out into the hall, Charlotte could not escape the fact that this side of the door still felt more familiar, more ingrained. Even though she hadn't been part of this world for many years, there was no real leaving it, however hard she tried. Archie always teased her about her airs and graces. He was well-respected, bright and no stranger to the Bohemian society of academics, writers and gentry. But Charlotte's mother had been Lady Rothesville, from a long line of

Rothesvilles, before she was married off to the financier Sir Richard. There was no breaking that ancient bloodline.

As Charlotte followed Heskins out, the great hall at Ravenswick Abbey echoed with their slow footsteps. Canvases stretched along the walls, setting out the Ravenswick's family tree in a grandiose vision of a room entirely populated by the faces of the family through the centuries. A suit of armour and long tapestries depicting battles hinted at past conflict and honours.

But this was a house shrouded in dishonour now. The Lord's heir had been murdered and no one had been punished. That would have been an unthinkable state of affairs for all these previous holders of the title arrayed throughout the hall, resplendent in armour, mounted and ready to defend the family name and honour.

The crest hung over the top of the stairs, a vast raven rearing into aggressive flight with wings that had not been clipped. Unlike those it now looked down upon.

A long and proud history had led to this point. The fabrics were frayed and moth-riddled, the dust was gathering and the fountain had run dry. The scent of decline wandered the hallways freely and passed through the walls like a ghost.

Ravenswick Abbey had become a poor relation, wearing handed-down clothes. Like so many old houses Charlotte knew of these days, pride and poverty sat uneasily side by side.

Heskins paused at a door flanked by two large spears that crossed above it as if to forbid any entrance.

The butler remained grave and knocked with a decisive pattern that sounded almost like a code.

"Come in." The voice was clear and certain.

11

It was not a hesitant woman who greeted them. There was a steadfast assuredness to Lady Ravenswick. An unsinkable look as she sat morbidly still in a chair by the side of a large picture window.

This woman was all contradictions. Rigid and pale, she had a bird-like, porcelain delicacy to her. Grave shadows blurred under her eyes. Line upon line of troubles were written across her parchment skin, each detailing her descent through the years. She seemed worn away as though if she were held up to the window it might be possible to see through her like a leaf. There was a certain dignified, condemned look about her.

Yet the water-blue eyes were far from weak. They had a hardened, ice-like quality to them as they followed Charlotte's entrance into the room.

"Your Ladyship." Heskins bowed in a way that wasn't just adhering to convention. This was real admiration, devotion even. "Miss Blood."

"Thank you, Heskins. You may leave us."

He bowed again before making his solemn retreat. Every movement, every look was performed with deep veneration.

Lady Ravenswick's gaze didn't falter. She had a cordial aloofness to her.

"Please, take a seat, *Miss* Blood." The emphasis on her title immediately hinted at more knowledge than Charlotte was comfortable with.

Charlotte drew closer and perched awkwardly on the edge of the green silk sofa opposite Her Ladyship. It was an opulent room. Small tables littered with trinkets and boxes were dotted around. Displays of china and other ornaments sat in cases along the walls and in every corner. In spite of the size of the room, it still looked cluttered. The paintings were of country scenes and places the eyes easily skimmed over.

"Heskins is a wonder," she mused. "It's still hard to find servants these days, ever since the conflict."

Charlotte had heard so many euphemisms for the war now. The world was full of ways to avoid saying death.

"We're very lucky to have held onto the staff we have though. So many houses didn't. But you know, *Miss* Blood –" she leaned closer and let her voice fall just above a whisper "– it does mean they're very, very loyal to the family. Discretion is a wonderful thing, wouldn't you say? We like to maintain the old order here. We respect their world, and they respect ours. No crossing the streams as it were, Miss Blood. It works. Always has." She sat back into the chair and the pale light fell on her face leaving a strangely cold, ephemeral impression. "Tell me, you wear a wedding ring I see, and yet you are a *Miss*. Is this another concession to the *modern* age we must now accept?"

Charlotte looked taken aback. "My husband is dead." She didn't offer any more.

"Surely you would still be Mrs in that event? Please, excuse me, the titles of the lower classes are as mysterious to me as ours must seem to you."

"There's no mystery for me, Your Ladyship. I am aware of the system."

Lady Ravenswick's thin eyebrows meshed and formed an intricate web of lines spreading out across her face. "I see, Miss Blood. You are a woman of many layers." She knitted her fingers together. "Journalism being the most recent." Those faded, alkaline-blue eyes still watched Charlotte closely.

"As a journalist, I prefer to be referred to as Miss. It's easier than being a widow."

The silence was important to them both.

Lady Ravenswick was the first to break it. "We are very familiar with journalists in this house." She waited for the words to take effect. "So, tell me about this publication." She searched for the name. "*The Ornithologists' Monthly*. It sounds riveting."

Charlotte frowned. "I thought the Ravenswick family were very keen on their birds."

"Well then you thought incorrectly, Miss Blood. My husband and some of my children do indeed adore the ravens. I think they are foul, savage birds that feed on death. My surname was also changed by marriage, Miss Blood. I am not a Ravenswick by birth. My eldest son was to have them shot when he became Lord. Sadly, that will not now come to pass."

The conversation had not gone how Charlotte had envisaged. If she was to tap into this family's secrets, here was the place to start, right at the heart. Lady Ravenswick had the look of a spider in the centre of its web, ready and alert to any movements. Charlotte couldn't let this opportunity slip. This was her chance. She pictured Fulman behind his desk, all bloated with disappointment.

Charlotte's mind stumbled through the possibilities. She tried to summon up the memories of all those afternoons of tea and cards, rigid backs and sharp conversations designed to probe and judge. Charlotte had always been masterful in her manipulation of the older grand dames and their demands for the utmost respect. She could charm the most acerbic of old establishment women. But Lady Ravenswick was different. She was utterly opaque.

Charlotte looked around the lavish room for inspiration. On the far wall was a large glass case filled with stuffed birds, all of them ravens in various poses, some even flying, others pecking at an animal's remains on the floor. It was a faintly disturbing little tableau and she could see why Lady Ravenswick might not wholeheartedly embrace the creatures. She had to steer the conversation away from birds, which wasn't going to be easy for an ornithologist.

Alongside the taxidermy bird case, there was a large bookcase filled with neat rows of leather-bound volumes that looked as if their purpose was simply decorative.

"The books –" she stumbled.

"Miss Blood," Lady Ravenswick batted the words away efficiently, "it's probably important for you to meet the rest of my family. We'd like you to dine with us tonight. You'll find Cook has an unvaried repertoire, but the wine is good."

This took Charlotte by surprise. She was consigned to the servants' quarters and yet they were inviting her as a guest to dine with them. She was again crossing a border that shouldn't be broached. They were keeping her as distant from the family as possible but then luring her in. There was only one possible reason for that, and it was to observe her whilst keeping her contained. She accepted the invitation immediately.

"That sounds too delightful! Thank you."

Charlotte was a firm believer that observation worked both ways. It had served her well so far, but the Ravenswick's were an old breed and all the assured faces looking down from the walls had been defending this way of life for centuries. It would take someone who knew it implicitly to breach those walls. Charlotte felt sure she was the woman for the job.

12

Lady Ravenswick made a few more glib enquiries about Charlotte's intentions with regard to the ravens article. It wasn't taxing and Lady Ravenswick seemed disinterested. Charlotte was dismissed in the same manner as Heskins had been and she left knowing very little about this guarded woman. It was going to take a lot more skill to find out about the goings on in this house. But, although frustrating in its closed nature, this initial meeting had whetted Charlotte's appetite. The secrecy was intriguing and, rather than averting suspicion, Lady Ravenswick's icy restraint only served to sharpen Charlotte's resolve.

Outside the room, there was an unsettling stillness. Hardly anyone moved around these vast halls, unlike the tiny, cramped warren below. A strange aroma clung to the cold, stone air. There was an old familiarity to it, something she recalled from every Sunday morning. It was heavy with church-like incense, that sweet, cloying smell conjuring up notions of death and decay.

A sudden, cold draught of air flittered round her ankles and, at the edge of her vision, over on the opposite side of the room, a movement caught her eye. It came out of the wall as if it had just emerged from one of the long portraits and slowly travelled across the stones.

Charlotte caught her breath. The shadow moved gently. It was a slender shape, curved over in penance as if bowing. Or perhaps praying.

She blinked once to clear her eyes. It had disappeared before she could fully capture the outline. Charlotte quickly searched the shadows. There was nothing but her own imagination. Her face gathered and she gave a little irritated tut. She had to keep a clear head here. There was no room for silly nonsense about ghosts. She still felt foolish for running from the figure in the mist earlier. She wasn't about to let anyone else scare her. Charlotte started walking across the hall with a quick, new purpose, pushing aside any ideas of fear.

But just as she reached the centre of the room, she saw a flicker of cream material over by the stairs. That was definitely real. Someone *was* there, half hidden in the shadows. They didn't make an effort to move or announce themselves, so Charlotte did it for them.

"Hello? Can I help you?" Her annoyance was barely contained. "You can come out any time you like." She folded her arms and waited, her eyes sharp with anger.

There was a pause. Then movement. The figure took one bold step out into the hallway. Standing beneath the dark banister was a man so tall he had been forced to stoop a little to fit in that space underneath the stairs. It was not a natural place to have wedged himself, and looked very much as though it had been chosen in a hurry.

He was imposing, with noticeably wide shoulders suggesting a powerful man beneath that curious, white tunic. He had a disguised look. Most of his face was hidden by a thick, black beard immaculately shaped around his jaw. There was a precision to him.

"I am Nicodemus Bligh, Lady Ravenswick's spiritual guide." He needn't have told her that. He was exactly the same as the photograph in the papers.

He held up his face defiantly. This man was used to being inspected and challenged. He was defensive before there was any need to be.

"How do you do? I'm Charlotte Blood. I'm here –"

"I know why you're here, Miss Blood." He gave a cynical smile. "We all do."

He used the "we" in an aggressive, closed way. They were a clan, a group he was part of, and, most importantly, she was not.

"I've been visiting the beautiful ravens only this morning. What a magnificent aviary."

"I'm very glad to hear it, Miss Blood." He leaned closer. "I must talk to you more about our little black souls."

She only recoiled slightly, but he saw it. Bligh seemed to enjoy that. He stepped nearer and held his hands together as though in prayer.

"It is their great responsibility here to escort the newly deceased from Earth to the afterlife." He had adopted a faint, spectral voice. "They are psychopomps."

"I see." She nodded slowly.

He waited for her to ask.

She sighed as if this was already becoming tedious. That seemed to spur him. In her experience, the biggest fear of all men like Bligh was to be thought of as boring. Charlotte knew just how to tease more information out of performers like him. Artists, writers and actors, they were all the same. Make it seem like she didn't care and the floodgates would open. They couldn't stop revealing increasingly salacious, private and inappropriate stories until she was worn down by the weight of their secrets. Nosferatu could have filled ten columns. And when their exploits were finally exposed, it was with a grim thrill that those people ran out into the open to repeatedly deny their exploits whilst ensuring that they were standing in the full glare of all that attention. They'd got what they wanted and so had Charlotte. The game worked both ways. Nicodemus Bligh was very clearly someone who played it well.

"I'm sure you know all about their special place here, being an *expert* on ravens, of course." There was a subtle sneer on the edge of his voice. He deepened the look of beguiling intensity, with every slight movement perfecting his image. If the word contrived didn't already exist, he would have invented it.

"A psychopomp, Miss Blood, connects the material world with the world of the spirits, a mediator, if you like, between life and death. They transport the souls to the other side –" he paused to deliver another knowing smirk "– and sometimes back again if they need to return to this world for unfinished business. Many people even think these psychopomps are the souls of people who have been *murdered*." He left the last word hanging, still staring wide-eyed into her face.

Charlotte didn't let her gaze falter. This was not a man to show one inch of fear or hesitation to.

He stroked a hand over his carefully slicked, black hair. It had an iridescent sheen to it, each spear layering flat against the next like feathers. As she studied him more closely, it was increasingly apparent that underneath all the careful disguise he wasn't quite as old as he looked.

"Well, good day to you, Miss Blood. I look forward to

seeing more of you." There was a subtle suggestion that she might not be aware exactly when that would be or that she'd even know anyone was looking.

"It was a pleasure to meet you too, Mr Bligh. Will you be at dinner?"

He looked affronted. "I always dine with Her Ladyship. Her diet is carefully monitored by me."

His clear eyes seemed perfect for *monitoring* everything.

"I look forward to it," she said in her most indifferent manner. Charlotte considered herself quite good at being dismissive when the occasion demanded it. She was, after all, her father's daughter.

Nicodemus Bligh gave one small, low nod in acknowledgment but kept those amber eyes on her at all times. She couldn't help but drift into them. They were searching eyes, the irises noosed with a clear, thin black line that defined them, creating an inescapable, mesmeric effect. Charlotte had to admit to herself that, although he may have been performing a carefully devised act, part of it seemed worryingly real. His lips drew back into a smile and the smooth white teeth shone from the shadows. "Miss Blood. It has been a pleasure to meet a fellow bird lover and also, if I may say, very… revealing."

"Good morning to you, Mr Bligh." Charlotte lifted her shoulders and walked away with quick little confident steps, but she could still feel those compelling eyes making their way along her spine. The feeling lingered long after she'd left the room.

13

If she was going to find out anything here, she needed to get to know these people more intimately. And, as her father always said, what better way to find out about someone than to listen to what they had to say under oath. Her father was a litigious man.

When she got back to her room, she pushed the chair under the doorhandle and pulled out the folder from her satchel. At the back, behind the press cuttings, were some records of the inquest into Charles Ravenswick's death. Written on the front page was "Open verdict." Those didn't feel like the right words here. Nothing about this case seemed open.

The first person to give evidence at the inquest had been Edward Ravenswick, the deceased's brother. As she read through, it was immediately obvious that his evidence ruled out suicide. It was very clearly murder and any other verdict seemed wrong.

The notes from the reporter in court were quite detailed and diligently taken. A lot of careful attention had been paid to this case by the newspaper. From the look of the file, there'd been a reporter in court every day. Fulman had obviously invested a lot in this case, so an open verdict and no answers must have been a source of enormous frustration. And still was. He was hoping for great things. The more she learnt about this family and the case, the more the weight of expectation settled on her.

Edward Ravenswick had given evidence that when he'd arrived at the lift, his brother Charles Ravenswick was there waiting, and they chatted about the reason for their attendance being required. Edward Ravenswick was asked what this was and he replied that they had been summoned to hear the new will, which arose out of the recent change in circumstances.

When he was questioned as to this change, he detailed the discovery of certain books and manuscripts, some of which had been sold, but there were the remaining ones which were also very valuable. This obviously had an impact on the estate and Lord Ravenswick had given instructions for his will to be altered to reflect this. It was thought appropriate that all those concerned should be gathered to hear the details redrafted by the solicitor, Mr Philip Pembroke. Charles had informed Edward that his mother, Lady Ravenswick, was already waiting upstairs with his father. Lord Ravenswick had been quite poorly earlier but was well enough to see everyone now and would like to raise a glass in celebration of the New Year.

Edward Ravenswick then gave evidence of all the other people in the lift and it concurred with what Charlotte had read earlier in the press reports. He acknowledged that it was a bizarre collection of people but, it being New Year's Eve, Lord and Lady Ravenswick wanted some of the long-serving members of staff to attend as there was some token provision for them in the will and there were also small gifts to be given out then as well. This was something they did every year. It used to be a much grander affair but, since Lord Ravenswick's decline, the celebration had been scaled back.

Charlotte always used to love the ball her parents held for the staff every year. Her mother and father would send out invitations at Christmas time and all the servants were gathered together for a party which their children would also attend. These events were a real highlight of the year and everyone adored the entertainer with his magic tricks and puppets. Charlotte, however, relished the opportunity to play with the children from the village. They were free and fun loving with none of the constraints the rest of the children she knew had placed upon their behaviour.

It was the one time her mother, the celebrated daughter of the Duke and Duchess of Rothesville, would dance with the steward. Every man in the room wanted to dance with her, except Charlotte's father of course. Frances, Lady de Burgh, as she was now, had been a PB – a Professional Beauty whose photographic portraits were displayed in all the shop windows. She was universally lauded. A great jewel in her husband's crown. He provided the wealth her family had run out of over the centuries. She was the old name. It was a system that worked for everyone. Everyone except for Charlotte.

On those nights when the veil between worlds came down and boundaries blurred, they all danced in the ballroom as the wine and beer flowed. The next day, order would be impeccably restored, no matter how bad anyone was feeling. Any indiscretions were forgotten.

Edward Ravenswick's evidence as to why members of the staff were in the lift that night may have seemed strange to the public following the case in the newspapers at the time, but it made perfect sense to Charlotte, who had grown up in this rarefied world of rules. It was disturbing to her how quickly she could still relate to it all.

Raven masters and gardeners standing alongside the family in a lift on New Year's Eve now seemed perfectly natural to Charlotte, particularly given that Lord Ravenswick was in no state to go to parties or even leave his room. She didn't even question why they'd put the elderly, infirm head of the household in the most inaccessible part of the house. He'd always been there, so why move him? The answer was of course to have a large, ornate lift fitted that was powered by an unreliable electricity supply and kept failing. It might seem like a looking-glass world to the newspaper readers, but not to Charlotte. She was beginning to understand it. Perhaps even sympathise with it.

This world was starting to make more sense. She wanted to delve deeper. The answer was here somewhere. Further on in the folder, there was more evidence put before the coroner's court as to the construction of this unconventional lift. A few large country houses had such mechanisms installed for invalid family members, but it was felt necessary to explain it in more detail for the assembled court and, in the articles, to the public at large, who were enthusiastically following the case in the newspapers with bewildered fascination.

The paper had made great show of this vast lift and printed the detailed drawings and photographs which had been shown to the court. These were all included in the folder. It was a beautiful construction, in shape not dissimilar to a bird cage, its scrolling metalwork and painted gold remarkably reminiscent of the aviary Charlotte had seen earlier. Its primary feature though was its size. It was as big as a room and could easily have accommodated all those people.

The court was informed that the occupants that night hadn't been in the lift very long before it stopped. This was apparently a perennial problem as the hydroelectricity produced for the house was not entirely reliable.

Edward Ravenswick gave evidence that where the lift stopped, they were surrounded by solid stone walls. The cage fit very snugly into the lift shaft. He was asked to explain in detail what the surroundings of the lift looked like. He said there was no space around the lift, the floor was solid and nothing could fit through the intricately designed bars in the roof and round the sides.

He was then asked if anyone else could have entered the lift and he replied that was not possible. No one could have got near it. The lift fit into the lift shaft as tight as a bullet in a gun. This seemed to Charlotte an extraordinary analogy to use, given the circumstances of the case, and jarringly flippant coming from the mouth of the victim's own brother. The court perhaps concurred as there was a note made that there was a long pause after this remark.

Charlotte pictured the court, silent as a memorial, picking over the last moments of a man's life, teasing out the details from a brother who watched him die. So many difficult, awkward moments had faced this family as a result of the heir's death. Their grief, their very existence and way of life had been dragged out and put on public display. And Charlotte was now becoming party to that, being asked to pick over that corpse again. What good would that serve? She told herself she was looking for an answer, it would resolve their pain to know why he had died and who was responsible. Too many men had died and no one was held to account for their deaths, no one was responsible anymore. There were no reasons for so much loss.

No ceremony followed Archie's death. Charlotte was only asked the bare details and even that was a torturous reliving. His wheezing had grown more pronounced, she'd recounted. The coughing severe. There had been blood, not much but it was brilliant red against his neat handkerchief. She went into no details about his final words. She would take those to her own grave.

That was all. No press. One announcement. A cold cemetery where it was hard to leave him on his own, to walk away from that mound of earth knowing the body she'd held so often was under there. Empty of anything that was him. He always hated the mud after he came back. Hated the thought of all those men he watched buried under it.

She wouldn't touch Archie again. Wouldn't hear his voice. Wouldn't see his eyes when they opened in a morning. No court would have had any time for all that. There was no need. There was no "victim". No mystery to why he died. Out of all the questions he'd left her, the biggest one that spooled in her head would always be "Why?" Even though there was a very clear cause, there was no sense, no reason to it at all.

In Charles Ravenswick's case, Charlotte could already imagine a number of reasons why people might have been driven to kill him, not least of all that he was the heir to Ravenswick Abbey. And one person who had benefitted from that was his brother, Edward, whose dispassionate retelling of the event to that courtroom told a lot more than he was saying.

Edward Ravenswick clarified that no one could have slipped between the structure of the lift and the walls. It had not been stopped for long when the lights went out. There was a little grumbling from the occupants but they were all accustomed to issues with the power.

Edward's emotionless evidence continued that Charles shouted, "No!" There was a bang. Something dropped to the floor which made a thud on the carpet. This was followed by a much louder, heavier sound of something else falling to the floor.

The lights came on and there, on the carpet in the middle of the lift, was the gun. His brother, Charles Ravenswick, was slumped on the floor. Edward was asked to describe him. A pause was noted in the evidence at this point and the question was asked again. It was also noted that the witness spoke so quietly that his evidence could barely be heard. He went on to recount that his brother, Charles Ravenswick's, eyes were stretched painfully wide and had the most terrifying look of...

Another pause was noted.

"...disbelief." It was a look, his brother went on to say, that he would never forget as long as he lived.

Charlotte thought about this statement for a moment. As long as he lived. The new heir to Ravenswick Abbey must have wondered about that and whether or not his brother had been murdered as a result of this position that he now occupied.

But it was almost a year later and Edward Ravenswick was still heir to the Ravenswick fortune. There'd been no attempts on his life. At least, none that had come to light.

14

The report noted that it had been necessary to take a break in the proceedings at that point for the witness to rest and gather himself.

When the court reconvened, Edward Ravenswick continued with his bland delivery of the facts. Any emotion had been dealt with.

Edward Ravenswick stated that the butler, Heskins, had checked for signs of life and confirmed that Mr Charles Ravenswick was dead. It was indeed a bullet wound and Charles Ravenswick had been shot.

His brother then recounted how there was a huge amount of unnecessary shouting and screaming. Charles's wife, Rachel, fainted and had to be revived. Mary Ravenswick would not stop shouting that someone in that lift was a murderer. She was quite hysterical. Nicodemus Bligh attempted to comfort her. Edward Ravenswick reported that there was so much noise and commotion it was hard to understand what was being said and who was doing what. He too took the opportunity to inspect his brother and confirmed that he was dead, shot, he clarified.

However cold the delivery had been, Charlotte could sense the chaos rising up out of his words. To be trapped in such a small space with a dead man and a killer, not knowing which one of them it was, must have been overwhelming, frightening. The confusion of panic-stricken voices, horrifying. A whole turmoil of emotions was unleashed in that moment. A man who at least some of the people in that lift must have loved, was dead in front of them, and one of them had shot him. Sudden loss instantly coupled with extreme fear in those frantic moments of disbelief. As soon as the light had exploded in their blind eyes, it would have exposed this scene. The confusion and disorientation instant. Devastating. Edward however had managed to give quite a coherent, almost impassive account of that moment. Nothing less than would be expected of the new heir, with his stiff upper lip already firmly in place.

His recount continued of how the lift started again very shortly after and carried them up to Lord Ravenswick's apartment where the police were called. Lady Ravenswick was utterly distraught. Lord Ravenswick was so frail and agitated he could hardly breathe, and had to be sedated by Mr Bligh.

Charlotte leafed through the folder. Various police officers' evidence had been given. Everyone was searched, as was the lift, and no other guns were found other than the one in the lift. In any event, the evidence supported the fact that Charles Ravenswick had been shot with the gun found in the lift, a Colt Derringer, and it was confirmed that that was definitely the cause of death. There were various photographs of the gun, lying on the carpet. There were no fingerprints found on it.

The lift had been analysed and the gaps in the bars were shown to be too narrow for the gun to have passed through. It had to have been in there already. Either someone took it in with them or it was already in there and hidden somewhere.

Charlotte fell back on the bed with the folder open. One of those people in that lift was a murderer, but it was utterly impossible to say who. It was perfect. The killer had devised a situation where the possibility of each person in the lift committing the offence was equal and there was no way of telling who it was. Which also meant that whoever the killer was, they were both clever and ruthless. She looked down the list of the occupants of the lift again. Apart from the dead man, they were all still here at Ravenswick Abbey. She glanced at the lockless door.

It was also very clear that this house would not only be deep in grief, but suspicion as well. Every person in that lift would suspect someone, except of course the killer, who was presumably watching their moment of silent success.

There were so many unanswered questions, including why someone would want to kill Charles Ravenswick. How did they know the electricity would fail at that moment, or was it just an opportunistic crime? Perhaps he shot himself, but there were no fingerprints at all on the gun which indicated it had been wiped clean and there'd be no need to do that if it was suicide, or, for that matter, to enact the entire elaborate scene.

There was also that extreme look of shock imprinted on the victim's face. That had been the only part of Edward Ravenswick's evidence which seemed to verge on emotion – the disturbing, dramatic look on his brother's dead face.

All the questions washed through Charlotte's head but

the major one was, how on earth she was going to ask any of them. She was here to investigate ravens, not dead men and, so far, she had been kept noticeably separate from the rest of the family.

Except for tonight. Tonight, she was to be drawn out for inspection.

The questions rolled over in her mind as she dressed for dinner. She needed this to work. It had to. It was the closest she'd got so far. She had to look the part tonight. This was her chance. The nerves were already rising.

She put on the little black dress she'd seen Clara Bow model that had cost a fortune, the dress she'd worn for many wonderful dinners with Archie but which had now, quite literally, seen much better days. All her dresses had, but she was lucky enough to have them. Nosferatu needed a good wardrobe to trawl the clubs and bars, exploring London's hidden nights to titillate her readers the next day and give the eager public their much-needed gossip.

Bottle parties, cocktails at The 43, cabarets at Café de Paris, all required "the look." And Charlotte had it. Or, at least, she knew how to look like she still did with the help of Mrs C. But her facade was wearing as thin as her shoes. Everything was. Not just the chiffon and silk; the appetite was waning as well.

There were fewer revellers at each party now. The guest lists were dwindling, the tables shrinking. She wasn't the only one in a reworked dress with paste jewellery. Some of the gang had gone back to crumbling houses in the country, some had to stay, their homes sold to pay groaning tax bills.

The public were growing a little tired of their antics. Car races through Piccadilly at dawn, shooting parties and oblivion, it had all been gloriously scandalous for a time, the names infamous. Now, the lens had refocused. She sensed the shift. Almost imperceptible at first. But there were more letters to Nosferatu now. More criticism of their wanton excess. Hadn't he – they always assumed the column was written by a man – looked out of his window recently? People were hungry. People were losing their jobs. What she was writing about was detached from reality, out of touch, alienated from the real world. Nosferatu was running out of time. Charlotte could see that.

Some of the old gang would always be there doing the same thing. They were estranged enough from the real world to remain indifferent. The likes of Jonty Merrybright and Lady Withers would carry on partying to the bitter end. But most had become exiles in their own country. They weren't leading the way anymore. They'd been left behind. It wasn't just the decade that was ending, it was their era.

And it was a relief. Even when Charlotte started as Nosferatu, she knew it wouldn't last forever, nor did she particularly want it to. She'd always dreamed of being a real journalist. The same round of parties and faces couldn't go on forever. She was in her own little locked room just living the same life over and over again. This job here at Ravenswick had to work. It was definitely time to find a new, more serious persona than a fictitious vampire who liked cocktail parties.

Charlotte carefully rolled on her last smart stockings, combed down her hair and slowly teased out some more of the old Max Factor lipstick and powder. Another disguise. Another person to be, to find out secrets and tell the world. But now it was more serious. Now it mattered.

She watched herself in the mirror with an absent air of distraction, trying to recapture that bored, decadent look. The hair was the same, the make-up similar. She could almost be that *It girl* again. Almost. She had to play the part well tonight.

15

Heskins was waiting to serve cocktails in the sitting room. It felt strange to Charlotte having him mix her drink when she'd emerged from the same door as him earlier tonight. He studiously avoided any form of pleasantries.

Most of the diners were already there, although Lady Ravenswick had sent word that she'd been delayed with her husband but would be joining them for dinner later. They were to start without her.

Heskins handed Charlotte a gin and Dubonnet without looking at her.

"Thank you so much. It looks positively lethal. I'll have to make sure I don't get too *splifficated*!" She gave her usual coquettish, nightclub look and injected a false note of fun. Heskins paid her no attention but the disdain was clear on his face. She began to think her efforts would be wasted here.

However, the man to her side laughed a little. "Is that ornithology speak or flapper girl?"

Charlotte sipped on the drink and eyed the man over the rim of her glass. "I suppose one can be both." His fine-drawn features were instantly recognisable from the photographs she'd seen in the newspaper reports.

"Edward. Edward Ravenswick."

She held the drink in her mouth for a moment and tried not to look too interested in the man whose testimony about his brother's death she'd just been poring over.

He turned to Heskins. "I'll take one of those too if you don't mind. I'm sure being *splifficated* with Miss Blood will be very interesting."

Edward Ravenswick's voice had a lazy elegance to it that lingered on every word just a little too long to be polite. There was admittedly an easy manner about him, a kind of languid, relaxed nature that should have put Charlotte at her ease. But men like him never put Charlotte at her ease. That indolent air he'd so meticulously cultivated was designed to be challenging.

There was an unwelcome proximity to his presence. He was only a few inches too close, but it made all the difference to her comfort.

The scent of cologne and cigarettes hung around him in a way that hinted he was a man who liked to do things to excess. She'd met a hundred Edward Ravenswicks in her time and hadn't liked one of them. Archie used to call them icebergs – there was only a tiny little glimpse on the surface of the kind of man, but beneath, there was a whole lot more going on. And generally, it wasn't good for anyone else sailing by. Archie was always a good judge of character. He knew the cut of a man in seconds.

He would have known the exact calibre of the man in front of Charlotte now. Edward Ravenswick drank heavily on the cocktail as though he was inhaling it. But she could not square the image of this man with the man in a lift standing over his dead brother, or the man in a courtroom recalling those terrible wide eyes. He was everything he should be, but there was definitely a lot more beneath the gloss of that suave surface, as if more than one man looked out from the same face.

Of course, he was dressed impeccably in white tie with immaculately shined shoes. Everything about him had an icy shine, his skin, those black eyes and his smoothed-down hair. Under the lights, he had a kind of rich glaze to him.

There was a theatre to all this. If she was honest, Charlotte had always loved the extravagant dressing for dinner. There was something faintly childish about it. Uncomplicated. Playing dress-up with adults. But in her experience, when it got to the dinners themselves, that was when they tended to lose their simple fun.

Archie had always looked very handsome in his finery. It was the only part of his wardrobe she'd kept, apart from the socks. The rest had been sold.

"So, how do you like our little Abbey?" Edward looked at Charlotte teasingly.

"It's very beautiful. I saw your aviary this morning."

"Oh, so you are interested in *all* the birds here." He laughed again with that mocking sound.

"Of course I am. That's why I'm here, Mr Ravenswick."

"Edward, please. *You* can definitely call me Edward. We're all terribly informal here, as you can see." He gave a sarcastic little smile that, as with everything else about him, had an almost cruel edge to it. "Now, come on. Let me introduce you to the rest of the flock. You can tell everyone what you think about *the birds*."

He guided her towards two women who were sitting as far away as possible from one another on the long sofa, resolutely not speaking. One of the women Charlotte instantly recognised as the youngest sibling. She had the look of a woman who'd had a difficult time emerging from the shell of childhood and had not managed to unfurl quite as effortlessly as the rest of them. It was not only bewildering to her but evidently the source of considerable frustration. Everything about her was awkward and ungainly. In spite of her severe look, adolescence seeped out of her like she was suffering from an illness.

"Miss Blood, meet Mary, my little sister."

Charlotte knew this patronising introduction all too well. Either Randolph or Bertie would always set her up to be inconsequential and ignored every time with a line like this.

"Hello." The word sounded very dry. Mary didn't offer anything else.

"And, the grieving widow," Edward winked at the woman perched on the other end of the sofa. "Rachel Ravenswick." Her dress fell in waves of silk shining crow-black under the glittering light. She clicked her long nails against her pearls restlessly. When she looked up from beneath feathery lashes, it was only directly at him. Her eyes didn't stray anywhere else. Clearly, Charlotte had not mastered widowhood quite as successfully as this lady had.

"This is Miss Blood. The ornithologist flapper."

The woman cast her a dismissive glance. "Pleased to meet you." She clearly wasn't. There was a lithe grace about her. Her limbs liquid as if she could just slip through a person's fingers. She was elegant but in a self-aware way. This was a woman who wanted people to notice. Most of all, she wanted Edward Ravenswick to notice, and she didn't care who saw.

There was no subterfuge here. These two were conducting a silent conversation with their eyes, but it was very obvious to Charlotte what they were saying.

"How do you do?" Charlotte used a meek voice. She was an ornithologist after all. "What a delightful gown." She sipped on her cocktail, attempting to look as demure as possible.

Rachel smirked. "Well, aren't you just adorable?" She held out a cigarette in a short holder and Edward leaned in to light it. Neither of them looked at the cigarette or the lighter.

They held each other's gaze until a sharper voice cut in. "I'm his wife, Elizabeth, although you wouldn't think it."

Charlotte refocused on the slightly more ruffled-looking woman sitting rigidly in a soft chair beside the sofa. She looked more careworn than the photograph Charlotte had seen of her. Elizabeth's eyes were ringed with the sort of puce, swollen skin that usually accompanied hours of crying. Maybe that was true, but she didn't look like the kind of woman to cry easily.

Edward immediately straightened as if called to attention. Rachel blew out a thin stream of blue-grey smoke before nonchalantly tapping the cigarette ash over the back of the sofa.

"Mummy says you're here to look at our ravens." The girl, Mary, had an unsteady voice, the kind that seemed to enter every conversation unsure whether it should be heard. It always sounded odd to Charlotte when people the size of adults used the word "Mummy." It gave the impression of an overgrown child still being squeezed into little girl words and clothes.

"I am, yes." Charlotte took another drink and tried to

ignore the fact that even she didn't think she sounded convincing.

"Why would you want to do that?"

"Well –" Charlotte took a preparatory breath "– they're just such fascinating creatures. Did you know they can speak?"

"Of course I do. We all do. We speak to them."

Edward cleared his throat in embarrassment at the girl's sudden directness. "Now, Mary, play nicely." He turned to Charlotte. "You must ignore our baby sis. She doesn't get out much or have any company... or friends."

The girl tutted and turned her head away, closing her eyes.

"We used to think it was quite fun to teach the ravens little things," Edward continued, "you know, silly things to say or rude comments about each other. It's great fun to watch people's reactions when they hear Aunt Mildred has a purple bottom."

"Really, Edward!" Mary exclaimed.

"Mary was too young to play with us." He sounded suddenly petulant. Even the adults were child-like here. It was as though they'd never been given the chance to grow up and had simply remained in this charmless stasis. Whether that was a choice or not was a different question.

Living together as they always had done with *Mummy* and *Daddy* still at the helm was a world Charlotte had found suffocating and could not escape from quickly enough. All those sons and daughters she knew living together in their vast mansions with Mama and Papa never giving them the chance to be anything other than children. All decisions and responsibilities were removed.

Life just continued as it always had. Sometimes a spouse would be added into the house, like a playmate coming over for tea who just never left.

It was the same at Bladesworth. First, her brother Bertie arrived home with Hen who was aptly named due to her constant pecking at her new husband. Then Randolph, her other brother, brought Blythe over the threshold and she just drifted around looking pale and miserable all the time.

But nothing was ever really *that* serious. All those important matters like money, jobs and the business of a home were dealt with elsewhere, with the dirty laundry. She and her brothers were doled out allowances like pocket money and, in turn, had to abide by the rules, forever dependent.

However small their little Bloomsbury flat was, Charlotte had relished being master of her own domain with Archie. In spite of everything, he'd taught her how to spread her wings and be free. She would never let that go.

Charlotte looked at the figures arrayed around the Ravenswick drawing room drama that was being put on for her. They were still children who'd never left the nest. Still with their playroom squabbles and pop guns, only this time the gun was real. And from what she'd seen so far, any one of these people could have pulled the trigger and then hurried off for tea-time.

A gong sounded somewhere outside the room, interrupting her assessment of them.

"Ah, dinner. I'm fam!" Edward announced before reaching down for Rachel's hand.

She slipped her fingers between his and looked at him

coyly. They smiled indulgently. The whole little scene was saccharine and, like everything else here, it had the decided air of being performed for someone else's benefit.

16

It was just as they stepped through into the large, ornate dining room that the lights glimmering from the large chandelier flickered then failed. It was nothing dramatic. They just petered out then died as if from old age. The reaction from the assembled party was similarly unimpressed.

"Oh, for God's sake, it's every other night now." Rachel sounded bored with the tediousness of it all.

But Charlotte's mind instantly leapt to the night of the lift. She couldn't make out any of the faces or even place them in the room. In that perfect, smothering darkness with no glimmer of light, the confusion and disorientation were easy to envisage. No one would have been clear who or where anyone really was and what they were doing.

The darkness here was immediate and absolute. There were power cuts in the flat in London regularly, but it was nothing like this. In the city, there was always some form of ambient light creeping in through windows or bleeding under doors. Out here, the world instantly reverted to another time, a darker time.

"Don't move around," Edward instructed, "you'll fall over something. I've got a lighter. Heskins, have you got matches?" He was efficient and perfectly calm, taking control immediately. The louche, sarcastic man she'd seen earlier was suddenly very much in charge, as if it came naturally to him.

"Yes, sir. I'm lighting up now. The footmen are here too."

It was all very routine and matter of fact. There seemed to be no urgency, but Charlotte could feel the steady rise of her pulse and the skin stretch tighter at the sides of her eyes as they widened.

"I do wish you'd get this fixed, Edward. Honestly, it's every time it goes dark now. Only yesterday –"

"Do be quiet, Elizabeth." His voice was commanding. "No one wants to know what you get up to in the dark."

"If they weren't so penny-pinching about staff for the turbine –"

"Be quiet!" Edward barked. As the match lit, his face grew out of the black, the hollows set in deep shadow, each contour darkly defined. Charlotte immediately saw that his eyes were set in an expression of fierce anger. This was not the easy-going fop he'd presented earlier. Another man was looking out from that face again.

He glanced around the semi-lit assembly, suddenly aware of the new light on him. His face changed in an instant and the mocking, supercilious version of him returned. "Aha! Let there be light!"

A sequence of lights were lit in turn like stars growing out of the night sky. First one, then more, each illuminating a new face until the room was glowing in candle flames.

"Apologies for the minor delay, sir," Heskins said calmly.

"Not at all, Heskins. Marvellous as ever! You've saved the day – or night, as it were." Edward gave a nod and a smile. Any trace of his earlier anger had effortlessly evaporated. "Now, let's all sit down to dinner by candlelight."

"I prefer it," Rachel hummed. "Very romantic."

"And much more forgiving on an older woman's features, wouldn't you say, Rachel?" Elizabeth pushed past her.

"Well, I hate it." Mary stomped to her place and sat with a petulant look. "It's very stupid and it needs fixing. Old Jeffers never does it and I don't understand why we haven't got the men anymore who used to work there."

"Because they're dead, Mary, dear girl," Edward sneered. "There was a war, if you recall."

Charlotte looked down quickly but Edward saw it. From his face, he understood immediately, everyone did. Every table in England had seen this look at some point in the last few years.

"Oh, Miss Blood, I do apologise…"

"There's no need." She kept her voice under control. She was used to it.

The familiar hole in the conversation opened up. They were less frequent these days but they still left some traces of pain. Not a lot. More a vague remembrance from a scar. It used to explode inside her when anyone clumsily mentioned the war deaths. The fire used to be almost unbearable that anyone could be so thoughtless with his memory, kicking it around like a deflated football in the mud. But now it was awkwardness that nestled into place as if a shameful secret had been exposed. She was a reminder of something it was time to forget. It had been over a decade but the world couldn't move on from its loss if there was always a grieving widow at the table.

"My brother and I both served, Miss Blood," Edward added with a new note of sincerity in his voice. It was surprising how seamlessly this man moved from fripperies to serious matters, as if he could see no difference between them. "We were fortunate to survive combat."

No one spoke, but behind every face the same thought was playing. Charles Ravenswick had survived the horrors of war only to be gunned down in his own home.

Wine was served in the difficult pause and the prospect of a forced dinner unfolded with the napkins. It was the beginning of a well-trodden, tired affair as the footmen walked around the table, serving. Both the food and the conversation seemed stale from the very beginning. Edward and Rachel were caught in their own world. Elizabeth looked aloof and when she spoke it was with a colourless voice. Mary fidgeted like a churlish girl at nursery supper, poking the food around the plate.

Although they sat in semi darkness, there was no noticeable effort to change the situation. There was a general acceptance that they would dine in the secular gloom. Perhaps servants had been tasked to sort out the problem, but around this table there was not even mild concern. They seemed quite happy to dine as all those faces that hung from the walls had done in bygone days. The large mirrors were gilded by candlelight, great ornate candelabras placed below them strategically to reflect the light. But they made only minor holes in the darkness. The smell of the candles was more noticeably potent than the light they gave off, a deep, waxy odour that seemed to burn all the air in the room. It coated the back of Charlotte's throat, leaving a dusty charcoal taste behind. The ecclesiastic half-light ushered in an air of melancholy, one Charlotte had experienced many times before. In spite of her father's best endeavours to enter the modern age, Bladesworth had to routinely rely on candles and oil lamps, as if the house itself was clinging to the darkness of the past.

There was a rush of relief when the tension was broken by the door opening to reveal Lady Ravenswick standing there, accompanied by Nicodemus Bligh. They entered as if they were being presented at court, she the grand dame, washed in diamonds still in their old-fashioned, ornate settings, her delicate limbs swamped with more swathes of heavily embroidered cloth and lace than would be needed for two dresses – even three, nowadays.

But it was Nicodemus Bligh who drew in all the attention like a croupier gathering in his cards. He was just as stately as Her Ladyship but there was something else. He radiated a hypnotic quality, as if he'd conjured some charm or enchantment to attract all the room's attention and bind it solely to him the instant he walked through the door. It wasn't just his imposing stature or the unusual plain white robes that flowed down him, there was a disturbing, wintry power to this man. He paused to enjoy the moment. This man was keenly aware of the attention he controlled.

17

Nicodemus Bligh surveyed the room with eyes that were the same perfect, mesmerising copper discs Charlotte had looked into before, reflecting the candlelight as if the flames were deep inside them. He seemed to command the light. When Nicodemus Bligh walked into the room, it was like a cloud passing over the sun.

Yet, in the way he held Lady Ravenswick's arm, there was an extravagant humbleness to him. He guided her into the room as though she was an invalid, frail and liable to crumble at any moment. Her skin was as soft and grey as ash. This weak person was not the same as the steely woman Charlotte had encountered earlier. The care he afforded her every move was so over-played, so attentive, as to look almost contrived.

"I'm so sorry we were delayed." Nicodemus Bligh used a soft, reverential voice. "His Lordship needed an immediate healing ceremony." He said it so sincerely, that for a moment it didn't even strike Charlotte how strange this selection of words was.

"He's not carrion yet, is he Bligh?" There was disdain in Edward Ravenswick's question. He didn't look at the man he was addressing when he spoke but rather at his mother.

"Thanks to my swift intervention," the mystic shot

with quick precision. He was clearly used to dealing with challenges incisively and putting them down instantly. Nicodemus Bligh was bold, unquestionable.

He gave the impression of focusing all his attention on Lady Ravenswick, seating her carefully with the required level of grandeur a child would show their favourite china doll. But he was alert to the room, aware of the scrutiny being afforded his every move. He gave a quick glance round the table before he settled into his own seat next to her. They were vigilant eyes that did not falter.

A discreet flurry of staff followed, liveried footmen, their gold braid glittering in the candlelight. The moment food was presented to him, Bligh immediately adopted a heartfelt face of gratitude, before drawing back his lips and lifting the small roasted quail in his fingers. He ate voraciously.

"Foul," Rachel murmured, and looked away in disgust.

His eyes settled on her, scorn burning out.

"I am a simple man, Mrs Ravenswick. I eat as man was intended to." He sank his teeth into the meat again but his eyes did not leave her. A thin trail of the bird's juices passed down over his chin and spotted the tablecloth.

"Edward, your father would like to see you later to discuss the sale of some manuscripts," Lady Ravenswick ventured. She had a borrowed look to her, hollowed out and unable to focus. When she spoke, it was in a detached voice. She ate nothing. Heskins attempted to serve her some wine but Nicodemus Bligh placed a long hand across the rim of her glass. He did not speak but the butler understood and moved away.

Lady Ravenswick fell into a gaunt, defeated look. White powder settled in the fragile lines of her face. She was a woman who had surrendered – what and to whom was becoming clearer by the minute.

"Flogging off more of the family jewels eh, Bligh?" Edward had not waved his white flag yet, though. He gave the mystic a supercilious look. "What would dear Charles have said?"

Lady Ravenswick's face instantly contracted into a pained expression. "Edward, my dear…"

"Don't concern yourself, Mother." He blew out a little faux laugh. "I have no interest in what tricks our resident magician is performing, much less in a heap of dusty old books no one ever reads. Charles may have had time to waste on arguing about rotting manuscripts, but I have much more… *worldly* pleasures to distract me. Perhaps my dearly departed brother should have paid more heed to that side of things." He smirked towards Rachel who gave a flirtatious face in response.

"*I* read them," Bligh said softly.

"Edward, my dear, we have a guest. From a *news*paper." Lady Ravenswick said it as if it was somehow an alien notion to her, this wife of a wealthy press magnate.

Her son laughed. "Our little *ornithologist*?" That constant mocking note still rippled under the surface.

Charlotte cleared her throat. "I very much enjoyed seeing the ravens and the aviary this morning, actually. I'm hoping to visit again tomorrow."

Nicodemus Bligh set down his napkin with great consideration as if readying himself to perform a sacred ceremony. The sermon was about to begin. "Were you aware, Miss Blood, that the Romans thought the ravens were bad luck because they associated them with Apollo, the god of prophecy?"

"All very scholarly, I'm sure. Thank you, Bligh." Edward flicked his hand in a dismissive gesture and sighed. The candles closest to him momentarily dipped.

"Ravens were originally white, you see." The keen-eyed shaman leaned in and assumed a conspiratorial tone. As he drew closer and the flame inspected his face, he seemed to take on an almost malign look. "But when one bird brought back the news that Apollo's lover was *unfaithful*, the god scorched its feathers and that is why they are now black." His eyes lingered pointedly on Edward then moved to Rachel, the flame lighting his black pupils. He didn't blink once.

There was a silence. Even Heskins ceased his shuffling around the room.

Charlotte broke the tension with a small laugh. "Oh, I'm not sure there's any truth in that. A very beautiful story though, Mr Bligh, thank you."

"Ha! Bligh," Edward exclaimed. "Scuppered by the raven *expert*!"

A mixture of sneers and awkward fidgeting circled the table.

"I don't think your opinion is required, Mr Bligh." Rachel spoke with an entitled condescension that sounded well practiced.

"I will determine that, Rachel," Lady Ravenswick cut in, addressing her as she might an unruly pet who needed to be reminded of the order.

The muscles around Rachel's mouth twitched and her eyes flared. She instantly looked towards Edward but this time he did not meet her gaze.

"And how is His Lordship?" Rachel gave an indulgent smile. The implication was clear to everyone. When the thread of the old man's life finally snapped, so too would Lady Ravenswick's authority. Her reign would be over, there would be a new order and the grand dame cast into her dowager days, as was the usual way.

"He is comfortable, thank you Rachel." Lady Ravenswick shifted her gaze serenely. "Tell me, Edward. How is dear Celeste? It is so gratifying to see a young child around the house."

Charlotte knew exactly where this arrow was aimed. She was well aware of the comments that followed childless women around like little ghosts. She watched Rachel squeeze her lips so tight they were ringed with white.

Elizabeth gave a gracious nod. "She is very well, Your Ladyship." She cast a glance towards Rachel. "Thriving. A child is a gift, is it not?"

Rachel slammed her glass down and the stem smashed. A footman circled and removed it in silence. "It was not me who was at fault in that department."

Mary straightened in her chair and spoke first. She'd been biding her time, waiting for a new possibility to open up for her to shine.

"Well, I too read a lot about ravens, Mr Bligh, but I prefer Poe's raven, I must say." The young girl set out her knowledge like a market trader, loud and immodestly. She gave a self-satisfied smile and poked her fork around the food. "There's such a beauty in that all-consuming love for his dearly departed spouse, don't you think Rachel, dear sis?"

Rachel's smile withered. Increasingly, she wasn't quite so perfectly beautiful. Under a harsher light, the painting was clearly flawed.

Around the table, the rest of the faces solidified in the candlelight.

Mary turned her cool expression on Elizabeth Ravenswick next, who was still playing the role of the vanquished wife quite flawlessly.

The young girl adopted a conceited look.

When Mary spoke, she lifted her head with pride. "'On the morrow *he* will leave me, as my Hopes have flown before.'" She paused, searching out more drama, before whispering, "'Then the bird said, "Nevermore."'"

An unreal silence descended as if the air itself had stopped to listen.

Lady Ravenswick was the first to end the illusion. "That's quite enough of your schoolgirl nonsense, Mary. Thank you."

Charlotte hesitated before she spoke, but something compelled her to say what was in her mind. "I believe Mr Poe's poem was about grief and loss rather than any other form of leaving, Mary." She stared at the tablecloth, remembering when she sought out such books in those first dead months when it hurt just to breathe in the air without any trace of Archie in it anymore. Charlotte stared into the flickering candle and its light danced on her eyes. "'Take thy beak from out my heart, and take thy form from off my door! Quoth the Raven "Nevermore."'" Charlotte's voice was almost inaudible as if she didn't care whether they heard her or not. For that secluded moment, she was no longer present.

But Nicodemus Bligh was not a man to shy away from private places. "Such glorious symbols. I fear death may have touched your heart deeply, Miss Blood."

Charlotte fell back into reality. "It has touched all our

hearts in some way or another I believe in these last years, Mr Bligh. Mine is a very ordinary tale."

Elizabeth took up a wine glass and twirled it, distractedly examining the deep scarlet stained glass lit from behind by the candlelight. "Well, I don't intend my tale to be. Let's stop all this talk of death. It's the Abbey we should all be thinking of and preserving its beauty." She drank heavily on the purple-black liquid.

"That's all you're ever interested in," Rachel was slurring a little now.

"I never suggested otherwise. The Abbey should be forefront in all our minds, as Ravenswicks. That's my concern."

"How perfect then that your husband is now the heir," Mary sneered.

There were so many rifts opening up here that Charlotte was too wary to walk into the conversation. Silence seemed the better option. But that wasn't going to be permitted for too long. She was, after all, the new specimen.

"So, Miss Blood," Nicodemus Bligh spoke her name smoothly, extending the sound of it. "You have an interest in literature?"

"I'm not an expert, I'm afraid. Just a very novice reader."

"I believe we are all novices in the eyes of the firmament. If we cannot delight in something new each day, we are condemned forever to see only what we know." His face was rich with self-gratification. "Come and see me in m–" he clenched his lips for a second "– in the library tomorrow and I will show you some of the wondrous books."

The shadow of concern immediately passed over Lady Ravenswick's face. "Is that wise, Nicodemus?" She sounded doubtful. Perhaps even distrustful.

"Oh, of course! I'm sure Miss Blood will delight in our spoils. Perhaps she'd like to include our treasures in her report. I'm sure we can find some texts on birds."

"'Our' is such a big word isn't it, Bligh?" Edward didn't look for an answer. He leaned back in his chair and drank with an air of contempt.

The spiritualist placed his hands on the table so precisely and slowly it could have been the prelude to a ritual. "Forgive me, I was unaware of your interest. I have not seen you in the library before. Your brother was always so keen. It is wonderful when someone suddenly finds a passion for books that has eluded them previously in their life."

The two men watched each other with unguarded derision.

"Ha!" Edward suddenly broke. "You have no worries from me, Bligh. I have no interest at all in your silly books. You and Mother can do with them as you please, so long as the coin comes in."

Edward leaned even further back in his chair.

"Your Ladyship," Heskins interrupted, "will you be leaving the gentlemen to port and –"

"Not a chance, Heskins!" Edward scoffed. "We're pretty light on *gentlemen* round here these days."

Bligh didn't react but remained with his palms down and fingers spread across the table.

"Thank you, Mr Bligh," Charlotte said. Attention switched again. "I would very much like to see the library."

A smile curled across the man's full lips. "Good. Good. I will see you tomorrow afternoon. After luncheon."

"Well, won't that be just delightful for you, *Miss Blood*." Rachel's voice was dark with sarcasm.

Edward Ravenswick spoke deliberately, as though he was thinking through each word before he said it. "Our aviary, then our library, Miss Blood, you really are seeing it all, aren't you? If we're not too careful you'll soon know everything about us."

"Everything might be quite a lot." Charlotte's smile was light, but the meaning was not. The look on all the faces gathered round that dark table suggested that they knew exactly what she meant.

18

The meal dragged on longer than anyone's patience at that table. Tempers were frayed and, as more wine was drunk, the barbed comments flowed freely into the tension. When coffees were brought in, that seemed to be Lady Ravenswick's cue to leave, assiduously enforced by Nicodemus Bligh, who held out an expectant arm to her. She gave a strained smile and departed with some comment about leaving the young people to enjoy themselves, which seemed remarkably inappropriate given the solemn-faced gathering.

Charlotte didn't wait long to make her excuses, and Heskins reluctantly gave her a candle. As she was leaving the room, Edward called after her. "Careful of the ghosts, Miss Blood."

Charlotte paused. "I'm afraid I don't believe in such things, Mr Ravenswick. I do not have a superstitious mind."

He laughed at her teasingly. "Well, aren't you just the thoroughly modern young woman." Edward tapped a cigarette and clicked the wheel of his lighter. For a brief moment, his mordant features were lit from below. He casually blew out a thin wisp of smoke. "Oh, we've got our monks around here and our fair share of bad ancestors too. Lord William Fortesque Ravenswick threw his own baby, not five minutes out of the womb, onto the fire, denying any servant girl could bear his child." He leaned in towards the candle. "And if you listen tonight, Miss Blood, you might even hear that babe crying on the cold, night wind."

The flame of the candle she carried obligingly bent with the draught from the open door. "Well, thank you, Mr Ravenswick. I shall be sure to listen for babies, monks and ancestors tapping at the window. And if they do appear, I shall be happy to inform them −" she paused and gave her sweetest smile "− that Miss Blood does not scare easily. Good night to you."

His mirthless laughter followed her out into the unlit hallway.

She had to admit to herself, however, that the journey to bed was daunting. The long corridors that tunnelled into black were deserted and cold with silence. She held out the candle in front of her, a thin line of wax dripping onto the small brass base. Occasionally, a droplet slipped over the edge and scalded her hand. The flame wavered.

She told herself there was no reason to be scared. There were no ghosts, otherwise surely Archie would have come back to her. But something played at the edges of her eyes, in that space where vision ends and imagination begins. Her mind sought out the slight shifts in the air, disruptions it could spin movement from. Almost imperceptible noises were unnatural, not part of the landscape of the house.

Charlotte walked quickly, her eyes searching the darkness. The candle created only a small pond of light that blinded her to anything beyond its circle.

She was grateful to be nearing the servants' area,

where at least, even if it wasn't friendly, there would be some sign of life. As she turned into the small corridor, glaring back at her from the darkness was a pair of sallow eyes that grew out of the emptiness.

The air stuck in her chest like a fist that seemed to push her back against the wall. The gazing eyes lingered in the black air, an unmoving luminous face steadily forming around them from out of the stones.

Holding a hand to her chest to calm her breathing, her eyes mirrored the perfectly circular whites staring back at her. Time seemed to expand to make space for all her fear. Charlotte bit down hard on her lip, trying to remind herself of reality. She watched the glowing eyes suspended in the darkness, motionless.

She tried to find calm. A shred of rational thought. The eyes just bored out of the wall in terror as if they had been walled up behind there and had found a small hole to peer through in horror. Charlotte closed her eyes. This couldn't be real. There were no ghosts. But when she looked back, the eyes were still there on the wall, unblinking.

She screwed her eyes even tighter shut. Her mind reformed the image, the face around the eyes, hanging there on the wall.

"Hanging on the wall," she breathed. "It's hanging on the wall." She opened her eyes and held out the candle. "A painting!" The face was there on the black wall. The frame was hidden in the darkness but she could see it now, and the old Ravenswick ancestor looked back at her from inside it. A benign, frozen face. She breathed out a few beats of laughter. "It's a painting. Just a painting. Of course you're a painting."

She moved the candle closer to the brass plaque below and read the inscription that formed in the darkness. Lord William Fortesque Ravenswick – the man Edward Ravenswick had said killed the baby that now haunted these corridors. Her gaze travelled back up the dark outline, back to those bone-white eyes burning their way through the layers of oil paint. There was a cruelty in that look, or was she just painting him with a new expression after what she'd been told? Whether the baby haunted the Abbey or not, he'd escaped justice for his crime. This family did not seem to be judged on the same level as ordinary men. Somehow, they were of a superior order.

She held out the candle and skimmed it round all the other dour portraits looking down on her. The Ravenswicks were everywhere, always watching. Even the dead ones. How many more of them were clustered in corners right now, watching her fear? Was the most recently deceased member of the family there, Charles Ravenswick, willing her on to avenge him? Or did he want her to leave him alone as well?

As she turned away, those shining eyes were still watching her. They were not the only ones.

Her heart was calming down, her breath slowing, when she heard the footsteps running. She scoured the darkness. A new cold river of air passed over her before the main door to the house slammed. A solid, deadened sound. Someone had just run outside. Instinctively, or rashly as she might later think, she followed. There was no time to think.

The candlelight threw a long shadow up along the wall, flickering quickly alongside her like an agitated friend. She paused with her hand on the large metal handle, before throwing back the door. The wind instantly took the candle flame, leaving only the dim glow of the coaching lamps.

Charlotte stepped out and called into the wind. "Hello?" Her hair was snatched back on the cold air.

The veiled moon cast a brittle light over the grounds, the wind shaking the black bones of the trees. There was no one here. She was chasing ghosts.

But as she turned to go, she heard more footsteps, running over stone. Fast footsteps. Close by.

"Hello? Is somebody out here?"

Charlotte stepped further out from the door.

The footsteps had died on the wind. But a strange scraping noise had taken their place.

She switched her head around. "I know you're here." If they were, they didn't answer. "You won't scare me this time."

Another scrape sounded before a sudden rushing sound, drowning out the wind. She frantically scanned the air.

Charlotte tilted her head back to see the grotesque face coming out of the black air towards her.

The huge, stone gargoyle hurtled through a gap in the darkness, the grey-white eyes boring out of the sky, fixed open, on Charlotte.

She dove forward and felt the vast hunk of stone skim past her heels before it embedded itself in the gravel. The thunder of stone being driven into the earth smothered every other sound, leaving a hole of silence in the air behind it.

Charlotte was rigid, her face buried into the gravel, feeling the beat of her heart pouring out of her chest into the ground. Her mouth was open but she didn't take a breath.

It was an eerie stillness, as if time had stopped, stretched out to make room for this lump of stone to fall through it. Everything paused.

The world slowly began contracting back around her.

Charlotte closed her eyes, blood flushing through her head, her body racing back to life.

She turned to look at the shattered, grotesque stone face staring at her with a broken malice from its newly formed hollow. One horn smashed, the wicked smile twisted into the ground.

Charlotte's eyes shot to the battlements above. Was there a dark shadow watching, before flitting across the eye of the moon? It was only a moment, then the shape was gone.

She looked back to the face of the gargoyle at her feet. A single devil eye stared up at her from the gravel with a sly look that said, "*Next time.*"

19

Charlotte left nothing behind her except the quick tap of the cobbler's nails on the stone floors. A current of fear raced through her veins like a new charge.

When she got to her room, she stood with her back to the door, her eyes wide in disbelief, her thoughts too fractured to settle, listening for those footsteps again. But there was only silence for company. She rammed the chair under the doorhandle again, feeling the flimsiness of its frame. That wasn't going to hold anyone back for long.

She sat on the bed, watching the door. Like a child braced for the nightmares, she slipped under the covers, still clothed, still rationing her breath, keeping it shallow in an effort to create as little disturbance as possible. Keeping that one thought at a distance: had someone really just tried to kill her? Or at least scare her off? This was an old house, crumbling at the seams. Perhaps the malign stone creature just couldn't cling to its plinth anymore. But there were definite footsteps. Although, she doubted even that now.

The room was white cold, the sheets brittle. Charlotte remembered nights in houses like this very well, when all the voices went silent, and the house started to make noises as if it was waking up the moment everyone else went to sleep. The windows rattled like ill-fitting teeth. Old floorboards woke, stretching and contracting, cracking and groaning as if invisible feet started to walk across them. Even the walls filigreed out fine lines that seemed to move with a fresh pulse spreading through them. Every stone lived and breathed in those dead hours.

Charlotte lay awake, listening to the house, the gusts of wind mewling round the walls outside, twisting their way down the chimneys. She thought of the demonic little face half-buried in the ground, that evil eye looking up to her window.

She couldn't bring herself to blow out the candle but still, she was wary of the line of yellow light that would be showing under her door. She reasoned that if someone saw it, she could just say she was doing research.

It was in fact the only thing to do now as sleep seemed like a very distant idea. It was the only refuge from the fear. The only escape was to find the answer to all this.

She glanced at the door again before shakily taking out the folder and opening it on the bed. She took a steadying breath and tried to calm herself.

The next section was from a reporter at *The Comet* who had been in court and made extensive notes of Mary Ravenswick's evidence in full. The picture it drew of the youngest daughter was very similar to the person Charlotte had encountered at dinner. Her responses were typically curt and Charlotte could easily recreate the scene of the surly young woman delivering her arrogant, clipped answers.

There was the usual swearing-in and then the bout began. Combative. Unhelpful even, in the face of an investigation as to how her eldest brother was killed. It was a cold, steel-hearted display.

Coroner: *Miss Ravenscroft, I believe you were in the lift the night of your brother's death.*

MR: *That's correct.*

Coroner: *Why were you in the lift?*

MR: *I was told to be there.*

Coroner: *By whom?*

MR: *Heskins said my parents wished me to be there.*

Coroner: *That would be Lord and Lady Ravenswick.*

MR: *They are my parents.*

(Long pause)

Coroner: *Why was your presence required, Miss Ravenswick?*

MR: *I don't know.*

Coroner: *Would it be because it was New Year's Eve?*

MR: *Maybe.*

(Long pause)

Coroner: *We've heard mention of there being a will. Were you aware of anything to do with that?*

MR: *I don't know anything about that. The family doesn't involve me with the money, I'm only sixteen. Like he said, what would I do with money? They won't increase my allowance because apparently I'm only a child.*

Coroner: *Who told you that, Miss Ravenswick?*

(Pause)

MR: *I don't know. I can't remember.*

Coroner: *Well, who oversaw the family finances?*

MR: *I'm not sure that's entirely relevant here.*

Coroner: *Perhaps you should leave it to the court to*

determine what is relevant, Miss Ravenswick.
Your brother, Charles Ravenswick was shot.
Someone must have had a reason to do that.
Perhaps money might provide a motive.

MR: *I thought you weren't here to apportion*
blame, sir. At least, that was my reading of the
Coroner's Court procedure.

Coroner: *Miss Ravenswick, can you tell the court what*
happened when you arrived at the lift?

MR: *I have already been through this with the*
police.

(Long pause)

Coroner: *Perhaps, Miss Ravenswick, you might indulge*
the court once more. I'm sure It's very painful
for you.

Charlotte could sense the sarcasm leaking off the page.

MR: *(Long sigh) Very well. I went to the lift. My*
brothers, Edward and Charles, were both
there. I got in the lift. Rachel turned up and
Elizabeth. Then the staff – George Jeffers,
Patrick Bartram, Heskins and, of course,
Nicodemus Bligh. I think they all arrived at
around the same point. I can't remember in
what order. They got in the lift. People were
chatting. It was all very normal and the lift
stopped. The lights went out as well. We were
stuck in the lift shaft. There are walls all around
so there's no possibility of getting out. You just
have to wait. It happens a lot. It's the power. I
couldn't see a thing, it was completely black. A

gun went off. I heard it thrown to the floor and then something else fell too, heavily. The lights came back on and we were all standing where we were before. No one had moved. There was a gun on the floor and Charles was slumped in the corner. I didn't know what had happened at first. Charles didn't speak. He didn't look alive. Heskins went towards him, bent over him and confirmed Charles had been shot and he was dead. There was a lot of shouting. Rachel fainted, which was no surprise. The lift started and when we got up to the top, Mother was distraught. Someone telephoned the police. Nicodemus had to sedate Father. We waited for the police to arrive.

Charlotte sat in the meek pool of light from the candle, the papers fanned out around her. This was a mechanical delivery of the girl's recollection. Was that to avoid falling into the trap of emotion? It unfailingly concurred with her brother Edward's account. But the unnatural nature of her evidence was the one thing that did shine out from off the page. It had a rehearsed feel to it, although in fairness, she had made it clear that she'd been called upon to recount the incident before.

Charlotte could easily picture the tart-faced girl she'd met at dinner sitting pin-straight in that courtroom, delivering the worst of details with the coolest voice. Her brother had been shot in a frighteningly dramatic incident but she could have been describing how he stumbled on a walk through the woods. Nothing more. It was a casual, pedestrian recount of the events. And it perfectly mirrored the atmosphere in the house. This was not a home in mourning, not a family less than a year from a sudden brutal death. That much was already clear.

Charlotte knew very well the lingering cloud of despair that settled over a house blighted by bereavement. It clung to the fabric of the walls, settled into the furniture, and looked out from every picture. Its taste even sank into the food. She remembered the first time she looked at herself in the mirror, after Archie had gone, after he would never see her face again. When was that? A week, two weeks later? She had no recollection. The doctor's parting words, when he left her alone with death, were still raw.

He'd placed his hand so gently on her arm. "What an angel you are to have married a man who knew he was dying."

She was too numb, too shell-shocked to tell him that the man lying on the bed, the man who had just made her a widow, had never told her this would be the end of their story. Her mind was loosening, her thoughts coming unstuck.

It had not been the first of his secrets. It would not be the last. Sometimes she feared he was a man made of secrets. They were his life. There was always a deep quiet about him. The silence of secrets. But, as she looked at his still face, so pale on the pillow, on their bed, there was a delicate peace to him now. A release. Whenever doubts would resurface, she still had this simple last image of him.

Time concertinaed in and out over that period. Long, everlasting nights. Months that just disappeared in a smoke of unremembered days. Less than a year later, how had she been? A void. She was still so pinned to his loss, so attached to it and scared to unpick it. Because when she did, she would have to let him go completely.

Here at Ravenswick Abbey, there was too much nonchalance, too much detachment. They had already closed in over the wound. There was no visible pain. They'd let him go so easily, almost as if it was a necessary sacrifice.

20

The night passed in uneasy dreams, broken fragments of the dinner, all the family arrayed around the table, their eyes star-bright from the candles. Wine slashed red in the glasses, staining their lips. The gargoyle face smiling out of the darkness above. The table was arrayed with all the gleaming finery, flowers and draped fruit just as she remembered. A strange garden of food set out but now with a new and disturbing addition. Standing amongst the opulence, down the centre of the shroud-white cloth, were the black shadows of the ravens, still and reverent. All their daunting eyes turned on her. Patrick Bartram was there now, standing by the family, judgemental and knowing. A single raven on his shoulder, its tar-wet eyes following her.

When she looked closer, it wasn't food on the table that the birds picked through with their thick, horny claws. It was a man. A chalk-faced man, dead and laid out in state. She recognised his face from the photographs. Charles Ravenswick. There was a serenity to him. A peace. A sense of wisdom. There were answers in those wide, still eyes.

A lone bird hopped up onto his face. It was almost a cheery movement, like robins in winter jumping onto the berries. His frosty skin did not move.

Nothing about him moved even when the bird took its

144

first peck. It had a harmless, natural quality to it as the head lowered, darted forward then pulled back.

Beyond her dream, in the real world where she slept, she felt her forehead sinking lower, her face fumbling for a reaction.

The bird went in again, the horn of its beak a precise instrument sinking into the open eye. A piece of it came away this time, dangling from the beak. The raven turned and flicked her a look, then continued with a fast savagery this time. Its head drilling down, claws turning into the fabric of his white shirt, the blood rising up through the cotton in a great opening wound.

"Half dead," another bird rasped. It was the phrase so many had used about Archie, whispered when they walked in a shop, murmured behind church hands on a Sunday morning. Even on their wedding day. How right they had been.

As the head fell to the side beneath the curling talons, it wasn't Charles Ravenswick anymore. It was Archie's face staring back at her through those gouged eyes.

***

Charlotte jolted into the mattress as if she'd been dropped from the ceiling. Her eyelids clicked open and the room was flooded with light. She held her hands to her face, damp with sweat. It stung her palms where the gravel scratches were. She raised her head slowly. The folder of papers was still scattered around her. She let her breath slow and held her hands flat on her chest to ease herself. Looking up at her from the drawings and photographs was Charles Ravenswick, his eyes peering out with a blind bewilderment as the photographer took the picture.

She sat up and began searching through the pages again. She didn't know what she was looking for but there was something in those reports that did not feel right. Something she'd overlooked.

The last of those night hours seemed to tick by in a slow heartbeat. She lay awake staring at the unlocked door and nursed her fears, diligently sharpening every sorrow, every terror, until each one was a perfect arrow.

When she heard the first movements in the rooms around her, it was relief that warmed her. She was being drawn back into the world of the living. Charlotte let herself have a moment of gathering, remembering who she was meant to be that day.

She washed the dirt from her face and hands quickly in the almost frozen bowl and looked out of the frost-white window. There were lights down by the old lake, drifting in and out of the mist. Bartram would be tending to the ravens soon. She should go back this morning. Continue with the subterfuge. There was something else down there, some more knowledge. He'd been in that lift, that night. He was part of it all, whatever "it" was.

She decided not to mention last night's incident but watch for their reactions to her presence instead. But there was only the usual brusque meal.

Breakfast was a quick affair of tea and some toasted bread. Heskins asked if that was all she required and Charlotte nodded as she hurried to the door, toast still in hand. She didn't care if his archaic judgement couldn't stretch to her taking away the breakfast. She could get a lot more done if she just carried it with her and ate it on the hoof. That should be more of a thing. She made a mental note to write a column on it.

She paused at the door. "Did anyone hear anything fall last night?"

There was no response other than a few indifferent looks.

She shrugged and bit into the toast.

Outside, the gargoyle had gone. There wasn't even a slight dip in the earth to show where it had been. She hadn't dreamt it. Her sore knees and scraped hands were evidence enough of that. So too was the space up above where the stone creature should have crouched.

She couldn't afford to lose a second. The journey over to the aviary seemed less intimidating today. There was a delicate light to the mist this morning. It was that pearl hour when time almost paused, and everything remained caught in that hinged moment between night and day.

Out beyond the structured hedges and lawns, she could see Dartmoor. The Abbey's gardens flowed into the landscape beyond with lines of trees leading into the great tors and vast open expanse. Ravenswick borrowed the view of the moor leaving no break between the imposed formality and the wilder land beyond, making it seem like they owned the horizon itself. Their ambitions were limitless. They even sought to tame nature and bend it to themselves. Life was theirs to control, and perhaps even death. Charles Ravenswick's death and maybe even the manner of it served a purpose. This was no random act. It was carefully and meticulously executed so that it could never be explained.

She could hear the rankling noises of the ravens loose on the air. It was a strange, unearthly sound. Charlotte paused at the edge of the fountain to gaze at the captive stone woman again. Perhaps she wasn't being dragged down by the coiling serpent after all. Perhaps she was escaping and rearing up out of the slimy depths. The expression of defeat said otherwise though.

There was such a hidden, unfathomable nature to all this. She lowered herself onto the stone-walled edge, thick with an encrusted rind of lichen. No one sat here very much anymore. It had an undisturbed air, as if its decline was ignored. Like most things at Ravenswick, it was a graceful descent into neglect.

But then she caught sight of something in the dark green mottled surface that suggested someone else might have been here. And recently.

A little carving in the rough contours of the stone. She peered closer, her eyes were still growing used to the dwindled light. She frowned as the markings pulled together into a recognisable shape.

Her name. *BLOOD* was carved on the surface of the stone, and recently, by the look of it. The white shapes of the letters were clean of moss and dirt. Next to it was a small drawing of a face, clearly a woman with short, bobbed hair.

She traced a finger through the grooves. Someone had sat here and spent time carving this repeatedly with some small, scratching implement. They had been here for a while creating it.

Charlotte looked over at the captive woman being dragged to her watery ruin. Who had those stone eyes seen lingering here as they worked away at their scraping? Someone came out and sat for a long, lonely afternoon and whiled it away drawing out her name. Were they thinking about her the whole time as they scratched away at the stone?

The ravens called out again. She could sense their

impatience. A tumble of leaves passed over the wall of the pond and spread across the still water. Another streak of morning light lifted in the sky. She should get to the aviary, but first she took a pencil and a piece of paper from her bag. When she was young, her father would take her to their chapel and teach her how to do brass rubbings. It had been a silent, contemplative time but even without words they'd connected over those afternoons. At least, it had seemed like that at the time and no power on earth would have compelled him to cast her out into the world penniless and unforgiven. She was wrong.

But she had the skills to preserve the stone carving. It felt like it could be important, perhaps even a warning that should not be ignored. This was the kind of place where details might easily go missing and she needed to have proof. She rubbed quickly and thoroughly over the letters, just as her father had told her, with a firm grip on the paper. When she had finished, it was a grainy image due to the rough surface of the wall, but there was a clear impression of her name. It had a strange, ancient look about it like an old woodcut. She studied its naïve runic features. Was it just an idle scribble? No, there was nothing idle about this. It had taken time and effort. She folded the paper carefully and put it in her satchel.

Over the treetops, she could hear the ravens growing restless. The voices raking. And for one disconnected moment, it seemed to her that they were carving her name into the air.

***

The birds landed on the carrion with ferocity. Jeffers had

shot a rabbit that morning and brought it over early. It had been hanging there, teasing the ravens.

"I like to stick to good hours with them otherwise they want food all the time and they'll seek it out whenever they want." There was a slight tone of admonishment in Bartram for her lateness.

He threw the flaccid carcass out to them. There was a momentary lull and then they plunged.

The beaks wrangled with the pink flesh, tearing off thin strips that dangled in the air. Her mind flashed back to the dream and the eyeless man. She shook away the thought.

"Will they eat again today, after such a big meal, I mean?" She injected a tone of genuine interest into her voice and watched the birds with fascination.

"Aye. Dinner time. They'd be too ravenous without that. It'll be a light meal though 'bout half six. A little minced meat or biscuit." He looked down at the ground and kicked the grass about. "You can come down if you want. I do all the packing up after then. Cleaning and that. Then I'm off home."

"It's a long day for you."

He nodded. "You staying long, Miss?"

She smiled. "Why, have you had enough of me?"

"No!" His response was a little too sudden. "I wondered if you'd got... all that you needed or if..." He left the word in the air.

She studied the side of his face. His beard formed rough swirls up the side of his neck. Thick lines sank down from his eyes. He glanced at her as if deciding what to say.

"No, I haven't," she answered quickly. "Got all that I need, I mean."

He took a deep breath, indecision troubling his face.

"Would you be able to help me with that?" she added. The crisp air deadened her voice.

"Depends what it is you want to know. I have to be careful, you see."

Charlotte watched the claws gripping hard into the rabbit's fur, gnarled black fingers curling round into the flesh.

One of the birds glanced up at her, the black stone beak streaked with gore. It watched her, tipping its head to the side. Inquisitive. Assessing.

"See, Blood?" its voice raked.

Charlotte's eyebrows drew down.

The bird jolted its head and stared.

Her mouth dropped open, lips parted, waiting for the words to arrive.

Bartram was quick to speak. "Like I said, they're just mimicking. They don't understand. It's not... you. It's the food." He was struggling.

"See, Blood," one cawed.

"Apparently they would beg to differ, Mr Bartram." She folded her arms. "And if they are just mimicking, then who taught them to say my name?"

He blew out his cheeks and shook his head. "I just look after the birds, Miss. Nothing else."

She raised her eyebrows. "Who would come here and train your ravens to speak?"

He frowned. "Anyone can come here. *You* come here."

"I'm *supposed* to be here."

"Are you, Miss Blood?" He watched her expectantly, every word heavy with meaning.

She attempted to look astonished but her face started to mottle in scarlet patches. "Whatever reason you think

I'm here for, I'm supposed to be here. Yes! And if I wasn't, what would happen then, eh? You'd all just go along as before, watching the birds picking over the carcass?" She turned to leave.

"Miss Blood?"

"If you've got something you want to tell me, you know where to find me." She walked away, conscious of all their eyes on her back.

21

She walked back to the house, angry and dissolute. Whichever way she turned she was frustrated by these people. They intimated that they knew more, that they were fully aware of her purpose, but no one helped her. Why? Surely they wanted to know who killed one of their own. But there was no getting through. This world, their world, made it so essential that they protected each other. There was a mutual dependence that made this device work. Was that what killed Charles Ravenswick? Had he in some way challenged that, stepped out of the intricate order of things and disrupted the balance to the extent that he had to be removed?

It seemed extreme, but this was a realm of order. There was a strict hierarchy to be observed and each strata played its part in that. Charlotte was all too aware of its workings. She was one of its casualties. There were layers to it but she was determined to peel those away, one by one, however painful that might be.

Charlotte stormed through the servants' hall, ignoring all their looks and judgement. What did she care? She'd be out of here soon and they'd all still be left with their unexplained death. That was the problem though, she did care. She cared very much and not just to please Fulman.

She needed to make sense of this. This couldn't be another senseless, unexplained death. Someone needed to be brought to account. There had to be blame.

She slammed through the door up to the bedrooms. Heskins was coming out of his butler's room and issued an impolite cough.

"And you can start being a little more helpful." Charlotte could hear her voice breaking.

"Miss Blood, if there is something –"

"There's everything! Everything you people have hidden."

"I'm sure I don't know –"

"What I mean? Oh, I think you know very well what I mean *Mr* Heskins. You were there. You gathered everyone. You told them to be there." Her face burned.

Heskins looked around quickly then back at Charlotte with a renewed sense of purpose. "Miss Blood." He had stripped his voice of any emotion. "You do not know what you're saying. I strongly advise you to go to your room and calm down."

"Oh." She widened her eyes. "Do you indeed? Are you going to throw more masonry on me?"

He looked confused.

"Well, bigger men than you have *advised* me to calm down and I can tell you, Mr Heskins, they have failed. Every. Single. Time."

They stood, silently assessing one other.

"Now, if you'll excuse me, Mr Heskins." Charlotte turned on her heel and began walking away with a firm purpose.

"If you require –"

"I think you already know what I require, Mr Heskins,"

she called without pausing or looking round. "Come and see me when you want to help."

Her pulse surged in great bursts. Although her eyes stung, she told herself not to blink, keep it all in until she got back to her room. She was well practiced in holding back tears.

When she finally made it to safety, Charlotte pushed the door shut behind her and leaned against it. She breathed in great lungfuls and sighed them out.

"I should never have come." She lifted her face and looked up to the ceiling. "I can't do this."

Whether the voice spoke in her head or out loud in the room didn't matter, but she knew the sound of it so well. *Yes, you can*, was all Archie said. It was what he always said.

She drank in each of his words then blew out a long steadying stream of air and held her palms to her eyes, blocking everything out for a moment. "Right," she whispered. "Come on then." She wiped her hands down the tweed skirt with a new, determined efficiency.

The chair was back by the side of the bed, and this time Charlotte left it there. She sat down on it and reached in her satchel for the folder. If moving the furniture was all they were going to do to help her, she could make use of it.

No one was going to willingly offer her assistance, or at least not openly. They were not going to be seen to break ranks. Order and structure would be assiduously observed to the death and beyond, each world respecting the line between the other. She was happy to acknowledge that, but she didn't have to be part of it.

None of this was simple or two-dimensional. There could be no stepping over those careful ranks. The trenches were far too deep. No matter how hard she tried, Charlotte would still be in that no-man's-land. She just had to find a way of using that.

As she leafed through the folder, what was becoming increasingly obvious was that the rules could definitely be manipulated or, at least on occasion, overlooked. Some people were using their positions to their own advantage, that much was clear. Lady Ravenswick in particular.

At the inquest, the coroner seemed to have been easily agreeable to Her Ladyship giving evidence remotely in the form of a short letter to the court. Admittedly, she hadn't been in the lift on the night in question, but she was the mother of the deceased. Surely her reasons for summoning everyone, and what she in fact saw herself in the aftermath, must have been of some material benefit in deciding how this man died. There were already pages of questions Charlotte wanted to ask Lady Ravenswick, each one of great importance in forming a picture of this house and its secrets. So why hadn't the court felt it necessary to do so? Lady Ravenswick was, after all, part of the reason Charles Ravenswick was in that lift in the first place. She presumably had knowledge of why they were all there and the contents of the will that had been referred to. She also knew about the manuscripts that had originally provoked the changes in the family's situation and, from what Charlotte had seen for herself, was the closest person at Ravenswick Abbey to the man who had discovered them all, Nicodemus Bligh.

There were a multitude of reasons for this woman to be questioned and yet the judicial system in all its wisdom had decided there was no need to inconvenience the grand Lady Ravenswick with the troublesome matter of giving evidence at her own son's inquest. It was agreed by all parties that it wouldn't be necessary to put Her Ladyship to the trouble of helping the court understand why her son was dead. Would that have been the same had she simply been plain Mrs Ravenswick? That was at least one question that Charlotte already knew the answer to.

The evidence Lady Ravenswick did provide the court with was basic in the extreme. A short note, that shed no further light on anything. The only thing it helped to confirm was how closed and secretive this family was. There was a very stilted nature to it, almost as though each word had been thoroughly thought out and vetted before it was committed to paper.

Charlotte read it with a sense of indignation and perhaps even injustice that she didn't know she possessed until then. It wasn't the first time she'd questioned this world she came from, but she surprised herself now with the strength of her own feeling. What struck home more than anything for Charlotte was that sense of remoteness and detachment which came through so strongly from the dead man's own mother.

I am Lady Violet Ravenswick, wife of Lord Melhuish Ravenswick of Ravenswick Abbey on Dartmoor. The deceased, Charles Ravenswick, was my eldest son and the heir to Ravenswick. His brother Edward Ravenswick is now the heir as the sole surviving son. I have a daughter Mary as well.

On New Year's Eve 1928, I had been with my husband all day as he was quite ill. Rather than going down, I called all the family to attend upon us, along with some members of staff who have been with us for a significant period of time. I had some small gifts for them which is a custom we observe every year. Mr Philip Pembroke, the family's lawyer, had been to the house earlier in the week for myself and my husband to sign a new will. We were going to inform the family of the new provisions. Some small bequests had been made to some members of staff.

My husband has been gravely ill after the effects of a series of strokes over the last two years. He is bedridden and requires twenty-four-hour care. Nurse Sidmouth provides his medicinal requirements. Lord Ravenswick occupies the entire top floor of the east wing, formally the astrology tower. A large lift was installed for him when he could move around in his wheelchair. However, following his last stroke, he is now incapacitated.

Those visiting on the night of my son's death, New Year's Eve, all took the lift to the apartments. Unfortunately, the power failed. It does this on a regular basis. Ravenswick Abbey obtains its own power from a hydroelectric turbine which was installed some years ago and can be somewhat temperamental. Often it needs some form of attention to reset it and, knowing both Heskins and Jeffers were left in the lift, I telephoned down to Mrs Thornycroft but she did not answer.

I had heard the lift stop and the subsequent commotion which ensued. I also then heard a loud bang.

The power was quickly restored, which is very often the case and there is generally no cause for alarm.

The lift then arrived. I was aware that there was a lot of shouting and screaming. My son, Charles, was slumped in the corner. There was blood on his shirt. My other son, Edward, came towards me and held me. He told me his brother was dead. Charles had been shot.

I'm afraid, at that point, I was rather upset, which in turn led to my husband becoming very distressed.

Mr Nicodemus Bligh, who assists me in caring for my husband, took the necessary action and sedated His Lordship to avoid any further unnecessary suffering for him or consequences resulting from that. The police were called.

As a result of my husband's severe illness and incapacity, I am unable to leave him and am not able to attend court.

This statement was taken under oath and witnessed by my solicitor, Mr Philip Pembroke.

It was a bland, straightforward recount of the incident. Again, there was that overwhelming sense that it was devoid of any real emotion. Such a witness statement was admittedly not the ideal forum for unbridled grief. By all accounts, she'd certainly shown a large degree of anguish at the time and from what Charlotte had seen of the woman so far, Lady Ravenswick was still living a very solemn life. She was disconnected.

Maybe Charlotte had been initially unfair on Lady Ravenswick. Perhaps the reason she did not attend court that day was that it was simply too overwhelming for her.

Charlotte was very familiar with the life of caring for a sick husband. Love becomes devotion as everything is eroded except for the need to see it through to the end. Every other emotion is consumed. It is existence that takes over, grinding out everything other than the here and now. Past and futures become irrelevant, lost in a sea of days that join up into the end of a life.

For Lady Ravenswick, when her husband died, it would be the demise of an era. The house should have passed to Charles, her son. Now, another of her boys would step into that place along with his wife, Elizabeth, or perhaps the duplicitous Rachel. What then for Lady Ravenswick? No longer in control of the domain she had sat at the head of with her husband, it would dissolve into a life in the shadows. Her husband's life spent, so too was hers. Charlotte knew that only too well. She knew what it was to be left alone without her husband, to be vulnerable.

Archie had been the biggest, boldest part of Charlotte's life until he was gone. She was a widow at twenty-two. One of many in the army of desperately young widows these days, consigned to those half-lives or to the indignity of finding a new husband. She wanted neither of those options. But as soon as he died, Charlotte was looking over the edge again, down into the life she'd escaped once before.

***

This time she was alone. In the aftermath of his death, she couldn't think, couldn't settle her mind to anything. The days were just unravelling. Mrs C had drifted around the edges with food, cups of tea and stronger. She even left out some books. They were the usual selection of detective stories. But in the days after his death, Charlotte hadn't been able to concentrate on anything at all, let alone read. She just distractedly flicked through the pages of The Mystery of the Yellow Room, turning the pages in a blur of meaningless words.

But her fingers stopped instantly when the letter fluttered out silently onto her lap as if that was its intended destination. She stared at it incomprehensibly, before picking it up like an unfamiliar object.

It was addressed to Archie at Mecklenburgh Square.

But the name was not the only thing she recognised. It was the familiar slant of the black, sharp handwriting that spoke to her with a voice she'd be able to pick out in any room. Her father's.

Charlotte turned the slim letter over in her hand, a bemused expression on her face as if questioning its very existence. The envelope was as incongruous in that room as the man himself would have been, standing over her, staring back with that fierce, confrontational look he always had. She opened it warily, as though there might be more than words waiting inside. It was not a long letter. There was no space for pleasantries here. The tone was set from the beginning.

Colonel Blood,

Your continual insistence on a speedy marriage to my daughter remains a source of great frustration to me. You are fully aware of the very imminent announcement of her engagement to Lord Naseby and yet you refuse to desist. It is shameful and dishonourable.

However, in light of our recent meeting and the information you have somehow come into possession of regarding my private business, I find I am left with no option but to acquiesce to your demands. But let me be very clear, I will not suffer you in my home again. Be under no illusions, I am not accustomed to defeat. You're a dying man, Blood. I will wait and bide my time. But make no mistake, I will retrieve what is mine.

Sir Richard de Burgh.

Charlotte lingered over every word in turn as if each one was being branded into her eyes. She turned the paper over and back again, searching for more, her father's name glaring up, resolute and furious. The inner sanctum of his business had never been open to Charlotte but that wasn't something that ever struck her as unusual. He had a lot of money and he wielded it like a hammer over everyone. That's all she knew. But Archie knew more. And somehow, he'd used it.

Yet, he was aware he was dying as well. Charlotte's face wrinkled. How could Archie have expected he'd achieve anything more than a temporary reprieve for her? Perhaps he didn't see any reason to think beyond his own imminent death. No, that wasn't Archie. Surely he would never have just abandoned her to this fate. Charlotte put that thought away before it had too long to settle and cast its shadow over her mind.

Whatever Archie knew, whatever his motivation, he couldn't help her now. It all died with him. She'd been granted a glimpse of freedom, but her parole was over the moment he died. One thing was certain, he'd left her a lot more questions than answers.

She let the letter fall and held her head in her hands. With every breath she could feel herself being dragged back there. It was hopeless.

The distant tapping at the door pulled her thoughts back. She quickly wiped the tears from her cheeks.

"Just thought I'd bring another tea, Duckie. That one on the landing looks a bit cold. How you getting on with *The Mystery of the Yellow Room*?" Mrs C looked at where the open book had been discarded on the floor and frowned.

"Oh, Mrs C." Charlotte let the tears fall freely.

"Come on, girl. He wouldn't want to see…"

"He knew he wouldn't have to see any of it!"

Mrs C sighed and put the tea tray down.

The anguish cut deep into Charlotte's face, her voice desperate and breaking. "I can't... how can I... I can't even pay you..."

"Oh, let's leave that this month, eh. 'Til you get back on your feet."

***

Whether Charlotte could be described as on her feet now or not, the years had just rolled on, and they'd resolved into a vaguely comfortable pattern, a way of life. The column paid some bills but there were more missed months than paid. Charlotte's choices had cost her dear so far. Going back behind the bars of Bladesworth and being condemned to a marriage of her father's making was a poisonous thought but it was never far from her. If she wasn't going to fall back into those dark waters, she needed this job to work. She had to start finding things out here. She threw the folder on the bed. It was going to take a lot more than some meaningless, pre-prepared statement.

Someone stood alongside Lady Ravenswick, guiding her. The self-appointed guardian of Lady Ravenswick's soul seemed like a good place to start. Nicodemus Bligh was waiting.

22

The library had the impressive kind of dignified quiet that immediately inspired respect. It was grave in an old statesman way but still with the comfortable air of a place where the artifice and ambition of the outside world could be left behind. At least that was, until Charlotte heard the dry voice of Nicodemus Bligh.

Her eyes scaled the towering shelves of books and ran along until she saw him perched, bird-like, on a long ladder, his ivory robes falling behind him and covering his feet, giving the impression that he was just floating up there, spirit like, flying beside the books.

"Ah, Miss Blood! So good of you to come." The smile threaded its way along his face. "You find me climbing the mountain of my endeavours again! But we must conquer these vast edifices if we are to dig for such well-hidden treasures." He pulled out a large, leather-bound book from the shelf, looked it over and held it close to his chest. He began the descent with the sure-footed awareness of a well-trodden path.

A slant of cool morning light cut across the room, letting the years of dust tumble through it, every grain another second from the room's past. Nicodemus Bligh seemed to bring his own flurry of particles with him, disrupting the rhythm of the air.

"Well, well, Miss Blood, what an honour." Everything he said had a tone of mockery about it. He placed the book down deliberately and drifted towards her, picking up another, newer book on the way. There was a very contrived nature about this man. He'd spent a lot of time perfecting who he wanted to be or, at least, what he wanted people to see. It was flawless.

"I couldn't miss your magnificent library. I've heard so much about it *recently*." She added the last word purposefully.

He paused before laughing. "Dear girl, it's not *my* library! Oh no, no, no. Not at all. It's the Ravenswick Abbey library, that is, if anyone ever really owns a library. It is also a much older source of knowledge than that. We are merely the custodians for the next generation of this great wealth of knowledge. We simply borrow it for a while."

She felt as if she was being sold something. There was a very compelling way this man had of manipulating his words. His movements mirrored the preciseness of what he said. Each step was carefully timed, each hand gesture calculated. He let his fingers slip through his finely combed black hair, grooming himself. In the sharp rays of morning light, there was a vaguely metallic sheen to him. She noticed how his yellowish fingernails were just a little longer than she would have expected, although they were immaculately filed into small, horned shapes.

"Unless, of course, you sell the books." Charlotte watched him closely.

His eyes narrowed slightly. "That is not my decision. I merely curate the treasures."

He waved the book that he'd picked up as he walked

towards her, a prop carefully placed. "Tell me, Miss Blood, are you aware of the works of Mr Aleister Crowley?"

"Is he local?" Charlotte, along with anyone who'd read a newspaper in the last few years, knew very well the name of this charlatan with his latest breed of religion that lured in the desperate and lost.

Bligh looked exasperated and waved the book again with an evangelical zeal. "His work is the most important that men can contemplate."

"Fortunately, then *I* do not need to worry about it."

She read the title and smirked. "*Magick in Theory and Practice*. No, I'm afraid I don't enjoy sideshows and circuses anymore, Mr Bligh. I've put away childish things."

His jaw clenched as tight as a fist. "I can assure you, Miss Blood, there is nothing childish about Mr Crowley's work."

There was a deep look of conviction forming on his face. A devotional look. An obsessional one. Charlotte had seen this before, the people between sandwich boards caught in the grip of religious fervour all professing a way to save everyone. Salvation itself was the new religion, by any means possible, and it seemed that Mr Bligh had found a fairly extreme one. One that he would defend with all his soul, if that didn't defeat the object entirely.

"Thelema is the answer!" he announced, his eyes as intense as a preacher's. He leaned closer to her face and she could smell the strange heady mix of spice and earth. There was a hypnotic, old quality to the scent, with remembrances of incense in church on a cold Sunday. It lifted from him in layers of wood and flowers, a cinnamon bark flavour to it that she could almost taste.

"It is the perfect magico-religious doctrine." His voice

was low, conspiratorial. There was a forbidden note there that dropped into a whisper. "We have entered the Aeon of Horus, Miss Blood."

"That sounds painful."

His eyes flared. "You may scoff, Miss Blood, but there is a greater power on this earth. Modern paganism folds together all the ancient knowledge and power, its magick and alchemy, with Western esotericism and scientific naturalism."

"A lot of *isms*, Mr Bligh."

With his finger and thumb, he pinched together the skin between his carefully manicured eyebrows, giving him a pained look. "You will see, Miss Blood. Our arcane knowledge was understood by the ancients. All the way back to the Druids, who knew the soul was immortal and passed from one person to another. You have known death, Miss Blood, have you not? You have sat close to it and wondered at its work." His smile was rich with clandestine excitement, as if he had opened up a little dark secret. Her secret.

Charlotte knew this conjuror's trick all too well. She'd fallen down that dark rabbit hole before. Seances and table turning, Ouija boards and tarot, they came and leeched off her desperation with every form of little sorcerer's game to bring back her husband's beautiful smile. *"Speak to us, Archie. Speak to us!"* She'd willed his voice to break from one of their leering mouths. But their shrill demanding voices were nothing like how her Archie sounded. The sound of him had gone.

Archie would never have spoken to those fraudsters and, when the fog began to lift, neither did Charlotte, and she vowed never to let the deceiving parasites back in.

The world was suddenly full of inscrutable, cryptic people who could speak to the air. But there were even more desperate people who wanted the air to answer back.

"I think in these last years we've all seen death up close, haven't we, Mr Bligh? And my wedding ring most definitely gives that away. Keen observation of the individual you're dealing with, put together with lucky guesses based on high probabilities and an air of mysticism, or whatever *ism* you choose, can be quite compelling, can it not Mr Bligh?" She folded her arms and didn't break with his gaze. "Particularly for the grief-stricken and bereft."

He drew back his head. "There are always the unbelievers. The blind who have no eyes for *augury*."

"What utter nonsense."

"Well, you may not believe there is a science to augury. But I warn you, Miss Blood –" he leaned closer again and lowered his voice "– look to the birds."

She let out a single, dismissive laugh. "Have you any idea how this sounds?"

"All you need to do, Miss Blood, is open your mind. Amongst these shelves is the answer. The truth that has been known for centuries. Hidden away from those who would burn it, desecrate it and destroy it."

Whatever nonsense pseudo-religion those books contained, they didn't need to be the scientific truth to be worth a fortune. Charlotte tried not to let her new interest show. She raised a sceptical eyebrow in an effort to tease out more. It worked.

"You will see, Miss Blood. You will understand. There is treasure beyond belief amongst these books. Pages handed down and concealed through the ages. The truth of man. The truth of existence. What they don't want people like *you* knowing. A fortune in –"

"Nicodemus?" It was Lady Ravenswick, her voice thin but clear. Although she sounded faded, there was still a dignified authority ingrained in her.

"Your Ladyship." It was the first time Charlotte had seen Bligh waver. "I didn't know you were coming down today. Is His Lordship resting?"

Lady Ravenswick had entered unseen and studied him. There was a brief clarity to her eyes but it quickly passed. "Nurse Sidmouth is with him at the moment. He's sleeping. I thought I might come and see how work is going in the library, but I see you have a guest." She nodded towards Charlotte in acknowledgement. "Miss Blood."

"Lady Ravenswick." Charlotte bowed her head in response.

"I hope you are finding your stay with us rewarding."

"Yes, Your Ladyship. Very much so."

Lady Ravenswick paused to look at Nicodemus. "Do we have any books on ravens?"

"I'm sure there will be something, Your Ladyship."

She gave a pallid smile. "I'm assuming it is ravens you are researching in here."

Charlotte pressed her lips tight together.

"Are you supposed to be over at the aviary, Miss Blood?"

"I went this morning."

Lady Ravenswick nodded slowly. "And have you everything you need?"

"I have, Your Ladyship, yes."

"Oh, so we will be saying goodbye to you soon, will we?"

Charlotte's mind stumbled.

"I..."

"You have everything. I assume Bartram has been his usual helpful self."

"I'm sorry, Your Ladyship, I thought you meant in terms of comfort. I have been very well accommodated. In terms of the ravens, however, there is much more research to be done, I'm afraid."

Lady Ravenswick gave a forced look of astonishment but her eyes didn't flicker. "Well, Miss Blood, who would have thought there would be so much to discover about our little family of birds? Perhaps we should not detain you further."

Nicodemus Bligh was staring at Charlotte intently as though he was memorising every feature.

The atmosphere had grown distinctly unenthusiastic for her presence.

Charlotte tried to smile. "I should be going. Thank you, Mr Bligh. It's been very enlightening."

There was too long a pause.

"It has been my pleasure, Miss Blood. Please feel free to visit again." It had the ring of insincerity.

As Charlotte left, their eyes followed her through the room, the only sound, the heels of her little one-bar shoes still ticking the parquet floor with that multitude of tiny cobblers' nails. The door closed heavily behind her.

23

Charlotte paused outside the door, her heart fluttering fast against her ribcage. Something held this house in a constant state of anxiety, and she was being drawn down into that with the slow certainty of quicksand. There was an unspoken language to everything as if secrets were being passed under the conversation like notes under a school desk. But there was nothing fun or mischievous about this. It was a dark, serious game they were playing here.

How long had Lady Ravenswick allowed Charlotte's meeting with Nicodemus Bligh to continue before she'd decided to put a stop to it? How long had the old crow stood in this corridor, listening? Waiting.

For such a large house, there was nowhere to hide. Nowhere to think. It was a crowded emptiness. There was always somebody there, and it wasn't just the family either. Her room seemed like it was open to everyone, furniture moved frequently and someone was going through her things.

She'd tried a few times to find a quiet room in the servants' area but that was a crowded nest. Every time she thought she'd found a moment of solitude, there was someone busying themselves, with the fire, cleaning or simply rearranging objects. Most of the time, it seemed they were finding things to do, aware that they should look occupied at all times to justify their place. The butler, Heskins, was all pervasive, his glowering presence in every corner, at every door. Mrs Thornycroft was endlessly bustling through rooms inspecting them. Maids performing various functions ran around the hive, in and out of spaces, when one departed a room, another came in to commence a new activity.

Even when she was in the main house, footmen strode around corridors, always on their way somewhere, delivering, tending, sorting. Everyone had a specific function and it had to fit perfectly alongside all the others. From a distance it seemed hurried, random, but there was an intention to everything. And the ultimate purpose was to serve the family, make sure their every whim was taken care of. Wake them, feed them, dress them, clean their rooms. It was a revolving structure carefully orchestrated and achingly familiar to Charlotte.

She heard a door closing somewhere in the distance. There was nowhere to even be alone with her thoughts. Charlotte stepped to the side into a shadowed alcove and sat in the window seat, half hidden by the frayed curtains. It smelt of schoolroom damp, the kind that settles easily into bones. She'd stayed in many grand stone houses like this where the dead, wet air constantly leaked out of the walls. But this one was the worst.

Charlotte looked out of the long bay window, the estate disappearing into the mist as if it was never ending. That was its whole point. To never end.

She remembered so clearly the stultifying feeling of being part of that. A cog with its place. Daughter of Sir Richard de Burgh, wealthy, and willing to climb any family tree to finally emerge into the sunlight of society and lose the brash sheen of his new money. Lady Frances Rothesville had the chestnut hair and china-blue eyes that would be the only thing Charlotte would inherit.

Charlotte had been destined to marry and finally sew their family into the fabric of society. She was prepared like a thoroughbred. Dresses and luxuries were lavished on her, polishing her. Finishing her.

And there was ample opportunity to wear them. As stern as he was, Sir Richard was canny enough to realise the importance of entertaining rich friends. Powerful, titled people were regulars at Bladesworth for parties, balls, cocktails and tea. Some would arrive by yacht and stay all weekend. An invitation to the great gilded palace was highly prized. With its vast stained-glass dome and opulent ballroom, it was a monument to elegant excess. Charlotte was expected to be charming at these country house parties. Whether at Bladesworth or elsewhere, she must be enchanting and entertaining for all prospective suitors. Tennis, swims, dances, sailing, fishing, picnics, piano recitals, everything designed to throw her in the way of a hefty title. There was never a private moment. Always somebody there. Always something she must do. Every caprice was satisfied with instant gratification in her great, ivory prison.

If she'd followed the future they had planned for her, would she still have been hiding in a window seat, desperately trying to find a moment alone? All that she'd done, every sacrifice she'd made, and it still pulled her back.

She picked at the moth holes in the worn fabric of the cushion and leaned her forehead against the cool glass, watching the condensation roll down in long streams. How many girls had sat here wondering what life far away might be like? This was a bleak, unchanging world that many people worked hard to keep that way.

"Ungrateful," that's what Charlotte was called. She had always known hers was a life of privilege. She'd seen the kitchen staff struggle, the local villagers scrape by. But it didn't mean she had to like her own world. Even if the cage was ornate and beautiful, she could still feel it every time her wings were clipped.

They didn't ask why she had no intention of marrying Lord Naseby. That was patently obvious. He was twenty-five years older than her and corpulent enough to have left her with a lifetime of frustration because he didn't just drop down dead. The finishing touch was that he was widely reputed to hate all women. His penchant for young men was expensive and had been hinted at regularly in the papers.

Charlotte used to sneak down to the servants' dining room to read the gossip, scandal and politics. Across those pages was a whole array of worlds every day, not just a single stifling one.

Her parents may not have needed to ask why she was rejecting this carbuncle of a man as the imminent love of her life, but the arguments rolled on for weeks. Her father didn't care if the man had "*hobbies*", as he so quaintly phrased it. That was a man's own business. He didn't care if there were rumours of cruelty. There always were and they were probably made up lies by *newspapers*. It was the "probably" that was the most frightening word in all of it.

"*Why can you never do as we ask?*" they said. Because she was never asked, just told.

It was the first bar Charlotte removed from the cage that convinced her she could fly.

These people here at Ravenswick would do anything to keep the bars in place, but would they have gone as far as to murder one of their own? Her father would rather his daughter have been dead than bring shame on the family. Charlotte was under no illusions about that.

She wiped her face quickly. She never felt unwatched here, and an ornithologist had no reason to be sitting in a window seat crying on her own. That would raise some suspicions.

As her hand rested on the wooden ledge, she felt something sharp. A splinter. She held the finger up and one small berry of blood inflated at the end. She sucked on it quickly and looked to where the wood was broken.

Roughly carved into its grain was one deep word. "*Sacrifice*". Charlotte stopped her breath for a moment then let it stream out slowly, misting across the window. She traced around the letters with her other hand, still sucking on the vinegar-sharp cut on her finger.

It was etched in short, stubby strokes just as the others had been by some sort of small, thin instrument. It had taken a while. Someone had sat here for a long time whittling away at that word, turning it over in their mind. Did they face the same bars she had? Charlotte imagined the faceless artist, finally sitting back to admire this anonymous note. The same someone who had sat at the lake?

She heard a door click and instinctively sat back, covering the word with her tweed skirt. It was Lady Ravenswick leaving the library. She drifted ghost-like down the corridor leading away from where Charlotte was sitting. Even if she'd walked right past, Charlotte doubted those transfixed eyes would have focused on anything much. She was a woman with her troubles set deep in every feature.

Charlotte felt the sharp pinpricks of wood beneath her hand and looked down again. She lifted her hand. *Sacrifice.* The letters wormed their way into the wood along with the slow rot. It was a household riddled with it as if some disease had taken hold.

She looked out aimlessly at the sky, heavy with rain. Distant thunder rumbled over the moors towards the house. Something was coming and the constant undercurrent of suspicion had firmly pushed her back into a strange no-man's-land. It seemed they could only let her in for a brief window before she became the interloper again to both parties. She kept circling back to the question of why they'd ever allowed her in in the first place.

The press was very much a monster to this Frankenstein family. They'd spent a lifetime involved in its creation. Then they had run from it and walled themselves away. And yet now, at their darkest moment, they chose to invite her in. To look at the birds? Surely even their beloved ravens were not worth inviting the beast back in.

Edward had openly scoffed at her being an ornithologist. They were suspicious from the outset. But still, they didn't ask her to go. Someone was even leaving these carvings now like it was just a game. Were they for her? They used her name. If there was something to uncover here, someone wanted her to do it. But which one of them? Not Lady Ravenswick. She was a closed book to Charlotte. And not Edward or his wife. They were too guarded. As was the ungrieving widow, Rachel. The strange, baleful Nicodemus Bligh had quite deliberately drawn his conjurer's curtain around anything he was involved in. He was naturally distrustful of any press, which wasn't surprising given the way they'd portrayed him as some malevolent fanatic. He'd been dragged through the pages as the malicious, deceiving influence at the Abbey.

She wanted to telephone Fulman and ask him who it was at the house that had agreed to her coming here, but every wall had someone's ear up against it, listening. To even attempt to use a telephone with multiple extensions all over the house would be tantamount to a public broadcast. No, she couldn't risk that. They may have their suspicions but she didn't want to openly confirm them.

Charlotte looked down at the word again. *Sacrifice.* She had no intention of ending up as the next one. There was still a murderer in this house, walking along these corridors, safe in the knowledge that nothing could single them out from the rest of the group. Equal suspicion, the perfect disguise.

She pulled out the folder from her satchel and looked down that report with the names all set out. Maybe it was one of the staff who had covertly summoned her. Although, they surely wouldn't have had the time or opportunity to sit whiling away on these carvings. But there were definitely others apart from the family present in the lift that night. The butler Heskins had that fierce automaton loyalty that would never have betrayed the family. He would have sacrificed himself first. Bartram was there that night, but his main allegiance seemed to be towards the ravens and he clearly had his suspicions already that she might not be a genuine ornithologist. Although, how he could have come to such a conclusion was beyond Charlotte, given her natural ability to go undercover.

Jeffers the gardener had been there in the lift, and no mention had been made of him in the reports or any of the inquest statements she'd read so far. Perhaps it wasn't felt necessary to call a mere gardener.

The family solicitor, Philip Pembroke, had been there earlier in the week as well, for the purposes of the new will. Presumably it had needed to be altered again since that day, given the heir had changed in such dramatic circumstances. There was definitely no possibility of an ornithologist getting hold of a copy of any sort of will though.

She closed the folder and cursed Fulman for his ridiculous choice of career for her. There was no necessity for her to do anything other than look at the birds and to go further than that would immediately attract even more suspicion. How did he expect her to investigate anything? She needed a way in.

And then she saw it. Skipping across the lawn as if life didn't matter. Someone who would definitely be more guileless and much easier to handle. Someone who might indeed have seen all this as a game. A child. She checked back to the file, quickly flicking through the pages, running her finger down the report. Celeste Ravenswick – nine years old at the time of her uncle Charles's death. Edward and Elizabeth's daughter had eluded Charlotte so far.

She watched the girl with her chicken-skin legs and heavy brogues prancing across the lawn. Bundled into a thick winter coat with her rough nest of hair standing on end, the girl was a barrel of information just waiting to be tapped.

24

It somehow seemed even colder than earlier in the morning. The sun hadn't ever really broken through the anaemic layer of cloud and mist. Now it was already edging its way back below the bare branches.

Charlotte had shoved the folder in the satchel and swung it over her shoulder. With renewed resolve, she'd been quick out of the house but there was no sign of the girl anywhere. Her keen little footsteps had left a trail in the damp grass though. They led off into the rough hedges. Leafless, with only the occasional holly bush, they were sharp and impenetrable. The footsteps ended where the borders began. Charlotte looked along the burley thicket of brambles and branches. The girl had simply disappeared.

The anarchic raven cries startled a group of rooks up from the skeleton of a winter tree and sent them wheeling off into the air, teasing the grounded birds with their flight. It shocked her momentarily and she stiffened. This was a cautious place where every living thing was on its guard and wary of one another. Charlotte looked back towards the watching house. It had already sunk into the background of mist and seemed quite far away now.

She was further out into the grounds than she thought,

Dartmoor's barren landscape of gorse and granite spreading far beyond the edges of the lawns.

Two unfamiliar environments forced against one another seemed to generate an unnatural dissonance constantly playing beneath the surface. The Ravenswicks made everything about belonging here but the simple fact was, they didn't. The monks had built their humble abbey here to separate themselves from the real world. They'd existed quietly alongside the land but generations of Ravenswicks had sought to dominate it. The moor was a place to overshadow with this vast statement of wealth. That was all slipping away now and the wilds of Dartmoor were slowly encroaching.

Out here, near the borders of their land, it felt so much closer to all that isolation. Charlotte's fingers ached from the cold. She cupped her hands and held them over her mouth, blowing out plumes of warm breath on the frozen air.

The clean sound of a branch snapped on the bitter air. She paused, her hands still around her face.

"Hello?" She sounded uncertain, her throat tight. Slowly, she lowered her arms. "Hello. Is someone there?"

She couldn't see far in the gloaming light.

There was no response except the swift crack of another branch.

She wasn't about to run again.

Charlotte dropped her hands and peered closer into the hedge. A new, hunted expression crossed her face.

"No one here but me, Miss." The voice was behind her.

She turned quickly, instinctively pulling back.

It was a man, old with a worn-out face that looked like it had spent a lot of time out in the hardened moorland.

His rough country clothes and parked wheelbarrow marked him immediately as the gardener, Jeffers.

"I was looking for someone." She spoke too abruptly. It sounded forced. Guilty. She leaned from foot to foot trying to spark some feeling into the toes.

"There's nobody out today. Too cold, Miss." He looked pityingly at her as she folded her arms in tight around the thin coat.

"I saw a girl. Running out across the lawn. The footsteps led to here." Charlotte was panting out each word breathlessly now in small, icy-white clouds that lingered between them. The cold had made her sound even more hurried than her nerves.

He studied her with a puzzled, doubtful look on his face.

"I'm Miss Blood." She made it sound like an apology. "I'm here about the ravens."

His eyes tapered. "Not about the girl, then?"

"I..."

He drew his hand along the stubble on his face making a sandpaper sound. "Best be going back to the house, Miss Blood, you'll catch *your* death."

Did he stress the word? She couldn't be sure but there was an ominous undertone.

"It's Mr Jeffers, isn't it?"

He looked taken aback. Then nodded. "Aye." He didn't add any more.

"The gardener." She said it as though she was running down a list.

"That's right. Been here forty years. Always been Ravenswicks at the Abbey."

"I see. So you know them well. The family, that is."

"Thought it was the birds you was 'ere for." His eyes crinkled at the edges and she noticed one of his grey eyes had a flaw in the iris. It was shot through with a seam of green that shone like a scar.

She smiled. "Of course. But the family who keep them is of great interest to our readers as well. They want to know what kind of people own such a beautiful aviary and keep such fascinating creatures." She surprised herself with her own ingenuity. She was growing into the role. "To leave out the Ravenswicks would be to leave out half the story. As you say, they've always been here. And you must know them better than anyone."

Even this world-weary man was not immune to flattery.

"True. They're good people." He said it solemnly. "Honest people," he added, which seemed unnecessary.

"I'm sure they think highly of you too."

He watched her. "I like to think so, Miss. They know I'd do anything for them."

She looked at him, a question paused on her face. The word rolled over in her mind. Anything.

"After forty years, it must feel like you're one of the family." She needed to tread carefully. "It must have been deeply upsetting to lose one in such tragic circumstances."

The suspicion lingered on his face. "It was."

"And shocking."

"Aye."

She was losing momentum. "Do you think the... the birds were aware? Of the death, I mean. Some people believe the ravens are very sensitive creatures."

"Sensitive? Now whose been telling ye that? Definitely not them wild ones out on the moor. Only t'other day I sees 'em executing one of their own. Bird had its neck in a tree between the trunk and the crook of a branch. And what do you think? Two birds is below the trapped creature and they has its legs in their beaks, pulling down on it from below they was. And one raven is above, jumping up and down on its head. Hanging it they was. They knows how to punish their own alright." He let out a rasping laugh.

She stared at him.

"Mr Bligh says they carry the souls of the dead to the after world."

He shook his head. "Well, I don't know about all that. Mr Bligh has his own ways." There was a new, evasive look about him. He picked at the edges of his old wool cardigan.

She nodded along in encouragement, adopting a deep expression of curiosity. "I see. Yes." She had to say something to keep him on track. "It must have been devastating for all of you to lose Charles Ravenswick."

He looked down at the ground, avoiding her eyes. "Was a sad time. For all of us."

"Oh yes, it must have been. And quite shocking for you, especially. Being there when it happened, I mean."

He didn't answer. She started to worry she'd maybe gone too far but his eyes drifted and took on a glazed, distant look. A new weariness invaded his face but then something seemed to take hold of his thoughts and, without warning, he started unpacking the moments of his story piece by precious piece.

"I'd been out all day," he said. "Been a wild one out here on the moor. Often is this time of year. Big, old tree come down right across a wall. Collapsed it like. I had to make it safe... for animals and the like. Always some victims of that moor's gales every winter. Horse chestnut this year. Took all day. Couldn't do no more. I was ready to go off home. Was dark when Mr Heskins came. He don't usually come out here so I knew it was important like. Said Her Ladyship wanted me right then, like. So I left my work and followed. I'd usually have changed my clothes, cleaned up like, but Mr Heskins said to make my way there immediately. He had to fetch Mr Bligh and he'd meet us at the lift. Said Bartram was already making his way over. We was to be quick. Something about the will and the family wanted to give us gifts." He stared at some faraway point. "They're very generous. Always take care of us staff. See us right."

It was as if Charlotte wasn't there anymore and he was delivering some sort of confession. She didn't dare speak or move for fear the spell might be broken.

"The family was all waiting when I got there. Went in the lift and then it stopped, sudden like and the lights were gone. Some of the ladies were frightened and then young mister Charles, he shouted and there was a shot and next thing was the light was on and there was a gun and he was sitting on the floor by the wall." Tears blistered in his eyes and he looked to the ground with a face full of shame. He sniffed. "Weren't nothing anyone could have done. Mr Heskins checked him. Shot alright and he was dead." Jeffers looked straight at Charlotte. "Someone in that lift killed him but I don't know who, Miss. I swear it. That's all as I know."

The air was still. She felt the rhythmic stream of her blood in the side of her neck. The wind raked through her hair, pulling it from her face, clearing her head and straightening out her thoughts.

Jeffers seemed to flicker with life as though the trance was lifting. "I don't know what happened with the birds but I do know the house ain't been the same since. None of us has." He wiped the back of his hand across his cheek and flushed a little. "Not the same."

"What's not?" A new voice broke the moment.

Jeffers suddenly looked agitated. "Nothing."

It was Bartram, striding towards them. "Telling tales of the good old days again, are you?"

"Not exactly," Charlotte said. "Not the good ones, anyway."

Bartram frowned at the old gardener before his eyes went back to Charlotte with a more accusatory look. "More birds research then, eh Miss Blood?"

"Mr Bartram, as I have just explained to Mr Jeffers, our readers want the full picture. Who it is that cares for these birds? How much do they mean to the family? They will want to hear about the custodians of these creatures. It would be –"

"I care for them. You can ask me. Leave old Jeffers out of it. Too honest for his own good, this one."

The gardener avoided Charlotte's gaze now, a sudden embarrassment flooding his face.

"Honesty is always good, isn't it Mr Bartram?"

He didn't acknowledge her question. "What are you doing out here anyway, Miss Blood?"

"I was looking for someone. A girl."

Bartram glanced around. "Well, there's no one out here and it's getting cold. Be dark soon. You best be getting back to the house."

A wintry breeze circled her ankles in agreement.

"Come on, Jeffers. Miss Blood needs to head home

now, don't you?" Bartram stood firm, watching her until she started to make a move.

Her shoulders fell in a long sigh. "Very well." She shoved her hands in her pockets. "I will come and see you tomorrow, Mr Bartram, if I may?"

He didn't answer immediately. He let her wait. Finally, he said, "If you think it will be of any use."

"Of course it will. I need as much information as I can gather."

"I can see that, Miss Blood." His voice remained toneless but his eyes were shrewd, studying her.

As she left, she could feel the prickle of their eyes on her. She set off briskly, the freezing mist clinging to her skin, her arms pulled up into the sleeves of her coat. Small drops of light from the old Abbey glowed in the darkness. From a distance, it was a perfect dolls' house, all neat lines of windows and great columns by the door. A preserved world she'd left behind many years ago. In that moment, she had an unnerving feeling that it had all just been waiting to pull her back.

Maybe she'd never really left all this. It had just been a temporary aberration as her mother so helpfully put it the last time she saw her. That had been at the funeral for Charlotte's father. There'd been no reconciliation, no relenting on the decision to cut her off if she persisted with the ridiculous idea of living *on her own* and working as a *journalist*. The phrase "our father's wishes" had been repeated by both of Charlotte's brothers with the solemnity of a prayer. The new custodians of the future would ensure everything remained the same as the past.

As she hurried back to the house through the fading dusk, Charlotte caught a movement in one of the ground floor windows. The figure paused, silhouetted for a moment in the lambent light. Watching her. If she could get back quick enough, this could be a chance to confront them. Given that they were making no effort to disguise their observations, perhaps they were even expecting her to. She half ran the last section back to the house.

Charlotte slipped through the servants' corridors, her presence either dismissed or ignored entirely, and entered the great hall via the green baize door.

It was easy to work out which room the figure had been in. But when she entered the small day room to the left of the hallway, it had a cold, undisturbed air. There was no trace of anyone having been there.

She walked towards the window where she'd seen the long silhouette. A small, cushioned bench filled the alcove below. It was frayed at the edges and had a large indentation in the middle, where someone had been sitting. The dull, floral curtains remained open and she saw immediately that beads of condensation were meandering down the grey windowpane. The droplets came from one small spot midway down as if someone had breathed out on the glass.

She reached towards the window hesitantly and touched it, following the droplets as they ran in chains all the way down to the sill. There in the wood below was scratched one word. "*Darkness*".

Charlotte ran her fingers over the sharp edges, careful this time not to catch a splinter. The carving had the same malicious, small strokes stabbed into the grain.

She looked up through the window that someone else's eyes had watched from so recently, out across the garden and down to the long, jagged hedge where she had been talking to Jeffers and Bartram not ten minutes ago. She pictured herself there, the eyes watching, reflected on this pane of glass, the breath pooling in a small, fogged circle then fading. But whose face would have been reflected? If she'd stood on the other side of this window and looked in, who would have stared back at her?

A thin line of anxiety traced down her spine. Whoever had sat here had done so for quite some time, long enough to do this carving. Long enough for the embroidered seat cushion to still be warm.

There was a movement behind her.

A sudden shuffle.

She turned.

It was no one again.

The wind played a long note down the chimney. Charlotte let her breath leak out slowly. Perhaps she was crafting phantoms from the air.

But the faint, sweet smell of lavender soap they'd left behind made that very unlikely.

25

Charlotte hadn't slept. She lay on the unmade bed in their flat – her flat, she corrected herself, just her flat now. There was going to be a lot of readjusting. She watched the first blinks of dawn and the dull patina of the sky rolling out again across London. It had been two nights. Two nights since Archie died. She wouldn't let sleep in until she was completely drowning in exhaustion. If she went to sleep, she'd have to face that first flash of waking and realising he was dead. The thought was poisonous. That would be another step away from him. Another moment in this aching, new world without him in it. Nothing about this was brave.

In those first days, Charlotte went over and over the last moments to make sure they were deeply embedded in her thoughts. Repeating them to ensure they didn't fade. Archiving every second so she could access them whenever she needed to.

Firstly, the seconds before his death. That smile. The kind of smile she had feared for so long. Defeat pulling it down in surrender. It had taken its time. But as his thin lips stretched out into that weak look of goodbye, she knew it instantly. An apology. A regret. So full of pitiful sorrow for her and all those days she would spend in loss.

The disintegration of a life can be so slow. Her husband's began the day he came home blistered and blind from Ypres. He told her he'd been in the Machine Gun Corps – the Suicide Club, he said they called it. But he didn't die, not there. He was one of the unlucky ones. She never met anyone else who'd survived that club. He didn't talk about it.

Part of him had recovered. Part of him never came back from France. His eyesight returned partially and the yellow oozing blisters healed, leaving the image of the same man who had gone out there. But something never returned. He looked at her with realisation, as if he was seeing her for the first time. A small fraction of his eyes looked jaded with life. She thought at first he might be tired of her, having seen all that excitement in France, but he held her closer than ever, as though he was attempting to shield her, keep her safe. To begin with, he could only see her if she was close enough for her to smell his breath. It smelt different, stale with a mouldering behind it. The scent of decay.

As the months ticked by, one after the next, no one but her would have known that the damage she'd seen come home had just retreated inside of him, into the deep crevices of his lungs, still as raw as those wounds were that she'd seen, stripped bare and scarred. Vulnerable. Perhaps she had just blinded herself to the truth when they married. But then there were other secrets, doubts to distract her in those early days.

Colonel Blood had a box filled to the brim with medals that he kept in a tin at the back of a drawer and never looked at. He never spoke about it. But she knew he'd seen so much more than most. He hid all that heroism away so he could just be Archie Blood again, the man who worked in some department at the Foreign Office. So he could be the man who married Charlotte. Every morning, he would leave their little flat in that Bloomsbury square, the rest of the world acting as if nothing had happened.

But it had happened, and it was there in front of them all.

There were fewer men.

There were broken men who shook, men without all the limbs they had before and then there were the men who just coughed. They were the ones who never left home without more than one handkerchief, who had to excuse themselves to hack up the contents of their ravaged lungs. They were the ones who would not last many years.

Charlotte made every year a memory. She held every birthday, every Christmas in her head, burning it deep. The slow and inevitable descent was as graceful as the man it took away.

She had time, time to fix in place all the remembrances and cherish every single one.

When the last day came, she knew what to do, what to preserve inside her memory, carefully curating every last moment. She had all her lasts. Her last cup of tea with him. Her last night. Her last embrace. His last words – "*It will all be alright.*" She never got the chance to ask how he could be so sure.

When his blighted lungs let out their last, laboured breath, she kept her lips close to his and breathed it in. She held it, savouring every moment as she watched her own image fade on his eyes. The life in that last look weakened, paled and gradually fell into darkness.

She stayed there until he was cold. Until all of him was gone. Until the muted stars seeded the sky, and she imagined him up there, one of those silver specks far away but still watching her.

Then it was time to make the call.

They swooped in great black flocks of mourning. His parents – weary and kind; hers stern and with a new agenda. But this next war with her family would only begin when he was safely in the ground. It was to be bitterly fought. Her marriage had granted her only a temporary reprieve. Now he was gone, it instantly seemed like she'd been left exposed and alone. She held her ground, clinging on to her life at Mecklenburgh Square, but her grip was so tenuous, her fate still dependent on others.

The memories trickled out. Time to file them away again. It wasn't good to follow the dark river of grief too far into the past. It would be too easy to drown.

Charlotte stared at the bare-walled room before turning back to the folder. The photograph of Charles Ravenswick was looking up. He had none of Archie's slow suffering. A single shot was all. But it still cut short a man's life and stripped away so many years. Someone took all those days, and they did so without punishment or apology. She looked down the list of names again.

Edward Ravenswick

Elizabeth Ravenswick

Rachel Ravenswick

Mary Ravenswick

George Jeffers

Patrick Bartram

Nicodemus Bligh

Heskins

Eight names. Eight possible shooters. Only one person took all that life away from that young man. Charlotte looked at a new sky beginning. She would find them.

26

Charlotte Blood had never been very good at sneaking around. She preferred a much more honest approach but honesty wasn't going to get her very far in the Ravenswick household, they'd made their fortune in newspapers after all.

As everyone else was busy with the restoration of another day, Charlotte attempted to casually drift from room to room, glancing at magazines, studying ornaments in glass cabinets, and giving undue attention to trinkets on tables. There was the usual corps of staff, engaged in all manner of strange and varied occupations – beating cushions, stocking coal scuttles and dusting down curtains. At Bladesworth, when she'd entered a room, even before nine o'clock in the morning, the maid would bob into a curtsey and scurry away. Here, they didn't know what to do with Charlotte. None of them acknowledged her or even appeared to have seen her. She was the kind of ghost who had no real purpose or place.

Charlotte was under no illusion though that her whereabouts were known and whispered about at all times. The busy little bees would no doubt be sharing everything they'd seen with each other. Gossip and intrigue were a currency amongst the servants. That was one of the few things her mother had taught her. As she grew up, it was drilled into her. Never speak about anything beyond the mundane in front of the staff. It was a natural part of the organisation of the house. And never, ever have the giant row in front of them about your future and the fact that your father was going to cut you off if you didn't tow the family line. That would definitely bring shame on your family, leading to an irreparable rift that would never heal.

Charlotte continued to flit from bookcase to alcove, waiting for a plan to form whilst attempting to look like a natural ornithologist just wandering around the house.

She was just about to give in to the tide of frustration at being so utterly hamstrung by her ridiculous bird-based profession, when she saw the young girl again.

This time she was in a small side room that had long, locked cabinets. It was, by the looks of things, what her mother always referred to as a smoking room. There were large stag heads and antlers on the dark green walls and comfortable leather chairs dotted around, so men could relax, admire their collection of weapons on display and fill the room with smoke. That's what her mother always said they did in such rooms. Charlotte couldn't imagine that would be particularly relaxing but then, growing up at Bladesworth, she didn't think many of the things adults did were and, given the expression on their faces most of the time, she was probably right.

As Charlotte stepped into the room, she immediately recognised the scent of dry wood and tobacco mingled with the remains of a late cognac. There was all manner of weaponry on the walls, presumably so they were easily accessible to whoever was having a nightcap if an assault on the house was mounted.

There were the long rifles either side of the large marble fireplace, but also three smaller cabinets filled with pistols and hunting knives. It was an impressive array of different implements one could use to kill someone.

In amongst all this mini armoury was the figure of the young girl Charlotte had seen running across the lawn. She was standing with her back to Charlotte now, adopting a stance that suggested she was fascinated by something outside the window, when clearly her attention was entirely focused on Charlotte.

"Hello," the girl spoke without turning around. She had an insolent tone, familiar with challenging people. She was trying too hard to be self-assured.

"Hello." Charlotte kept her voice neutral. She didn't want to scare the girl or risk losing an opportunity.

The girl leaned her head in vague intrigue but still didn't turn around. She was analysing Charlotte's reflection in the gun cabinet's glass and smirking.

"An impressive collection." Charlotte paused, holding her hands behind her back, adopting a firm stance.

"Quite." The girl had a clipped, military way of speaking. "All present and correct." But when she turned around, she was very far from the sophisticated woman she'd attempted to portray. She was a ruddy faced child, saddled with an irritated little scowl.

She could immediately see Charlotte's amusement with her immaturity. This was a young girl who wanted to be thought of as more than a child, but they still kept dressing her like a doll. The checked pinafore stuck out at just the wrong level and her bruised knees looked doughy and pale below. The thick glasses didn't make her look any more studious or serious, just angry that she had to suffer them. Everything about her was irritated and out of sorts, as if she'd woken up to discover she'd been put in someone else's body, someone else's life. She clearly had no choice in anything to do with the way she looked and was vastly overcompensating for that in all the little details of herself. The way she acted, the way she spoke, all the tiny nuances she'd adopted were all devised as a way to be taken seriously. But somehow undermined her.

"You must be the Blood woman." The girl still held her head at a defiant angle and attempted to look disdainful in a way she'd obviously observed in the other members of the household.

"I am Miss Blood." Charlotte gave a half-smile.

"Not going to run away this time, then?"

Charlotte's smile evaporated. "That was you in the mist? Why didn't you answer? Why did you run at me?"

"Wanted to see if you'd scare easily."

"And was that why you hurled a gargoyle down on me?"

The girl frowned. "I don't know about that."

Charlotte raised an eyebrow.

"I see you are wearing a wedding ring, Miss Blood." She waited for Charlotte to acknowledge how astute she had been.

"I'm a widow."

The girl tutted. "How unoriginal."

Charlotte's face darkened. "I'm not sure I'd describe any death as *unoriginal*. Although some are definitely more original than others, wouldn't you agree?"

The girl suddenly looked disconcerted. "They all hated Uncle Charles," she blurted.

Hearing her refer to him as Uncle Charles was a reminder that this was just a naïve, young girl. This was her uncle. A man she would have grown up with, lived with and seen most days here, in her home. Now he was gone.

Charlotte softened her voice. "I'm sure *you* didn't hate your uncle."

The girl looked down at her childish shoes. A flush of colour spread through her cheeks, the suggestion of tears in her eyes.

"Your name is Celeste?" Charlotte asked tentatively.

The girl met her with a brazen look. "Well, aren't you the sleuth?"

Charlotte looked slightly patronising which irritated the girl even more. "Now, where did you learn a word like that?"

She lifted her chin. "I'll have you know I am a great reader of detective novels."

"Is that right? And which detectives live on your shelves?"

The girl paused and seemed dubious, weighing up whether she should share this with Charlotte. "Well, of course, I admire Mrs Christie greatly but I've got a couple of very excellent books by Anthony Berkeley and I managed to get a book by a lady called Dorothy L. Sayers. I get them from Mary's room. She loves clever murder mysteries. She says she's going to devise the perfect one herself and nobody will ever be able to solve it, but I don't think she's clever enough for that. Mummy doesn't like me reading detective novels though so I hide them. I put different dust covers on them. I've just got hold of a copy of *The Seven Dials Mystery*. That one is disguised as *Dr*

Dolittle which I'm not sure Mrs Christie would approve of, but Mummy does."

Celeste's shell had cracked and below was a fresh individual. There was a keenness to her that was so spirited in contrast to the snide little girl Charlotte had first encountered. The young face bloomed with genuine enthusiasm.

"I'm quite a fan of detective novels too," Charlotte said encouragingly. "We must compare notes one day." She thought of Mrs C and how enthused she'd be at this point. Charlotte tried to channel a little of that into her own face.

It seemed to have the desired effect. The girl looked sincerely pleased at the idea and quite surprised by any of this interest. "I take notes too," she confided.

Charlotte's mind landed on the carvings. "I see. And do you *leave* notes too? Clues?"

The girl frowned. "I'm going to write my own detective novel one day based on *real life*."

Charlotte tried not to appear too desperately eager. This was definitely the kind of girl whose suspicions could rise quickly. She couldn't risk losing this chance. "I see," Charlotte said. "And have you got very far with it?"

"Oh yes! I think I might be close to knowing who did it."

A stunned look flashed in Charlotte's eyes.

Celeste seemed to like that she was finally making an impression on someone in this house. She leapt on the moment with a thrilled face. "Yes, that's right. I've gathered the clues and I've worked it all out." That self-aggrandising look filled up her young face again. "It's quite simple, really, if you just use your brain."

"Celeste! What are you doing in here?" A new voice had invaded their little conspiracy. There was a clean, surgical edge to it. And by the look on the girl, it was a very familiar and very daunting sound.

27

Celeste instantly reverted to her dark surliness.

The woman obscuring most of the light in the doorway had a concentrated face, stern in an efficient way that seemed to be continuously inventing new ways to look harsh.

"I'm talking to our guest, *Nanny*."

The woman gave Charlotte a dismissive glance before focusing back on Celeste. "You are not supposed to be in here. You are aware of that, young lady. I feel we shall have to make you aware of it once more." There was a deep malevolence about Nanny. She placed her thick, brutish hands on her hips. "I suggest you explain this to your mother later and she will decide upon your punishment."

The girl soured and started for the door but as she passed by Charlotte, she whispered, "Four o'clock. Lake."

The nanny took a hard breath before grinding out another command through her teeth. "*Now*, Celeste!"

The girl's thick brogues plodded across the wooden floor begrudgingly and out into the stone hallway.

The woman didn't move for a moment, studying Charlotte intently. "I believe the ravens are being fed, *Miss Blood*." She threw out each sharpened word with precision.

Charlotte recalled mention of this nanny in the press reports at the time.

"Thank you, *Miss Austin.*"

She looked taken aback at the use of her name but quickly readjusted her face. "Good afternoon to you, Miss Blood." She turned and left as if it was Charlotte who was the member of staff being dismissed.

Charlotte waited, listening to the resolute steps drift away with the harsh sound of Nanny Austin's words.

Charlotte was alone in the new silence. This was an uneasy room. It wasn't just the array of weaponry, or the animal heads staring down at her from the walls alongside photographs of various people holding up carcasses. There was something else. Something claustrophobic about this small space devoted to death. She looked more closely at a framed picture on the polished side table next to her.

Edward Ravenswick was there looking disdainful and dignified, which seemed to be a permanent expression. She recognised Charles Ravenswick from the photographs in the press clippings. Slightly older but no less assured than his brother. They stood either side of a giant stag, its vast antlers filling the centre of the photograph, the pathetic eyes glazed into that last scene of the shot being fired.

Another, older man sat resplendent on horseback behind the two brothers. He was staring into the camera with an undeniable look of power. Charlotte instantly recognised him as Lord Ravenswick. Which serious journalist wouldn't? But he'd been out of the limelight for years now and those days of the conquering news hero were very far behind him. Rumours abounded of his pitiful state. Each stroke had left him more debilitated than the last until he could barely move. Stories circulated about how he was unrecognisable from this once proud man. The rival papers delighted in tales of this Hercules, shorn of his powers, brought low and weak. There were always a few new articles running around every month on how damaged he was. Degraded. They threw his deflated name around in some vile sport. Fulman and the rest of them knew what sold papers. To them, they were just servicing a requirement. Lord Ravenswick would have done the same and back in the day, he had. Charlotte was well aware he'd ruined many a reputation, broken stories of infidelity and bankruptcy in his morning papers like they were just another boiled egg being cracked at the breakfast table.

All this empire had fallen on the shoulders of the two sons when he could no longer hold himself up, let alone the weight of his newspaper. And now, it all came down to just the one. Edward Ravenswick was, for all intents and purposes, the new head of the family.

She looked closer at the photograph of him. A gun was slung over the crook of his arm and he was looking straight into the eye of the camera, defiantly unapologetic. But Charles Ravenswick wasn't. He was looking at his brother.

Charlotte reached to pick up the photograph but as she moved it a little, something else caught her eye. Gouged into the glossy smooth veneer of the table were two words: "BANG! BANG!"

It was so stark and sudden that it felt as if the words had grown a voice and shouted out at her from the wood.

The breath caught in Charlotte's throat. She frowned, her hand still resting on the photograph, looking down at the jagged lines of the carving. It was such a barbarous act. The table was ruined by these crudely cut, childish words. Who would do such a thing? This was no idle act. She ran her finger through the rough grooves. There was malice behind the hand that had done this, a spiteful determination that drove the instrument in deep.

It was the same as all the other carvings she'd seen. Had the girl done that and left it here for her to find? Surely not. Even she wouldn't be so brazen, would she? However surly she was, Celeste did exactly what the nanny told her to. There was no denial. No challenge. She'd shown no real acknowledgement when Charlotte mentioned leaving clues. And in any event, Celeste wasn't standing anywhere near this table when Charlotte came in. This had taken some time. Perhaps the girl had been here a long time. But Nanny seemed to keep a tight rein on her.

Charlotte replaced the photograph, making sure it was exactly where it was originally, obscuring the carvings. Somehow it felt beholden on her to hide this nasty little act of destruction, part of the blame finding its way onto her.

She hurried out of the room as though she was the one who had just committed a crime.

As Nanny had reminded her, the ravens were being fed. She had to be there for that. After all, she was still an ornithologist. For the moment, at least.

28

They were vicious, circling creatures, black as death and just as cold. Their faces all gathered into one judgement.

"You will come back to Bladesworth House, that's an end to it." Her father wasn't one for answers, or even questions for that matter. Commands suited his military bearing much better.

Archie had barely been in the ground an hour before they began the process of burying Charlotte's previous life. Burying her. All the life, all the world she'd lived in would be covered over and dug so deep that she would never get out again. She'd managed to escape once.

Whatever had compelled her father to agree to her marriage had died with Archie and no longer seemed of any use to her. Now Archie was dead, they had to reclaim whatever was left of her despoiled life. Who was going to take on a young widow who'd chosen to marry outside her world? Clearly, there had been a rebellious streak. What dangerous, dark thoughts might have been planted there during that strange, Bohemian life she'd been living amongst artists and writers – and in *Bloomsbury* of all places? What corrupt ideas had the outside given her? This was going to be a big campaign by her family to dig her out of her husband's grave.

She couldn't possibly stay living in a *flat* on her own in London. After the funeral, she must leave with them.

"No." Her voice was quiet and calm.

It was not a word her father had ever grown used to.

"I've got a job, and Mrs C is very understanding about the rent."

Mrs C nodded as she placed down the tea tray. "She'll be safe here, sir. I promise."

It didn't help. As grateful as she was, Charlotte thought it might actually have made it worse, if that was possible. Mrs C didn't know the kind of man her father was.

In a controlled statement, he explained the consequences as if punishment was being metered out in accordance with the law of the land and it was his solemn duty to see that it was observed.

Her mother did not protest. Charlotte was glad that she was saved that hypocrisy at least.

This was *"for her own good"*?

Her two brothers looked on, silent and grave in solemn agreement, two extra heavy weights to pull down on her legs as the life was being strangled out of her. But she attached no blame to them. They'd known nothing else. They'd been raised into this and any thoughts of a mutiny were killed off out there in France.

They'd both returned from the war, with no visible valour or injury. A bunch of medals their father dismissed, and some fractured nerves. Whether they'd taken the nerves out to Flanders with them or not wasn't something anyone questioned.

Bertie, the youngest, returned surly and bitter that he would never inherit. The war had presented an opportunity for many a second son, but not him. He was the unluckiest of young men. Cursed with a brutish father for no real gain.

The last Charlotte knew, Randolph's milk-faced wife, Blythe, bore him a son and then inconveniently died. There was an heir but no spare which was always a risk. That pressure would weigh heavily on Randolph.

Here at Ravenswick, they all still lived entwined in one another's lives, stumbling over their feuds and duties every day. There was no escape other than the way in which Charles Ravenswick had gone. Had he embraced that option? From what she'd read so far, there was no suggestion that he'd taken his own life. If he had, it seemed a remarkably elaborate staging, and for what purpose? Of those who benefitted, no one attracted any blame.

His adulterous wife and brother now had the run of the place. Edward was arrogantly enjoying his new status and Rachel was clearly happy with the new arrangement. Elizabeth was the future mistress of Ravenswick Abbey, so that suited her.

Charles Ravenswick's death had become little more than a parlour game to them, a mystery story waiting to be solved by his little niece Celeste. His mother was utterly absorbed by her invalid husband and the charlatan who now seemed to control her.

It was very evident how little Charles Ravenswick was missed. Life just continued as if he'd never existed.

Would that be the case at Bladesworth now? Perhaps Charlotte was just consigned to being an image in a few photographs in dusty corners of the house. Maybe they'd even removed those now. She wasn't dead to them, she just never existed.

But here at the Abbey, someone was interested in her. There was a quick flash of movement outside the door to her room. A momentary darkening of the white line of light around the doorway. Charlotte ran towards it. She'd catch them this time. But as she threw open the door, there was no one.

"Hello?"

No answer. But she could feel that familiar presence again. She could sense their eyes peering through the darkness, feel their breathing disrupt the air. The tap of a shoe on stone, the rustle of material, was becoming a constant companion, and they weren't trying very hard to hide their presence now. They were growing bold. The fresh, wet footprints on the stone floor leading away from the small room and along the hallway were proof enough of that. All Charlotte could console herself with was the thought that if they had wanted to cause her any harm, then they would have tried again. Perhaps the gargoyle was merely a warning. But they were watching alright, that much was very clear.

29

It seemed like an interminable wait until four o'clock. Charlotte watched Bartram feed the ravens and worked hard to muster some enthusiasm for their sickening meal. She was growing tired of the subterfuge and the raven master was now making no effort to disguise the fact that he'd seen through it. He hoiked the chitterlings and carcass remains out to the birds without any acknowledgement of Charlotte's presence. He noticed though every time she glanced at her watch.

She kicked at the dirt like a bored child, fiddling with the buckle on her satchel. When enough time had passed that it wouldn't appear rude to leave or look like she had no interest whatsoever in the birds, she announced her intention to go.

"Well, thank you so much for that. That's been fabulous. Our readers will be gripped!"

He gave her a casual look.

"Thank you. It's been…"

"Don't tell me… *Fabulous*!" He laughed mirthlessly. "I can see exactly how interesting you find it, Miss Blood. But obviously you're going to need to stay around a little longer as you need more… *information*."

She sealed her lips, holding back any quick response.

"Can I ask you something, Miss Blood?"

"Why not? After all, I'm an ornithologist and you're a raven master." She gave him a pinched little smile.

"Have you considered another profession?"

Her hand paused on the satchel. "Like what?"

She watched his face hover between a smile and something more serious. "I don't know. Anything! This is dangerous, you know, and you don't seem... Well, I mean, journalist is a little..."

"Oh, I see." She dropped the smile. "Because there are just so many options for people like me to choose from, aren't there? Let's see now, judge, surgeon, spy... Why not Prime Minister? It may have escaped your attention, but those positions are filled, and not by twenty-nine year-old widows."

His mouth had fallen open a little and the rest of his face creased into an awkward expression. "I didn't mean..." he winced.

"We both know what you meant. Now, if you'll excuse me, I'm going to go and do my worthless job and talk to a member of the family about the recent unsolved murder at Ravenswick Abbey." Charlotte didn't wait for a response. She readjusted her hat and slung the satchel over her shoulder. "Good day, sir."

***

When she got to the lake, there was no one there. Its surface was a perfectly undisturbed, dull mirror reflecting the wet slate of the sky. Charlotte waited, perched on the low wall, a thin, cold wind circling her feet. The damp stone was quick to sink through her clothes, settling into her bones as if it knew its way there very well now.

She thought about whether her outburst to Bartram had been wise. She'd lost her patience. She was human, after all. Presumably even his precious birds had a temper. They definitely looked like they did.

A tree of crows rattled and croaked high above where the aviary was. She thought of the ravens, great ambling creatures only able to look up at the skies and those daily tormentors who could fly. Bartram clipped their wings. He took away their ability to soar above all this and fly out across those moors. What use was a bird that could only dream of lifting into the sky and flying where it wanted?

Bartram had also been in that lift on the night of the murder, his presence requested by the family. Years of service to the family, tending their ravens, doing whatever was necessary to keep them hostage here. Would he know the family secrets? He was hinting at more and he certainly knew why Charlotte was here. He'd made that much obvious. She'd been rash to walk away. And perhaps very unwise to have said what she did. But if she just kept on the same parallel tracks, she was going to find out absolutely nothing. She needed to get hold of this and shake it until something came out.

It was past four o'clock. She couldn't just keep waiting around for something to happen. There needed to be action. Charlotte was just beginning to stand and brush the specks of crusted lichen from her skirt when she saw movement in the bushes. The crows lifted in one great curtain of black wings, squalling off into the darkening sky. The remnants of the day were already falling away into another unforgiving dusk. A chill passed through her.

She peered closer and the bushes moved in response. If it was Celeste, why didn't she just come out?

"Hello? I don't want to play chase again." A hint of frustration was finding its way into her voice. These people seemed to inspire it though. It was like lighting a candle in a storm. Every time a possibility took light, it was blown out. But irritation and exasperation would not encourage an unruly girl, Charlotte was well aware of that. She tempered her voice slightly. "Hello?"

The bones of the trees lined the edges of the lawn in one long spine. The fat black nests of the crows hung like charred Christmas baubles from the leafless branches. Perhaps it wasn't Celeste out there after all. Perhaps it was her constant watcher. A ghostly monk maybe. She smiled to herself, but the bitter gust of wind immediately wiped that away.

A cluster of bushes paused, then parted. And finally, the girl stepped out in a thick coat belted round the middle that gave her a solid, trussed-up shape. It had the look of a rehearsed entrance. She'd timed her moment and had clearly been observing Charlotte's mounting impatience.

A long smile opened up across the girl's round face. She looked very pleased with herself, walking with a self-conscious aloofness. Charlotte couldn't help but smirk. She wiped it away quickly though. This wasn't the kind of girl who enjoyed being mocked. But what was becoming increasingly interesting with every step the girl took towards her was that Celeste was holding something in her hands, clutching it to her chest. A large, brown leather book, bulging so fat that its binding looked like it might split. She gave a conspiratorial look. She'd been waiting for this moment.

The girl gestured towards the far side of the lake. She was clearly enjoying her new covert role. "We won't be seen from the house there." Celeste looked round and held the book tighter. Charlotte could see a label stuck to the front and scrawled in childish script one word. *Diary.*

Charlotte followed without questioning her and they sat on the edge of the wall by the lake, distant from the eyes of the house. Charlotte looked down at the well-stuffed notebook.

"This –" Celeste held out the diary ceremoniously "– is the sacred book."

She widened her eyes in exaggerated awe until they were two perfectly smooth, wet pebbles reflecting Charlotte's face back at her. "All the answers you seek are contained within these pages." The girl had adopted a hoarse whisper that was faintly comical, but as she opened the front cover, Charlotte was captivated.

Inside were drawings and timings, notes and small clippings all diligently pasted in. The book was bursting with meticulous details and all manner of observations from this young hand.

"I like to observe," the girl said simply. She offered the comment without apology or shame. "I watch and record my findings." There was, in fact, a distinct element of pride in her presentation. "I write them all in here." She handed over the book with reverence.

Charlotte looked at her in amazement before edging the book gently onto her lap, ensuring Celeste could see the care she was taking when she handled it.

It was in a diary format but far more extensive than any Charlotte had seen before. It was intricately detailed. On the first day, the girl had illuminated the date – 1st January 1928. Any one of those ghostly monks would have been proud. The hours of devotion were plain to see. It was quite beautifully ornate, as were the shapes of the letters below, a kind of childish calligraphy. But the words themselves were far from delicate.

The first entry alone set the tone for what was to come.

Saw Aunt Rachel at it with Daddy again today. Twenty minutes this time. The usual moaning and groaning. All so disgusting. She's quite pretty but not when she pulls that face. She looks so funny naked! Took one of her stockings as a souvenir. She'll be frantic looking for that, worrying if she's left it where Mummy will find it. I'll make sure she does in a few days.

Glued in next to the writing, there was a small rough square cut from a silk stocking. It had a very stark, charmless look to it. A brutality. There was undisguised vindictiveness in these pages.

Charlotte turned to the girl who still had a look of pleasure ingrained on her face. She was clearly proud of this disagreeable record. There was no hint of embarrassment there. She'd worked hard at this and the rotten fruits of her labour were now being exposed. This was presumably a moment she'd imagined many times, the unveiling of her vile project – the look of appalled curiosity she would inspire that now played on her audience. Charlotte had filled her role perfectly.

The girl nodded towards the book, encouraging Charlotte to continue. She dutifully turned the page with slow hands, instantly compelled. The next page was no less disturbingly fascinating.

Marvellous news today! Uncle Charles found out about

their dirty little secret. Can't imagine how that happened!

Here she'd drawn a small self-portrait with a mischievous smile. The innocent little coloured pencils she'd used somehow gave it another, more sinister layer.

He flipped his lid completely. It was wonderful. There was so much shouting. Adults do like to shout. Aunt Rachel denied it but he had proof. A witness. He didn't name me but I wouldn't have minded if he had. She changed tack then and started screaming how it was his fault for "neglecting" her. That all she wants is a child and he can't even give her that. No wonder she has to look elsewhere. And he should be grateful that if there is a child, at least it will look like him. Goodness, Aunt Rachel does need a lot of attention! And they say I'm demanding and difficult! Then she said she wished Uncle Charles was dead so she could marry the real man of the house who could at least father children. This is dynamite! If he's killed, this would definitely be excellent evidence. They'll all want to hear what I know then, won't they just?!

She'd drawn another small cartoon, this time of Rachel Ravenswick shouting at her husband Charles and a childish little speech bubble coming out of her mouth with the words, "I wish you were dead!" scrawled inside it. She'd made each letter bright red and finished it with a little skull and crossbones.

Charlotte looked at her in disbelief. "Celeste?" She spoke cautiously. The girl had a wide-eyed excitement to her that sat in stark contrast to the words on the page. Instead of this sneak-thief account of a tawdry story, she could so easily have presented her with a painting of a posey of flowers and expected the same response. There was such naivety in her face that clearly didn't mirror the inside world of this girl.

"How many people have seen this?" Charlotte had to tread carefully. She didn't want to scare the girl. For all Celeste's swaggering and sharp bravado, she was still a child, and a sulky one at that. One wrong step and Celeste could storm away with all these precious pages of information, information that was opening the door into this family and what happened that night.

"Only you," she said. "No one else so far." There was an eagerness there, a need to impress Charlotte. She could capitalise on that. "Because you're a journalist. That's why I persuaded Grandpapa that you should come and report on the ravens. He's not been very well and he loves them. He loves me." She looked down in embarrassment.

Charlotte paused with her hand on the book.

"I'd seen the letter asking if an ornithologist could attend. I read most of the letters that come here." She fixed Charlotte with a gaze. "It was someone from the outside world. I had my suspicions, but when I saw you, I knew you weren't here for the birds."

Charlotte didn't answer that one.

"But, Celeste, you know this could be quite dangerous, don't you? I mean, I'm not sure a young girl should be…"

Celeste's face took on a churlish look. "Well, if it's no good to you…"

Charlotte had to manoeuvre quickly. She couldn't lose this.

"Oh, I'm not saying that. It's utterly marvellous. It's just that I've never been privileged enough to see someone's diary and certainly not one that is so beautifully illustrated." She chose her words carefully, watching Celeste's reaction closely. "There's so much... detail here. It's really very wonderful, Celeste."

The girl clearly liked flattery. The satisfied grin spread quickly. "Nanny always says, if a job's worth doing, it's worth doing well." She nodded. "Shame she doesn't practice what she preaches." There was a prissiness about her, a fastidious nature. She was also quick to embrace anger. "You can find a lovely little moment on August the eighth when I paid Nanny back for being too rough when she brushed my hair." She giggled a little behind her hand. There was a sharp sound of glee to it. Charlotte made her own note not to cross this girl.

"Celeste, this is a great work and you should be very proud of yourself. I wonder..." She intensified the grave sincerity that was clearly appealing to the girl. "I wonder if I might have an evening to study it in depth?"

The girl's features tensed, and doubt began to settle in.

"I'll take incredibly good care of it, I promise. I just think something so wonderful and *literate* as this needs a lot more attention and study. There is so much to... *enjoy* in here and it would definitely be of great use in my piece." Charlotte was grave, earnest. "A great work of detective fiction."

The girl flushed. She liked that, not just the flattery but the sense of inclusion, of being part of this scheme. Even from the small snippet Charlotte had read of the diary, Celeste was keenly aware of how nobody wanted her around. She was a pest. An annoyance. Something to endure. To dismiss. Charlotte must be very careful to make this girl feel important. Wanted.

"There would definitely be an acknowledgement in it for you." It was a gamble. Although this girl obviously liked admiration, was it too early to suggest complete exposure for her cherished diary?

Celeste took a breath. It was a leap for her but one she was very willing to take. "OK." When she smiled, Charlotte could see all of the girl's crooked little teeth.

Charlotte placed her hand on Celeste's. The girl noticeably stiffened. She obviously wasn't used to being touched, not with kindness, at least. "Thank you," Charlotte whispered. The air was full of sincerity and Celeste lapped it up.

Charlotte held the book close to her. "I will keep it so safe. You have my word, Celeste. You are doing a very important thing. A very *brave* thing."

The girl puffed up her chest. "Glad to be of service, ma'am!" She saluted.

Charlotte smiled. Celeste had found someone to please, someone who at least acknowledged her. It seemed like a very new experience for her, one she obviously enjoyed.

"I must go." The girl gave a tentative look towards the house. "Horrid Nanny Austin will be calling out the guns." The girl jumped to her feet. "And we don't want any more shootings now, do we?" She gave an unsettling laugh.

Charlotte shook her head and forced out a smile.

The girl gave one last parting glance to the book, then ran, with her arms still pinned firmly to her sides. There was so much bitterness, so much resentment in that young shape as it disappeared across the lawn. How had this family created all that lonely spite in so few years?

Charlotte watched the squat little body of the girl

swaying from side to side, proper schoolgirl shoes and a menacing little mind to match.

Charlotte had always wanted a younger sister. One she could bond with and guide. One to share secrets with, pains and silliness. Bertie and Randolph were never ones for silly. The world was a dour series of necessities and duty for them. Perhaps that was Celeste's motivation in all this. Fun. She said she liked to observe. Perhaps that made her feel more involved, at least from the outside, where she could watch them and record them as if she was somehow part of it.

Who was there here for a young girl? The two brothers had nothing but responsibility and the burden of Ravenswick Abbey and the estate, just like Charlotte's own brothers, keenly aware they were custodians of the future. The only women anywhere near Celeste's age were her mother, Elizabeth Ravenswick, a distant woman; Aunt Rachel who spent more time with Celeste's father than Celeste ever did; and Aunt Mary, who had scourged herself of all joy and any glimmer of *silliness*, if there'd ever been any at all.

The young girl had clearly amused herself by analysing their world from the outside – outside, where she had been left. She watched them like they were specimens in their cage. Finding her fun in their misery and anger.

The thick, well-worked book sat in Charlotte's lap full of all its secrets and revelations. The question Charlotte kept returning to was, how much of it was fact, and how much the creation of this bored, malign little girl?

30

It was the kind of bleak afternoon made for tea and fires but there was none of that here in the austere world below stairs. In Charlotte's old dolls' house, a large door used to swing open to reveal a whole world in cross section, from music rooms and nurseries to the kitchens and scullery, every detail was there in miniature. If Charlotte could cut right through Ravenswick Abbey, it would be that same perfect scene of opposites. A picture with its negative, down here, amongst the servants, an absolute inverse of everything that could be seen in the world above.

The heartening glow of fires tinting those rooms was not the only reverse of this biting winter air. The open, deserted spaces in the land above were poles apart from this overpopulated maze. Above, whole rooms and corridors echoed to the sound of silence and abandonment. Whereas down here, there was a constant clamour to perform duties quickly and efficiently. Jobs were plentiful in comparison to the apathetic boredom running through the lives above.

Charlotte remembered how long the days were, especially in winter as a child, confined to the sombre atmosphere of the house. She would hear the staff occasionally when she passed the green baize door, shouting, sometimes laughing. She saw their footsteps traced through the snow and longed to go out, but it was never permitted. It was not deemed appropriate to roll in the snow.

She knew exactly how precious it was that first winter when Archie came home and they threw snowballs and laughed until he nearly choked from coughing. That was the first time she saw his blood, so vibrant and raw on the snow. Perhaps she'd known then that time was too fragile. Charlotte blamed herself for making him laugh but he made her swear she would never stop doing that. She was the fun, the life he craved.

More than anyone, Charlotte understood that stultifying boredom of an isolated childhood Celeste would be suffering. The young girl peered through those same bars of her cage that Charlotte had. And she watched other people's worlds. Charlotte held the heavy journal in her hands. Here was the testament to a child's savage loneliness. It was liberating, in some way. The girl didn't need to be polite or even nice in these pages.

Charlotte sat in her bed, the covers pulled up high to preserve what little warmth there was, looking down at that fat, stuffed journal resting on her lap. What exactly was waiting in here? The small extract she'd read so far was brutal and coarse, an unfiltered journey through the girl's bitter thoughts. Was there worse to come? What more was this young, unrepenting girl capable of? Perhaps there might be a confession. Charlotte banished the thought. However vicious the girl was, she was not in the lift that night.

She turned the thought over. It was New Year's Eve and Celeste was the only member of the family not there. Although the serious business of the will was to be discussed, it had all been presented as a celebration with presents being handed out. That must have been infuriating to a girl like Celeste, to be excluded from such a gathering. Her inquisitive, snooping nature must have been incensed at being absent, not just for a New Year's Eve gathering attended by all the rest of the family, but for what turned out to be the most momentous meeting this house had perhaps ever seen.

Charlotte opened the first page cautiously and leaned back against the pillow as if its secrets might suddenly stir and reach out to her.

2nd January 1928
No one ever wants to play here. It's deathly dull. Mother had another headache; father was busy with Aunt Rachel doing the usual in the conservatory; and Mary said I should just dry up and blow away. She was in an awful funk today. I heard them, Mary and Uncle Charlie arguing in the study. She wanted more money, as usual. Why? She's got nothing to spend it on and she certainly wouldn't spend it on nice clothes. She always looks like a mare's backside.

There was then a childish drawing of a horse's rear end with a mouth and eyes. It was labelled "Aunty Mary is a horse's arse."

3rd January 1928
Saw Nurse Sidmouth come out of the lift and wander off into the gardens. She'd gone for a smoke. I know what she does. Bligh went up in the lift, the sneaky rat. He wasn't up there for long though, probably spouting some more of his nonsense hocus pocus. Grandad can't hear him anyway.

At this point, the girl had drawn a magician with a spiteful look and long, pointed fingers as thin and white as fish bones.

4th January 1928
Went to see Grandad today. He's so unwell and he doesn't even look the same. He used to play so nicely but now he can't even move himself to play chess with me. He just stared through me as if I was the ghost. I wish he would come back. I miss him so much. Nurse says I shouldn't tire him out. It wasn't me, it was that Bligh creature. He'd been up there again for ages.

The ink was smudged here and some of the words ran down the page.

The wind tested the windows again. Charlotte paused and looked out at the bleak lawns rolling away down to the lake. The light was dwindling and another day had almost passed. The hours seemed to compress here until it left only half a day. Charlotte remembered the crushing feeling of being suffocated by this world, frozen into an existence where all the days were just exactly the same over and over.

Then it struck her. What if she never got out of this place? She knew quite a lot now and this diary would tell her even more. Members of the household had already made it obvious that they doubted she was here for the birds, and someone was suspicious enough to go through her things. There was a murderer in this house, one who was capable of killing the heir to the family fortune.

Not a soul in the world would worry or even notice for quite some time if she didn't come back from this. The only people who knew she was here were her boss and her landlady. Fulman probably had no memory of her the minute she walked out of his office, and her flat could easily be rented out by Mrs C.

Charlotte looked down at the incriminating book. If this was found in her possession, she would be a very big threat to the killer. There was only one thing to do. She needed to know everything.

5th January 1928
Another blazing row today! Granny, Daddy and Uncle Charles this time. The scene of the crime was the smoking room, not a smart place for an argument, I'll say, given the number of weapons in there! I was lucky enough to be in the room when it started and managed to get behind the sofa as quick as a hare. Didn't want to get caught in the crossfire!

Here, the girl had drawn a little picture of a gun firing at a startled rabbit. It wasn't intricate, but more in the manner of an idle doodle as if she'd sat daydreaming about the animal being shot.

I'm getting very good at hiding. I slow my breathing right down, just how Bligh taught me to. I love making him think he can hypnotise me. The man is such a clown!

She'd illustrated this with a tiny cartoon of a wicked clown, again with those talon-long fingers.

I stayed as still as a hawk hovering, waiting, listening to them and their silly grown-up prattle. They argue all the time. No wonder they look so glum. Today was the same as always. Money. Money! Money! It's all I hear. Goodness knows what they spend it all on. When I have this place all to myself, I will keep my money much safer than these fools do. Uncle Charles doesn't want to sell off the family silver, well, books. All those nonsense manuscripts Bligh finds. Who wants them anyway? Granny says they must sell them for the upkeep of Ravenswick. Daddy agreed. Daddy doesn't care much for the books anyway.

Then it all got heated. Uncle Charlie said it was his decision, not Daddy's, because he was the eldest son and heir. He was the only one thinking of the family name. If it came out, they would be ruined anyway. Granny said it was still Grandad's decision. Uncle Charlie was then very rude and hateful. He said Grandad had no business running the family estate as he was incapable. That was such an ugly word to use. I hate ~~that~~ Uncle Charlie ~~said that~~.

Celeste had neatly scored through those words as some sort of afterthought, leaving only the words "*I hate Uncle Charlie.*"

I love Grandad. I'd do anything to get him back. I just want him to be how he was.

Granny is so weak. I wish I could help. If she wants to sell the books then she should. They're her books! Why can't grown-ups just be less stupid. When I'm a grown up I'll not be stupid at all.

Through the net of mean thoughts, Charlotte could still detect something familiar in this girl's feelings. How many hours had Charlotte spent wishing away her childhood, dreaming of the promised land of adulthood with all its freedom and choice? But no child can imagine just how the constraints tighten as you grow. As a child, Charlotte had yearned to choose her own clothes, her own food and hairstyle. Little did she know that in place of that there were much bigger things people would want to choose for her – who she would marry, how she would spend her days, where she would live. The sanctity of childhood had protected her from any knowledge of what they expected her, as a woman, to submit to.

Celeste was in that unblissful period of ignorance, when the land on the other side of the fence seemed much more exciting and liberating. Presumably the Ravenswicks already had a match in mind. The bloodline would be maintained, even if the name would die with her. There were no little boys in this stable. Clearly that was a source of contention too, especially for Rachel Ravenswick.

30th January 1928
Miserable day today. Everyone is so out of sorts. It's so cold and damp and Nanny refuses to let the fire be lit until after four. She says it's a waste and I'll get too lazy. Like her, she means. She's just like a great big pink rat with those black studs for eyes, always watching me. Disapproving of me. I'd feed her to the ravens if I could. Ha! Circe would like that!

Here, was a small drawing of a black bird pecking at a large woman who was lying on the ground.

Spoke to Granny about her again but she always says the same thing. "Nanny is part of the family. She is so devoted to the family. She looked after your father and your uncle and they've both turned out very well." Silly old woman, she must be blind. She certainly can't see what Nicodemus Bligh is up to. Uncle Charlie can though.

Hid in the cupboard in the library today. They were arguing, Bligh and Uncle Charlie. I couldn't hear so well but Bligh was saying something about it being a necessary evil. Uncle Charlie accused him of being a fake. That's rich! He's always so dramatic and ridiculous. It was about money. Everything here is these days. Grown-ups are so obsessed by it. Everything is so unfair. When I grow up, I wish that I could live here all by myself. They'll all be dead and gone. I could spend my money on me and no one else. Nanny can go hang herself!

There was then a drawing of Nanny hanged from a tree in the garden and a small girl dancing around underneath. It was an unnerving image drawn with obvious delight. As Charlotte studied it, the words echoed in her head. Not just the callous "Nanny can go hang herself," but there was something else in amongst that childish scrawl.

31

It was dusk when Charlotte woke. In those first moments of consciousness, she thought she could smell his body next to hers. But it wasn't that odour of an unwashed body, half-destroyed by exhaustion. This was the man from the beginning of their story. Taut, lean and a warm mixture of sleep and cigarettes. His chest rose and fell in untroubled waves. She didn't know then, as they lay on that Autumn lawn, how precious those perfect breaths would be. They'd met two weeks before he had to go back. Another last push in those final months of the war.

Time is not a regular beat. It stutters, expands to accommodate the moments. Those two weeks before he had to go back soaked up so much space in her memory that they could have been years. Every day was a new world. A new excitement. Even then, at the time, she knew somewhere deep in all that happiness that this couldn't be how the rest of time would look. There wouldn't be enough space in her head for all that. From the beginning, that bliss felt so transient, so intoxicating.

She knew every moment of that party the night before Lady T's shoot. Less a party, more a piano recital with dull drinks afterwards. But Charlotte's family had dressed her like it was another opportunity to snare a husband. It was. Just not the one they wanted.

Charlotte kept every detail of that night so she could turn it over again and again, wearing the memory smooth.

He'd been by the window, polite and inattentive, with a group of older men, their wives conducting their own version of boredom elsewhere in the room. Archie nodded along to the conversation's ebbs and flow, absently turning his glass. His ungreased hair fell down over one eye and he pushed it back. He moved with modesty, a sensitivity, keen not to impose himself too much. He was a man who could easily blend into the background. Archie didn't seek out her attention.

His eyes absently wandered, looking out of the window. But they never got as far as the garden beyond. His focus was caught on the foreground. The reflection of a woman looking back at him. Charlotte. Her hair so dark it had become part of the black glass. Her eyes intent.

It was a deliberate look. She didn't turn or glance away as most women would. She let him study her. There was a provoking nature to her that fascinated him.

She inspired him, he would say later. To what, he never told her. It couldn't be that she inspired him to be a *better* man.

When they spoke, she was captivated by his undisguised interest. He didn't look away and made no effort to hide his intrigue. From that first moment, he always looked at her when she spoke, and that never changed, not in all the time he knew her. Just over four years, it didn't sound long when she said it out loud, but that look lasted much longer. She could still see it even now, as clear as his eyes.

Even when his lungs were breaking and breath should have been his only thought, he focused on her as clearly as he had on that first reflection. *It will all be alright*, he'd said. A lovely dream.

He always appeared an unsurprising man, but there was an eloquence to him. A beautiful rhythm to his life. He would walk down the little lane every morning, the rising sunlight glowing through the little cloud of cigarette smoke that trailed along behind him above the hedge. He would catch the same train to work every day. The same train home, his briefcase in the hallway as she came down the stairs on time, on the cusp of that moment that he built his day around. A minute she always timed impeccably.

At the weekend, he would read the paper by the fire. Whenever she looked up at dinner, he was there with his smile that said "wouldn't it be nice if this could last forever?" She still believed Archie's first morning thought was for her and his last every night. His very last thought in this world was for Charlotte.

The intensity of his regard for her seemed so solid and unwavering that it needed great armies to take it away.

But she knew all along that a man as good as Archie would never come out unscathed from that hell. Nothing as rare and simple as a decent soul could come back unchanged. That wasn't ever going to be the story. She'd always known that he'd change.

Charlotte remembered her first thought after they were married. *What will I do when you are gone? How will I ever live without you?* She'd known, of course she had, there would be some years without him, she just didn't realise there'd be so many and how they would be so interminably long, rolling out in that long, black ribbon of grief. The days had stretched so far away from him now, far from that one daily moment when he would come home from work and she would drift down the stairs. They had lost so many stories that never got a chance to be told.

Charlotte often wondered at all the stories she didn't know the endings to. His stories. No man is without his secrets. As time went on, he just seemed to gather more than others.

She'd seen him once, so out of context that she doubted it was him at first. They'd only been married a month and Charlotte had gone shopping for cups. She loved the feeling of the daily mundane tasks, of building a home and a life with him.

He'd gone to work as usual. The clock had ticked with a regular beat that day, right up to that moment when her pulse stalled. It was him, Archie, entering that house, greeted on the doorstep by the enthralling woman with hair as auburn as the sunlight. It was that look they both gave, furtive, glancing around, that engraved itself on Charlotte.

She never knew how long he stayed there. She ran. She didn't stop. She ran all the way to Mecklenburgh Square.

Mrs C heard the tears and brought the tea, and she listened.

Charlotte never spoke of it again, not to Archie, not to anyone, and she would only ever go back to that house one more time.

These days, she didn't share her life anymore except with Mrs C, who left her tea and books, darned her stockings and drank whiskey on Sundays. Charlotte lived a lot of her life on her own. Unshared moments just became things that happened, moments Charlotte felt no need to remember. She never paused on the stairs anymore. She just walked down them.

For a while, after he'd gone, she used to come downstairs at the same time. It wasn't even a conscious decision, just an impulse. Sometimes she wouldn't even realise she'd done it until she saw the clock in the hall. Mrs C would come out with a cup of tea then.

Later, Charlotte would sometimes forget to be on the stairs, but her eyes would be drawn to the clock suddenly and she would look to the door. There were so many tales of missing soldiers, believed to be dead, coming home having been lost for years, either unable or unwilling to get back. But Archie had come back.

Every night when Nosferatu went out in search of another story, she would pause and look back up those empty stairs. This had been his view when he came home, his eyes never leaving her. They never left her in that last second. She could see them now, just as entranced as they had been watching that first reflection on the window at the party.

So many times she'd woken herself up whispering, "Don't be dead. Just don't be dead." It was the one thing he couldn't do for her. She closed her eyes and said it again now into the cold void of that room at Ravenswick Abbey.

Archie wasn't coming back and not one person was to blame because it was so many people's fault. Charles Ravenswick wasn't coming back. But Fulman wasn't interested in sorrow. He wanted blame. Someone had to be responsible. And Charlotte would find them.

There were no footsteps to announce the tap at the door. Had someone been there all this time, listening? She looked down and the diary was still open on the page she'd left it on, the chair still under the doorknob.

There was a dry rustling, a pause and then the quick sound of a retreat. Charlotte leaned forward on the bed and in the dim light on that bare floor was a single black feather. Beneath it was a piece of paper.

She paused before walking to the door. The feather was soft, almost weightless in the palm of her hand. The note was written in elaborate, cursive script.

Please join me in the library this evening before dinner. Your servant, Nicodemus Bligh.

She twirled the feather and ran it across her cheek. "Well, Mr Bligh, I shall be delighted to attend."

32

Charlotte hurried along the barely lit hallways. These walls didn't encourage lingering. Her worn shoes made very little sound on the thick carpet. She flitted along, her reflection travelling on each mullioned window next to her like a spirit following closely alongside. The black silk soaked up the light. The long string of pearls she'd managed to hang on to, when most of the other jewellery had been pawned, was cold against her skin. Her mother always had the maid wear her pearls to warm them up before she wore them.

Charlotte held her hand to them and remembered their wedding anniversary when she opened the box from Archie.

"*Pearls for thirty years, silly!*" she'd said. "*Not two.*"

Archie didn't answer that.

Charlotte had hoped for a better occasion to wear them again than visiting Mr Nicodemus Bligh.

Her satchel didn't quite go with the coal-bright silk, but she wasn't about to leave the diary and the folder unguarded. She decided it probably gave off the right ornithologist-going-to-dinner look.

The library was deserted and full of shadows. She wandered through the vast, high room, glancing at the rows of books, great worn, leather-bound volumes, each waiting for the magician's hand to discover another lost treasure.

There was only the maudlin light from the moon falling through the long windows. A cloud passed over its face, sending a beat of darkness over the room.

When it lifted, the grey moonlight touched on the glass of a display cabinet, half open in the centre of the room. And there beside it was the unmoving, luminous face of Nicodemus Bligh, oppressively still and watching her.

A strange, serene look lingered on his face. There was a disturbing calmness about him. He didn't speak immediately but examined her unashamedly before holding his hands together in front of his long white robes in a deliberate, sanctimonious act. Everything about this man reeked of being meticulously contrived, not least of all his voice.

"Miss Blood." He lingered on every sound, enjoying it.

"Mr Bligh."

Both were treading carefully now, a distrustful air between them.

He moved towards her, into the new light that seemed to loosen his rigid features. He attempted a smile and his face momentarily slipped into being that of a younger man. If all the confidence and disguise were swept away, what would be left? An unsure man? Perhaps even a concerned man? To have so many layers, there must have been something he needed to conceal.

His hands remained clenched before him in semi-prayer. But what was already becoming obvious was that this man saw no one else in the role of god.

"I have prepared some items for you to inspect." He used that same patronising, learned tone she'd heard him use before.

"Her Ladyship and I have concluded that given your interest in the ravens, you might be intrigued to learn we have many texts on these spiritual corvids, some of which have only recently come to light as a result of my investigations." It increasingly had the distinct feel that she was being manoeuvred towards something else.

"Come! Come forward. Let me show you. They are very valuable."

He beckoned with a hooked finger. She hesitated and he saw it.

"Come, Miss Blood! I don't bite."

She gave a tight smile. They were not encouraging words. "What makes you think I don't, Mr Bligh?"

He grimaced. "Your interest in these amazing creatures is entirely understandable." Bligh flicked on a small table lamp beside him. The fringed light seemed to empty his eyes of any kind of expression. On closer inspection, his arching eyebrows had been pencilled darker for emphasis, the hair dyed. He had the look of a malevolent conjuror about to perform his next trick. He stared, unblinking as if he was attempting to mesmerise her.

She shifted her attention away from him, towards the many ancient looking books in the case.

"Miss Blood, you are more coy than you would like us all to think," he laughed.

"Oh, I suppose we're all putting on a performance of some sort, aren't we?"

Bligh's face hardened.

"You will have heard, I presume, about the legends of these great birds. Gods and scholars have revered them for centuries. See this picture here." He nodded down at an illustrated text carefully displayed in the case. The book sat in the crook of a small seat emphasising that this was a very special, precious item. "The Vikings thought Odin himself kept two ravens as pets."

The faded medieval depiction on the page was of a powerful man with one eye. On each shoulder perched a vast, black bird.

"Huginn." Bligh pointed to one of the portentous creatures. "He is Thought. And this –" Bligh's hardened, yellow fingernail travelled over to the other bird "– this is Muninn, or Memory. You see, Miss Blood..." He stood up, so close that he was looming over her. "The Vikings were not such uncultured beasts as history paints them. The Dark Ages were a time of great thought and study, which has sadly been forgotten or lost. Their teachings were more enlightened than many of our modern ideas. They forged an alliance between the spiritual and the naturalistic world." He leaned in and whispered, "They had made the connection to our earth that has been lost for centuries... Until now."

It was easy enough for Charlotte to see she was being angled towards something other than birds. She had the sense that the real reason she had been summoned to see Mr Bligh was beginning to be revealed. There'd been very little preamble or subterfuge about it. The atmosphere had grown decidedly business-like. He knew she was a journalist and that had its uses. Its publicity.

"Tell me, Miss Blood, have you heard of the library of Iona?"

Charlotte was happy to go along with him. She shook her head slowly. "No, I'm afraid I haven't, Mr Bligh. Does it have a specific relevance to ornithology?"

He shook off the question quickly. "Iona, that small,

Scottish Island, inhospitable to so many, beloved of the spiritual and pious, was once home to one of the greatest libraries known to man."

"And woman?"

He gave a deprecating look. "Innis Nam Druidneach, Miss Blood! The Isle of the Druids. It housed the written records of the Druids themselves. Their ceremonies and laws have been lost, some were thought to have never been recorded. You see, Miss Blood, it was a very oral-based set of laws and customs. But there are some who have always believed the ancients *must* have made some record. Iona was one of the greatest centres of learning in Dark Age Europe. *The Book of Kells* itself was created there. Yet why would only one book survive from such a magnificent library? Hector Boece himself..."

"Hector?" she puzzled. "The same Hector caught drinking champagne out of Tilly Bossington-Carr's shoe at The 43?" She looked at him teasingly.

He batted this away. "He was a fourteenth-century Scottish philosopher."

"Oh, that's a pity." She was toying with him now.

Bligh's expression glazed over. He continued regardless. "He wrote his book *History of the Scottish People* based on a mysterious tome he found on Iona. If this library were ever found –" he gave a wry little smile, almost to himself "– it would be of huge historical significance. It contained the history of the Celtic Church of the Culdees and of the Druids themselves! In 410 AD, the Scottish king, Fergus II, plundered the great libraries of Rome. There were a host of illuminated religious manuscripts, ancient Greek and Persian philosophers' texts and even the lost books of Livy."

Genuine excitement lit in his eyes now. Charlotte's presence seemed almost irrelevant. She tried to look interested in the same way she did when Mrs C was plotting out a new novel.

"It was said to perhaps contain one of the greatest lost books of all time, Aristotle's book on magick." His voice was barely above a whisper now. "To find that would be the key to the door between our world and the world of the supernatural. The natural philosophy of the true *Magi* – the magicians or priests, if you prefer. All their wisdom. Imagine what that would mean?"

"Money?" Charlotte offered in a knowing voice. "Fame?"

He paused and a distrustful look passed across his face. "Miss Blood, these texts, I believe, were all part of one of the greatest libraries the world has ever known. The Druid Library on Iona. There is definitive proof that the monks at the monastery there hid the books and spirited the majority of them away when news of the Viking raids reached them. Even *The Book of Kells* was lost for a time but then discovered under a sod of earth. Many are thought to be buried, preserved in the acidic peat bogs and mires of Ireland. It conserves the velum, you see." He leaned closer, leering into her face for a sign of recognition.

She nodded as if she did.

"Other manuscripts were taken over the water by courageous monks who saved them and hid them in monasteries all over England." He leaned closer and she could smell the strangely spiced scent he had drenched himself in. "And what was Ravenswick *Abbey*, Miss Blood?"

He stood back, his hands still folded in reverence. "A

monastery, Miss Blood!" he announced. He injected fresh drama into his voice. "But books are never safe. Great books that tell of the truth are a threat to many and have always been. Wars and reformations, plagues and witch burnings, books have always been victim to the next great upheaval and ritually destroyed. At the Dissolution of the Monasteries, the monks hid the books to the best of their abilities, but sometimes they were not even capable of hiding themselves! Nor were they wealthy and so often had to reuse what they had to hand. Many old manuscripts were used to create prayer books or were even repurposed for book binding. Tell me, Miss Blood, are you aware of palimpsests?"

She shook her head once. The more he spoke, the more she found that, in spite of herself, she was being drawn in. His voice was like balm.

"Look, I will show you." He leaned toward the cabinet and extracted one of the leather-bound volumes. It was small but with thick, heavily illuminated pages. The dim light caught the strands of gold and lifted them from the text as if the letters themselves swam up from the page and spoke out down the centuries.

He held it humbly. When he spoke, it was as if he was wary of waking something. "This, Miss Blood, is an intricately crafted book of hours. As fabulous as the workmanship is, there are many in existence. But look." He offered it with an air of divinity.

She craned her neck forward and inspected the elaborate page. The pages were thick yet delicate. Richly coloured letters emerged from the page, curling round one another and over the smallest of painted creatures. Birds glided around the edges, words nested in the entwined vines. Fruits and flora draped through the text.

He held it out further as an offering. She looked uncertain but he nodded. "Take it."

The thick leather had an inner warmth to it, a softness that seemed organic, as if it was a living thing. It was heavier in her hands than she'd imagined, but there was a distinct fragility, a frailty that spoke of how tenuous this book's existence had been.

She raised it closer and the scent of the past lifted in waves. The perfume of the woodland soil seemed to drift up from the intricate forest design. It mingled with the camphorous smell of the monks' ancient inks, rising from the page as fresh as the day their fingers carefully worked them. Small animals, squirrels and deer appeared from the thicket of words and foliage. Berries and delicate blossoms touched the letters. It was a complete world in a single page, as clear and living as the day it was finished.

"It's beautiful," she whispered, entranced.

There was a worthy, craftsman's pride in Bligh's smile. A satisfaction that she too could see the splendour and significance of what she held. How many hands had this book passed through to ensure it survived so that it could remain simply untouched in this glass case?

"But this is not the real treasure." His eyes widened and uncreased at the corners. It was as close as this man's face would ever get to open and honest. "Look!" He spoke with unrestrained wonder.

Bligh turned the book in her hands, brushing her skin with his thin fingers. He didn't acknowledge that he'd touched her or even seem to care. The book was his sole interest.

"Look closely, Miss Blood." His voice drifted in and out hypnotically. "Closer. Do you see? Do you see, Miss Blood? Do you see Blood?"

She glanced into his face, the words familiar, the eyes in front of her swimming in a sort of trance.

"Look." His hooked nail hovered over a section of the text. "Look below what you see. Here! The ghosts of other words. Another book!"

She peered deeper, under the forest floor of words. He was right. Pale letters whispered beneath the ink like scars on the paper.

"From the original document. You can still see the imperfectly erased words."

Charlotte stared in amazement as the secrets slowly lifted and wove along the page. She looked back at him. "There is another book. You're right."

He nodded once and stood upright in confirmation. "And that's not the only one like that. These books haven't been touched in centuries. Their magick has been hidden for generations. The words have slept in these pages, many thought to be lost or destroyed. But they were *here* all along. Sleeping. Hidden in the best of places. In another book."

She looked down at the small, innocuous little book laid bare in her hands. "What is it?"

"This one, I do not know yet. Two of the ones that the family chose to sell were small pages that had been used in the binding. One on Roman augury with origins dating back to Flaccus, and another on questions of Roman ritual. But if I'm right, those texts formed part of that greater library I told you of, pillaged in the fifth century from Rome and brought back to Iona. To the Druids' Library. I believe the monks brought some of the texts here, to Ravenswick Abbey, when the Viking raids began. Hidden in the bindings of other books or simply reused over time, those books are buried in here, in Ravenswick Abbey's own library, safe from the centuries and now within our reach. Think of it – Aristotle's dialogue on the true art of magick, one of the most magnificent lost books. Details of the Druids' ceremonies, long lost and forgotten, all their practices and laws. How they became Druids. The answers to questions we thought could never be solved are all here in these pages. Their magick is in here! The secret of *real* magick."

He took a steadying breath. "If I'm right, Miss Blood, you are standing in the greatest library ever built." He held out his arms as if soaking in every word on the shelves.

Charlotte stood, beguiled, with the precious book open in her hands, her eyes wandering along shelf after shelf. All the years laid upon one another, waiting for this man to peel back each layer. If what he was saying was true, and there was little room to doubt this genuine display of enthusiasm and excitement, the Ravenswicks were sitting on one of the greatest treasure troves ever to be discovered. There was wealth here beyond their wildest dreams. Or nightmares. There was certainly enough for someone to kill the heir to it all. She thought of Celeste's own book and the arguments. Charles Ravenswick had set himself up in opposition to their sale. These once silent, devout pages could very easily be restitched into one enormous motive for murder.

But one thing that was becoming very clear to Charlotte was that she'd not just been permitted to remain at Ravenswick to tell the story of the birds, or even find out who killed Charles Ravenswick. She was definitely here for more than one purpose.

They needed the world to know about this discovery, but in a controlled way. They'd sold some, but there were clearly more. The treasure buried in these shelves could change everything for the Ravenswicks and it was very possible that it had already led to the death of one heir. Even if Celeste was telling the truth, and it was her who had originally brought about Charlotte's presence, Bligh and the Ravenswicks, or at least some of them, had perhaps spotted an opportunity to make use of her. No one would dare to banish her now for fear that the finger of blame might point at them for the murder. Was it possible that if she had to stay, Bligh had perhaps decided to attempt to utilise her to create a new and more profitable narrative around their potential discoveries? A story through the family's own paper wouldn't be as convincing as an independent investigative source stumbling upon this remarkable tale. That did make some sense, she thought, if anything made any sense at all in the strange goings on at Ravenswick Abbey. One thing was sure though, there were many conflicting interests at work here. Each of them had their own agenda and Charlotte could not entirely put her trust in any of them.

33

After she'd eaten dinner in the jaded opulence of the dining room, Charlotte returned to sleep amongst the very people who had been serving her. This was a strange, ambiguous world where, in spite of the rigid adherence to place and roles, no one seemed to be entirely what they should be. She was sinking deeper and, more importantly, alone. Suspicions were rising, and the only ally she had was the disturbing young girl who liked to draw cartoons of people being hanged and shot. Charlotte needed a lifeline to the outside world.

It was essential that she got news to Fulman. He'd specifically tasked her with finding out more about the strange manuscripts coming out of Ravenswick. If Bligh was telling one journalist about his discoveries, it was perhaps only a matter of time before the rest of the world knew and she would be left behind in their dust. Charlotte was no fool. She knew when she was being used for publicity. When Bingo Reynolds suspected Monty might be Nosferatu, he played up all the more and ended up dressed as Napoleon in the fountain at Trafalgar Square. Charlotte certainly wrote about it, but with more emphasis on the straining waistcoat and unflatteringly tight trousers. Bingo was not happy, and even less so when he became known as Full House.

Charlotte's main concern now was that she had to get news of this groundbreaking development to Fulman. If they really did have all these treasures here, she had better be the first to let the world know and see her name on the story. She had to tell Fulman and fast. She was settled on that much at least. The question was, how to do it without alerting the entire house?

Charlotte had seen telephones in two locations – Mrs Thornycroft's room and above stairs in the sitting room where she'd met Lady Ravenswick. She couldn't say how many more there were but that was enough on its own to know that her conversation could be carefully monitored from various locations in the house. She'd have to get a telegram to Fulman but anything she wrote down here and gave to a servant would be passed through so many hands she might as well have made a public announcement.

The only way to ensure complete privacy was to do it herself. She'd passed through some villages out on the moor with post offices and stores. All she needed to do was make her way to the nearest one. It would be that unearthly cold she'd come to expect out here, and the terrain had looked decidedly inhospitable, but if she could do Goodwood in three-inch heels for an entire day, she could certainly manage a brisk walk. Charlotte had been out on many a shoot, enduring hours of trouping around moorland watching men blazing away at various birds and attempting to look impressed by their heroics.

She had to risk it. After all, if this worked, if she broke the story, all that she'd sacrificed for so long would finally have been worthwhile. It might be a challenging journey over the moors, but it was difficult to ignore opportunity when she'd got holes in her shoes.

Mrs Thornycroft, however, did not share her enthusiasm for the journey. Charlotte passed her room on her way to bed and knocked at the door.

When the housekeeper answered, her face looked as predictably bleak as the moors.

"Mrs Thornycroft, I was considering a walk tomorrow morning. Could you tell me where the nearest village is?"

The old woman's face gathered into a frown. "That'll be Widecombe."

"Good, and I am assuming they have a general store, a church, that sort of thing. Perhaps a post office. My editor requires the occasional telegram to update him."

"Yes?" A question was rising in her voice.

"On the ravens." Charlotte smiled agreeably. "Well, I think I will make a journey there early tomorrow, if someone could supply me with a map. Just something basic and perhaps –"

"You'll either freeze or fall in the mire." Mrs Thornycroft delivered her heartwarming verdict in a suitably flat voice. "Where rushes grow, ponies fear to go."

Charlotte paused. "I'm sure I shall be fine."

The woman blew out her contempt. "All those who don't come back say that on their way out the door. Let me tell you, young miss, when you hear a voice calling to you from out of the mist, ignore it. Even if it is a young child."

Charlotte frowned.

"Under no circumstances follow that voice. It's the Devil alright, luring you into the mire." This deathly serious woman looked at her without a trace of irony. "If you see a woman sitting on a tor, that'll be Vixiana. A witch. She'll send down a thick mist and shout out to you, "follow my voice." Don't! She'll lure you into the featherbed as well."

Charlotte looked confused.

"Dartmoor bogs." She paused. "The mire."

"Tell me," Charlotte began, "is there any way of ensuring that one isn't lured into a mire?"

"Aye."

Charlotte waited expectantly.

"Don't go." The old woman turned and retreated into her room, closing the door without another word.

Charlotte paused, unsure of what she'd just heard and the intentions behind it. This was a woman who ran a large household and was responsible for many members of staff. She was a sensible, grounded woman, organised and meticulous in ensuring the smooth running of the house. And yet here she was expounding superstition as if it was the latest front-page news. Her unwavering belief was astonishing. It was an unshakeable truth to this woman, however strange and fantastic it seemed to outsiders.

As Charlotte walked away towards the stairs, Celeste quickly slipped around the corner out of the shadows. It had the feeling of an ambush.

Charlotte glanced back at the housekeeper's door. "You shouldn't be down here," she whispered. She knew the rules better than anyone, and to be found in the servants' halls after hours would definitely invoke some form of punishment for the girl.

"I must speak to you!" There was that same wide excitement of youth in her eyes. She grabbed Charlotte's arm and pulled her into the small boot room. "Don't try and go out over Dartmoor on your own."

"Were you listening in, Celeste?"

The girl looked pleased. "I told you I like to observe. I assume you're enjoying the fruits of my labour. Have you read much?"

"Some of it." Charlotte looked anxiously towards the door. She thought of the cruel image of Nanny hanging from a tree that Celeste had taken great pains to draw.

Celeste scowled. "Dartmoor is a wicked place."

"I'm a little old for –"

"For what? Death? I doubt that, Miss Blood. Not everyone has your best interests at heart."

"What's that supposed to mean?"

"Everyone knows why you're here."

"Do they indeed?" Charlotte didn't add, *because I certainly don't know anymore.*

"Surely you of all people have read what Sir Arthur Conan Doyle says about Dartmoor. We are only two miles from Hound Tor itself."

Charlotte smiled. "It's just a book. It's fiction, Celeste. There are no great phosphorescent hounds out in the dark, just as there is very little chance of a genius in a deerstalker hiding out on the rocks or a curse that will take the Ravenswick family to its grave."

Charlotte immediately wished she hadn't said the last part. "I'm sorry."

"There's no time for that. You are in danger and you must not cross that moor. Old Thornycroft is right. The stone cairns and rings are full of evil magick. I know they are. I've seen Bligh going out there in his robes."

"Look, I've no time for all this superstitious nonsense. Witches, evil magick and devilry, it's just not for me."

"Not for you? I know the Devil came down to

Widecombe Church and seized a boy who'd fallen asleep at congregation!" The girl folded her arms defiantly. "Wouldn't catch me going to Widecombe this side of never."

Charlotte laughed. "And who told you this? Nanny? To make sure you stay awake in church?"

"I don't listen to anything that old goat says. Probably in league with the Devil herself. I know there's things go on out there on the moors. I've *seen* them. I've seen the light from the torch. Bligh goes out there all the time."

This was more intriguing to Charlotte. More salacious perhaps for the readers. They'd lap up a tale of legend laced with modern deceit and strange practices. She could see the headlines: *Devilry and Dark Magick at the Abbey of Death.*

"Goes out there communing with the witches, I bet."

"I see."

"It's where they perform their rites, up by the stone circle, the old cairn."

"Do they indeed."

"And –" the girl leaned closer "– some say when the sky is moonless, he summons up old Lady Howard and she rides out in her carriage made of the bones of her four husbands, a skull on each corner and her whisht hound seated beside her."

Charlotte nodded. "I shall be sure to avoid any carriages made of bones, and all hounds, glowing or otherwise."

"You can laugh all you like but something goes on out there, I know it. Bligh knows it!"

"Well, I'm sure Mr Bligh knows a great many things that I do not."

"He knows why you're here, that's for sure."

There was a pause.

"To report on the ravens," Charlotte said flatly.

Celeste giggled. "We both know that's not true, don't we Miss Blood? And that's definitely not why I asked you here." She had a cruel look of conspiracy on her face, and it began to occur to Charlotte that this girl might not be someone to yoke herself to entirely.

"It would seem some people have other motivations for keeping me here."

The girl looked bewildered.

"There are perhaps more agendas at work here. But I must go to bed, Celeste, and I suspect you should have done so yourself some hours ago."

Celeste was stung. The role of the child in this family sat so uncomfortably on the spiteful young girl.

"I only meant…"

"I know exactly what you meant, Miss Blood. But you'll find I'm much smarter than you think I am. Just you wait till you read my ending! You'll see." The girl then stuck out her fat tongue and ran down the corridor, her heavy brogues tripping on the uneven flag stones.

Charlotte stood alone in the dingy corridor. It was important not to lose her allies. She would have to work hard at soothing the girl tomorrow. But, for now, she needed sleep if she was to do battle with the Devil, his witches, and noble women who rode around in carriages of bone.

34

The next morning, she couldn't face another round of tea and judgement in the servants' hall. Instead, Charlotte spent an extra hour in the warmth of her bed watching the droplets of condensation travel down the window as she formulated a plan. She looked out the window at the frosted day glistening back at her. What to say to Fulman? She made a few scribbled notes. No extraneous detail was necessary. She would organise a time for a longer call if she could find a suitable telephone. For now, all she needed Fulman to know was the basics. "Mind-blowing news!" No, that sounded too frivolous and gossipy. "Stop the press!" Perhaps not.

She scrawled down a few details of what she needed to include. The walk would hopefully clarify the rest. "News from Ravenswick! Just too exciting! Discovery of valuable books. Possible motive for murder. An affair. Arguments over money. A diary." She thought for a moment. "Blood." She looked at the note then added, "Charlotte," paused and wrote, "journalist," in case he was in any doubt.

Yes, that would do very nicely. She was getting good at this undercover reporter role.

Charlotte leaned back against the pillow and admired her work before crossing out a few unnecessary, expensive words. It would definitely pique Fulman's interest. She could see the presses rolling out, readers' faces captivated, checking to see the name of this daring news reporter who'd broken the story. She smiled and threw back the covers.

Down in the kitchens there was a dull murmur of post breakfast routine. A pause before the next round of chores and duties. The sour odour of hard-working bodies had already settled in for the day.

She passed through hurriedly. In the corridor, two maids were busy with their daily trawl through secret gossip gleaned from upstairs. They stopped to watch her pass by, their eyes distrustful. She smiled and one of them merely cocked her head to the side insolently.

Charlotte had no time for pleasantries anyway, not this morning. She had to get to that village. At the post office she could also enquire as to the use of the telephone. It was all falling into place. She just had to get over the moor.

She had heard the stories, of course. She'd read the book. Who hadn't? *The Hound of the Baskervilles*. Mrs C loved a good Sherlock story. Although, as with all the books she read, she annotated them with her own suggestions.

"He needs a love interest," Mrs C had decided. "And a dog. All great detectives should have a dog." She made a note on a slip of paper. *Would be better with a pet.* She paused with the pencil poised on her bottom lip before writing. *And a woman.* Mrs C sat back and admired her work, then popped the note along with her fully edited version of *The Case-Book of Sherlock Holmes* into an envelope addressed to the publishers. It was just something Mrs C did with many of the old detective novels she'd read. She never received a response.

Charlotte was sure there were no ghostly hounds out there on Dartmoor, but there could be worse terrors – animals, mires and even possible murderers, although Ravenswick Abbey seemed the more likely location for the latter.

First of all though, there was a more imminent adversary to overcome. Heskins had positioned himself next to the door and adopted a pose that was very much a statement.

"If you'll excuse me, Mr Heskins, I'm off for a jolly good walk." She tried to look nonchalant.

"Mrs Thornycroft was good enough to inform me of your intentions. I'm afraid I cannot permit you to go out there on your own, Miss Blood." His voice was stripped clean of emotion. "It's dangerous and without a guide you will lose the path," he added.

"I'm quite capable of looking after myself, thank you very much. I was raised in the countryside, and I have lived under Mrs C's roof for many years. So I know all about stoicism." She gave him a firm look.

Uncertainty flickered across his face, whether from being challenged or from this slightly odd insight into her life, wasn't clear. Charlotte continued to put on her hat and gloves with an obvious determination. She slung the satchel over her head and shifted the strap across her body with a sense of finality.

"If you'll excuse me –"

"A woman such as yourself should not be on her own."

"But I am. So, there we are."

"You don't know the way, Miss Blood." He gave

her space to realise he was correct. "Young Meadows is a moors lad and knows the route. *Widecombe* –" he emphasised the word. He knew where she was going and possibly, therefore, even why "– is perhaps a two hour's walk on a fine day. There's rain coming and the mist is falling. Many a stronger man than you, Miss Blood, has been caught out there on the moors and perished."

Her face flushed. "Mr Heskins, if your intention was to deter me with such a statement, I can categorically say that you have failed. I do not require anyone to accompany me, least of all a *young boy*. I shall be perfectly fine. I promised my publication regular updates as to my progress with the ravens. They have heard nothing so far. I must think of my readers."

"Miss, there are the house telephones…"

"I am fully aware of that, Mr Heskins and that is why I am going to the nearest village. I would prefer my readers to hear the news from me first."

She pulled her glove down firmly and headed for the door.

"At least permit me to assist with directions."

She stopped.

"You will need to know *where* you are going, at least, won't you Miss?"

Charlotte had to admit it was probably a good idea. "I do have quite a natural sense of direction," she said. "But a map might be of assistance."

Heskins looked sceptical and was already pulling out a piece of paper and a pencil from inside his jacket. He leaned on the nearest shelf and drew silently.

Charlotte waited awkwardly at the front door.

Finally, he held out the paper expectantly. She stepped

closer reluctantly looking at where he was indicating. It was a fairly detailed drawing of the surrounding moors, complete with tors and various landmarks clearly marked. She had to admit it would be very useful.

"Do not take this road." He placed the pencil on an area of the map near where he had marked Widecombe. "It is perilous in this weather. This is the route you need." He drew along with a steady hand. "Follow this road up and through the old quarry. Do not go near the ponds that have formed there. They are from the abandoned tin working and very dangerous. Some are bottomless. Stay on the path over past the ancient hut circles, then turn right. You will soon see an old granite cross. There are many out there. They were to help the monks navigate across the moor from abbey to abbey. To guide them. The land rises here into Bonehill Rocks. Keep that to your right." He paused and looked at her, his pearl-grey eyes unwavering. "Avoid the mire, Miss Blood, over here to the right of the rocks. That'll easily swallow a man on horseback whole. Be sure to turn left. And stick to the path." He folded the map and handed it to her. But he did not let go immediately as she reached for it. He stared into her eyes intently. "If you feel the journey back is too arduous, stay in Widecombe. There is a telephone at the Post Office. Someone will be sent to collect you."

They both paused holding the map between them for a moment before he stiffened and let go.

"Thank you for your concern, Mr Heskins."

She walked towards the door, putting the map in her pocket.

Heskins called to her. "Would you like me to request some –"

The door slammed.

"– tea?"

The air was frigid. An insipid light darkened with the threat of rain. Somewhere in the distance, the sky let out a single groan. Charlotte pulled up her collar and shoved her hands deep into the pockets. The rising winter sun was no more than a listless, white outline struggling behind the thick layer of grey cloud.

At the end of the long gravel drive she stopped to look into the hard face of the moor. She felt the cold grip her bones. The wind stalked towards her over the barren landscape of granite and gorse. It ripped through the frost-blackened skeletons of ferns and bracken. It's just cold, that's all, she told herself. She'd known enough of that. But as she stood in front of that desolate landscape rolling out endlessly, she couldn't help but hear Mrs Thornycroft's warnings ringing in her head.

Charlotte looked back towards the house, with its lights lingering in the mist, it drifted there in its own world.

She had to keep moving. It wasn't that far, and she had the map.

Charlotte lifted her shoulders and set off.

The road stretched out, tunnelling into the grim distance.

She'd felt so determined last night, in spite of all their superstitious tales of devilry designed to scare her. But now, as that desolate moor opened out in front of her, and she saw the grey shapes of tors rising cathedral high through the hidden mist, all those warnings didn't seem quite so fanciful.

Charlotte used to love the scary places most of all. When she was young, she was forbidden from going down to Pisky Cove on her own. So that's exactly what she did whenever she could slip from under the watchful gaze of the household. They told her all manner of strange stories to frighten her away. Those treacherous shores hid creatures that would drag her into the murky depths. Spirits were gliding under the surface of the green water ready to ensnare her. What they really meant was that the footmen up at the house could see her swimming.

People were the only threat Charlotte could ever conceive of. Not monsters, ghouls and spirits. They were the fictional beings that lived in the pages of her books. The controlling beasts that stalked her childish world were very much human. The wrath of her father, the disapproval of her mother, the carelessness of siblings, and coldness of those paid to look after her, they were the thing to dread.

After her family, Charlotte thought nothing would ever be frightening again. But as she set out onto that moorland on her own, she had to admit to just a little trepidation. Not fear though. Never that.

She held the satchel tight, her fingers tracing through the grooves of their initials.

The road ahead drew out to an invisible point. An ominous sky was sitting heavily over the land now as though it could crush everything if it just lowered a few more feet. She'd have to be quick to make it to the village and back before the weather drew in. She pushed on with renewed purpose and tried to clear her mind of all those terrifying stories, real and unreal.

As she turned from the main path onto the smaller one, it felt like a bold move. She checked the map again. It was disorientating out here with very few features and those that there were seemed interchangeable. There was very little difference between one giant tor and another, at least not to Charlotte's eyes. At the house, they had been very clear in their warning to stick to the path. She had no problem with that logic. It was just which path.

"Where rushes grow, ponies fear to go," Mrs Thornycroft had warned. The mires. A constant source of peril. They were at least a real and recorded occurrence rather than witches on high tors and tales of pixies and demons.

A dry-stone wall followed alongside the path beside her. Drifts of yellow gorse lined the hills. Ahead, just visible over the descending mist, were the rocks she was aiming towards. Bonehill, Heskins had called it. A suitably disturbing title.

An uncomfortable layer of winter damp had already settled between her skin and the thin clothes. She'd hoped the walk would have lifted her pulse by now but the rough wind came incessantly across the open wilderness. The air was heavy with the peaty smell of wet soil, rich and acidic.

She pushed on, keeping herself distracted by turning over the words she would send to Fulman. They had to enthral him. Grab him by his jowls and set his eyes wide enough to see her name all over that front page. *The Secrets of Ravenswick Abbey – full story inside*. She smiled to herself, and the thought drove her on with renewed purpose.

Charlotte's little heels dodged between the granite boulders, skipping past patches of dense scrub. White skeins of mist were settling. The constant drizzle growing heavier.

Her legs were frozen now and ached with the cold. Her face burned.

The path dipped down into a gulley and past a high thicket. A few trees twisted their way up through the severe thorns. Wind ravened around their stripped black branches.

Charlotte lowered her head and continued.

Gorse constantly snagged at her stockings. As she neared the top of the slope, the fog gathered, closing in around the path. Visibility was dying, the cold brume clinging to her.

Her shoes were damp and claggy from the mud. And out of the grey air came a single dark figure. Charlotte squinted against the constant fine rain. She could just make out an outline, a shape cut from the air, standing there beside the path. A gnarled old stone cross, weathered and disfigured by time. Lichen grew along its rough creases. It was becoming easier to see how so many tales of ghosts and phantoms stalked this land. Heskins had said the crosses were used to guide the monks. If those poor, pious souls could do this without giving in to discomfort or the incessant bad weather, so could she.

When she reached a stone circle, Charlotte was grateful for the bare, cold stone to sit on. The boulders were half-buried now by the scrub and crusted over with moss and lichen.

Charlotte's eyes travelled around the circle. Each stone marked out the small area, distinct from the rest of the moor.

The light was waning and she felt no closer to Widecombe, even though it seemed like she was a lot further away from Ravenswick Abbey than might be wise in this weather. She took out the map and found the stone circle. Marked nearby was a short pathway off to the left. Bonehill Rocks lay just ahead.

The wind drove more layers of fog towards her, spreading in thick cobwebs down the slopes. And there below in the valley, just peeking above, was the tower of a church.

"Widecombe," she breathed.

There was a faint whispering around the circle as the wind picked its way through the grass and ancient stones.

She shoved the map back in her pocket. She must be near now.

But, whether it was close or not, Charlotte was not going to reach Widecombe today.

35

The ground was growing thicker as she headed into the lower, damper area. The air had an overripe, mouldering edge of decay to it.

It didn't take long for the path to peter out. She was sliding through swathes of wet mud, the ground waterlogged from the constant rain. Her shoes were sticking in the soil. Charlotte had to drag her feet now with every step.

The air smelt foul, the mist meandering in thick clouds low over the ground. Charlotte could barely see more than a few feet.

Ahead, there was a shape, caught in the mud. She paused, her feet tentative in the puddling earth. In the centre of what had been the path was a wide pool of black sludge. Rising up from the soil were the bleached bones of a small horse, perhaps a pony, its skeleton embedded in the ground, half shrouded in mist.

Charlotte paused in quiet horror.

Mrs Thornycroft's words rolled out through her head, one after the other. "Where rushes fear to grow, ponies fear to go."

She moved to go round the pitiful beast. Her body leaned but her feet did not follow.

The black mud had climbed over her shoes and reached

up higher than her ankles. When she shifted again, her legs slipped a few inches deeper. Charlotte felt nothing beneath her thin soles. She was floating. No, she was sinking.

Twisting her body around, left, then right, the slightest movement seemed to pull her further down. It was over her knees.

She jerked her whole leg from the hip. The opposite leg sank and fell deeper.

The mire.

She looked over at the remains of the stricken animal, the black holes of its eyes staring back blankly.

"Damn this!" Charlotte writhed, twisting and jerking, each movement sending her lower. Her first thought was to throw the bag with the file and the diary clear of the swampy earth. It landed on dry stones only a few feet away from her.

That stench of putrid soil rose up. A thick sucking noise puttered alongside her quick breaths.

"Anyone! Please!" she shouted.

The drag down was heavier than anything she'd felt before, soft muddied water, gripping tight around her ankles and pulling.

The black silhouette of a large bird soared above. It circled once then glided away back towards Ravenswick with a distant call echoing behind. It couldn't have been one of the house's ravens, but there were wild ones out here, Jeffers had told her about them. An image of that sorry raven, with birds pulling on its legs, ran across the surface of her mind. Charlotte quickly banished it.

Her body dropped a little lower, the ground tightening around her.

"God! Anyone!"

Archie's face drifted into her head.

He'd never have come here. He had a morbid fear of mud. After he came back, they never went on the woods walk again. Part of that was his breathless lungs. But the mud, the thick, cloying feel of the earth beneath his boots, was too much.

It was a desperate sensation. There was an inevitability to the draw of it on her legs, circling her waist and pressing tight.

She had to find some calm. It was only mud. She was not far from the house. It was only up to her...

Chest.

The crushing sense of the earth swallowing her was overwhelming. It pushed down into her ribcage, into her spine, threatening to shove both up against each other. The mist meandered in and out between her and the ivory horse bones. Charlotte was almost on the same level as the calcified remains now. There was a desperate, spent nature to the way those bones had settled. Exhausted, the beast had lain down in surrender.

She screamed into the mist. The tears burning in her eyes, the sides of her mouth cracking.

Her voice echoed off the hills.

"Hello?"

Someone was out here.

Her breath was rapid, sticking in her throat. Her blood hammering in her ears. "Help! Hello? I'm here." Her voice was too weak.

"Hello!" The answer came out of the fog.

She *had* been heard.

"I'm here! I'm in the mire! Please, help."

A jolt of panic went through her, and she began

squirming and turning which only led to her sinking lower. She felt the cold mud tighten all around her and pull down further.

"Dear God! Please, come. I'm sinking. I'm…"

"I'm here!" the voice appeared through the mist. Bartram stood there holding out his hands. "Stay as still as you can, Miss Blood."

He flung down a thick coil of rope from off his shoulder.

"Please." The tears rolled down her cheeks unchecked. She couldn't move her arms, couldn't feel her fingers. "Please help me. I'm…" she panted out the words.

"Alright. It's all going to be alright, Miss Blood. I'm going to get you out." He started to turn.

"No! No, don't go."

"It's alright. I'm not going. I need to find a rock. A boulder to tie this around."

He picked up the frayed end of the rope and wrapped one end around a stone. Then passed the other around his own waist.

She screamed as her legs were pulled down harder.

"Miss Blood, I'm going to need you to stay as calm as you can and not move." He spoke softly in the same voice she'd heard him use with the birds.

"Calm? I'm drowning!"

"Well, technically it's not drowning. It will suffocate you. The peat, you see." He finished tying the rope around himself with one hard tug then dropped to the ground and lay down. "I need you to grab my hand, Miss Blood."

"That's it?" Her mouth hung open. "A rope and a hand?"

"What were you expecting, a Rolls Royce and a cocktail? Take a hold."

"I can't... I can't get my... my hand is stuck."

He frowned. "You're going to have to try, Miss Blood."

"I am trying!" She closed her eyes tight and sensed the mud dragging her hand back down. "Please!" She felt the thick matter filter through her fingers as she lifted her hand up through it. It surfaced, with pink patches of skin visible through the soil.

"That's it!" he called, and shuffled on his belly further towards her holding his arms out.

She lunged for his outstretched hand and missed. As she did, she sank another few inches. "This is a hideous place!" The panic rose in her voice.

He held up both hands and spread his fingers in a calming gesture. "Don't fret. We'll have you out. Happened to a pony only recent."

She glanced over at the crippled skeleton. "Not that one, I hope."

He didn't respond.

"Now then. You grab my hands this time, Miss." He set them out on the surface. "Come on, Miss. No time left."

Her eyes widened and she lifted herself as hard as she could, stretching her arm taut.

She missed again. He lowered his head in frustration.

As she fell back, the mire pulled down even harder and her chin touched the surface. A wash of fetid water slipped over her lip. The sudden flood of foul water in her mouth made the idea of her head being submerged a real and very imminent prospect. Charlotte spat and coughed. "Help me! Please." There was desperation now. "Please!" She was choking. The thick liquid fell over her lips again.

Thoughts surfaced of those men Archie had seen buried under the mud.

"Miss Blood. This time. We do it. Come on!" he barked the command at her. There was a new ferocity in his eyes. "When I shout grab, you do it. You understand?"

A tear traced through the crease at the side of her eye and onto the surface of the mud. It was instantly lost. She tried to control her fast breath.

And then she quietly slipped under the mud completely. There was silence.

Her hand was the last part of her to sink below the surface.

Seconds passed, and Bartram lay across the mud, his eyes wide in disbelief, searching. His face collapsed in resignation.

In one explosion, she reared up like a frightened horse. A mouth retching out of the murk, her arms flung out to him, white searing eyes peering through the caked mud. She pushed forward and caught hold of his hands.

The ferocious concentration never left his eyes. He gripped Charlotte with brutal hands. And dragged. The tendons on either side of his neck stood proud as bone.

She was dragged from the mire, inch by inch, moment by moment, unfurling in a ghastly shape, thick with filth, the leaden weight of her, soaked with earth. The rope cut deep into Bartram's stomach and back.

Her hair was plastered down to her skull, her ears filled. She gasped for air.

"Pull, girl. Now!" His voice broke with the strain.

She slithered up over the surface. The hole left behind by her body in the mire closed over behind her like a wound.

He dragged her in jolts, rocking back and forth. Her head was to the side, slaring in the dirt and, in one final lurch, he flung her onto the harder earth beside him.

They lay spent on the ground. The only sign they were alive, the heavy sound of their breath.

Slowly, he untied the rope from himself. It had ground deep into his stomach. He spun over onto his back and his head lolled over to the side to look at Charlotte.

She didn't move, lying in a confusion of dank clothes and mud, her face slick with earth and hair. She made no effort to wipe it back.

"Thank you," she coughed.

The satchel. Her eyes darted round the rocks. Bartram followed the line of her vision.

"What?

"My bag!"

"Safe." He pointed to an area of stones nearby. "That was a close one, that."

She paused before nodding. "Yes."

"Mire's no place for sightseeing."

"No." She pushed herself up onto her elbows.

"Should stick to the path, Miss."

"I did."

He glanced over. "Beg your pardon, Miss." He leaned back and reached into his pocket, his breath still labouring. "You better…"

He held out a scrunched-up handkerchief.

She gave him a bewildered look.

"Your…" he motioned round his own face. "There's a little…"

"What?

"Mud."

"Oh." Her fingers quickly explored her cheeks and forehead, coming away with thick clods of black earth.

"It's clean." He held out the small, puckered

handkerchief with streaks of browned blood on it. "Well, it was this morning. That's just from the birds."

Charlotte gingerly took the handkerchief.

"I did stick to the path," she insisted. "Mr Heskins told me the route. The direct route to Widecombe."

"There's a road straight there."

"Well, some are too perilous this time of year."

"Not as perilous as a mire."

She didn't answer that.

"You've not listened right then, Miss. Old Heskins has been walking these moors before even the piskies was 'ere. He knows every step."

She felt in her pocket for the scrap of paper. When she pulled it out, all that remained was a soggy, limp blank. There were a few markings but none that were sensible anymore.

"Hard to remember every turn, it's not your fault, Miss."

But she knew Heskins had not marked the mire here on his map. His words rang in her head again. "Turn left." Left into the mire.

36

It was an arduous journey to Bartram's cottage. Her clothes were heavy, dragging her down. Her shoes filled with silt and debris, clinging like a wet vice to her feet. Every step was an exhausting effort.

It was very easy to disappear under the moor.

Bartram's home was meek against its landscape. Nestled beneath an outcrop of a granite tor, it looked so insignificant but she was grateful to see the solitary line of smoke curling up from the chimney.

Two small ponies wandered near the wall.

"Yours?" she breathed.

"No, they're wild. Live out here. Let's get you inside. Fire's on."

She wondered how any creature could be native to this place. It would take a certain kind of mind to exist in this isolation. A certain desire to be alone.

The house was sparsely furnished but with splashes of unexpected delicacy. A vase of small marsh flowers. A painting of the moor.

"Are you alone out here?"

The single chair at the table was answer enough.

He glanced at her. "Aye."

Charlotte's face flushed and she was glad of the muddy

layer that was hardening now. She had intruded on his private world and that was clearly something he was uncomfortable with.

The fire was healthy and smelt of the strong, acidic peat he was burning. It blended the house into the moor, blurring the border between them. He hadn't set himself up in opposition to this land, he was part of it.

"You'll need to wash and change, Miss." He didn't look at her.

"I..."

"My wife's clothes are still in the cupboard."

That one word – "still" – didn't need any further explanation for Charlotte. Archie's things had been "still" everywhere for a long time. "Still" in the wardrobe. "Still" in the coat cupboard. His cigarette "still" in the ashtray and his smell "still" on the pillow. Everything was still.

She nodded and went into the room he motioned towards.

"There's water in the jug. Boiled it an hour ago. Might be warm. There's a towel below." He closed over the door.

It was a room Charlotte was instantly familiar with. One side of the bed immaculate and untouched. A photograph on one of the bedside tables.

Inside the wardrobe, the dresses were hung neatly. Some hangers were empty now. Shoes were lined up with a thin layer of dust on the leather. Charlotte took down a plain, black wool smock and small particles of dust floated out from it.

The water jug was over by the dressing table on a stand. She carefully stepped out of her clothes, trying to avoid letting too much mess fall. It was unavoidable and heavy lumps of earth littered the wooden floor. When she touched the ewer, her hand left a smear of dirt. It was painful how much she was invading his quiet world.

She washed quickly, desperately trying not to soil the small towel too much. It was all so personal. Even her once pink chemise was filthy and clung to her muddied body. She peeled it back, before glancing to the door. This was a room that had grown unused to a woman undressing.

There was a mirror above the dressing table and she caught sight of herself. Dirty, a mess. Her hair lank. Bones clear now down her back. She hadn't been taking care of herself.

She held her hands to her head, closing her eyes and drawing back her filthy hair. Charlotte looked back at the reflection. "Now what? What would you think of me now?"

She wrapped the small towel around herself and rummaged in her satchel. There were a few essentials she always travelled with just in case she lost everything in a moment.

She called it her Emergency Blood kit. Comb, tissues, soap, cologne, toothbrush, small face flannel, chemise, cami and slip, lipstick, powder, latest detective novel. Any man who happened to glance down into her bag often got the wrong idea about the kind of woman Charlotte was.

She tried to clean the floor a little, but it made no difference.

There was a knock.

"Miss Blood?" He sounded hesitant. "Would you like some tea?"

"Yes. Yes, please."

He paused. "Don't concern yourself about the mud. I'm used to it. Just... if you –" he cleared his throat. "If you pass out the clothes, I'll hang them by the fire. It'll dry the mud so you can take them back."

She opened the door and saw his thoughts pause as she stood in the dress he'd only seen on a hanger for a while now. He didn't say anything.

He handed her a mug of steaming tea and she sat by the fire.

The dirty water dripped from the points of her hair.

"What you doing out here, Miss?" He settled into a chair.

"You can call me Charlotte. I think we might have reached that point."

He gave a self-conscious laugh. "Alright, Charlotte." He didn't offer the same. He looked more like a surname kind of man.

"Why are you floundering around on the moors dressed in those London clothes with no idea?"

"I've got a lot of ideas!"

"I'm sure you have, but I meant what is an *ornithologist* doing out here?"

"Looking at birds."

He laughed. "Alright, Charlotte the ornithologist." He drank his tea and sat back in the chair.

"Aren't you lonely out here?" she asked abruptly.

He hesitated. "As lonely as anyone. Person can be just as lonely in a big city."

She looked down at the surface of her tea.

"Anyways, I got my birds. Don't need any more than them."

"They must mean a lot to you."

"They're my world now. More loyal than people, that's for sure."

She paused. "Depends which people."

"Most, in my experience."

"Trust is just a word." Her voice was thin. Unconvincing. She remembered searching his bag, his desk, rooting through Archie's belongings like a stranger. She didn't even know what she was looking for. Confirmation of the woman? What would that look like? A name? A photograph? Letters with their love spelled out in curling script? The stark telegram cut her down in her tracks.

B YOU WILL HAVE TO TELL HER SOON STOP SHE SAW YOU STOP SHE SUSPECTS = L

It had been sent to a hotel Charlotte didn't recognise two days after she'd seen him entering the woman's house.

Charlotte slumped down to the floor, her eyes fixed on the wall.

The steps on the stairs were heavy. His. She'd quickly pushed the telegram back in amongst his papers and pushed the bag away. She'd only just stood up as the door opened.

"Darling?" Archie gave her a puzzled look.

She cleared her throat. "Let's eat." Charlotte gripped her hands behind her back so he couldn't see how much they were shaking.

"Are you alright?"

"Perfectly." She made a sound like a half laugh as she watched him lift his eyes and shake his head in mock amusement.

"Come on then, you. I'm starving."

He turned and walked down the hall, the low light settling on his bent shoulders.

That was the moment Charlotte decided she had to confront the auburn-haired woman.

"Miss Blood?" Bartram's voice was quiet against the background of her thoughts.

She gave him a weak smile and took a long drink of tea, feeling its warmth reviving her.

"How well do you know Heskins?" Charlotte asked, running her finger around the rim of the mug and carefully avoiding his eyes.

His forehead bunched into a knot in the middle. "As well as I know any of them at the house."

"It's just... I was on my way to Widecombe. That's where I asked directions to."

"And Mr Heskins..."

"Told me to take that route."

37

Charlotte rested a little in the chair and watched Bartram pottering around doing various chores. It was calming to see a normal home being tended to, cups being washed, a plate put away. The minutiae of his daily existence was taking place regardless of the great house over the moor and its cabinet of curious people.

"Does anyone from the house ever visit here?"

He frowned. "Why would they?"

Charlotte shrugged. "I don't know. Maybe they would like to know where their staff live, at least. Check you're alright from time to time. Talk to you about the ravens, maybe."

Bartram laughed. "It's only the old Lord who likes them really, and he can't get out to them no more. Mr Charles was going to get rid of them the minute he took over." He stopped and let the smile fall. "They got no need to be coming out here. Only Bligh comes out on the moors."

"To visit you?" She knew very well that wasn't the reason.

Bartram paused and watched her as if deciding on something. "He goes digging, Miss Blood."

She frowned. "Digging?"

"Aye, like he's looking for something."

She looked confused. "Does the family know?"

He shook his head slowly. "I ain't getting involved in nothing to do with Mr Nicodemus Bligh. That's for the family to deal with."

Charlotte thought of Bligh's comment about digging for treasure. She'd assumed he meant in the library. *The Book of Kells* he'd said had spent time buried in the acidic bog soil. Was he alluding to the fact that, when horror was heading their way, the monks might have buried their treasured books out here on the moors, somewhere under that peaty soil of the mires? Had Bligh discovered something about the whereabouts of that precious book he was searching for?

"I got to go see to the birds. I'll be back later. You stay here. Rest." It was more a command than an invitation. "Your clothes will be dry then and I can take you back to the house. Weather's too rough to get any further."

Charlotte didn't question it. She'd taken enough chances.

The house and its hidden killer were safer than crossing this moor.

When he'd gone, there was only the sound of the rain pattering at the window. Charlotte was suddenly very aware of being alone with the disconcerting thought that someone in that house might have tried to send her to her death. Why would Heskins do that? She knew she could be rather testing sometimes, but killing her off seemed a bit extreme. Surely, they could just ask her to leave. That's what a weekend host would usually do with a difficult guest. So much easier and less complicated than murder. Maybe not everyone did want her to leave. Bligh seemed keen to use her for publicity for the book sales, and presumably that was in the best interests of the whole family. Celeste had even arranged to get her here to show Charlotte her very own book and be part of the solving of her uncle's death. It seemed there were more people who wanted her here than didn't. Perhaps she was seeing foul play and conspiracy where there was none. Perhaps Heskins had just made a mistake with his directions. Perhaps the gargoyle falling was an accident as well.

She took out Celeste's diary and ran her hand over the worn leather cover. It was a strange notebook for a young girl. There was no adornment, no flowers or animals. It was a serious book.

Inside was the same contradiction. Such solemn words disguised in that childish hand. The small drawings were immature, but their subject matter grave. She thought back to Celeste's last words to her: *Just you wait till you read my ending.*

Charlotte looked doubtfully at the book. It was breaking every rule to read the final chapter now, but time was not her friend out here and she was in danger of not making it to the finish at all if she didn't work quickly.

She turned to the final entry. New Year's Eve 1928.

Dull. Dull. Dull. Dull.

The girl's petulant voice instantly surfaced.

There was then another of her macabre little drawings with people shooting, stabbing and strangling one another. Charlotte assumed these represented various members of the family.

I've been reading the latest Lord Peter Wimsey and it's not bad. I could certainly do something much better, I'm sure. Maybe one day I will write a great novel and then Bligh can shove that in his library. I need to start my new diary. Only six hours to go! Must get a new one.

That mean old bugger Bligh just told me off for stealing. Stealing! How can I steal from my own home? It's not his. He's got hundreds of the bloody old things. I shall tell Granny immediately. She'll put him in his place.

Charlotte closed the book over for a moment and held her hand to the old worn leather cover that she'd thought so inappropriate for a child's diary. At least that explained why she had such a strange-looking book, but a much bigger question was germinating now. Bligh had hundreds of notebooks.

Charlotte carried on reading. She could hear the petulant clomping of the young girl's chunky shoes lifting up from the page.

Blast this place! Everyone is in such a foul mood. They're arguing again! Poor Granny. Always the same thing. Blast Bligh and his bloody books!

She'd drawn a picture of Bligh being blown up by a large cartoon bomb and the pages of his books fluttering all around him.

Worse news still! Mary says there's going to be a NYE party in the tower and I'm not invited! I'm too young apparently. So I get to sit here on my own to round off the year while everyone goes up for a big argument in the tower. I'm not sure which is worse! Maybe they'll all just kill each other and leave me everything! I shall see in the New Year, by myself with my diary. I am lonely.

She'd drawn a big clock with a heart at the centre that had a sad face and a single tear tracing down it. The hands were great big swords she'd stabbed down from the heart. For all her sullen spite, this was still a very young girl who was repeatedly pushed away by her family.

Five hours to go and lazy old Nanny has forgotten my cocoa again! It'll be in there going cold as usual. It's almost as if I don't exist at all here. I shall have to ring for it to be sent up. That's three nights in a row I've had to sort myself out and Mrs Thornycroft gets awfully cross whenever my bell goes off. She says that's Nanny's duty. If kitchen have made it, Nanny should see to me getting it. The maids shouldn't be disturbed by me. So, I have to trog down the hallway to fetch it myself from the hatch! It's just not acceptable.

Charlotte remembered the clashes between nursery and kitchen very well. Everyone had a function that must be clearly defined and stuck to. It often meant she fell through the gaps just as Celeste did.

She pictured the child, uninvited to the party and so desperately lonely that she was being pushed further into her world of vicious words.

Charlotte sat with the diary open on her lap. Celeste had waited a long time to find someone to entrust with this precious book. Charlotte disliked being used, particularly when it was by a child, but she too had her way in now and the doors were starting to open, even if it wasn't a particularly pretty sight behind them.

38

Bartram wasn't gone long and when he returned, he seemed keen to take Charlotte straight back to the Abbey. More bad weather was coming, he said.

They walked towards the main path, the one she had been diverted from, and back in the direction of the house.

Charlotte decided to make use of the opportunity. She had to start taking some risks if she was to get to the answer first.

"You were in the lift that night, weren't you?"

She saw him take a long breath and sigh.

"What was it like to…"

"You want to know what it was like hearing a gunshot in the pitch black, trapped in a lift? Then seeing a man dead on the floor, knowing one of those people had just murdered him?"

"Well, I can imagine –"

"Can you? Can you really, Miss Blood?"

She looked at him. "I'm sorry. Truly I am. It must have been –"

He stopped and turned to her. "Terrifying, that's what it was. They were all screaming and shouting. Standing round his body shouting. Mobbing, that's what they call it, what ravens do when one of 'em dies. Gathering around the dead, all aggressive."

A tortured look entered his face.

"I'm so sorry, Mr Bartram. I really am. But wouldn't it be better if his death was solved?" She'd taken her chance and now she waited for the response.

He shook his head. "Police couldn't. How could anyone? We couldn't see a thing. It could have been any one of them. Court said there was no way of knowing. Now we all share the guilt."

It seemed like a very strange phrase to use but perhaps that was what he'd settled to, what they'd all accepted. Would it be worse to unearth one culprit now after all this time? Those words appeared in her head again, *for her own good*. But what *good* was she doing here opening up this wound?

"Mr Bartram, can I ask you one last thing?"

He waited and then, with a resigned look, nodded once.

"Why were you there that night?"

He didn't answer straight away but waited, assessing whether he should. When he spoke it was as if he was back there, on that day, not out here on the desolate moor of his home.

"I was told I was needed. There was some business with the will and Her Ladyship had gifts for some members of staff. It was Mr Heskins came out to tell me."

"Mr Heskins." She gave him a sceptical look.

"He's a good man. Been here decades. He's devoted to them. Very loyal, he is. He'd do anything for the family, he would."

"Even –"

Bartram held up a hand and shook his head. There were clearly boundaries he would not pass.

"I'd just fed the birds their dinner. I'd been cleaning up and was about to go home. Mr Heskins appeared, came walking over and told me to go straight to the house. Be at the lift for seven. He was going over to fetch old Jeffers. He'd been off shooting rabbits."

She frowned.

"For the ravens, Miss Blood."

"Yes, of course."

"You saw how much they like them."

"Yes, Mr Bartram, I'm aware of their dietary requirements. I'm an ornithologist, remember."

He smiled. "Who happens to have an interest in murder."

She nodded. "That's right, Mr Bartram. Who happens to have an interest in murder. I like that. Perhaps I'll use it in my by-line. Now, if you don't mind, I should be getting back to the house. I'm sure they're missing me enormously."

***

They paused at the aviary where Bartram said goodbye to her. "You going to be alright, Miss Blood?"

She nodded. "Bit of mud never hurt a girl. It's actually quite good for the skin, I'm told."

He turned the corners of his mouth down and shrugged. "I wouldn't really know, Miss."

"No," she said slowly. "Perhaps not."

His face fell.

"Sorry, I mean…"

"Time to go, Miss Blood."

"Yes, quite right."

"I think you know your way back to the house now. Don't think you can get in too much trouble from here."

She nodded. "Thank you, Mr Bartram. For the whole life-saving thing. That was very... helpful. Very helpful indeed."

"Glad to be of service. And next time, remember to stick to the path, Red Riding Hood."

"Oh, don't worry, Mr Bartram, I'm not afraid of the big bad wolf."

"Well, I'm glad to hear it, Miss Blood. And by the way."

"Yes?"

"If I don't see you again before tomorrow, happy New Year."

She looked momentarily confused. "It's New Year's Eve?"

He nodded.

"I'd lost track of the days."

"Easy done out here."

Charlotte looked up into the heavy, enclosed sky and the rain started again. This was a strange capsule of a world. She was losing her bearings.

As she walked away, she heard the voice of the raven behind her repeating her words, "Big bad wolf."

39

If they were missing her back at the house, they were doing a very good job of disguising that. When Charlotte returned, there was only a lone figure silhouetted in an upstairs window, the outline short enough for it to be obvious who was watching her return.

Celeste didn't wave or make any acknowledgement. She just waited, a dark outline against the gingery light.

In the servants' area, it was a different matter entirely. The first two footmen she encountered looked at each other and raised their eyebrows in amazement before laughing. It only occurred to her at that moment that she was standing there in another woman's dress, wearing no stockings and her hair hardened with mud. She smoothed her hand over her head and felt the hard, crisp edges around her face.

It was unfortunate that the next person she saw was Mrs Thornycroft.

"Miss Blood, I don't know what kind of standards are acceptable for *ornithologists* but I can tell you right now that this –" she drew back her head as if recoiling from Charlotte "– *shambles* is not appropriate for Ravenswick Abbey."

Charlotte lifted her shoulders. "Mrs Thornycroft, you may be unaware of the fact that we ornithologists are sometimes required to conduct field work."

The woman kept her keen eyes on Charlotte. "Whereabouts, Miss Blood, a pig farm? I was under the impression your profession involved the study of birds."

"You can find birds anywhere, Mrs Thornycroft." Charlotte looked at her defiantly and the housekeeper seemed suitably repelled. "All you need to do is look up."

Mrs Thornycroft's face turned rigid.

"Now, if you'll excuse me, I have a little grooming to attend to."

"Well, don't be late. They're expecting you upstairs, this evening." It was very clear which side of the baize door she thought Charlotte belonged. There was no ambiguity as far as she was concerned. Mrs Thornycroft was not an ambiguous kind of woman.

Charlotte looked bewildered.

"Mr Bligh wanted everyone assembled before he began."

"I'm afraid I don't..."

The housekeeper shook her head in disappointment. "The séance, Miss Blood. Your presence is required tonight."

The slow realisation spread. She knew very well no one had mentioned this to her. She would definitely have remembered that, given what happened to her at the first and only one she'd ever attended. If someone was meant to pass on the message that her attendance was required at this event, they certainly hadn't. Someone here had set Charlotte up to fall, or perhaps had assumed she'd never come back from her ill-fated trip to Widecombe.

"Thank you, Mrs Thornycroft. I presume someone will be sent to my room to escort me there at the relevant time." She'd attempted aloofness. That didn't meet with Mrs Thornycroft's approval either.

"You can get yourself to the library, young woman. We've got enough to be doing down here. Some of us *work* for a living." She turned on her heel and didn't wait for any further requests.

Charlotte hurried along the stone corridors, avoiding the shocked and disapproving glances from other servants as she passed. She'd have to brave the bathroom. When she arrived in her room, it seemed more of a sanctuary. She held the satchel close to her chest. Now what would Archie think of her, in borrowed clothes and covered in mud? She knew very well what he'd think, and it gave her even greater resolve.

He'd always made her brave. In the depths of her doubt, as her tide of suspicion was rising, she pictured his face entering that woman's house again and it spurred her on. It would be the only time she ever followed him. Charlotte went back, keeping a cautious distance between herself and the figure of her husband. Strangely though, somehow it didn't feel brave. It felt like she was the deceitful one, the one betraying their trust.

She watched him climb those steps to that house, the one she'd reimagined so many times that it had now become achingly familiar. The glossy black door opened and the face that had burned its way into her dreams was there, framed with that auburn hair. The woman was subtly different this time, more assured, less wary. Archie nodded and she stood aside opening the door fully.

Charlotte could see inside a little to where two, maybe three other people were seated in the hallway. No, that was the wrong word. It was more of a reception area. Archie entered and as the door began to close over, she saw the woman settling herself behind a large desk.

Charlotte stood alone on the street, looking at the closed black door. By the side of it was a brass plaque. Without a thought for who could see her, she walked towards the house until she could read the engraving.

Dr M R Shepherd

There was the usual string of letters after the name that all dissolved into a blur, each one stamped into the metal like a judgement on her. Charlotte studied it with a bemused look. How had she missed that the first time? She pictured the moment when she'd first seen him go in with that woman. Charlotte had just run, not stopping to look. If only she'd seen the plaque then, these days of heartache and turmoil would never have happened. She'd been so busy looking at the woman, too caught up in creating a whole guilty picture around those seconds. How could she have doubted Archie so easily based on just one moment? Charlotte looked across the road to where she had stood before, with all those new and terrible thoughts about her husband pounding in her head. She wanted to go over there and point to that obvious brass name board, shining out into the street.

Charlotte didn't run that day. She walked home slowly in a fog of confusion and self-doubt, occasionally shaking her head and whispering, "How could I have got it so wrong?" "Why didn't I look?" He'd told her he visited a doctor about his cough. That was no secret. And yet, it had only taken a beautiful face to blind her reason so easily. Charlotte vowed to herself that day that she would never question him again. But sometimes she had to remind herself of that vow, when the candle of doubt would flicker in her darkest moments, and she'd think of that telegram again. She even looked for it once, but it was gone, and how could she ask him now?

Charlotte remembered how she'd sunk into the bath when she'd got home to Mecklenburgh Square that day. It wasn't doubt that she felt then. It was relief travelling through all of her with the warmth of the water. She'd looked at those painted Chinese birds that lined the bathroom and imagined floating in the air, flying alongside them.

She sat in the cold bath now at Ravenswick Abbey, surrounded by that hospital-white tiled room, and looked down at the dirty, brown water.

She needed to act quickly before the hideous séance. There was still time to research the loyalties of the man who had almost sent her to that filthy, muddy death. And if there was one thing Charlotte never wanted to do, it was to die dirty.

Afterwards, in her room, she immediately opened the folder. Heskins' testimony to the court had been delivered in a suitably military style.

The inquest heard evidence of the initial moments. Charlotte read quickly over the preamble. It was identical to everyone else's evidence in most respects. He'd been tasked with quickly gathering the staff. He went to fetch Bartram, then Jeffers and Bligh.

When they arrived at the lift, the family were all assembled. They entered and not long after they had started to ascend, the lift stopped and the lights failed. All was simple and clean in his telling up to that point. Word perfect, one might say.

Coroner:	*Can you tell the court what happened next?*
Heskins:	*Yes, sir. There was a gunshot.*
Coroner:	*How did you know that's what it was?*
Heskins:	*I served, sir.*

Coroner: *I see. And what happened next?*

Heskins: *Well, sir. I heard a small thud, followed by a very large thump that sounded like something heavy had hit the ground. Some of the ladies were distressed and there was a lot of shouting. The lights went on and Mr Charles was half slumped in the corner against the wall. There was a gun in the centre of the lift on the floor.*

Coroner: *Thank you. Can you tell the court what you did?*

Heskins: *Yes, sir. There was a lot of confusion and noise but I am... well, I have experienced that before. I went towards Mr Charles.*

Coroner: *How did he look?*

Heskins: *Sir, he wasn't moving. He was very pale and had the most terrible look on his face.*

Coroner: *Terrible look?*

Heskins: *Yes, sir. He seemed...*

Coroner: *Mr Heskins? Mr Heskins could you describe the look on Charles Ravenswick's face?*

Heskins: *Well, it was disbelief, really. Shock and...*

Coroner: *And?*

Heskins: *Sadness. Yes, I'd say sadness would be the best word, sir.*

Coroner: *I see. Was there any sign of life?*

Heskins: *No, sir.*

Coroner: *How can you be sure of that?*

Heskins: *I've seen a lot of dead men, sir.*

There was a pause here.

Coroner: *Of course. Forgive me, but the court needs as much detail as possible. What did you do?*

Heskins: *I searched for a pulse but there was nothing. His eyes were staring out. Not moving. I looked down his body and then I bent him over. There was blood on his shirt, sir. He'd been shot. I sat him back against the wall and then the lift started to move again. It didn't take us long to arrive upstairs. There was a lot of shouting and crying, especially from Lady Ravenswick. We got the door open as quickly as possible and telephoned for the doctor and Mrs Thornycroft. His Lordship was also in a great deal of distress.*

Coroner: *Did anyone telephone for the police?*

Heskins: *I think the doctor must have done so. He arrived very quickly. He lives out on Dartmoor not far away from the Abbey. He's been the family doctor for a very long time, sir.*

Coroner: *Thank you very much for assisting the court today, Mr Heskins.*

Charlotte looked up from the folder. It was already dark outside. There seemed so little gap provided for the day here. This was a house caught in perpetual gloom. The lights were always on, faltering and threatening to fail again. They seemed to live with the constant threat of being plunged into darkness without notice. It made for a very unsure world. They were on edge all the time, waiting in fear for another power cut, knowing what could happen in those lightless moments. Somebody had used that darkness to hide the worst of crimes. It hid a killer who was still here, waiting for the next moment when nobody could see.

40

Charlotte dressed quickly. The things she'd worn when she was dragged into the mire were still in the bag Bartram had given her, thick with dry mud, a reminder of how close she had come to disaster and how someone may well have intended that to be the outcome. She would take them down to the kitchens later when everyone had gone to bed and wash them herself. She looked at the dress Bartram had given her, she'd been careful to fold it neatly over the chair and would make sure he got it back tomorrow. But for tonight's engagement, it was too plain and old.

She'd brought the green silk cocktail dress with the beading. Mrs C had recently replaced all the broken beads and added some more to the neckline so it looked almost as good as new. She was well-practiced now in restoring Charlotte's old dresses so Nosferatu could still look the part for the necessary round of parties and bars, even if the role didn't even pay for the costumes. The pearls would do again. She carefully dotted the red lipstick on her lips. It had served her well but there was precious little left now. She hooked the strap of her satchel over her shoulder.

"Yes." She nodded into the mirror. "A perfect ornithologist off for a séance."

The halls were almost deserted and still barely lit. An occasional member of staff appeared along the edges as if they were forbidden from coming out too far into the room.

A séance. She'd sworn she'd never succumb to another one of these absurd charades.

There was so much desperation to connect with death these days. No one could leave it alone. Grief was on every corner.

When the charlatans first came knocking, keen to leech off Charlotte's loss, she sent them packing. But their promises glittered in the darkness of grief. Surely it couldn't hurt to give it a try. There might even be some answers to all the questions he'd left behind. It would be temporary, an interlude that would ease her mourning, sustain her. They wore her down. And as her family closed in, she felt weaker. She relented. Once. The supposed communicating with *the other side* was a painful farce built primarily around a woman wheezing out some words that Archie would never have spoken. It was Mrs C who eventually gave the velvet fringed fake her marching orders, refusing to give the woman a penny. Mrs C then set about the job of coaxing Charlotte out of her misery with whiskey and understanding. Ever since Archie's death, Charlotte had tried so hard to stay afloat, but it was in that moment she felt the tiny boat of her soul capsize.

"He's never coming back, Mrs C." Charlotte shook as if the walls of her heart were shattering all over again. "I'll never speak to him again. Never hear his voice. Not ever."

"I know, dear. You won't. That's the truth of it," was all Mrs C said, and it was enough.

Ever since that day, Charlotte vowed to herself she would never surrender again to the spiritual circus that so many were lured into. But now she found herself at its mercy again. With one small difference this time. She did not believe it or want to.

They were all seated and waiting for Charlotte when she opened the library door.

It was a dark tomb inside that room, and she could barely see the outlines of the bodies. A weak pool of light from the small lamp in the corner cast everything else beyond its sphere into deep shadows. There was very little room between the cluttered shapes. Chairs and small side tables had been pushed to the edges creating a space in the middle of the room where a large round table had been set.

The stiff silhouettes perfectly arrayed around it moved with a disjointed, marionette nature. They had the look of shadow puppets against the dull amber light.

There was a sudden rip of a match being struck and one of the faces appeared in its red glow. Nicodemus Bligh had an intense look of concentration boring its way through his eyes. He lit the candle nearest to him and the outline of more faces surfaced from the darkness.

"Take a seat please, Miss Blood." He blew out the match. "Quickly! We have kept the spirits waiting long enough."

Charlotte moved warily towards them. She'd seen enough desperate people suffering seances, Ouija boards, automatic writing and Tarot, searching the Deadlands. With the uncompromising help of Mrs C, it hadn't taken Charlotte long to realise that even in the unlikely event that any of those swindlers could take her on a journey to the underworld, she did not belong there. *"Lost souls should be left in peace. We will discover them soon enough,"* her landlady had decreed. *"You're safer staying here."* It was a painful realisation for Charlotte that, even if she could, she should not see Archie again before their allotted moment.

Charlotte had sworn a lot of oaths and made a lot of vows not to do this sort of thing again. She gripped her hands together and approached the black birds perched around the table. Their inquisitive heads turned to watch her approach.

Lady Ravenswick, thin and cadaverous in the dark light, sat next to Nicodemus Bligh. She clung to his every movement, watching him closely and responding as if she was tethered to him. Rachel and Edward Ravenswick were there but with none of the solemnity of the other faces. Edward was still sporting that languid, weary look, Rachel, a cruel sense of self-worth. Elizabeth, his wife, was dour enough for everyone.

The younger sister, Mary, sat upright and prim, judging each person in turn.

One of the high-backed, ornately carved seats was empty and Bligh widened his eyes towards it. Charlotte paused, looking around the assembly.

"Tonight, we will reach across the borders of our world and communicate with our dear brother, Charles Ravenswick."

Charlotte had an unconvinced look in her eyes. No one appeared to be disagreeing with the intention to rake through a dead man's bones. Was the intention merely to speak to him or was there a deeper purpose at work here? Were they really intending to solve the crime by conducting a séance? Or was someone about to be framed by the slippery Nicodemus Bligh?

Perhaps they really did believe they could speak to Charles Ravenswick. Lady Ravenswick looked fragile enough to try. The year since her son's death had taken its toll. She was a dried-out flower, faded and delicate. It would only take one touch for the petals to fall and crumble.

"Sit!" Bligh commanded. He nodded to the empty chair.

As Charlotte approached, she could feel the eyes boring their way through her.

It was a strange, unnatural atmosphere in the room. A mildewed air of damp left an almost tainted smell lingering.

Everyone was turning to Nicodemus Bligh, his face reverent and imposing. He seemed to soak up the light from the meagre candle and radiate it. His face was a concentrated lens, magnifying everything, all the intensity of emotion, the fascination.

Charlotte perched on her seat like all the other birds.

"We will link hands." Bligh didn't leave room for questions.

She reached for a hand on either side of her. Rachel Ravenswick's slender fingers studded with rings slotted between hers. Mary with a much more spartan, scrubbed-dry skin took Charlotte's other hand.

The table fell into an oppressive anticipation.

Charlotte could hear the ebb and flow of breath, the rustle of material on the thick velvet seats as people shifted with slight, self-conscious movements. The run of her pulse sounded in her ears. The wind rushed outside, circling the house as if it was trying to find a way in.

Bartram was right. More bad weather had been on the way. Waves of rain fell across the black glass. No one had closed the curtains, leaving the night to watch at the window.

Charlotte tried to calm her uneven breath in the dull silence.

There was a noise behind her. A distinct movement. Her back stiffened, her body rigid. She could sense a ripple in the air, a breath, a chill. Lady Ravenswick's eyes flickered and seemed to focus behind Charlotte for a moment. She squinted into the darkest corner of the library. A creak responded. A step.

Charlotte sat motionless, staring ahead at the old woman's blank eyes reflecting the flame. Next to her, Bligh seemed utterly unmoved, maintaining his solid look of certainty. The strongest belief this man had was in himself.

Another step moved behind Charlotte and she summoned up some courage. Turning her head a little, she saw a face grow out of the darkness.

Heskins was right there, hovering behind Charlotte's chair.

She gasped and let her grip on the two women either side of her slip. Charlotte held her hand to her chest as if holding everything in.

Heskins seemed to enjoy her moment of surprise. He stood sentry-still behind her chair, leaving the very distinct impression that he had been stationed there to prevent any attempt at escape.

"You shocked me," Charlotte blew out the words.

"Miss Blood." He nodded and looked straight ahead.

"Remind me to thank you later for the directions you provided."

His jaw tensed.

She turned back towards the table but could still feel his presence behind her.

Nicodemus Bligh lifted his head and closed his eyes. "Spirit, we call upon you to make yourself known."

There was a mild shuffling around the table, an uncomfortable atmosphere settling in.

The candle flame dipped in response. A common trick performed by even the most novice of mediums, a quick blow out of air down the nose that has already been raised for that distinct purpose. It was why men like him all began with such a reverent lifting up of the face.

"Spirits, hear me. On this evening, one year ago, we lost a much-loved member of this family."

It didn't escape Charlotte's attention that again he spoke with the confidence of someone who considered himself part of that inner circle, applying a subtle emphasis to that all important word – "We."

Someone cleared their throat. It was a doubtful sound. Not everyone at this table would have described Charles Ravenswick as "much loved," especially, it would seem, his widow.

Charlotte glanced at Rachel now. The wife of the dead man was smirking at Edward. Her finger gently ran along the edge of his hand, suggestively. Charlotte didn't need to look under the table to know their feet, maybe even legs, were touching. She could see their bodies sway a little, twitching with excitement.

"You better hope that your brother isn't watching." Elizabeth's voice was sharp.

Bligh called out again for the dead husband and brother. Would he really come back here to witness this betrayal? Maybe that might be an added incentive. But Elizabeth was right, these two were taking a chance with divine providence, that was for sure. To sit with this so-called mystic and attempt to conjure up the soul of the man both had cheated upon could be seen by some as too much of a gamble with the afterlife.

Another blast of wind rattled at the windows and Lady Ravenswick drew in a sharp gasp. Her head switched over towards the outside world, as if she'd seen something skim across the edge of her vision.

The rain drummed heavily on the glass. Bligh lifted his voice over the interference. "Charles Ravenswick," he announced, his voice silvery and clear, "we call upon you!"

Lady Ravenswick let out a small groan and closed her eyes.

"Are you among us, Charles Ravenswick? Speak to us now. Speak through me."

Bligh jittered slightly. The usual display. The knuckles of his hand shone white as his grip tightened. Lady Ravenswick frowned a little and glanced at him.

He didn't waver from his game. "Charles Ravenswick –" his voice sunk lower "– I command you to come into this body! Speak to us. Tell us what we demand to know. We must have an answer! Tell us, now, who…" He inserted an extravagant pause before rekindling the force of his voice. "Who shot you, Charles Ravenswick?"

There was a very audible gasp from someone and a noise of disapproval from the only other man round the table, Edward.

The dead man's brother started to speak in a terse, weary voice. "I really don't –"

"Edward, please," his mother whispered.

"Do not break the circle," Bligh ordered. "Charles Ravenswick, are you here with us?"

Charlotte felt Mary's hand grip a little tighter. Was there a genuine belief here that this dead man would just walk into another's body and begin the tale of his death? Rachel Ravenswick shifted a little in her seat. The fear that was surfacing was certainly authentic, if nothing else was.

A cold draft flurried around Charlotte's ankles. She shivered a little and Mary glanced at her, as if to acknowledge her apprehension.

"Charles Ravenswick!"

Bligh began the inevitable thick breathing to the backdrop of the tapping rain at the windows. Charlotte heard someone stifle an exclamation, in disbelief or readiness, it was impossible to tell.

There was a pause. A lull in the sound as if everything had focused in on that particular moment, waiting for it all to come raging back with even greater force.

The long doors blew open and slammed hard into the walls on either side. The wind poured in, cold and shocking around their faces. The candle was instantly quenched, the darkness fierce. Charlotte was immediately blinded. Either side of her, both hands let go. Wind rounded the table in a furious, cold river.

Someone was shouting. Lady Ravenswick was making distressed noises.

There was a thud. It sounded as if something had landed on the carpet somewhere in the room. Charlotte's eyes searched the black air.

And then another voice rose above all the noise.

Charlotte couldn't tell who it was. It was broken and indistinguishable as male or female. It murmured some vague noises before one simple word surfaced through the undercurrent.

"Murderer!"

It could easily have been Bligh's strained voice pretending to have entered the spirit world. Equally, it could have been any one of the voices around the table.

"Heskins." Edward's shrewd voice though was easily identifiable. "Get those doors shut."

"Do not break the circle!" Bligh shouted.

"We need some light in here," a female voice urged.

"The light is within!" Bligh called out.

Again, the word seemed to come from above them. "Murderers."

This time it was more distinct and clearly aimed at more than one person.

"Seal the circle," Bligh commanded. "Rejoin hands. It is a malevolent spirit." There was a pause. "Quickly! He comes!"

Charlotte felt both her hands being snatched on either side.

"For God's sake." Edward's frustration was barely contained. "Get some light in here, Heskins, and get those bloody doors shut."

"Silence! Let the spirits speak! Charles Ravenswick is that you?"

The darkness was oppressive, the cold wind brazen in her face. Charlotte could feel the feverish shaking of Mary's hand in hers. Rachel's was calmer but still there was a distinct tensing. Charlotte was beginning to feel as if she was being restrained rather than held.

"Murderers." The voice was rough.

Charlotte could hear shuffling behind her. Presumably Heskins. There was some movement across the room. Then a sudden thud, as if a body had fallen to the floor.

It was followed by a low, guttural moan and then two distinct bangs. The wind was suddenly muted. There was a pause, before light flooded the corner of the room and illuminated Edward's face standing there.

The acid-white light flared across Charlotte's eyes. She squinted against it but could see Edward by the long French doors which had been closed. Everyone else was still seated at the table. Charlotte turned. Heskins had gone.

Bligh let out a long deflating sigh. "The circle has been broken. The spirit is gone."

How he could have been so sure so quickly was one of the wondrous things that only those who inhabit the spirit world are privy to and mere mortals must accept without question. Charlotte was full of questions. Above all, where was Heskins?

She looked back at Bligh who was extravagantly demonstrating his fatigue. Lady Ravenswick beside him was pale and distressed. The two women either side of Charlotte were noticeably disturbed.

Rachel Ravenswick pushed back her chair and went over to Edward. Elizabeth, his wife, made no such movement, her face firm with disapproval.

In those opening seconds of light it seemed easy to place everyone in the room and there was certainly no sign of a spirit or any other unearthly manifestation. It was the usual family picture of bitter recriminations.

It was only when Charlotte finally managed to find a

space on her own later that evening, after the storm had subsided, that she realised everything was definitely not as it should be. The diary and the folder had both gone from her satchel.

41

Heskins was clearly not the sort of man who responded well to being challenged, particularly about a theft. His face was granite, his eyes unblinking, focusing on some point just above Charlotte's head. He'd told the court, in the evidence Charlotte had read, that he fought. His military shoulders and battle-hardened look were enough to pin that medal on him.

"I am unaware of the existence of any such notebook, Miss Blood. Your query should be directed to Nanny Austin, she is charged with the control and discipline of young Miss Celeste."

Those words were chosen with care. Control. Discipline. There was no prettiness to this girl's upbringing. He made it sound like training, in every military sense of the word, rather than childhood.

"I'm afraid, Mr Heskins, that both the notebook and folder in question were very clearly in my bag at the séance and they are no longer there now." Charlotte was determined to stand her ground. "Only you left the room. Short of it being some pilfering spirit, I see only one explanation."

They both let the accusation settle between them. Lines were drawn.

"If you wish to make a formal complaint, Miss Blood, there is a procedure."

"There's always a procedure. I'm sick of *procedure*. I don't care about that. I just want the notebook back. It doesn't belong to me."

He lifted his eyebrows. "As you said, Miss Blood, it is the property of a member of this family. Indeed, the youngest member, Mr Edward's daughter. Perhaps you could tell the family how you persuaded her to give up her precious diary to you, a journalist."

"I didn't tell you it was a diary."

He pursed his lips, his eyes challenging. "Nevertheless, Miss Blood, I have no knowledge of any such item."

"What about my folder?"

"Folder, Miss Blood? What folder would that be, then?"

"A work folder."

"I see."

"As you know, I am here as a journalist researching the family ravens."

"I know very well what you are here as, Miss Blood." He watched her with impenetrable eyes. "Perhaps we should go and tell Her Ladyship about this folder and the fact that you seem to have had her granddaughter's diary in your possession for some unspecified reason."

Charlotte chewed on the side of her cheek. "I can specify a reason if you require me to."

"Very well, Miss Blood."

She glared at him.

"Miss Blood, I would advise you to leave the child alone and stick to the birds."

"I beg your pardon?" she said in a faded voice. "Yes. The birds. I see what you mean."

This was going nowhere and the diary was drifting further from her reach. "Listen Heskins, that notebook was in my bag and someone has taken it from there. How it got there in the first place is between me and Celeste. I would be very grateful if whoever took it would give it back so that I can return it to its rightful owner."

"It's very late, Miss Blood. The family have retired for the evening. Perhaps it would be more appropriate to deal with this matter in the morning. That will give you time to decide if you wish to pursue a formal complaint. I bid you goodnight, Miss Blood." He walked away with unshakeable authority down the corridor.

"Well, I might just do that, Mr Heskins," she called after him.

"We shall see, Miss Blood." His voice trailed away.

Charlotte was alone.

It was late, but she had to get to Celeste. She had to find out what all these childish, little coded messages were about. Why the girl had to keep alluding to things and not just telling her, she couldn't understand. Notebooks, birdspeak and carvings. If the girl knew more, why didn't she say? It was very clear this girl liked the game – the puzzle of it all, as if it were no more than a detective novel.

But perhaps she didn't know more. Perhaps she was trying but her young mind couldn't sew it all together. Fear can be a powerful debilitator. As a child, would Charlotte have had the courage to stand outside the circle of her family and tell a journalist what she knew about a killing? It had been hard enough for Charlotte to slip out from the bonds of her own family as an adult. Celeste had seemed very confident and self-assured, like the rest of the Ravenswicks. But behind it all, there was an unbreakable system of control that kept them all in line here at the Abbey, unable to ever leave.

It would take a lot to persuade the girl to tell her exactly what she knew. But more importantly, first of all, she had to impart the news that the girl's precious diary had gone missing. Maybe she'd leave that part until last.

42

Charlotte crept along the corridors and out through the baize door into the dead world above. No one stirred up here. The lights were down in most areas. Doors were closed. Except for one. The smoking room.

A wedge of pale light fell onto the stone floor from the open door. The thin drizzle of blue smoke snaked out.

"Busy, busy bird, aren't you, Miss Blood?" It was Mary Ravenswick's voice. "Building your little nest."

Charlotte peered at her from the doorway. Mary's face was paper white in the circle of light from the table lamp. She picked at her fingers methodically. Beside her on the table, a cigarette was burning in the ashtray. It had the look of a very carefully set scene.

Mary Ravenswick sat in the centre of it. Her unruly hair and childish clothes incongruous amongst the sophisticated setting she'd created.

"Have you worked it out yet, Miss Blood?"

Charlotte looked at her sly little features.

The girl gave a mirthless laugh.

"*You* have, I take it." Charlotte kept her voice flat.

The girl smirked. "Perhaps." She picked up the cigarette and held it like a pen.

Charlotte resisted the urge to laugh.

"Aren't you a little slow for a journalist, Miss Blood?"

"I'm reporting on the ravens. I'm an ornithologist."

The girl snorted. "Really?"

Charlotte raised an eyebrow. "Well, if you'll excuse me. I need to go and see Celeste." She purposefully added emphasis to the name. Celeste was the important one here. "I should leave you to your *smoking*."

It provoked the intended reaction. Mary immediately balked and gave a spiteful look. "You won't be seeing my little niece again, Miss Blood. She's gone."

"Gone?"

Mary sneered. "Yes, they took her away earlier after you returned from playing in the mud."

Charlotte stiffened.

"Oh, we all had a jolly good laugh about that."

"I could have died."

She shrugged. "My brother was shot right next to me, so what makes you think any of us would be concerned with a grubby little journalist like you disappearing? What you should be asking is, would anybody care, Miss Blood? Would anybody even notice you'd gone?"

The words stung Charlotte as only the truth can. "Where is Celeste? Where are they taking her?"

Mary shook her head. "Have you not realised yet, Miss Blood? This family was never going to let you in to its secrets. They would never permit that. And anyone who does, is dealt with efficiently." She looked directly at Charlotte. She was clearly working hard to make every word heavy with meaning. It cast her in a slightly absurd light. "Do you understand?"

"I'm not sure I do. Perhaps you should –"

Mary held up her hand. "Celeste has been taken to a

family friend's house and from there she will go directly to boarding school. She will not return here until you are far away and she has learned her lesson. She's fortunate that is her only punishment."

Charlotte frowned. "But she didn't... She's just a child. A child whose uncle was murdered and nobody was doing anything about it except for her. You people, with your closed-in world, have let him die and let his killer escape without punishment." She turned and began to walk away.

"What makes you think they've escaped, Miss Blood? They have to live *here*."

Charlotte turned back to her. "If you know something, you should –"

"And risk what, Miss Blood?" She put the smouldering cigarette down. "Being sent away myself? Married off with immediate effect? Read the signs. Work it out. You have been given enough clues. Now you're on your own. Celeste won't be back."

Charlotte studied her face. Anxiety ran through Mary's eyes. Unlike Celeste, this wasn't just a game to her. She knew the penalties.

Charlotte walked slowly at first and then broke into a run, heading to Celeste's room. Through the dark halls, the faces of lost generations stared down at her intrusive footsteps. The narrow, half-lit corridors made it feel like they were closing ranks around her.

When she got to Celeste's room, she paused before opening the door. The curtains were open and the moonlight fell across the empty bed. The girl was indeed gone.

Charlotte stepped into the abandoned room and

imagined the tearful scene of a forced departure. She tried to block it from her mind. The young face pleading, resisting, overwhelmed. Celeste had ventured outside the family circle and there was no going back. Charlotte knew that only too well.

She looked down at the childish remembrances around the room. Teacups on a low table, china dolls left unattended. A hoop cast aside. Would the girl ever come back to play with these things, or when she was finally permitted to return, would she have outgrown them?

Charlotte touched the mane of the lonely rocking horse that stood by the window looking out for its owner's return. Under her hand was one word, etched into the horse's neck.

Fake.

43

It was becoming clear to Charlotte that this was a house under someone's very tight control. The constriction was achingly familiar. Perhaps even the heir had fallen foul of it. Celeste certainly had. She'd been silenced and all the words she'd written taken away too. Words were powerful weapons to this family. Currency. Their fortune was built on them. They'd been a dwindling, grand old family that would perhaps have faded into the past before Lord Ravenswick revolutionised their finances with his empire. Decades of newspapers, hundreds of column inches written by them and about them. But now the Ravenswicks chose to disappear behind a wall of silence.

Only they couldn't. The noise was always around them.

Now, even members of their own family were testing the walls of the cage, this time from the inside. It was death that chained them together. The loyalty that had always bound them into this house was faltering. How long could the conspiracy of silence last? That had to be their main concern now. How many more of them would have to die or be sent away before the very family they were seeking to preserve was fractured beyond all belief? And all for what? To maintain this world and its dying king?

She thought back to the picture of Lord Ravenswick with his two sons, a ruler surrounded by his subjects. The tales of his diminished state now were legion. It was time for her to see this broken king for herself.

As the house slipped into the quiet of night, she left her room, careful to stuff a pillow under the covers in case those prying eyes came back tonight.

The report had said his room was at the end of the house in the astrology tower. It was almost as if they'd chosen the furthest point from everything to hide him away. He'd been there when he could still move around, hence the installation of the vast lift at the centre of all this. But the reports and illustrations she'd seen so far could not have prepared her for what she was about to see.

In the large open area at the bottom of the tower stood a structure that resembled a vast bird cage. The intricate metalwork scrolled round all the sides, tapering up and meeting in a point at the top. The green-gold paint echoed the design of the ravens' aviary. But it was the size of the contraption that was the most awe-inspiring part of it. Standing in the centre of the room, it filled a large section of the base of the tower.

In the ceiling of the lift, the low-glowing lantern picked out the intricate patterns of the bars, sending a complicated web of shadows out across the tower walls. She imagined the scene that night, the light failing. A cry. Then the terrible sound of a life being taken. What must it have been like to be caged in the pitch black? Worse still, when the lights came back, they were trapped in there with the anonymous killer, looking down on the dead man with them. The fear was unthinkable. The horror and disbelief. It was no stranger dead on that floor. It was a member of their family. The heir.

The gate to the lift stood open like an invitation. Charlotte walked slowly towards it.

Inside the lift, it was a large, empty space with no sofa or chairs, even though there was ample room. Although ornate from the outside, it was a stripped-back, blank area inside, devoid of any unnecessary adornment. This was a functional contraption, not an eccentric addition, or some flight of fancy. There was a very clear purpose, even though that had been so extravagantly gilded. There'd been some reference in the folder to a large wheelchair that Lord Ravenswick moved around in when he was still able to. The structure had presumably been designed to accommodate that comfortably along with any other necessary people. Nurse Sidmouth had been mentioned and Lady Ravenswick seemed to spend most of her time up in the tower with her husband. Then there was the Machiavellian Bligh practising his arts, the foremost of which seemed to be maintaining his influence over Lady Ravenswick. Who would Charlotte find up there with His Lordship? Did they already know she was coming? They somehow knew her every move before she even made it.

As she stepped into the lift, the noise of her feet on the floor was dulled by the deep red carpet. Sections of it still bore traces of the once plush pile, but it was worn in parts with a smattering of bald areas. There were the tell-tale signs of the same moth larvae at work that were eating away below the surface throughout the rest of the house.

The dim, algae-green light cast a sickly air over the space, as if it had been tainted. The bars were so tightly woven in the ornate design, that, once inside, Charlotte could see very little beyond the cage.

She closed over the gate, the dull metal sound reverberating as if to confirm she was now locked in. It echoed around the circular room and lifted away into the tower. She looked up, following the noise as it disappeared beyond the light, far above the lift. Charlotte stared into the vast filigreed dome of the lift's roof. The shaft above was completely obscured by darkness.

On the left side, near the gate, was a control panel with two large buttons – one with an arrow pointing up, one down. There was nothing to stop the lift from the inside, so that idea was dead. Nor was there any facility to turn off the light.

Her finger wavered over the button. She hadn't really thought this through. What was she even going to say to explain her unannounced presence? Why was she going to see this sick, old man at all? According to Lady Ravenswick, he loved the birds but he couldn't see them anymore. Readers would undoubtedly want to hear about Lord Ravenswick. He was, after all, their owner and head of the household. But they would want to hear about a lot more than just his passion for ravens. What they'd really want to know about him was his condition and, most of all, his thoughts on the death of his son.

Charlotte had to take the chance now. Celeste had already been spirited away to stop her *observations* and both the diary and the folder had gone. Someone was definitely aware of Charlotte's interests beyond the birds and they were working hard to shut that down. It seemed like her time at Ravenswick Abbey was running out and she'd still come no closer to finding out who killed Charles Ravenswick.

Charlotte shuddered to imagine him dead in this lift, slumped on the floor. She pictured him now, sitting there just as the witnesses had described him, staring out, his eyes set wide in that expression of horrified disbelief. The gun on the floor in the centre, silent as to who shot it.

She pictured them all standing round this lift, looking back at her now, only one with the eyes of a murderer. But which one? She'd just witnessed how devious Mary Ravenswick liked to think herself. Celeste had told her Mary professed she would devise her own fiendish murder one day. Had she really gone this far? She'd been very frank about how little money he'd allowed her and Charlotte knew all too well how that always led to a woman's independence being taken away. Was this Mary Ravenswick's bid for freedom?

It was Edward Ravenswick, though, who benefitted most from his brother's death in so many ways. Not only was he the new heir but he was now free to conduct his affair with Charles's wife, Rachel.

Charlotte saw Rachel there too, looking down at her dying husband, the man she didn't love who couldn't provide her with a child – an all-important heir to Ravenswick Abbey. Rachel didn't run forward. According to the evidence Charlotte had read, she didn't even touch her dead husband.

It was Heskins who went to him and confirmed his death, the loyal butler who nearly sent Charlotte to her death in the mire, had it not been for Bartram's quick reactions, had he not been there at exactly the right time to drag her free from the mud.

The sad, bereaved raven master was one of that closed circle of faces in this lift, looking down at the dead Charles

Ravenswick. One of the perpetual suspects who could not escape the burden of their joint suspicion until the murderer was finally unmasked. The joint ordeal of the innocent. All except one.

Could the unquestionable loyalty of the staff here have led to one of them performing this terrible duty? Even when Charlotte had spoken to Jeffers the gardener out in the grounds, Bartram was quick to appear then as well and shut down anything Jeffers might say.

There was, of course, one more face staring back at her from those arrayed in the lift that night, the ever-present spectre of Nicodemus Bligh. He had to be there. He was always there at the important moments for this family, dominating and controlling Lady Ravenswick. Charlotte saw those feline eyes now, glittering back at her from the darkness. He was very believable as the killer of Charles Ravenswick. There'd been arguments about his precious books. With Charles Ravenswick out of the way, he only had to worry about the younger brother, who openly professed his boredom at the thought of the books.

All those faces formed now out of the shadows. Only one was the killer. Charlotte pushed the button and she began to rise.

44

The lift jolted into life and began its slow ascent. The mechanism, although loud and clumsy, felt precarious. It did not move smoothly, but with an irregular shuddering that sounded very unreliable. As soon as the lift set off from the base of the tower, it entered into the shaft where the structure fit so snugly that Charlotte could only see the stone walls surrounding her on all sides. The weak light flickered in the ceiling and, for a moment, she imagined the lift grinding into a halt, and the darkness descending. She could feel their fear that night. It said in the reports that the lift had failed soon after it had set off. That would have been about now.

But the cage continued its unsteady haul up into the darkness above, the irregular movements magnifying every sound, every pause. It was as if it was being lifted simply by human hands on the end of a rope and she dangled, helpless, at the bottom. One slip, and she would plummet to the bottom or, worse, be stuck somewhere in this great stone lift shaft unable to escape.

The air was thin. Dust from the walls filtered through the light as if she was excavating her way through in this strange machine, boring through the stone. The bars rattled and groaned, every joint and hinge stretched to its full capacity. The overwhelming feeling was of being trapped, a spider under a glass. What must it have been like with nine people in here? Even with the size of it, there would have been little space for movement. And then after, with Charles Ravenswick's body sitting, staring out and a wave of fear collapsing over them. She closed her eyes and imagined the scene of horror and panic. The screaming. Rachel had fainted. Accusations and fear filled the air, chaos echoing up this stone tunnel all the way to Lord and Lady Ravenswick. Something terrible had happened. They waited to be told the worst of news.

As the lift finally began to slow, a line of light from the room at the top pulled through the bars, slowly filling up the lift. Whoever was in there would see the lift surfacing, its great green and gold painted dome first, then the long length of its bars before finally seeing who was arriving.

There were doors to the lift's entrance into the room at the top, but they'd not been closed. As the room opened out in front of Charlotte, she could immediately see that it was the mirror image of the dimensions below, large and round. But this was a heavily decorated room, filled with furniture and paintings, tables full of curios and bookshelves lining every wall. It was hazily lit with soft side lights that gave no more than an elegant glow. All the dark velvet curtains were drawn, closing in the circular space like a fortune teller's tent.

And there in the middle, was a large, four poster bed. Thick, carved wooden columns held a great canopy aloft. Matching crimson velvet fell from it in vast folds. Lying in the centre of the bed was a figure – unmoving and ivory-pale, the skin shining out of the darkness like a ghost.

The figure didn't move or acknowledge the arrival of

the great, clanking lift. As it came to a stop, Charlotte remained inside, watching, deciding if she should just go back down without a word.

She opened the lift tentatively, her other hand gripping the satchel close to her like a shield. The hinges of the gate groaned as she pushed the bars back.

"Hello?" she stepped into the room.

There was no response. The figure in the bed didn't stir. She moved a little further into the room. There was a strange, decaying smell mingled with that astringent, medicinal scent she remembered so well from Archie's last days. A table beside the bed was littered with bottles and potions of varying sizes.

"Lord Ravenswick?"

As she drew closer, Charlotte could see his fine cotton hair, so white it was barely distinguishable from the pillow below. The skin was drawn taut across the bones of his face, his eyelids so transparent she imagined him watching her approach from beneath the skin. Tiny blue veins threaded through his gauzy face making him look like a delicate marbled sculpture laid out on a tomb.

"I'm –"

A weak rasp lifted up from his throat. The thin lips cracked open, his mouth barely a slit in his face. His lashless eyelids attempted to flicker open and failed.

He was covered in a thin white sheet through which she could make out the skeleton of his frame. The hands twitched and a finger fell from beneath the covers, its sallow skin mottled like rind, the nails thick grey claws.

"Miss Blood."

Charlotte swung around to confront the voice.

"Lady Ravenswick."

Her delicate features were ethereal in the gloom, those pale-water eyes unblinking.

Another ruckled breath lifted from the shape in the bed.

"I'm not sure you should be here, should you?" There was a strange, sinister thread running through her voice.

"I wanted to ask His Lordship about the ravens," she stammered.

Lady Ravenswick analysed her closely. "And you did not think it prudent to ask me first?"

"I do apologise, Lady Ravenswick. I'm just not used to –"

"Oh, but I think you are, Miss Blood. Did you not grow up at Bladesworth House? Are you not Sir Richard and Lady Frances de Burgh's daughter? And do you not drift around London society busily gathering gossip for your column? Nosferatu, I believe is your alias, is it not?"

The only sound in the room was the difficult breathing coming from the bed.

It was broken by the noise of the lift starting into life again. Charlotte watched as the light flickered and then the great contraption began to descend.

"You see, Miss Blood, we do not like infiltrators here. We are a very private family, as you have seen. We value loyalty and honesty above all else. And we do not like being lied to. My granddaughter may have thought it was a jolly good idea to summon you here on the pretext of watching the foul ravens, but she is being educated in the ways of preserving a family's privacy."

"Perhaps she was trying to find out who murdered her uncle."

Lady Ravenswick paused, watching Charlotte as closely as if she could see all her thoughts.

The ruckling noise lifted again out of the body on the bed. It was the only sign that there was any life left in the fragile man.

"Shh, my dear, we have a guest." Lady Ravenswick's voice softened. "An unexpected guest."

Another noise grew out of the thin figure on the bed but this time it had a familiar sound to it. The lips parted more and tried to move as if attempting to form a word. His frail eyelids fluttered like moth's wings before opening to reveal the dull, ivory stones inside. His skull fell over to the side and his milky eyes settled on Charlotte. They were diluted but there was just a small remembrance of some of that power she had seen in the photograph with his sons.

"Charles?" he wheezed.

Lady Ravenswick moved towards him, sorrow invading her sharp features. "No, my dear. No. Charles has gone."

"To war?"

She took a long breath, fortifying herself. There was a deep weariness to her as if she was very used to searching for moments of strength and calm. "Rest, dear. You must rest. Nurse Sidmouth will be back with your tonic soon."

"Tonic. Tonic. Tonic. I want... I want to see... my son."

Lady Ravenswick glanced over at Charlotte and then quickly back to her husband. She held him so gently as if frightened his thin hand could easily turn to dust in hers. "Edward is..."

"Charles," the word rasped out of him.

There was a movement behind Charlotte. She looked quickly towards the lift. It was still only a black hole. No one had come up there. The small panel on the right indicated it was still at the ground level. Whoever it was, they were still down there.

A figure stepped out of the shadows. He must have been in the room all along, watching from the dark, but Nicodemus Bligh appeared with the suggestion that he had been conjured from nothing more than air.

"Miss Blood." He spoke with authority and instantly locked those hypnotist eyes on her.

"Nicodemus," Lady Ravenswick was not shocked by his presence. "His Lordship is distressed. It would appear that Miss Blood's unexpected arrival has caused him some concern. Perhaps you could assist."

He let his eyes linger on Charlotte before nodding once with feigned humility. He approached the bed serenely as if his feet did not need the ground. The long white robes trailed back from him as he sailed seamlessly across the room. He walked as though he was attempting to cause as little disruption to the air as possible, perfecting the art of going completely unnoticed.

Bligh paused at the bedside table and looked at the array of potions and bottles, but the syringe he pulled from the sleeve of his robes was already full and primed.

Lord Ravenswick's eyes widened, stretching his thin, papery skin to a translucent film. He looked to his wife in confusion, then back to Bligh with fresh fear. "No."

"Melhuish, we have spoken about this. It is for your own good."

The phrase cut Charlotte to the bone.

"Nicodemus, if you would, please." There was a note of finality in her voice.

Charlotte looked into those desperate, failing eyes of the man in the bed. The needle caught a small droplet of light on the tip as Bligh held it out. He leaned over towards the horrified face in the bed.

"Wait!" Charlotte took a few quick breaths. "This doesn't seem..."

Lady Ravenswick let go of her husband's hand and turned her sharp eyes on Charlotte. Bligh pivoted towards her, the syringe still raised.

"This is none of your concern." Lady Ravenswick spoke in a detached voice.

"It's a concern if a man is being drugged who clearly doesn't welcome it."

They both watched her impatiently. These were not people used to being challenged.

"Charles... they took him away," Lord Ravenswick insisted. He attempted to lift himself. "The books..."

Lady Ravenswick looked with new fear at Bligh. "Now!" was all she said.

"No, please. Violet, please. I'm so..."

"Nicodemus." There was a hint of urgency rising in Lady Ravenswick.

Bligh stepped closer to the bed and took the old man's arm in his hand. The mottled skin hung limp from the bone and Bligh's strong fingers sunk deep into the flesh.

"Please, no..." Lord Ravenswick looked up to his wife in desperation and then towards Charlotte. "Whoever you are, girl... It's the damn books. They're..."

His face clouded over as the needle sunk into his arm. There was a moment of confusion before the tension in him released. His face collapsed as his eyes began to surrender. There was a momentary, weak attempt to keep them open that ended in one last word. "*Fake*."

45

Lady Ravenswick and Nicodemus Bligh remained still. Their eyes met, in silent conspiracy. With unwavering purpose, they finally turned towards Charlotte. She was caught.

Charlotte looked quickly in the direction of the empty lift shaft. There was no sign of whoever was at the bottom, if indeed they were still there.

"Miss Blood." Lady Ravenswick's voice was emotionless. "I believe you know far too much about my family." She glanced across at Nicodemus Bligh, who concurred. "And I cannot allow that. I have told you before we value our privacy above everything and everyone."

"I won't tell a soul. What you do with your books is of no concern to me."

She gave a petty laugh. "You still do not seem to understand, Miss Blood. No individual is greater or more important than the Ravenswick family, not you, not my granddaughter, not my son or even Lord Ravenswick himself. We are merely the custodians of the name and that name must never be tarnished or fade. With the aid of Nicodemus, we have done what is necessary to save this family from certain destruction. We must all shoulder that." Tears pricked her eyes and she placed a hand on

325

Bligh's arm. "I could not have done any of this without you, Nicodemus. You are my rock."

Bligh gave a gracious bow, the syringe still poised in his hand. Her husband groaned from the bed. It was a defeated sound.

"Your Ladyship, I am forever your servant." He turned his gaze on Charlotte. "You must understand, I did what I did for the family. It was for the best." Those words again. "The family were desperate. With His Lordship's failing condition, the newspaper was falling into decline and so were the family finances, even before the Crash. All investments plummeted. The rot was deep. The cure... expensive. It has cost us all a lot." He stepped closer towards her. "I still believe the library of Iona is here somewhere. My work was merely a temporary measure to give the family a reprieve."

His eyes were full of compassion for Lady Ravenswick.

"We couldn't get rid of you, Miss Blood, without raising suspicions, so I thought I'd make use of your presence to publicise my... the new texts. Her Ladyship warned me not to get you involved."

"Oh, Nicodemus, you have been the loyalist of them all. I will never be able to thank you for *all* that you have done." Lady Ravenswick shook her head. "You see, young lady, you can never understand what it is to make the ultimate sacrifice for your family. You turned your back on yours. Here at Ravenswick Abbey, we prize loyalty above all else. It is our lifeblood. It is what has sustained our name over generations. We have survived and will continue to do so."

"By having your son and heir murdered? Is that the ultimate loyalty, Mr Bligh? Did Charles Ravenswick find out your secret and object? Was he going to put a stop to it? Edward couldn't care less about the books or the library. He makes a far easier, more compliant heir, doesn't he?" Charlotte's heart thumped in her chest.

Lady Ravenswick shook her head slowly. "Miss Blood, how naïve you are. The world is such a simple place to people like you. You think you can decide what is wrong and what is right then shape the rest of us around that. Ravenswick Abbey has far more shades to it than your silly black and white world. I know the world you work in. I know the press better than anyone, all those reams and reams of words. But this is the reality. Survival."

"At any cost? When I leave this place far behind, you will still be trapped here."

She locked eyes with Charlotte. "Oh, no, I'm afraid you know far too much to *leave*." She smiled. "Nicodemus, I believe our guest is feeling a little unwell. Perhaps you could assist her to calm down."

Bligh nodded once and lifted a fresh hypodermic needle from a side table. He started to approach. His face so calm.

"What a wheeze! Scare the girl, eh?" Charlotte laughed. "Really? You're going to kill me. Just like that. You don't think they'll miss me?"

"Do you?"

Charlotte pictured her empty flat. Her family at Bladesworth had moved on. Even Fulman would probably have forgotten her by now. She stood alone here, knowing the answer to the question. No, she didn't think she would be missed. She'd sacrificed everything, abandoned her family and a home for a life of loneliness and hardship. When she thought of it now, it seemed like a very foolish thing she'd done.

"This won't hurt, Miss Blood." Nicodemus Bligh was taking hold of her arm and pushing up the sleeve.

She tried to snatch it away but his hands gripped with an unshakeable strength.

"Now, now, Miss Blood. It's better this way. Less painful"

"What are you doing?" She squirmed.

"I should have thought that was obvious to a trained journalist such as yourself, Miss Blood." He leered into her face, the needle resting on her soft arm. "I am injecting you with a mild sedative so that you do not feel any pain. We're not barbarians, Miss Blood."

"Just killers," Charlotte said defiantly, and felt the first sting of the needle. She tried again to pull her arm away but his grip was too tight.

A cold wave passed through her, infecting every limb, pooling in her brain. The room blurred. Bligh's grip melted from her arm. A white, rushing sound filled up her head and the room bent in and out of her vision.

"Murderer," she murmured.

"Protector," was the last word she heard him speak.

46

Charlotte's eyes opened and the darkness rushed in. She felt weightless, suspended in a void. She could feel something beneath her, but it wasn't the floor. Hard, rigid bars were digging into her side. She could see a speck of distant light up above, as far away as the stars.

A sharp pain burrowed deep into her hip. Her head was hot, her thoughts clouded as if her brain had been filled with steam. Her face gathered, part with pain, part confusion. The memories filtered back, all jumbled and in the wrong order. Nicodemus Bligh, the silver spike of the syringe approaching. The washing away of thoughts, of her ability to move. She was lifted. Thrown. She remembered sailing through the air, down into the darkness like a stone heading for the ground. The bone-splitting thud as she hit the bars, each one playing a different note as her body struck it. The sound vibrated through her body.

Charlotte tried to sit up. Every joint felt out of place. Where she'd landed heavily on her side, there was a searing pain flowing all the way down her flank. It was such an uneven surface on the struts of metal that she could barely move without falling back. The bars below her curved away steeply. As her eyes began to adjust to the faint light and the fog in her mind started to lift, the slow realisation began to dawn as to where she was.

She was on top of the lift. They'd thrown her down the lift shaft. Panic flooded in. She was shaking, her head twitching from side to side, trying to make sense of her environment. She was surrounded. Sealed in by the stone walls all around. Her breath started to stutter. Her hands gripped the cold metal bars.

Charlotte turned over onto her stomach, the pain shimmering through her hip and down her leg. The lift was dim below, with only the same dull morgue light she'd seen when she'd travelled in it. There was no one in the lift. Whoever had called it must have gone. She had no idea how long she had been down here but the dull buzz in her head spoke of the long, thick sleep of the drugged.

She tried to find a pocket of calm, taking deep breaths, closing her eyes. Her thoughts spooling out of control.

Then she found a small emblem of how to be brave. As soon as her fingers touched the familiar nap of the leather satchel, Archie was there with her. His calm face in her head. He'd said it would all be alright. How, didn't seem to matter. It just would.

She pulled in one more lungful of the dusty air. "Right, Blood. Let's do this."

Charlotte stumbled to her feet, feeling the sharp turn of the scrolling metalwork spiking every part of her that it touched. To get up, it necessitated pushing down even harder against the unforgiving bars. She used the satchel in part to protect her hands but her knees were bruised and pierced by the wrought iron.

When she finally got to her feet, unsteady as a newborn

foal, she managed to reach out to the nearest wall for support, her hand slipping at first on the damp stone. Her eyes were becoming more accustomed to the drab light seeping up from below. Small shadows formed and seemed to crawl along the wall. She floundered a little, finding her footing on the new rungs.

The wall was plastered smooth. She'd been hoping for a rough, raw edge to the stone to offer some footholds or grip, but, wiping her hand across the slick surface, there was nothing. Holding her head back in frustration she saw a tiny segment of light coming from between the doors in the upstairs room. They'd closed them. Even if she could get up there, what would be waiting? The people who had done this to her? Would they still be there? She didn't even have any idea how long she'd been down here.

She crouched and peered below into the lift. The reports all said the bars were too small to even fit a small gun through them. There were no escape hatches, even though the mechanism repeatedly failed. They couldn't have known how temperamental it was going to be when they installed it. By all accounts, they used to have more staff to ensure the power was maintained correctly, but still, who would install such a structure in the blind belief that it would never fail? That spoke volumes of this self-assured, delusional family.

What could she do? She clutched her knees to her chest. These people thought nothing could touch them. Nothing would ever fail. This was a family here at Ravenswick Abbey who refused to sink. Clearly, they'd do anything to maintain that. They would push any head under to stay afloat, even one of their own if the sacrifice was necessary. One of those carvings had said "sacrifice".

Charles Ravenswick's fate. And if they could do that to their heir, they would not flinch at dispatching her.

Charlotte thought back to what she'd been told, her mind desperately trying to piece it back together. The drugs still clouded her mind, the moments pulling in then fading out. What seemed clear above all else now was that it was Lady Ravenswick's instrument, Bligh, who had shot Charles Ravenswick. The books were forgeries. Celeste's diary had made note of the arguing about them. Charles Ravenswick had disagreed with them. But his personal code of honour stood in direct opposition to the financial survival of the family. It was a convincing reason to kill him. But what was also very clear to Charlotte was that now she'd found that out, she would have to be disposed of too. There was no chance they were going to let her escape with this knowledge.

She had to do something. Charlotte stumbled to her feet again and started to feel along the wall, trying to map out her surroundings. The shaft was an entirely curved tube that the lift fit inside snugly. There didn't even seem to be enough room for light. Whoever had designed it had used every inch of available space. Her hands travelled along the wall, searching for something. Anything. There was only a small hole that she circled. She pushed her finger inside, hoping to pull away some stone, create a foothold. But the wall was solid and unforgiving, the tiny cavity only shallow. There was nothing.

Then the lift began to move.

47

At first, she was elated. Someone was there, operating the lift.

Charlotte bent and peered down into the lift, trying to peep through the thin gaps in the bars. She couldn't see anyone. There was no movement.

No one was there.

She fell backwards heavily on the sharp bars. The pain ran up her spine.

It was when she looked up that a fresh surge of panic washed through her. There was very little room in the top of the astronomy tower. Once the lift got to the top floor, the conical shape of the roof would only just house the ornate dome of the lift. With all the apparatus and chains there'd be no room for anything else between the two. Anything, or anybody, on top of the lift would be crushed against the machinery in the roof.

The great cage clattered on, juddering through the lift shaft. The noise grew louder as they travelled towards the mechanism. The thick chains pulled taut as they slowly heaved the immense structure up.

"Hello?" Charlotte's voice was tentative at first. Then louder. "Hello? Can anyone hear me? I say, if you've started the lift would you mind stopping it. I'm a little bit trapped." She paused for breath, the disturbed dust from the walls clouding round her and filling her face. "I'm on the roof." The relentless progress didn't slow.

She looked around frantically. The smooth stone walls slid past, lit only by the dim green light from below.

"Help! Please! Anyone." The only response was her own voice echoing back down the tunnel of stone.

The grinding noise of the machinery grew louder moment by moment, the cage inching its way up the walls. She had to think. Fast.

The door to Lord Ravenswick's quarters was approaching. If she could somehow open that as they passed, she could throw herself out. Back into the room where her would-be killers were. Not the best survival tactic, but the only one on offer.

It was her only chance. It was slim, but there was no way she was going to survive being ground up by the great metal cogs above.

She was almost level with the door. The tiny network of bars was sharp and uneven beneath her feet as she stumbled into position. She readied herself, her heart pedalling fast now. She wiped her sweaty hands down her skirt and slung the satchel over her shoulder. This was it.

Charlotte was poised, her feet rocking violently on the sloping roof. She crouched a little to give herself momentum and as the roof rose up level with the door, she lunged forward hard with her palms splayed on the wood.

The door was locked.

Charlotte recoiled, staring in disbelief. She looked up at the grinding engine above. She had to get those doors open. She drove her shoulder into the heavy wooden doors. They didn't move. The lift didn't pause but continued its unrelenting journey. Her face was now above the level of the door. Then her chest. She kicked out with as much force as she could muster but the wood just rattled against the frame.

She lost her balance and fell. The door was disappearing below the level of the roof.

"Please," she breathed desperately. "Please, someone. Anyone!"

As she drew closer to the giant mechanism of cogs and chains, it grew unbearably loud.

A great noise of grinding metal filled up her head. She closed her eyes and braced herself, clinging to the satchel. The last word she whispered was, "Archie –"

The lift stopped and the light went out.

Charlotte lay on the roof, unable to move, her eyes searching the new, thick darkness.

"The power," she breathed, the smile breaking across her face. "The power," she shouted again in relief. "Thank you. Thank you. God, thank you."

Light flooded into the lift shaft as the door to His Lordship's bedroom opened and she felt a firm hand grab her leg and pull her down. Her body dragged along the bars, her face grazed against the upper edge of the door frame as she lowered her head to fit through the gap. She landed heavily on the floor.

"It's not God. It's me!"

Charlotte stared up in disbelief. "Mrs C?"

The familiar face looked down at her. She gave Charlotte a quick wink. Mrs C stood with one hand on her hip. The other was on a gun pointed with a surprisingly steady hand at Lady Ravenswick and Nicodemus Bligh.

"Take a seat, please, Your Ladyship. You must be worn

out." Mrs C waved the gun at them. "And your sycophant. You can take the weight off too."

Bligh gave her a hard look before lowering into the chair beside the bed. Lady Ravenswick sat slowly on the edge of the other chair.

Charlotte rubbed at her face. "What are you –"

"Doing here? Keeping you safe. You didn't think I was going to let you come out here with these lunatics on your own, did you?" She held the gun out a little further towards the room.

Charlotte frowned. Her eyes swam in and out of focus, but it was inescapable that Mrs C was dressed in a maid's uniform.

"The new seamstress, m'lady." Mrs C bobbed low into a quick curtsey.

Charlotte looked at her open-mouthed. "But how did you –"

"Get up here?"

Charlotte nodded in wonder.

"The stairs." She watched Charlotte's bewilderment. "You didn't think this dilapidated old lift was the only access, did you?"

A look of faint embarrassment crossed Charlotte's face.

"You see, I told you. You need to start thinking like a detective writer. I called the lift earlier but then I got to thinking it might not be such a good idea to just announce myself as a maid."

Charlotte gave a weak smile and gingerly started to haul herself to her feet, wincing with the pain. She shot a fierce look at Bligh and then at Lady Ravenswick. "You tried to kill me."

Nicodemus Bligh lifted his face defiantly. "I don't know

where you got that notion from, Miss Blood. You were unsteady on your feet and you fell down the lift shaft."

"But then you started the lift."

"Nonsense. The mechanism fails regularly."

Mrs C laughed a little. "Well, thank goodness I was on hand to stop it. Otherwise, Miss Blood here might have been living up to her name in a way that she might not welcome." Mrs C glanced down. "You alright, Duckie?"

Charlotte nodded. Every part of her hurt in succession, her legs, her hip where she'd fallen heavily onto the roof of the lift, along her side. Then she looked at her hands, raw from scrabbling around in the dark on the sharply designed metal. Her head pounded from whatever they'd pumped into her. As she stood and looked down, she noticed that not only were her knees grazed and bleeding, but the precious stockings Mrs C had mended so often were hanging in shreds.

She pulled at the laddered material then looked at the two guilty faces. "You're going to pay for that one."

Bligh shrugged. Lady Ravenswick did not respond.

"Never you mind about that." Mrs C winked. "We can sort those out. But what we're going to do now, Your Ladyship, is we're going to go on a little journey."

"You impudent –"

Mrs C shook the gun at her in reminder. "I can be as impudent as I like standing behind this. So you just sit there and get ready for a trip back in time, to a year ago, and we are going to reveal what really happened."

Lady Ravenswick noticeably bristled.

"I believe the first job, Your Ladyship, is to gather a lot of suspects together, is it not? Just like you intentionally did last New Year's Eve."

"I have no idea what you mean." Her voice was as bitter as her face.

"I think you do." She waved the gun at her again.

Charlotte held her hand to the side of her head, closing her eyes and wincing as she felt the open cut.

"Sit down before you fall down," Mrs C said in a low voice to Charlotte.

"Alright." Charlotte lowered herself into one of the chairs around the large table to the side of the room.

"Now, Lady Ravenswick," Mrs C continued. "If you'd be so kind as to telephone your lapdog, Heskins, and get him to round up the exact same people who were on your little guest list when your son died."

Bligh was rising from his seat. "How dare you speak to –"

"And you can get back in your cage, Houdini. You're already up for attempting to murder Miss Blood."

His eyes drew into long, thin lines. He paused, staring at the outstretched gun, before lowering himself back into the seat.

"The phone, Lady Ravenswick." Mrs C waved the gun at the bedside table.

Her Ladyship paused before walking towards the table. Her hand reached out.

"No other little surprises either, if you please."

There was a silence in the room, punctuated only by the arduous breathing of her husband in the bed. He was oblivious to this whole drama being played out around him. The drugs sat heavily over him, pushing him down into the deepest of sleeps. Bligh had sedated him very efficiently and Charlotte could only be thankful there'd been so little of the dose left when he'd administered it to her. A small enough amount perhaps that it would have been undetected in whatever would have been left of her after the lift reached its destination. She had no appointment. She wasn't expected. Who could have known she'd be on top of the lift when they started it? It could so easily have been a terrible accident.

"Hello, Heskins?" Her Ladyship said.

There was a pause.

"I want you to gather all the people who attended on New Year's Eve last year. Yes, in the astrology tower."

She listened and then turned to Mrs C and Charlotte before adding, "Please ensure they use the lift."

Mrs C nodded and flicked the switch on the control panel. The grating mechanism fired into action again and through the doors Charlotte watched as the lift continued the final moments of its journey up to the top of the tower where it stopped. Charlotte watched the green light glowing through the open doors. It had taken very little time to complete those last few moments.

Charlotte looked at Mrs C. "Thank you," she whispered.

Mrs C nodded. "To business!"

Lady Ravenswick spoke into the telephone. "Yes, and straight away, thank you." She replaced the receiver. "They are on their way."

48

Within half an hour, they were all arrayed on the seats at the table in front of Charlotte and Mrs C. Charlotte's eyes travelled around the arc – Edward Ravenswick, cultivating his usual air of nonchalance; Rachel next to him, all indolent good looks; Elizabeth with her disdainful appearance; and Mary still wearing her childlike surliness. They were as unchanging as the Abbey itself, caught in a timeless world, even after the death of a brother, husband, uncle.

Lady Ravenswick sat stiff and unmoving, surveying this nest. By her side, as ever, was the murderous-looking Nicodemus Bligh. Then Heskins, with his air of unquestionable loyalty. Jeffers fiddled with his cap uncomfortably. And finally, the last face in the row, silent and pensive, Bartram the raven master. He sat with his still eyes settled on Charlotte.

"Oh, I do like this moment," Mrs C said with undisguised excitement.

Charlotte leaned over. "It's not one of your novels, Mrs C. These people have lost someone."

"But they don't look like that though, do they?" Mrs C raised an eyebrow. She'd put the gun in her pocket when the lift brought the others up but she shifted her hand a little now to make it very clear to Lady Ravenswick and Bligh that her finger was still firmly on the trigger.

"Shall I begin?" Mrs C said eagerly.

Edward cut in. "Who the hell is this?" He looked up and down Mrs C's uniform. "Are you *staff*?"

"I'm the new seamstress, sir." She'd adopted a bizarre accent that was unplaceable. "But really, I am…" She removed her hat theatrically. It made no difference to her appearance.

"She's my landlady," Charlotte said, apologetically.

"And detective writer!"

The faces looked back in bemusement.

"Yes, that too." Charlotte felt she should agree.

"I write the Burnt Rose series?" Mrs C added, hoping for some acknowledgment.

She looked around the blank faces.

"Rose the mortuary worker, music hall entertainer and sleuth?" she said, expecting a great wave of recognition.

There was none.

"Famous for solving the Piccadilly Creeper case? Heads in picnic hampers?" Mrs C held up her free hand. "Don't worry, I can donate some signed copies to your library. *Genuine* copies," she added, pointedly.

Elizabeth Ravenswick sighed extravagantly. "Are we going to get on with this? Whatever *this* is?"

Mrs C looked at her tartly. "Why? Do you have some other pressing engagement? Because, from what I've witnessed so far, the only thing occupying your days is spying on your husband and Rachel Ravenswick."

Edward Ravenswick looked irritated, but the shadow of a smile crept over Rachel's face as she placed an obvious hand on his knee. Elizabeth looked away.

Lady Ravenswick and Nicodemus Bligh both noticeably bristled.

Mrs C gave a little shuffle in readiness. Then began. "You see an awful lot when nobody sees you." Her audience was reluctantly intrigued. "I was like a ghost, spiriting my way around your rambling house, and I saw plenty. You are very trusting, or perhaps very ignorant of those around you who serve." She raised an eyebrow towards Lady Ravenswick, who did not flinch. "I could see many things. Things that were perhaps not meant for me."

Heskins began to stand. "I'm not sure this is appropriate."

"The time to worry about what's *appropriate* has passed, Mr Heskins," Charlotte said. "It's time for the truth before anyone else gets hurt."

"Hurt?" Bartram raised his head. "Who's been hurt?"

Charlotte was suddenly very aware of her dishevelled state. She knocked some of the dust off her blouse and rearranged her skirt. "No one… yet. But there's a killer in this room and it's time to stop protecting them. What has complicated this from the beginning is that everyone had a motive, didn't they, Mr Heskins?"

The butler stiffened with his usual military stance.

"It was you on that first night who pushed the gargoyle from the roof. Were you trying to kill me then?"

"No, it…" He stopped himself.

"Oh, just a warning shot then. But it's true, isn't it, that you sent me the wrong way on the moor, directly into the mire, in an effort to stop my investigations? In an effort to kill me."

He looked straight into Charlotte's face, his eyes unwavering. Finally, he cleared his throat. "I must have been mistaken, Miss Blood."

She laughed. "A mistake that could easily have cost me my life if it hadn't been for Bartram here."

"Heskins?" Lady Ravenswick looked at him in confusion.

He pulled his shoulders back. "I will always be loyal to the Ravenswicks."

Charlotte turned to the raven master. "Mr Bartram, thank you. You were on the spot immediately, weren't you? Out there on the moor." She paused. "Charles Ravenswick made it clear he would have shot the ravens when he was the head of the household."

Bartram's expression darkened. "You wouldn't... you wouldn't be suggesting I killed a man to save some birds?"

Charlotte shook her head slowly and smiled. "No, Mr Bartram. I would not." She let the smile fall as she turned to the rest of them. "There are much better motives in this room. Edward Ravenswick, the second brother, for instance. I myself have two brothers. It was always a point of sadness to my younger brother that the older one came back from the war."

The look of condescension was finally slipping from Edward's face.

"More than anyone else in this room, you had a motive for killing your brother. You would be the new heir and very soon inherit all this. You would be free to conduct your obvious affair with his wife, Rachel. There's no subterfuge any more is there. Elizabeth is reconciled, so long as she will be Lady Ravenswick of Ravenswick Abbey." She looked directly at Edward's melancholy wife.

"How dare you?"

"How dare I? Because a man is dead and no one is being held to account. A death requires a reason otherwise it is pointless. Those to blame for ending a young man's life should be exposed."

Their faces were all sombre, absorbed in thought.

"I was about to stand by and watch a man be killed so his widow could take my husband away? How ridiculous." Elizabeth looked away.

"You yourself said your only interest was in Ravenswick Abbey."

She didn't answer.

"You are all bound to this place by loyalty. The assurance that there will always be Ravenswicks at the Abbey is of paramount importance and just as the ravens' wings are clipped to ensure they remain, so too are all your lives. There is one goal, maintaining the family at *this* house."

"And what would you know of such things, Miss Blood?" Lady Ravenswick's voice was clean and cold. "You abandoned family and home. You have no loyalty."

"Ah, Lady Ravenswick. Loyalty." Charlotte smiled. "Such a big word."

The old woman looked at Charlotte with dead eyes.

"You were willing to let your son die and his killer go unpunished. Yes, loyalty is everything in this. Not least of all for you, Mr Nicodemus Bligh, with your chronic dedication and control of Lady Ravenswick. Shall we tell everyone about your scheme? Perhaps they already know."

Charlotte surveyed the faces. Edward Ravenswick's jaw tightened and he looked to his mother. She simply shook her head in resignation.

"Oh, I see that I'm right. The little conspiracy was known about in the family. At least by some of you. The library of books that were the family's lifeline – faked by Bligh."

Some maintained stony faces, but some were wrinkled in uncertainty. Charlotte continued. "You couldn't stop His Lordship before he uttered that one word, could you? *Fake*. If that ever came out it would ruin the Ravenswicks and their name forever. His Lordship didn't like it, but he was easy to control. Charles, however, less so. Isn't that right, Lady Ravenswick?"

Her Ladyship's eyes remained fixed on Charlotte.

"Celeste heard the arguments," Charlotte continued. "She observed you, that was her hobby, *and she wrote it all down*. She knew the arguments were about the books. I assumed it was just selling the treasures but really, Charles Ravenswick disagreed with selling *forgeries*, didn't he? And thought it would ultimately end up damaging the family even more. Why else would Celeste write that he said '*He was the only one thinking of the family name. If it came out, they would be ruined anyway*'?"

Mrs C cut in. "And it wasn't just Celeste who had her suspicions about why he'd been killed either, was it Mary?"

The young girl shifted uncomfortably in her seat, rigid, with a bloodless look about her. She glanced at her mother, who did not return her gaze.

"I don't know what you mean." But from the churlish look on Mary's face, she clearly did.

Mrs C reached into the other pocket of her uniform. Triumphantly, she held aloft a number of bent and deformed fountain pens. "Looks like I'm not the only scribbler here. But, unfortunately, this writer chose not to use paper as her notebook. Behold, a mauled Parker duofold." She tutted and shook her head. "A very beautiful Swan Mabie Todd – complete with a severely mutilated nib. And, perhaps the greatest sin of all, the Sheaffer Radite – destroyed." She gave Mary a school-ma'am look. "Sometimes, the pen is not quite as mighty as the sword. Perhaps a pocketknife would have been a better idea." She threw the ruined pens on the table in front of Mary. "You were too frightened to break the circle of your family, so you left behind these clues instead.

"You left the carvings didn't you, Mary? *'Sacrifice.'* *'Fake.'* You *knew* your uncle had been sacrificed but, like everyone else here, you were too afraid to break ranks. You couldn't risk that."

Mary shrugged but the fear was already in her face. She looked quickly to Nicodemus Bligh and then to her mother. "I didn't…"

"Like children," Charlotte said in a distant voice.

Mrs C looked a little frustrated by the interruption. "Yes, dear. You've had a terrible shock. Perhaps sit quietly."

"Like children." Charlotte's eyes settled on Bartram. "When you said 'like children' about the ravens, you didn't mean that the birds are childlike, did you?"

He shook his head.

"You didn't use the word 'are.' You didn't mean the birds are childish. You meant that they *like* children. If it had been Celeste teaching the birds, she would definitely have taken pride in that. She would not have let that go unmentioned. But if it *wasn't* Celeste, it was the only other person in the house who Mr Bartram would think of as childlike. Mary Ravenswick." She turned to look at the watchful girl.

"You weren't just leaving the carvings. You taught the ravens your clues too. You are the childlike one here. Always cast as the baby sister. In court, you referred to being too young to be given any money. You couldn't speak to me directly for fear of what would happen, but you could leave your clues. Just like in the detective novels you adore so much, you set up a puzzle."

Mary looked to her mother again, but the old woman refused to return her gaze.

"Oh yes, you knew a lot more than just the fact that this was about sacrifice and the books. You were there that night in the lift. You'd seen the execution and elements of it bothered you. Things didn't make sense to you, did they, Mary? And you taught them to say more…"

The ravens' words fluttered in her head again. "*See, Blood.*" The birds had said that. Charlotte closed her eyes and imagined the black-eyed creatures looking up at her, their beaks poised, open on those words.

She whispered it again to herself. "See, Blood."

"Are you sure you're alright, dear?" Mrs C murmured. "You've had a…"

Charlotte opened her eyes and looked into the blank wall opposite. "See, Blood," she said. "See, Blood. See, Blood." She chanted it quietly to herself like she was saying a rosary.

All along, she'd been seeing it through the prism of herself. Her own name. But Mary wouldn't have known Charlotte's name before she arrived. How could she have started teaching it to the birds? Charlotte herself didn't know she was coming until the day she travelled down.

It wasn't her name. Charlotte drew out the words in her head. First of all, she removed that misleading capital letter. "See, blood." Almost. Something else. She let the words stand alone.

A very different meaning was looking back at her now.

Charlotte breathed the words out. "See blood."

"Mary, when you taught the ravens to say 'See, Blood?' I thought it meant 'Do you see, Miss Blood?' But that wasn't what you taught them to say at all was it?"

The girl shrugged half-heartedly but the panic was in her face. She'd spent so long devising her little puzzles that she hadn't considered what would happen if someone worked them out.

"No, you meant 'see blood.' As in someone saw blood."

"Of course they did!" Edward sneered. "My brother was shot. We all saw blood."

"So why go to the trouble of leaving that as one of her clues?" She paused and looked around the room. "Because it had to be someone who *should not* have seen blood."

Mary's eyes widened as the realisation began to dawn on her what she had done. She had stepped outside the circle.

49

"It's in Heskin's evidence to the inquest," Mrs C began.

"Wait, you read the file?" Charlotte looked confused.

"Yes, of course I did. How else was I going to help you?" Mrs C shook her head. "You were stumbling along aimlessly. I had to get involved. I sat by your bed some nights, reading the file."

"It was you? Why didn't you just tell me you were here?"

"Because you'd have sent me away. Also, I could see things you weren't party to, listen to the servants' gossip."

Charlotte's head felt like it might crack open and all those random ideas she'd had would just spill out onto the floor. Mrs C, in contrast, was solid and assured. And she had a gun.

Mrs C radiated confidence. "Heskins."

Fresh doubt clouded his face.

"You gave evidence to the inquest that you were the first to examine Charles Ravenswick. Let me just read that to you." Mrs C felt in her old handbag and pulled out the file. Charlotte's file.

Charlotte gazed in disbelief.

"Be a love and read the section of evidence I'm talking about would you, dear? I've only got the one hand." She winked at Charlotte.

The group looked to the other hand she resolutely kept in her pocket.

"Where did you –"

"Stole it from Bligh." Mrs C handed Charlotte the file. "Come on, read deary. I've marked it up."

Bligh was dumbfounded. "This is –"

"Evidence of the fact that you stole a file because you were trying to hide the fact that you shot someone? Yes. Continue, Charlotte. Mr Heskins' evidence, if you please."

Charlotte paused. Then flicked to the relevant page and began to read. "*I looked down his body and then I bent him over. There was blood on his shirt, sir. He'd been shot. I sat him back against the wall and then the lift started to move again. It didn't take us long to arrive upstairs. There was a lot of shouting and crying, especially from Lady Ravenswick. We got the door open as quickly as possible.*'"

She looked up at Mrs C.

"Now read Lady Ravenswick's brief account, please."

Charlotte flicked to the relevant page. "*The lift then arrived. I was aware that there was a lot of shouting and screaming. My son, Charles, was slumped in the corner. There was blood on his shirt. My other son, Edward, came towards me and held me. He told me Charles was dead. He had been shot. I'm afraid, at that point, I was rather upset, which in turn led to my husband becoming very distressed.*'" Charlotte glanced up.

"And finally, Edward Ravenswick's."

Mrs C was guiding her through like a conductor.

Charlotte dutifully obliged. "*Heskins had checked for signs of life and confirmed that my brother was dead. It was indeed a bullet wound and Charles had been shot.*'"

Mrs C waited. "Sometimes it is what we are not told,

the things that are not said, that are important. It is those little usual parts of life we take for granted, that are missed out or overlooked in a recount of a dramatic incident simply because we just expect them to be there. We assume everyone knows that is how it is. For instance, he has two arms. Two legs. Nobody says that, but it is the case." Her eyes remained on Charlotte. "Tell me, which part of a visit or social occasion do you most enjoy?"

Charlotte was slightly surprised by the question. "Well, the dressing, I suppose. The clothes."

"And the dressing gong would not have happened yet. That occurs usually at seven, but the visit to His Lordship interrupted that."

"Correct," Heskins agreed.

"However, at this time in an evening, with the whole family gathered together alongside various members of staff to pay a visit to His Lordship on New Year's Eve, tell me, would Charles Ravenswick have *only* been wearing a shirt? Would he have just been in his shirt sleeves?"

"Good heavens, no." Heskins looked appalled at the idea. "Of course not."

"Of course not," Mrs C repeated. "There is no conceivable way he would have done that. Of course he wouldn't. Like all the gentlemen of the family in the lift at that time, he would have been wearing a jacket. That's correct, isn't it?"

"Of course it's correct." Edward interrupted, increasingly irritated at the idea this was even being discussed. "We maintain standards here."

Mrs C stood gravely in front of the congregation. "From your evidence Mr Heskins, it is clear Charles Ravenswick was shot in the back. You bent him over and his jacket...?"

"As I bent him forward it pulled up over his back and I could clearly see his shirt and the blood. Immediately! Just as I said. I saw the blood on the shirt straightaway. It was obvious."

"You then returned him to his seated position."

"Yes!"

"And Lady Ravenswick confirmed that." Mrs C recounted the evidence again. "My son, Charles, was slumped in the corner. There was blood on his shirt." Mrs C leaned towards them. "He was slumped in the lift with his back against the wall and wearing a jacket. So there was no conceivable way Lady Ravenswick could have seen that there was blood on his shirt when the lift arrived before the door was opened. Her hysterics are mistimed. She has gone too early with her reaction. The only possible reason there can be for that, is she knew it was her son who was going to be shot. Because she planned it in advance."

Lady Ravenswick's lips faltered but she did not speak.

"See blood," Charlotte whispered and looked at Mary who would not meet her gaze. "She couldn't have seen it."

"And I think if we look at the small display of guns here, we can see one of them is missing." Mrs C nodded towards a case of pistols on the far wall. Clearly one was missing.

"All present and correct," Charlotte murmured.

"What's that, dear?" Mrs C frowned.

"Oh, just something someone said in the smoking room. It's not important."

Mrs C continued regardless. "You see, Celeste had said they were arguing. She says it's always the same thing they argue about. We know from her previous entries, that's the books. Bligh's fake books. Lady Ravenswick can only know in advance that her son would be shot if she'd sent someone in there to do it. Their elaborate scheme was devised to divert blame onto everyone." Mrs C looked around the astonished faces.

"And if you're still in any doubt at all, another clue you left us, Mary, was power, wasn't it? That didn't mean power within the family or control. You meant the electricity. That part didn't add up to you either, did it? They couldn't possibly know there'd be a power cut at that exact moment when they intended to shoot him. Because there wasn't. In your attempt to dispose of Miss Blood –"

"Mother?" Edward said in disbelief.

Lady Ravenswick didn't answer.

"Oh yes. You didn't think Miss Blood would survive so there was no need to disguise what you were able to do from up here in your little tower." Mrs C held out her arm to the control panel with various buttons. "You can stop the lift and restart it. You can turn out the light."

"We know that. We all know that," Edward said. "But it doesn't mean she did. There are often power cuts here. This is nonsense."

"Celeste's diary..." Charlotte said vaguely.

"Oh, you mean this." Mrs C reached in her bag and, like a magician, pulled out the diary. "Stole it from Bligh."

"What?" Charlotte had a look of mindless astonishment on her face.

"Never mind that now, girl." She held the diary out towards her. "If there's something in there..."

Charlotte took it and leafed through to the end. "On

New Year's Eve, she was writing in her diary. She called for cocoa. There were five hours to go and she hadn't had her cocoa."

Edward sighed and lit a cigarette.

"Mr Bartram, you'd just fed the birds and were clearing away. You told me that you feed them at six thirty. From what I saw, that takes about ten to fifteen minutes. It's then ten minutes back to the house. What time were you at the lift?"

"Seven o'clock. Heskins said I was to be there at seven."

"So you all met at the lift at seven. Got in the lift. Then the power cut happened. Correct?"

No one answered.

"Celeste's cocoa meanwhile has been forgotten. It's not been delivered. That's right, isn't it? She doesn't want it sitting there getting cold. So, she set about getting it herself. She rang for the cocoa." Charlotte looked around them. "Mr Heskins?"

He looked up.

"What sort of servants' bells do you have here? The old bell and string mechanism?"

"No." His voice broke. He looked at Lady Ravenswick.

"No, you don't do you. Tell us what it is, Mr Heskins."

"It's an indicator board."

"Powered by? Electricity?"

He nodded.

"Now, the cocoa isn't delivered to her room. She says she goes out down the hallway to pick it up. But why would someone do that? No one would go all the way up from the kitchens with the cocoa just to leave it down the hall. Why would someone leave it sitting there when it's just as easy to take it to her room? Because there is no one, is there, Mr Heskins? The girl sees no one. No one took it up."

"No."

"No person took it up. She says she will '*have to trog down the hallway to fetch it myself from the hatch!*' So it's delivered via the…" She left a pause for him to fill.

"Dumb waiter."

"That's right. It took me a while to realise why the girl had to go out down the hallway to get it after it was delivered. And please, just for the sake of completeness, Mr Heskins, the dumb waiter is powered by what?"

"Electricity."

"Electricity. That's right. So we know at seven o'clock, when they'd been told to be at the lift, the girl can see to write in her diary, she's able to ring for a drink via the electric servants' bell and it is then delivered via the dumb waiter powered by electricity. At no point does she say there was a power cut. Because… there wasn't one."

"Good." Mrs C nodded.

"Thank you."

"Lady Ravenswick…" Mrs C continued. "I return to my earlier assertion. You can, and you *did*, stop the lift. There was no power cut."

The faces were dumbfounded watching. Mrs C was relishing her moment and gearing up for the final pronouncement.

"Yes, this was your little conspiracy, wasn't it? You had to get rid of Charles Ravenswick as he was standing in the way of your plan for the survival of Ravenswick Abbey. Without which the family faced certain disaster. There would be a new heir – Edward, who cared little for the books and was only interested in the finer things in life and, of course, Rachel. Oh, the second son would be much easier to control." Mrs C paused and stared intently at the stern-eyed woman. "Lady Ravenswick, you sacrificed your son for the survival of the Ravenswicks. For the survival of the Abbey. You set up the party, gathered everyone in that lift, then sent your assassin to shoot Charles Ravenswick in the back, in a darkness of your creation. When the lift finally made it to the top, of course you already knew he'd been shot, because you were the one who arranged it in a way that would perfectly disguise the identity of the killer. They would all be caught in a conspiracy they had no idea they were party to and one they would never be able to leave. All for the sake of the Ravenswicks."

The room stalled, every face along the line bewildered.

"Your loyalty was put to the ultimate test, wasn't it, Nicodemus Bligh? Would you kill a man for the survival of the family, to ensure your work and, more importantly, what you'd done, was not exposed?"

He was silent.

"I think we have our answer," Mrs C said quietly.

For those assembled, watching a drama they had unwittingly been part of, their hatred seemed easier to shift onto Bligh than any other person. He was a man built for loathing.

He fidgeted uneasily in his seat, his eyes fixed on Lady Ravenswick.

"Your Ladyship," he whispered. There was a desperate, almost pleading look to him now. "They will hang me."

She remained as unmoved as ever.

"They will hang *you*," he added.

"No!" It wasn't Lady Ravenswick's voice. It was Mary's. "Mother. I never meant…"

Lady Ravenswick turned to Mary. "And yet you did. Your foolish little game, your silly notes and clever trail of breadcrumbs. It has led them straight to me. And now I will be punished and this family will fall. *You* will fall." She straightened and fixed her eyes ahead.

Mary's eyes glistened with tears and she looked in savage anger to Mrs C. "You... you..." The girl stumbled and wiped her sleeve across her face before shouting, "For a detective writer, you really don't know the rules of the game, do you?"

A baffled expression passed over Mrs C. Charlotte looked down at the diary and the folder. They'd been her guidebooks so far. Mrs C's reasoning was faultless.

"How do you mean?" Mrs C said slowly.

The girl leaned back in her chair and folded her arms. "You have chosen the clues that fit your theory. But it doesn't work if you do it that way round. There were more! It's not right. It doesn't work. It doesn't work! You have to use *all* the clues."

50

"Mary." Edward's voice was faltering. "If you know who did this, you have to say now. The family is depending on you. This... this *buffoon* of a woman is going to hang our mother. Speak, for God's sake. Who did it?"

The girl let her head fall. In a weak voice she simply said, "I don't know."

Edward's face reduced to anger. "What do you mean, you don't know? You've been leading this bloody woman up our garden path with your silly clues and now she's here, at the door, ready to bring down the axe. For God's sake, Mary, grow up! Now! You have to say."

She lifted her head defiantly. "I said, I don't know. I saw things. I left the clues because I wanted this woman, this so-called *journalist* –" she stared at Charlotte "– to find out who killed my uncle. This wasn't supposed to go like this."

Edward laughed bitterly. "So you were groping around in the dark and just setting it all out there without any idea who was going to get hurt."

Charlotte's mind stumbled. Mary was right. Mrs C had cherry-picked the clues. There was more. They had been arguing about the same thing they always did. Celeste had said so in her diary. She'd been out and about, spying on her family again. But who had been arguing? A nagging idea was growing. Something was there. She'd seen it.

"It doesn't work," she mumbled. "Something's wrong."

They looked at her in confusion.

"He couldn't have done it," Charlotte said, almost disbelieving herself.

"What do you mean?" Concern entered Mrs C's face now.

Charlotte looked up at her. "I don't think Bligh could have done it."

"What?" Mrs C looked wounded. "Why? Lady Ravenswick knew her son was going to be shot. She stopped the lift and turned out the lights for it to happen."

"Bligh wasn't there."

They all stared at her, one of them through killer's eyes.

"Of course he was!" Rachel said.

"I mean *before*. Before the lift. You weren't there Mr Bligh, were you?"

"So what?" Rachel shrugged.

"Because he wasn't there when they were arguing."

Rachel still looked unimpressed.

Bligh didn't speak but there was a silent relief in his frightened look.

"Celeste went to fetch a new diary and *you* told her off for stealing one of your notebooks, didn't you?"

He nodded once.

"Heskins went to get you."

She looked at the tight-lipped butler.

"In fact –" Charlotte frowned "– Heskins went to get all the staff that were in the lift. It was the staff party, apparently. But this was only a handful... a random selection that seemed to have no thought to it. Where was Mrs Thornycroft, Nanny

Austin, even Nurse Sidmouth? I used to wait weeks for the staff party. The planning was endless." Charlotte paused. "But Mr Jeffers didn't even have time to get changed. This wasn't a pre-arranged, organised party. This was a hurried gathering of people. We're told there was something to discuss about the will. Yet, the solicitor who drafted that had been days before. If you have an invalided, sick man and you're organising a party for the staff and family around him, you'd organise it more than half an hour before hand. Quite the opposite of being a carefully planned out crime, you hadn't planned this at all, had you?"

The room was silent.

The next noise was the distant cry of a bird.

Something snagged in Charlotte's memory. She closed her eyes and threw her mind back to that first moment with the ravens. Their black beaks were wide, that strange, unnerving creaking sound had lifted from them and formed into words. It was such an unbelievable moment, hearing a bird speak, that she hadn't landed on the words themselves until now. She heard them again as one said, "Shot in the dark."

"What did you say?" Elizabeth asked.

Charlotte opened her eyes to see Mrs C leaning closer.

"Are you alright, dear? This is your drugs, Bligh. You'll pay for this." Mrs C gave him a piercing look. She held Charlotte's hand. "Duckie?"

"The ravens said, 'shot in the dark.'" Charlotte's eyes widened. "Was this something else that didn't make sense to you, Mary?"

The girl didn't answer.

Charlotte started flicking through the folder, her fingers frantic. "Mr Jeffers."

The gardener looked suddenly scared.

"Now then," Bartram cut in. "He ain't done nothing wrong."

"This is time for the truth. Mr Heskins?"

"You're just scatter-gunning blame, now." Edward slumped back into his chair.

"Mr Heskins, where did you find Jeffers when you went to tell him to come to the house?"

Mr Heskins reluctantly spoke. "He'd been mending a wall. A large tree had come down."

"Is that right, Mr Jeffers?" Charlotte asked.

Jeffers looked around helplessly. "Aye. Happens a lot. Wind comes over the moors. Had to make it safe. I ain't lying," he said, panicked.

"I know. I know." Charlotte looked at him kindly. "Mr Bartram, you thought Jeffers was out shooting rabbits for the ravens. That's what you told me, isn't it?"

Bartram nodded.

"Why?"

"I'm sorry?"

"Why did you tell me that?"

The man folded his thick arms. "Because it's the truth. I don't tell lies. Not for anyone."

"And yet, it wasn't true. He was mending the wall."

They all watched her with suspicion.

"You *thought* he was shooting rabbits. Why? He hadn't told you that."

"I... I..." Bartram was clearly struggling to remember. "I heard his gun."

"Mary." Charlotte shifted her sights again.

The girl jolted.

"You said..." Charlotte riffled through the file. "At the

inquest, it was completely black in that lift when the power went."

The girl gave one nod. "It was. Everyone here knows that."

"You also carved, *Bang! Bang!*"

"Yes." She nodded her head at speed as if willing Charlotte on. "Yes, I did!"

"Edward Ravenswick."

The man sighed. "Are you just going to go through my entire family and staff in turn accusing them of murder?"

"It usually works," Mrs C said sagely.

Charlotte looked down at the file. "You told the court that Charles shouted, 'No!' There was a bang. Something dropped to the floor which made a thud on the carpet. This was followed by a much louder, heavier sound of something else falling to the floor."

She paused and looked up.

"The lights were out."

"Yes, dear," Mrs C said slowly. "Lady Ravenswick had full control of the power to the lift."

"If the lights were out and it was completely black, ask yourself one thing. How did Charles Ravenswick see that someone was about to shoot him in the back? Why did he shout 'No!'? He wouldn't have been able to see that someone was holding out a gun."

51

"So, you're saying he shot himself in the back?" Elizabeth leaned back dismissively.

"No." Charlotte paused, letting the thoughts settle. "I'm saying we need to look at what we know. *All* that we know." She counted them off on her fingers. "One, Bartram thinks Jeffers is shooting rabbits. Two, Charles Ravenswick sees the person about to shoot him in the back. He shouts 'No!' even though it's pitch black and no one can see anything. Three, Lady Ravenswick sees blood on his shirt even though Charles Ravenswick was shot in the back and was slumped with his back to the wall when the lift arrived."

She looked around. "And finally, four. Celeste knew there was arguing after six o'clock. When there were only six hours to go, she was excited to start a new diary so went to get another notebook. She wrote that Bligh was in the library and told her off for stealing. *'I shall tell Granny immediately. She'll put him in his place.'* After that, she found them all arguing about the usual thing. The books. Only one person argued about that – Charles Ravenswick. Celeste also said, *'Poor Granny'*. Charles Ravenswick wasn't arguing with Bligh, he was arguing with you, Lady Ravenswick. But the real question is... where?"

Charlotte paused to pick up the folder. Then she read. "'*On New Year's Eve 1928, I'd been with my husband all day as he was quite ill. Rather than going down, I called all the family to attend upon us, along with some members of staff who have been with us for a significant period of time.*'" You were here. In the tower. If Charles Ravenswick was arguing with you about books and you never left the tower, then he must have been here too. He was already up here just before the party. So why was he even in the lift at all?" Charlotte looked around. "Mary, you carved 'Bang! Bang!' Mr Bartram, you heard a distant shot. That is true. A gun was fired earlier. But it wasn't Jeffers shooting rabbits."

A cautious murmur travelled round the group.

"That's right, isn't it, Lady Ravenswick?" Charlotte stared at the stately woman, her mind reeling. "It was Charles Ravenswick being shot. Your son was shot before he ever went into that lift, wasn't he?"

The old lady didn't move.

"That's ridiculous!" Edward shouted. "I saw him. He was alive and talking to me."

"Alive maybe. But half dead."

Edward frowned.

Charlotte rose unsteadily to her feet. "He was already here, arguing. He has no reason to go back down and come up again. But he does. Lady Ravenswick stops the lift and turns out the light. And then –" Charlotte looked around everyone "– the already fatally wounded Charles Ravenswick shouts 'No!' and shoots the gun before throwing it into the centre of the lift. He slumps to the ground. The lights come back on, and there is the heir to the family, dead. Shot in the back."

"But why?" Elizabeth said quietly. "Why on earth would he do such a thing?"

"For one very powerful reason. To protect the person who shot him."

Lady Ravenswick stood with all the grace she was born to. "You have no proof, Miss Blood." She walked away from the table, turning her back on Charlotte.

"Oh, but I do." Charlotte's voice was cold. "The gun was a Colt Derringer. I wouldn't be my father's daughter if I didn't know that particular model fires only one shot. That shot is in the wall of the lift shaft. I felt one perfect, thin hole in the smooth wall when I was down there, frantically trying to scale the sides. It was a bullet hole. To think, if you hadn't thrown me down there, I would never have seen where that bullet ended up – a second bullet no one had been looking for. The inquest said he was shot with that gun.

"If the gun can only fire one shot and that shot is in the wall of the lift shaft, then Charles Ravenswick had to have been shot with a different bullet and, given there were no other guns on anyone in that lift, and there were no other shots fired after the lift shot, he had to have been shot outside the lift, before he even got in it.

"He didn't die instantly from the wound. Tonight, it took about thirty minutes to gather all those same people in the lift. Celeste heard arguing after six o'clock. We also know what time the party was organised, since Celeste drew her sad clock." She held up the drawing. "With the swords stabbed from the heart of it downwards. The hands of the clock. Six thirty. At that point you've stopped your arguing and suddenly decided on this random gathering, hastily pulled together for an impromptu, unplanned party. All unwittingly drawn together to be suspects." Charlotte put down the diary and directed her next comment to Lady Ravenswick. "A dying man who had been shot would only willingly enter into such a scheme for one reason. To protect someone he was enduringly loyal to."

Charlotte stared at the old woman. "His own mother."

Lady Ravenswick paused her slow walk across the room and reached out a hand to steady herself. There was a static energy in the room that no one dare break. All eyes were on the old lady.

"Mother?" Edward began to stand.

She didn't speak but simply collapsed across the bed. "They've found me out," she said in a worn, broken voice. "What do I do now? What can I do?" The desperation was raw. "How I wish I didn't have to be the strong one anymore."

Charlotte thought of the photograph she'd seen in the smoking room. And she looked at the defeated figure in the bed. Brought low by...

Charlotte's bleary mind shifted. A pain shot through the side of her head. Whatever they'd given her was still swimming in there. She rubbed at her temples, trying to find clarity. There was something more here. Something that didn't fit. A cloud of deceit and superstition had obscured everything, from ghostly monks screaming, foretelling imminent death, to mystics with fake books. But the answer was there.

She stopped, her eyes wide. The answer *was* there! It was right there in her own head. She rested her fingers on her pounding temples.

"Brought low by drugs."

Charlotte sounded like she disbelieved herself.

"Bligh, you sedated Lord Ravenswick *after* you came up in the lift. Why did you do that?"

He didn't answer but simply looked away in shame.

"Because you had to! You had to silence him. You were drugging him."

She paused. "And... and the scream the servants reportedly heard earlier wasn't any ghostly monk foretelling an imminent death. It was you, Lady Ravenswick. You *screamed*."

The old lady didn't move.

"Because of what you *saw*. You screamed because you *saw* your son being shot. You witnessed it and screamed out. But if it wasn't you who shot Charles Ravenswick, there was only one other person it could be who was here." Charlotte paused. "Your husband. Lord Ravenswick shot his son, didn't he?"

Lady Ravenswick cast one sad smile back to Charlotte before lifting the syringe to her husband's neck. "Such a bright young thing, Miss Blood." She turned away. "So it is time, my Lord."

The small, metallic gleam of the needle caught the light.

Lord Ravenswick stirred in the bed. "No," he whispered. "I can be good, I promise."

"I know, dear. It is not your fault."

He winced a little as the needle slipped into his skin.

Lord Ravenswick's eyes flickered momentarily, then a look of release spread through his face. "I'm so sorry, my dear. I do love Charles, you know that. I just couldn't stand to see him treating you like that. All that shouting and incessant *arguing*. It's not his place to speak to his mother, my *wife*, Lady Ravenswick, in such a way. I just went a little mad. Sometimes I do, you know. Can't control it. Thought it might help things along, you know. Help with your lovely little books. Give him a scare. What!" A devious laugh gurgled out of him before instantly dissolving into a rasping cough.

"Shh," she said. "It's all over now. You sleep, my darling. Nothing to worry about now."

He nodded. "Awfully tired today. Might go for a hunt later. Get the old ticker going, you know. How's Charles? Is he up for a ride out yet? Still sulking, I suspect. It was just a little flesh wound. Pea shooter. Should be fine now."

"Oh, yes," Lady Ravenswick said in a voice barely above a whisper. "Nothing really. I should think he'll be ready for that, darling. I'll get three horses saddled up and I'll come along with you. Let me just deal with a few things first."

"Oh, that will be marvellous. Just like we used to. Get Edward out too."

She shook her head. "He will have business here to see to. He's going to be very busy now."

Edward Ravenswick was standing slowly, a look of stunned disbelief etched on his face.

"Next time perhaps, my Lord."

"Alright, dear." Lord Ravenswick's head fell to the side. A slight, pathetic smile caught the edges of his mouth. It was a tortured look in his eyes as they finally lost focus. One thin frond of breath escaped through his pale lips, a thread on the cold air before it disappeared into nothing.

Lady Ravenswick waited, the only movement her frail frame lifting and falling.

The rest of them watched, transfixed in disbelief. Shattered.

Lady Ravenswick lifted herself carefully but remained with her back to the room. "So now you know. My darling husband's brain was ravaged by illness. He often went into terrible fits, shouting, growing increasingly violent. It had grown worse. He had little memory of any of it after the event. It wasn't his fault. We had to hide him away, up here, where he could do no harm. At least, that's what I thought. And I loved him you see. No one could know what he'd become or what he had done to his own son. Charles knew that too. He was loyal to the end."

This fine, delicate lady, as white as porcelain, turned and looked at each face in turn. In the dim light, with the pale remembrance of the woman she once was, there was an almost spirit-like look to her. A captured nature. And Charlotte's mind went to that night when Bligh told them all of the white ravens, scorched black by the gods.

It was only when Lady Ravenswick's body had completely turned towards them, that another small, silver syringe could be seen sticking out of her wrist, similar to the one she had used in her husband's neck and just as empty. Her eyes failed a little at first but she gathered herself.

"Charles did indeed make the ultimate sacrifice. But quite willingly. He devised our little plot as he stood there bleeding. Nicodemus, dear Nicodemus, I am sorry if any blame fell upon you. This family owes you a great debt. You were willing to make the ultimate sacrifice."

A troubled look of doubt had settled on the mystic's face.

"Dearest Nicodemus, you dealt with His Lordship so well after... after the incident. I will never forget your kindness. I'm so sorry that I was so ready to let you take the blame. But the family must be protected. You understand that."

"Your Ladyship." Tears coursed down his cheeks. Whether in relief or sorrow it was impossible to discern. Perhaps even he didn't know.

"My husband was delirious and still ranting. He could not know what he'd done. You must see that."

She appealed to the room but no one responded.

"Charles was adamant." Lady Ravenswick shifted a little in pain and gasped. "His Lordship must be protected. But no one person could be accused. He told me we must all carry this together. He was firm about that. Dear Charles, he was the bravest of souls."

Edward took a tentative step towards her, but she held up her hand.

"We had to act so very quickly. Charles was in difficulties. He knew he was dying, and this way no one would ever be blamed. The household would shoulder it equally. I dare say if we had asked you all, you would have agreed. I am in no doubt of that."

Charlotte looked around the circle of troubled faces. There was nothing but doubt there.

"I die in the assurance that this household would have stood firm." She drew another difficult breath. "So, I kissed my son goodbye, my darling Charles, and he took the gun with him, reloaded it and went down in the lift to wait at the bottom. I knew I didn't have much time. It was high risk, but it was all we had. Heskins would not fail me. I made sure he gathered you all quickly, as many names as I could trust and as fast as possible. When I heard the lift start, that was my cue." Her eyes closed momentarily.

"I stopped it and turned out the light, just as Charles had said to. And then I heard it. The shot. The fall. The screams. And I knew he was gone. My darling son. Sacrificing himself for his family. His name."

She paused and looked at her remaining children. "Dearest Edward and Mary. I am sorry to leave this burden to you. It is for the best. But we must be brave. We must always be brave. For the Ravenswicks." She fell sideways onto the bed without another sound.

52

An aching silence hung over the room. Shock lingered on some faces longer than others. To move would in some way be an acceptance of it all.

Nicodemus Bligh was the first to approach the bed, tears already blistering in his eyes.

"Get away from them." Mary's voice cut in, vivid with anger. "You've done enough."

Bligh looked confused. "I've only ever tried to help."

"By lying? Cheating? *Forging* books in our name?" Edward Ravenswick's voice was sharp with derision.

They were already turning.

The image of that executed raven landed in Charlotte's mind again.

"I wasn't even there when he was shot!" Bligh insisted. "I was willing to take the blame for it all. You saw that!"

"I saw no such thing." Rachel joined in now. The family stood in a line of firm, unforgiving faces. They had found their villain.

Mary ran towards her mother in a great display of grief, throwing herself onto the two bodies and wailing.

"Heskins," Edward said efficiently. "Perhaps if you could call the police."

Heskins rose and walked towards the telephone.

"That's already been taken care of." Mrs C was solemn.

"What?" Bligh looked aghast.

"Don't concern yourself, Bligh." Edward looked at Charlotte. "This is for the sad, mutually agreed suicide of my beloved parents who have struggled with my father's condition for so long. Isn't that correct, Miss Blood?"

Charlotte's gaze was still fixed on the final drama on the bed. Their bodies were such delicate shells of what had once been powerful souls. Lord Ravenswick, the great hunter in the photographs, god of the press. Lady Ravenswick, an impenetrable, proud force by his side, unquestionable in her devotion to the survival of Ravenswick and the maintenance of this old regime. They seemed so diminished now. Nothing.

"I am very aware of what I saw and what I heard, Lord Ravenswick." Charlotte was the first to acknowledge his change of title.

Edward Ravenswick raised a speculative eyebrow. "Meaning?"

"Meaning, Your Lordship, that this house, this family, has been in the grip of a lie for so long and that has caused nothing but destruction. All of you –" her eyes travelled around the assembly "– have sought to maintain a dying world through utter, unquestioning devotion. You call it loyalty. I call it lies." She looked at Mrs C for confirmation. Her solemn nod was enough. "I am a *journalist*! I was sent to uncover the truth and that is what I will do."

"You can't mean that?" Elizabeth said in disbelief. "It will ruin us."

"The seeds of your destruction were already sown. An ancient family, falling into decay, desperately clinging to a faded world by any means possible."

"My father was a very sick man!" Edward protested.

"He was. And whether or not that led him to do what he did will be for others to decide. Perhaps he and his illness should not have been hidden away. How many countless elderly and sick are spoken of only in whispers? They are treated as shameful and hidden in your high towers and low places, away from the eyes of the world. A weakness to the proud heritage. Perhaps if you had not isolated him, drugged him and kept him in this half world, he might not have shot your only brother."

Edward's nostrils flared.

Charlotte looked around at them in turn. "You were all so desperate to support this realm that you never stopped to ask if you should. Heskins, you put me in danger twice because of your misplaced loyalty. Bligh, you forged the ancient texts so close to your own beliefs. Mary, you knew there was some untruth here but rather than speak out, you resorted to a childish game of messages. Even your new generation was forced to consign her thoughts and suspicions to a diary. Celeste would sooner seek out a stranger to come here and hand her book to rather than give it to one of her own. You have all become consumed by the family. So much pride and poverty!"

Edward raised himself up into his new role of Lord. His face set in fierce grandeur fitting for his elevated station. "And what would you know of family, Miss Blood?" His tone was defensive. Accusatory.

She gave a rueful smile. "I know that out of love, you have crafted fear. Devotion has become slavish loyalty."

Charlotte watched their impenetrable faces. She was undeterred. "You are all ruled by this place, this name, forever tied to this ship, even as it sinks. *That* is the true master here. If you do not break with it now, you will forever be enslaved. All of you."

Edward's eyes betrayed no emotion.

Charlotte pointed to the bed where the old Lord and Lady Ravenswick lay, their bodies already empty with death. "You call it loyalty. But the poison is deep, infecting every soul. You will lie and cheat and kill for it, so the world will see only the might of the Ravenswicks. It is time the doors were thrown open to honesty. I am free. Free to tell the world the truth, even if you are not."

The new Lord took a step forward.

Mrs C cleared her throat, watching the faces fill with bitterness and spite. She drew out the gun from her pocket and pointed it towards them.

Edward Ravenswick's face darkened. "So you think the world will listen to you over the words of a Lord?"

"Some won't," Charlotte admitted lightly. "But many will. I am going to write the truth. People have had enough of the lies, rules and trenches built simply to protect you old families. Your genteel art of deceit and corruption has had its day."

"Then Charles died in vain," Rachel said bitterly.

Charlotte shook her head. "Quite the opposite. Your husband's death will pave the way to the truth."

Rachel laughed. "And your own renown. We're very familiar with the motivations of the press here."

Charlotte shrugged and closed the folder. She pushed that, along with Celeste's diary, into the familiar, soft satchel and ran her fingers along the grooves left by the bars of the lift before flipping the front over. She flung the strap over her shoulder. "I'll take my chances with my own reputation, thank you. I am in control of my own life. Who knows, there might be some sympathy for the fact that I was almost killed by a lift."

"You have no proof," Edward said.

"Oh, but I do. The bullet in the wall of the lift shaft, shot from the Colt Derringer." She smiled. "And of course, the dying confession of Lord and Lady Ravenswick, whom *you* would never wish to defame."

The fury was deep in his eyes.

The sound of the lift starting silenced everyone. Serious, officious voices lifted up through the lift shaft.

"The police," Mrs C said confidently.

As Charlotte looked along the line of anxious, disbelieving faces, her eyes were drawn to the space where one of them should have been. Nicodemus Bligh had performed one last trick. He had disappeared. In the chaos of death, he'd seen his chance to save his skin.

Perhaps some might see it as magick. What kind, would remain a mystery, as would the whereabouts of the strange, mystic man who once lived at Ravenswick Abbey.

53

PRIDE & POVERTY
The "Locked-Lift Mystery" of Ravenswick Abbey is
solved by The Comet*'s own intrepid journalist!*
Charlotte Blood

Recent events at Ravenswick Abbey might be more at home in the pages of a detective story, but the truth about the murder of the heir to the Ravenswick family is stranger than fiction. Along with renowned crime writer, Mrs Ella Crossity, I was on the scene to solve the mystery of who killed Charles Ravenswick and how this carefully constructed lie has baffled detectives for a year. Police have confirmed that they discovered a second bullet lodged in the lift shaft at the abbey which was shot from the same Colt Derringer used in the incident – a single-shot pistol. Full details of their scheme and how I, Charlotte Blood, unravelled it, are inside.

Fulman threw the paper down on the desk, sending up a small flurry of dust into the air. Charlotte looked down at her own name there in bold letters at the top. He wedged the stub of a cigar into his slack mouth and leaned back on the chair that always looked like today might be the day it collapsed.

"So, you did it, Blood," Fulman said out of the unoccupied side of his mouth. The rolls of skin were flaccid and shone with sweat on this bitter January morning. There were no seasons in this office. "That was a good article. Lots of sales under your belt."

"Thank you, sir." Charlotte sat down before she was asked and swung one leg over the other, admiring her fine new silk stocking, her face the picture of satisfied delight. She was tempted to lean back and rest her feet up on that great big, cluttered desk. But that could wait a little longer.

Fulman narrowed his swollen eyelids until they looked like he'd gone ten rounds with Dempsey. "Never thought you could pull it off, Blood."

She gave him a smart smile. "Thank you, *sir*."

"It's good." There was a tone of reluctant admiration in his voice. "Sales are up. You're a hit, Blood!"

She smiled and flushed, those forget-me-not eyes sharper than ever today against her cheeks.

Fulman suddenly adopted a serious look and leaned forward over the desk, his elbows sitting like two ham knuckles on the leather. "They've put Ravenswick Abbey up for sale," he said abruptly, searching her face for a reaction.

She shifted uneasily in her chair, the smile diminishing. "I know."

"They're being investigated for fraud, but that phoney Bligh is still missing. Looks like they're out of time, Blood. Creditors at the door."

"I see." She breathed out heavily, pushing the thoughts away.

"After this, they ain't good for no one's money."

"If they ever were," she said shrewdly.

Fulman settled back, switching the cigar around in his mouth.

"I told the truth. That's what we're here for, isn't it?"

He turned the corners of those fat lips down and shrugged. "If you say so, Blood."

"I do." She folded her arms with absolute conviction.

Fulman leaned across the desk. "What *I* want to know is, have you got the stomach to do this again?"

She lifted herself up in the chair. "Yes, sir!"

He paused, his eyes assessing, and blew out a thick, deep fug of smoke. She could taste all that woody tobacco in the back of her throat.

"Right, Blood. Some archaeologists have found a tomb. Say it's some queen." He rooted around the piles of paper on his desk. "The Iceni? Bou…"

"Boudica, sir," she said keenly, her face lit with anticipation.

He looked impressed. "Well, let's see what you've got." He threw her the folder. This one had slightly more stains than the last one. "People seem to like you, Blood, although God knows why." He sighed. "They want you there for the opening. They've sent an invitation to the launch event."

"One?"

He looked perplexed. "How many do you need, Blood? It's not one of your gin parties. This is work!"

"I know, sir. I shall need one for myself and one for my side… my assistant, Mrs Ella Crossity. As I've said in the article, she was involved in cracking this case. People like her too. And anyway –" she widened her eyes innocently "– you can't very well send me off *on my own* into a tomb. That wouldn't be fitting at all, now would it?"

"I imagine, Blood, that you'd survive very well indeed. It's the dead I'm worried for!"

"I'm not going without her."

He frowned, drumming his tuberous fingers on the desk. "Alright. Alright. You can take the woman with you. I'll send someone down to sort out another invitation, but I expect results, Blood. None of your cocktails and nonsense."

"Sir, if it gets results..."

He threw up his hands. "I'll sort out some expenses. Some! I won't be held to ransom."

"I'll need a new dress... or two."

"Out, Blood! Now, before I change my mind."

She stood and picked up the folder, wedging it under her arm determinedly. "Yes, sir."

His eyes widened. "Leave, Blood!"

She skipped quickly out of the room. And this time her new one-bar shoes didn't clip with the rhythm of a hundred cobbler's nails. She couldn't wait to tell Mrs C.

54

At home in Mecklenburgh square, Mrs C read the same headline again with a keen interest.

PRIDE & POVERTY
The "Locked-Lift Mystery" of Ravenswick Abbey is
solved by The Comet*'s own intrepid journalist!*
Charlotte Blood

Recent events at Ravenswick Abbey might be more at home in the pages of a detective story, but the truth about the murder of the heir to the Ravenswick family is stranger than fiction. Along with renowned crime writer, Mrs Ella Crossity…

Mrs C's shrewd eyes travelled along the words, seeking out any further references to herself. Charlotte had been generous to include her but there was no question raised as to why the journalist's *landlady* had been present. That much had been overlooked. But then Charlotte had *overlooked* many things.

Mrs C was very aware, however, that this would be subject to careful scrutiny in other quarters. Any mention of Colonel Archie Blood, or B as they knew him, always was. The Service was ever watchful. An agent's widow writing for a newspaper would always be subject to surveillance but the inclusion of a retired agent, Ella Crossity, or L, would definitely set alarm bells ringing.

There'd been those who'd raised concerns at the time about B putting a retired operative in place to watch over his widow and keep her safe. But L was keen and had been out of the service for years. It seemed fair that a man who'd given so much of his life to the service might at least be extended this. Charlotte's guardian angel hadn't gone, he'd simply handed over the role.

Mrs C had already taken a risk after his death planting that letter from her father in a book. Charlotte had to know that the man who knew he was dying had good reason to act quickly in marrying her before she was forced into an unhappy marriage. It wasn't just a selfish act. She wanted to tell her that he'd set all this up so it wouldn't be a temporary reprieve either. But Mrs C had to step carefully. Each bit of information she fed her always led to more questions, always took Charlotte another step towards finding out and that was too risky. Too dangerous. Mrs C had promised a dying man that she'd keep Charlotte away from all this. Keep her safe. But in Charlotte's new investigative journalist role, that was going to prove a lot more difficult.

There'd already been one early misfire in the scheme which had to be covered over with a doctor's plaque and a waiting room. Charlotte had never mentioned the telegram again, from L to B. She knew Charlotte hadn't forgotten. She'd seen Charlotte looking for it. Mrs C had immediately burnt it, but she still saw that far away puzzled look come over Charlotte every so often. There were too many unanswered questions for Charlotte to ignore. One day she'd have to know everything. But not today. Today was for celebrations.

Mrs C looked at the newspaper again and Charlotte Blood's name right there at the top. Archie would have been proud. She could see his smile now. *"Let her enjoy this moment. And keep her safe."*

She glanced at the clock. Time to go.

55

Outside, the London morning fog clung to the air, blurring out the faces hurrying by. Charlotte pulled her new scarlet wool cape around her and readjusted the satchel over her shoulder. There was a distinct purpose in her quick, little steps. On the corner of Fleet Street, a newspaper boy shouted indecipherable words in a feisty voice. It was hard to know what he was saying but one word lifted above all the rest. Ravenswick.

Charlotte paused to look at the board. *"Ghostly Monk Seen on Dartmoor! Local Man Sees Figure in White Digging Near Bonehill Tor."*

Charlotte smiled to herself. So Bligh wasn't giving up, at least. Maybe he had been telling the truth. Whether he had or not, he'd become one of the ghost stories he'd tried to scare her with.

Ever since Charlotte's article, the papers had been filled every day with revelation after revelation.

Below on the board, in smaller letters, it said, "Lord Ravenswick divorce." She fished in her purse and handed a coin to the boy.

He passed her the paper with a mischievous smirk. "Looks like them toffs is for it. Good riddance!"

Charlotte frowned and a flicker of guilt passed over

her face. She looked down at her polished shoes and silk stockings. What wages were these? She ran her hand over the satchel, her fingers instinctively going to the initials. *AB + C.* Would Archie be proud of what she'd done? Pride wasn't something he was given to, usually.

"You alright there, Miss?" The young paper boy enquired.

She found her focus again. "Yes, yes. Sorry."

"I shouldn't go getting all misty-eyed for them buggers. They wouldn't bother burying you if you was dead."

Charlotte raised an eyebrow. "Quite. But fortunately I am not." She moved a little further down the road and spread out the front page of the paper. As she read the opening lines, any feeling of shame died. Edward Ravenswick had already put large sections of land up for sale, and an anonymous buyer had been found for the Abbey. The new Lord Ravenswick was now resident in an apartment in the South of France with Rachel Ravenswick. He and Elizabeth would soon be divorced. Their daughter, Celeste, was to remain in England at boarding school. Charlotte thought of the round-faced impudent girl, and her diary, now in the hands of the police. She wondered if she'd be angry or, in fact, pleased about the importance her work had taken on? Charlotte already knew the answer to that.

When questioned by reporters, Mary Ravenswick had said she would also remain in England, having come into a small trust which she would be using to take herself to university in Oxford. Would she be grateful for this new turn her life had taken, or would the memory of where those childish clues had taken both her mother and father forever be a weight around her?

It wasn't Mary Ravenswick though that Charlotte was looking for. In a small corner of page five, she finally found a reference to them. The ravens. There wasn't much except for a statement from the family that the birds had been relocated to Mr Bartram's home on the moors. When asked for a comment by one journalist, Mr Bartram simply said, "Don't go near the mires." Charlotte smiled to herself and thought of Bartram's small cottage, with its lingering memories of his wife, now playing host to these strange companions. She was pleased he would not be stranded in his loneliness anymore. Perhaps he might even talk to his new houseguests, although Bartram hadn't been that much of a conversationalist.

A small announcement had also been made in the births, marriages and deaths page.

"In view of the circumstances, The Comet *does not believe it is appropriate that there should be an obituary for either Lord or Lady Ravenswick. The funeral was sparsely attended, although the family said that was intentional. They were not buried in the family crypt due to the fact that Ravenswick Abbey will soon be under new ownership. The new owners do not wish Lord and Lady Ravenswick's graves to be on their land."*

It was a heart-punching blow to the family honour. They had tainted the name forever. They would always be the Lord who shot his son and the Lady who oversaw the forgery of ancient books. All for the sake of their unsinkable beliefs.

"Penny for them," the voice beside her cut in.

Charlotte turned quickly to see Mrs C, resplendent in a new velvet-trimmed hat. Mrs C's face filled up with a smile. It was the kind of smile you couldn't help returning.

"I think a pot of tea at Lyons is in order, and perhaps

a bun," she said, glancing down at the Ravenswicks splashed all over the papers again.

Charlotte nodded. "I have news."

Mrs C looked inquisitive. "News? Haven't you had enough of that? Dangerous business, these newspapers. You did almost get squashed by a lift, dear."

"Another assignment." Charlotte folded the paper and pushed it inside her satchel.

"Assignment?" Mrs C said.

"For Fulman."

"I see. I presume I will be accompanying you."

"Oh." Charlotte laughed. "Do you indeed?"

"Who else is going to keep you safe?"

Charlotte frowned. "Why do you say that?"

"How do you mean, Duckie?"

"Just... that phrase. Never mind." She shook her head as if shaking the thought away. "Just something someone once said. We're going to find a tomb, Mrs C, an archaeological dig to uncover one of the greatest discoveries of all time – Boudica's tomb! There's a party for it and everything."

"A party. I see. And when might this be?"

Charlotte hadn't read the invitation properly until now. She slipped it out from her satchel and glanced down before looking back at Mrs C. A smile began to form on Charlotte's face. "The party is tomorrow night."

THE END

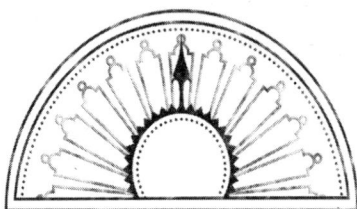

Author's note

The rugged beauty of Dartmoor remains a constant source of inspiration. A long history unrolls across its vast landscape, along the spine of its granite tors and round its stone circles and tombs. It is easy to be transported to a different world, where echoes of another existence remain in the long-abandoned settlements. The outlines of ancient, deserted villages are visible beside burial mounds and sacred Druid sites where pagan rituals were said to be performed. The remnants of those who once inhabited this environment persist in these pockets of largely untouched archaeology. Quarries from the old tin-making industry are now reclaimed by nature with their deep excavations forming reputedly depthless pools. The rusted old machinery is embedded in the ground and overgrown.

It is unimaginable how stark the lives of these various inhabitants would have been through time. The exposed environment can be profoundly bleak, the weather changing in an instant. It took me three attempts to make the journey to Wistman's Wood as the fog descended so fast that the path simply disappeared. It is disorientating how quickly a clear day can turn to rain and mist, dissolving every landmark and route. Once there, it is unsurprising that "wist" derives from the word "wisht", meaning eerie or uncanny. Or that the legendary Wild Hunt and its hellhounds is associated with this part of Dartmoor.

As well as the elements, the terrain can also change in an instant, the exact position of marsh ground and bogs frequently shifting. A physical map, not just a mobile phone, is a necessity, as reception is often non-existent. Mires are marked on the detailed Ordnance Survey maps and should be avoided. Many authors have been inspired by these wild, challenging places and the perils they contain. Just as with Sir Arthur Conan Doyle's Grimpen Mire in *The Hound of the Baskervilles*, the mire in this book is fictional. It is, however, based upon real mires nearby. The area itself is situated on thick, marshy ground. Bonehill and Bonehill Rocks are real, as is the marsh ground below.

Although inspired by the landscape, I have also changed some aspects, and others are entirely fictional, most notably Ravenswick Abbey. Sadly, this eccentric, crumbling house does not exist, nor does its aviary.

Wild ravens, however, do inhabit the moors, as do Dartmoor ponies. They are hardened beasts that exist in an environment where the wind can cut to the bone. Winter's teeth bite hard out on the moor.

It creates a unique atmosphere of isolation. Although quiet, it is far from peaceful. Finding yourself alone, surrounded by miles of harsh terrain beneath that low brimstone sky, can be unnerving. There is a suspension from reality which has attracted many authors over the years, not just Sir Arthur Conan Doyle. Agatha Christie chose it as the place where she finished writing her first novel, *The Mysterious Affair at Styles*, staying in The Moorland Hotel at Haytor, very close to where I have situated the fictional Ravenswick Abbey. She would return to Dartmoor as a setting in her work over the years in such novels as *The Sittaford Mystery*, which perfectly captures the atmosphere of bleak isolation when the guests become snowed in. This is a genuine hazard out on Dartmoor, The Warren House Inn being cut off for around twelve weeks in 1963 by snow drifts over twenty feet high.

Conditions where people are so exposed to the elements, and at the mercy of nature, have frequently led to darker influences being ushered in. What we cannot see or do not understand often resolves into the spiritual or supernatural. Out there at night on Dartmoor, it is not difficult to see why. A multitude of myths and legends have arisen to explain what might lurk in the black gulf that lies beyond the light. The mystical is easy to conjure given the fear this place can elicit. Grisly stories, such as that of Lady Howard, which I have included in the book, are rife. She was said to ride out in a carriage made of her husbands' bones, a skull from each one on the corners. Her companion was a great black dog with burning red eyes – a wisht hound and one of the inspirations for the hound of the Baskervilles. In reality, she was a woman greatly wronged by many of these husbands and labelled as a *wicked lady* to account for her actions.

Folk tales and horror stories abound in Dartmoor's history. Sadly, I could not include them all. That would be a different book. But a land of ghostly hands, figures that appear at will, witches, curses and devils, is fertile ground for a murder mystery. Superstition and belief are more easily manipulated in this lonely, all-consuming darkness.

In 1929, many parts of Dartmoor did not have electricity. Large manor houses often produced their own, and still do, via hydroelectricity. That, in turn, led to such innovations as the electrically powered indicator board rather than the traditional old servants' bells. Some went further. The great lift featured in this book was inspired by those which were installed in some country houses at the time for the elderly or infirm. These lifts were often unreliable and frequently broke down. In various accounts from people who experienced this, the overwhelming sense is of how disturbing it was to be trapped in such a cage in the darkness, unable to escape.

The people in this book are all in their own way trapped, their wings clipped and powerless to see any way out, except for one.

If you are tempted to explore Dartmoor further, safe travels. But remember, always take a *reliable* map, stick to the path and never go on your own after dark.

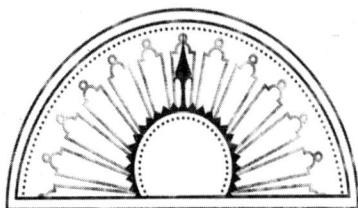

Acknowledgements

This book has been a labour of love for me. The Golden Age of Detective fiction has always been a passion of mine. It was my dream to actually set a book in that period. To do it justice, however, has taken an awful lot more than just my fancies. It has required a host of very skilled and patient people. Their insight, knowledge and ingenuity were necessary to make this more than just an imitation of those books I adore. I didn't want Charlotte to walk into the world as nothing more than a woman in a 1920s fancy-dress costume. She had to be real. It required the assistance of a lot of people, and for that I am eternally grateful.

Thank you to my agent, James Wills, who first showed enthusiasm for Charlotte Blood and whose wonderful ideas breathed life into her. Your suggestions opened up a whole new layer to her story, which lifted the entire book.

To my fabulous editor Ella Chappell, thank you for believing in this book. From our very first meeting, I was amazed by the passion you had for this series. Every step of the way you have given so much support and encouragement for this book. I cannot express how much that means to me. For any author to know they have someone who believes so keenly in their book is a true gift. Thank you. It means the world to me.

Thank you to everyone at Datura who have been endlessly supportive and kind. To Eleanor, Gemma, Caroline, Amy, April and all the editors, thank you for everything. It's been an amazing journey. I am so happy to be one of Cal's crew.

A particular thank you also to the amazingly talented designer Alice Coleman, whose work on both the cover and the illustrations is so beautiful. It is an absolute dream to have such fabulous artwork accompany my book. Thank you.

Writing is a solitary pursuit. Without the support of other authors, I would be lost. Thank you to Bonnie MacBird and Sophia Bennett for the glorious lunches that have kept me afloat. And to all the Transatlantic Writers, especially Antony Johnston, Miguel, Barry, Bryan, Jim and Alexandra. You know I would have lost faith in this without you. Your kind words and encouragement pulled me through the doubts. Also, thanks to Vanessa O"Loughlin, who is the biggest champion of other writers. And thank you to Emma for always being there for our wonderful coffee and crime sessions. You were where it all started.

To everyone at the CWA, thank you for your encouragement and support. This is the greatest group of authors who are endlessly helpful to others. Also, thank you to fellow Golden Age enthusiasts and writers. I never knew I would find such a wonderful community of people through my love of these books. Huge thanks to Martin Edwards. To have the support of someone I respect so much is something I could never have dreamed of.

Thank you. Thanks also to Tom Mead and Tony Medawar, both of whom are tireless in their enthusiasm for other people's work. Also, as ever, a huge thank you to all the D20s. You have been there from the very beginning and many of you have become great friends. Thank you for keeping me (relatively) sane.

A very beautiful and unexpected part of being a crime writer has been becoming part of the Agatha Christie community. They are the most welcoming, fabulous people and have taken me into their delightful world. Thank you to Matt, Jo and all the team at the festival. And, of course, to the wonderful Kemper Donovan. To be part of something that has always been so close to my heart is an absolute honour.

Thank you to all the bookshop owners, librarians, bloggers, reviewers and readers out there. The joy of seeing someone with your book never fades.

And thank you to all my family and friends. At the beginning, I said this book emerged from my love of a Golden Age. It also came from somewhere not quite so golden and bright. It was not the easiest time to write a book that has so much grief in its pages. Thank you, all of you, for guiding me through the storm.

To my darling sister, I hold you closer than ever. Writing this book, the truth that life is fragile and precious has never been so stark. By the time this book comes out, I hope we will have surfaced and that you will be by my side at the launch. No matter what, we will always have our books.

To my mother, who faced the unimaginable with dignity and still had time to keep the stories safe.

To my Jimmy, thank you for your constant, enormous

heart, your kindness, love and unfailing encouragement. You are the best of men. Also, thank you for the Lego models you create for the books, which I think might be more popular than anything else!

To my wonderful, clever daughter, Delilah, who writes like an angel and edits like a demon, thank you for always being so incredibly brilliant and supportive. You shine, my love. I am so proud of you and all that you have achieved. Seize every moment.

And, finally, to Kev. More than ever, this small piece of writing hidden at the back of the book is also part of the story. When the sky quite literally came crashing down and when the walls around me thundered and shook every single day, when my heart was split and my head heavy with all those rocks, you were there. How others alter our world has never been clearer to me than while I was writing this book. Often, I found myself adrift with the thought that "Hell is other people". But I found the other side of that. For every hell, there is a heaven. This book could never have been written without you. You gave me a room of my own, which thankfully was soundproof! You held back the storm and brought peace to the raging chaos. You gave me a reason to write this book and all the others that await. The blank page is not empty, but a sea of possibilities. Now, I start each page as I start every day, with the thought: where will this story take me? Thank you for showing me that heaven is other people.